Year of the Angels

By Erika Madden

Erika Madden

ISBN: 1460937546
ISBN-13: 9781460937549

In loving memory of

Dieter Rasp

1937 – 1951

ACKNOWLEDGMENTS

This novel, once my dream, evolved into reality thanks to the Hard-Nosed Zealots Writers Critique Group of Stanwood/Camano: Gloria, Mary, MaryAnn, Peggy, Margo, Lani and Karen.

And thanks to Leonard Smith, who with three little words, "write your book," gave me the push I needed.

I thank you all for your gentle, constructive critique and encouragement.

Special thanks to Heidi, my daughter and editor, and to Daniel, my son, who created the wonderful and personal cover art.

Most of all I thank my brother and escape companion, Dieter, whose imagination took us into a world of fantasy and make-believe that made life during World War II bearable.

He still inspires me to this day.

CONTENTS

CHAPTER 1

June, 1992: The Homecoming

"Lisl, please come home. Papa passed away last night." Kurt's words still echoed in my mind. Why couldn't I cry? I blinked–my eyes dry and gritty from lack of sleep–as I peered through the airplane window.

A colorful quilt of fields spread over the landscape below. Small towns with red tile roofs and high church steeples lay like toy blocks, sprinkled in clusters, among the fields. The land seemed so foreign to me now.

I remembered running barefoot through the fields, playing with my brothers and sisters, surviving the war as best we knew how. That *little* Lisl felt like a stranger to me now. *Please fasten your seat belt*, the sign flashed.

After exiting the plane in Frankfurt, I dragged my suitcase through customs check, looking for a familiar face. The welcoming smiles, however, were not for me. I regretted asking my brother, Kurt, to meet me at our parents' house instead of the airport.

Disconnected, I trotted through the airport maze to the train station where I took an express to Wuerzburg. There, I boarded a local train to Mainbernheim–my childhood home. Small towns appeared for brief moments along the route like long-forgotten dreams.

"Kitzingen," the conductor called as the train rolled to a stop. This was the town where my grandfather had lived. The scent of beer and bratwurst and the sound of music and laughter brought wisps of fleeting memories. Scenes I once had been a part of I now saw through the eyes of a stranger. I leaned against the window as the train moved on.

A little girl stood in a wheat field waving to the passing train. Her hair–like ripened wheat–blew in the warm breeze, her smile as cheerful as the wild poppies she hugged against her chest.

Fragments of sounds and visions blurred together like an old movie out of focus, back to a time when *I* was that waving girl.

The rhythmic clatter of wheels along the tracks played its hypnotic song. The memories I had carefully hidden in a forgotten corner of my mind invaded my thoughts.

"Next stop, Mainbernheim." The conductor glanced my way as if to remind me of my destination.

The train slowed to a stop. Reluctant I peered through the window, not sure how to cope with the emotions of my past. When the porter handed my luggage to the driver of a shuttle, I followed my suitcase to the small empty van.

"Where to?" the driver asked.

"Muehlenweg 21."

As he drove along Bahnweg, I could almost smell the sweet scent of lilacs, although they were no longer in bloom. My brother Dieter and I had walked this road as children. And on Mother's Day we charmed women into parting with some of their lovely flowers.

Memories of Dieter, his arms filled with lilacs, were interrupted when the driver tried to engage me in conversation–his loud words carefully formulated in English. Had I changed that much, or did he assume, by the nametag on my luggage, that I was American? Though irritated, I answered in English. Just as well–it would have taken me longer to find the correct German words.

I had expected Mainbernheim to have changed over the last thirty-five years, but the town looked as though I had left yesterday. The shuttle rolled slowly along Muehlenweg. Nothing had changed there either. The old five-house neighborhood, nestled against a hillside, appeared as though it had been waiting for me all these years.

Although my parents' house and garden showed slight neglect, the loving care once applied was apparent. I expected Kurt to greet me at the door but found the house deserted.

Surprised at how instinctively I grabbed the key from the bathroom windowsill, I unlocked the door, and when I walked in, I almost called out, "Mama, I'm home!" Somehow I expected my mother to come rushing from the kitchen, wiping her hands on her apron, ready to hug me. I knew she had passed away a year ago, but for me Mama was here. Was it because I was unable to attend her funeral to say my last goodbye?

Too tired to sleep, I walked through the house like a lost child and stopped by the window. The garden path descended onto Muehlenweg. On the other side of the road spread a meadow where the mill creek twisted its silver ribbon between the willow-lined banks. Beyond, wheat fields rippled softly in the breeze.

Mama had kept her eyes on us from this window when we, as children, played by the water. I tried to whistle the way she used to call us to dinner, but tears stuck in my throat.

I leaned out the window, closed my eyes and inhaled the scent of fresh cut hay. The warm summer wind touched my face. I felt my mother's presence beside me. I had huddled against her, stunned, staring across the fields at enemy tanks in the early morning mist. How clear my recollection of that April morning, back in 1945.

Haunted by that little girl, I turned from the window only to see little Lisl again, watching her mother prepare a meal from three potatoes to feed five hungry children.

"I'm too tired for this."

The basement door was ajar. Slowly I opened it all the way, staring into the darkness, and then closed it softly as not to disturb the memories waiting there for me.

Every room I entered, sounds of cries and laughter echoed in my thoughts. And when I stood in the doorway of my parents' bedroom, an invitation to rest was clear by the turned-down covers and crisp white sheets. On the pillow was a note from my brother: "Sorry I couldn't be there to greet you. I will bring you a surprise in the morning. Sleep tight. Love Kurt."

I drew a bath and soaked until the water turned cold. Only then did I summon enough energy to go to bed.

∞

The song of a robin announced a new day. My mind was still, not quite awake; sleepily I reached out, expecting my husband beside me. The scent of hay and cows drifting through the open window and the hush of the morning awakened me fully to my childhood home.

It was ten minutes past six. I tore the front door open and stood barefoot in the doorway, and for a moment I felt like little Lisl had upon waking. My mother had asked me once, "What do you expect to see?"

"A pretty morning," I had said, and she smiled knowingly.

The rising sun sparkled through the trees. The big cherry tree, contorted with age, a table and chairs beneath, gave invitation to linger in its shade. Perhaps today I could cope with my childhood memories.

My thoughts were still in English. While dressing, I forced myself to think in German so that I could converse in my native tongue without stammering.

I missed my American family the minute they waved good-bye at SeaTac Airport. Depressed and lonely, I felt like a foreigner in the house where I grew up. Jet lag, I thought, it will pass.

I walked down the flower-lined garden path with sweet memories of Sunday mornings and Mama. Even in her good dress and on her way to church, she could never resist pulling a few weeds between the flowers.

In the stillness of this sleepy country setting, little Lisl emerged. I remembered puffs of dust between my toes as I ran barefoot with my brothers and sisters down this road.

A few new buildings outside the Mainbernheim wall stood out of place in the old Bavarian-style surroundings. But when I entered the town through the high-arched tower gate, I stepped back in time.

This small Bavarian town, dating back over a thousand years, had withstood time's passing.

The eighteen towers built into a high stone wall surrounding the town had once been effective lookout posts. The moat had long been replaced with little garden plots. Years ago my grandmother had grown delicious vegetables and berries in one of them.

A fairytale from a storybook I had read to my children came to mind as I walked through the cobblestone streets of Mainbernheim. Now I saw my home town through the eyes of a tourist.

The main street, Herrn Strasse–called Adolf Hitler Strasse during Hitler's reign–connected large towers on each end of town. The heavy wooden doors in the high arched entries were locked at night in olden times.

When I was a child, my father told me of trucks that got stuck in these entrance towers as auto traffic increased.

Until 1938, when Bundesbahn 8 was built, all traffic between Wuerzburg and Nuremberg had to go through this little town.

The old stone fountains stood like monuments of times when horses and oxen drank from their basins on their way to the fields. Now, decorated with flower boxes and sparkling water spouting like centerpieces among the blossoms, the fountains seemed like tourist attractions.

Freshly painted store fronts brightened the old Bavarian buildings like picture postcards–giving no hint of the war that had once raged through this little town.

Why did the terror from long ago creep so vividly into my mind? Maybe seeing the old town after thirty-five years brought back sadness or maybe my guilt for having left Germany.

Almost out of habit, I walked to the old schoolhouse beside the church, and discovered that it had been converted to an apartment building. A few blocks away, outside the town wall, stood a brand new school with all the modern conveniences. The old schoolyard served as a town park with tall trees and shrubs shading park benches and swing sets.

I strolled across the park and pushed a swing into motion. Its haunting, rhythmic squeak brought back my brother's smiling face as we soared high into the air.

On my way back through town, a few people hurried along the streets.

"*Guten Morgen*," they greeted, along with curious looks.

"*Guten Morgen*," I replied, my first German words since I had arrived.

A delicious scent of fresh-baked bread escaped the bakery as I passed. Backerei Klein–the name shield dangled from a big, wrought-iron pretzel. Ownership had changed, the sign in the window indicated, but oh how well I remembered grumpy old Herr Klein, although I no longer could recall why I feared him so.

A few houses down stood the blacksmith shop. The large wooden door stretched almost across the entire store front, making it the largest part of this two-story building. As children we watched Herr Seidel hammer at the glowing metal, forming horseshoes to fit the hooves of patiently waiting horses. Dieter's face came to mind as he squinted at high-shooting sparks that eventually lost their glow on the ground.

A window above the shop swung open and a woman, curious, peered down at me, and then hung a feather comforter halfway through the window to let the morning sun work its magic. I turned away from the closed blacksmith door I had been staring at.

Instinctively I took the shortcut across the fields to my parents' house, the route Dieter and I had taken so many times on our way home from school.

The scolding voices of German soldiers echoed through my mind when we, back in 1945, had accidentally stumbled onto an artillery attack on enemy tanks. I ran along the narrow, overgrown path, but could not escape the memory.

Only when I stopped to catch my breath did I realize I stood at the edge of the quarry Dieter and I had treasured as our playground. Our magical sunken amphitheater was now a landfill almost reaching the level of the surrounding fields. My eyes shut, trying to visualize the stone break the way it used to be–our secret place where we could dream and escape reality. Our quest to find that perfect petrified seashell wedged between the rocks was often interrupted by air-raid sirens. But the dream of being famous archeologists, however, was not extinguished by flames of war throughout our childhood.

Now I felt ready to face my memories.

Shortly before nine, I returned to the house. In my search for a phone to call Kurt, I discovered boxes of my parents' belongings stacked in the corner beside the china cabinet.

One carton contained the beautiful crystal ornaments I had loved as a child. I took one out and twirled it slowly on its string. Rainbows danced across the walls when sunlight caught in its facets.

Christmas of 1944 replayed hauntingly in my mind. Memories of cloud angels, the scent of fresh-cut spruce, the hush of winter, but most of all Dieter's smiling face, took me to that special time.

CHAPTER 2

Christmas Eve 1944

Scattered pink clouds drifted across a violet-blue sky in the evening glow. A wintry silence settled like a soft blanket as Lisl and Dieter pulled a sled toward Willanzheim.

"Look, Lisl, gold." Dieter's eyes sparkled with Christmas magic as he scooped up a handful of snow and let it escape between his mittens.

Lisl brightened. "It's a falling rainbow."

The sunset painted the frozen landscape with magical colors. Snow-covered trees glistened in the evening sun like decorated Christmas trees. Lisl squinted into the orange ball as it crept toward the hills. "We'd better hurry or we won't make it home before dark."

Dieter brushed the snow from his mittens and jumped on the sled. A dark-blue knit cap, fastened tightly under his chin, framed his red face. He did not seem to feel the cold; neither did Lisl.

Lisl quickened her pace. "Let's hurry. Herr Schweitzer might leave early because it's Christmas Eve."

Dieter frowned. "I hope he's still there."

Herr Schweitzer worked in the signal shed and often searched for coal along the railroad tracks. Sometimes engineers lost chunks off their shovels while feeding the locomotives. When Schweitzer gathered enough coal to fill a sack he traded it for food.

Lisl frowned. There was no flickering light through the little dirty window. Schweitzer had probably gone.

"Oh please let him be there." She crossed her fingers. "I don't want to be cold on Christmas."

Dieter cheered. "There he is."

Slowly Schweitzer came limping toward them. "*Guten Abend, Kinder.*"

"*Guten Abend, Herr Schweitzer,*" they greeted in unison.

Schweitzer grabbed the wooden sled and hoisted it up the embankment toward the shed. His old army cap pulled low onto his brow and coal dust smudges across his pale thin face made him look frail. But Lisl saw a twinkle dance in his gray eyes, because Mama had promised him and his invalid wife some eggs.

Mama had saved the eggs in a glycerin barrel for him in exchange for coal to assure a warm Christmas. It was a great sacrifice for a family of six, especially in winter when the chickens were not all that enthusiastic about laying and the food supply in the pantry was getting low.

Schweitzer hauled a big sack of coal onto the sled and tied it down with a rope.

"I hope it's not too heavy to pull it through that mess," he said. Slowly he lowered the sled backward down the embankment onto the road. He looked at Dieter. "How old are you?"

"I will be eight next month." Dieter raised himself to his toes.

Schweitzer smiled and turned to Lisl. Before he could ask she said, "I'm almost ten."

She took the bag with the eggs from the knapsack and handed it to him.

"*Vielen Dank und frohe Weihnachten,*" Schweitzer said.

Lisl already felt warmer at the sight of the big sack. "*Danke shoen.* This will keep us warm all through Christmas," she smiled as she pulled on the sled handle.

Dieter pushed on the back, but it would not budge.

Schweitzer lifted his cap and scratched his head while watching for a moment. "I think you need a little help to get you started." He pushed with Dieter for a few meters then stopped and steadied himself. "*Gute Nacht, Kinder.* Don't take too long or you'll get caught in the dark," he called through his cupped hands.

"*Gute Nacht, Herr Schweitzer.*"

Darkness crept across the landscape, chasing the sun behind the hills, leaving a red glow on the horizon. Blackout had been a way of life for several years now. But Lisl still remembered the bright nights when Mama had kept the window shutters open and the warm glow of the chandeliers lit up the garden. The house was warm and cozy then. Now the garden lay dark in mysterious shadows at night while an unwelcome visitor called "Frosty Chill" made himself at home in every room of the house.

Blackouts were strictly enforced–especially after the Schweinfurt bombing a few months earlier. Many towns had been bombed. Although these attacks were not too close to Mainbernheim yet, Lisl and her family had spent many nights in an old wine cellar shelter as air raids became more frequent. Street lights remained dark and getting around was an adventure, especially with thick snow hiding familiar landmarks.

Lisl and Dieter struggled through the deep snow going up hills. A thaw earlier in the week had melted the snow on the road where farm wagons had cut deep grooves into the slush. But with the drop in temperature these grooves transformed into high frozen ridges. So staying on the side of the road, even through thick snow, made their journey easier.

They stopped periodically to catch their breath. The pink clouds had turned a glowing white, drifting in strange shapes across the deep blue sky. Dieter gazed skyward, leaning against the sack, gasping for air. "Look Lisl, an angel."

"Oh look, that one has long wings." Lisl pointed at yet another cloud.

Dieter wrinkled his brow. "Do you think the angels are here because it's Christmas Eve, or are they the children who went to heaven when they got killed?"

Lisl watched the slow flight of the angels. "Come on Dieter, let's go." They tried to pull the sled. It had frozen to the ground. After pulling and pushing they eventually got it loose and moving again.

When they reached the top of the hill, Lisl thought the worst was over. But going downhill created a dilemma as well.

Dieter stood on the back of the sled runners until the sled gained too much speed. He jumped off, grabbed onto the rope-tie and dug his heels into the crusty snow to slow it down.

The sled, however, sped after Lisl who could not outrun the load. She let go and jumped out of the way.

Tenaciously, Dieter held on. Snow sprayed from his heels like sparks as the sled raced to the bottom of the hill where it crashed into a snow bank. Dieter fell off and lay motionless.

Lisl ran to him. "Are you all right?"

Dieter laughed, looking cozy cradled in the snow. "Wow, that was a wild ride." He got up and brushed off the snow.

Lisl was grateful that Herr Schweitzer had tied the heavy sack onto the sled. It was too heavy for them to lift. After a lot of pulling and pushing, they finally got the sled free.

At last they reached the level road. "Phew, we made it." They stopped to rest.

"Look Lisl. Stars. Let's make a wish."

Lisl closed her eyes. "Please let Papa come home for Christmas." She watched her whispered breath rise toward the sky. But in her heart she knew he could not come. The fighting on the Russian front was too far away. Yet, she believed in miracles and wished with all her heart–just in case.

Dieter looked at Lisl and each knew what the other had wished for.

In the frigid, dark stillness the stars seemed magnified. A row of tall snow-laden trees lining the road appeared like frozen ghosts.

"Look, the angels." Dieter pointed to the sky.

Lisl squinted, and then cupped her hands around her eyes. "How bright they are."

"Well, Lisl, because it's darker now."

"I wonder what lights them up?"

They stood in awe, watching wispy cloud angels glide between the stars.

"When we get shot will we become angels, too?" Dieter asked, without breaking his gaze.

Lisl wondered what made him think of that. "I don't know. Maybe." Lisl searched the sky and pointed. "I would like to be that one."

"Wouldn't it be fun to float in the air?" Dieter's breath escaped in short bursts like the steam from a locomotive. "Do you think it hurts a lot when we get shot?" he asked, stuffing his hair under his knit cap.

"I don't know . . . it all depends."

"Depends on what?"

"If we get shot in the head, we won't feel a thing because we're dead before we could feel it."

Dieter looked puzzled, rubbing his forehead, but his frown turned to a smile when he gazed toward the glistening trees.

What if the enemy fired through our bodies? Would we die instantly? Lisl wondered. Norbert and Heinrich, her classmates, had told her that it would take many painful shots before you die. She wrinkled her nose. They had probably made it up.

She had punched Norbert in his chest when he took aim at her head with his finger. He had laughed and called her a scared rabbit when she ran away. Stupid boy, he didn't know the difference between angry and scared.

Lisl hoped the boys would not tell the shooting stories to Charlotte, her oldest sister; she was easily frightened and might believe them. But Lisl did not want to think about the mean boys or the war anymore and Dieter seemed to have forgotten about the idea of getting shot. They watched as more and more stars became visible between the clouds.

"It's so quiet," Lisl whispered. There were no blaring sirens, no bombers in the sky, and no aerial fighting. "Maybe the soldiers are taking a Christmas break."

"Maybe they're fighting too far away for us to hear," Dieter replied.

"I hope Papa is still alive," she whispered. Where would he spend Christmas? "Please God, watch over him."

July was the last time they had seen Papa with no word from him since. If only he would send a letter to Mama. Lisl's heart ached when her mother rushed to the post office, only to return, slowly and empty-handed, hiding her tears. But Lisl could tell when Mama had been crying. Her beautiful brown-amber eyes always turned hazel-green.

Dieter shivered. Lisl, too, felt the cold now from standing still too long.

"We'd better go, Dieter, before *we* freeze to the ground."

Dieter pushed from the back and at times caught a ride on a downgrade, standing on the sled runners.

Dark outlines of the high wall and towers that surrounded Mainbernheim rose from the frosty haze. They passed the tower gate outside on their way. Lisl saw shadowy figures. People scurried along the cobblestone streets and disappeared into dark doorways or alleys within the wall. Yet the town appeared deserted, shrouded in darkness. Not the smallest glimpse of light escaped through a doorway or window. Even Adolf Hitler Strasse seemed dark and mysterious.

Lisl remembered a Christmas when the town was decorated with fresh spruce garlands strung from lamp post to lamp post with colorful lanterns. She still felt the excitement when her sisters allowed her to go to the store with them. Then, the shops still had some toys and candies. The storekeeper would give them little chocolate bells. That was over six years ago. She smacked her lips, but could not remember the taste of chocolate. She feared she might also forget her father's smile and thought of him every day to memorize his face.

They left the main road and turned onto narrow Muehlenweg. The sloe hedge along the side the road guided the way when darkness hid their earlier sled tracks. There was no sign of light. They barely saw their house.

Lisl had always enjoyed their big garden because they lived outside the town with lots of space to grow fruits and vegetables. But lately the air raids had become more frequent, and she felt vulnerable, isolated in their five-house neighborhood.

When they reached their garden, Lisl cringed at the sight of the steep path. "I think we need help."

Dieter ran up and into the house to find his sisters.

Thirteen-year-old Charlotte and twelve-year-old Ellen came running and slipping down the snow-covered path.

"What took you so long?" Charlotte's scolding could not hide her relief. Now she did not have to go out looking for them.

"Well, it looks nice and soft *here*, but you should have seen the road, all slippery with crusty ice. It wasn't easy pulling the sled over that mess," Dieter said.

"You sure you didn't go sledding first?" Ellen said, pushing while Charlotte pulled with Lisl.

They got the sled up to the basement door, cut the rope off the sack, pulled it into the cement-floored hallway and slid it under the stairway leading upstairs. A laundry room with a cement floor was beside the stairway to the left and a root cellar with a dirt floor but thicker walls to the right. The root cellar served as an emergency shelter when they had no time to make it to the air-raid shelter.

Charlotte had warmed the water in the laundry room so Lisl and Dieter could wash off the coal dust before going upstairs.

In the kitchen the scent of spruce and fresh baked cookies filled the air.

"Where's Mama?" Lisl asked.

"Shh, she's in the living room getting ready for the *Christkind*," Ellen whispered, her finger to her lips. Her blue eyes sparkled with secrets that made the Christmas spirit come alive. Charlotte covered a plate with a towel, hiding another secret. But the biggest secret was behind the door when Lisl heard her grandfather's laughter. "Opa is here." She smiled, rubbing her hands together.

Mama had converted the sitting room to a guest room. Opa, Lisl's blind grandfather, and Papa's sister, Tante Anni, had come for a Christmas visit.

"The *Christkind* will bring me a rocking horse with a red mane, Opa said so." Four-year-old Kurt grabbed Lisl's hand. He pulled her along, hopping through the kitchen, riding an invisible horse. With every jump, his blond curls bobbed up and down, his bright blue eyes danced in anticipation. Dieter's baggy hand-me-down pants kept bouncing on Kurt's skinny frame even after *he* had stopped.

Lisl laughed. Her little brother had not been this happy in a long time. Since the bombings in their area had increased, Kurt spent most of the time close to the little wooden bench in the kitchen corner. Every time he heard the warning siren he crawled under it and pressed his hands tightly over his ears.

Kurt kept his eyes on the living room door and when the crystal bell rang, he tore into the living room with his brother and sisters right behind. Opa and Aunt Anni brought their gifts and joined them.

Mama always opened the window as though the *Christkind* had just flown away. The curtain billowed in the breeze and Kurt's little face brightened, but quickly changed. "We missed the *Christkind* again," he pouted.

The white flickering candles on the tree in a darkened room set everyone's eyes aglow. Mama closed the window and looked into her children's faces. Her thick auburn hair was tied with green ribbon. Her soft brown eyes shone like precious amber. Lisl smiled back into her mother's happy glow.

The sparkling Christmas tree near the window reached way up to the ceiling, where the golden angel smiled down from the tree top. Kurt, fascinated by the crystal ornaments, set one spinning and it reflected the candle flames in its facets.

Softly Mama started a carol and the family joined in.
> *Stille Nacht, heilige Nacht,*
> *Alles schlaeft einsam wacht.*

Mama's eyes turned hazel as she looked at her family even though she was smiling. Grandfather blew his nose and dabbed at his eyes as he tried to sing along.

Lisl wondered why Opa looked so sad on Christmas Eve. Maybe he worried about the war that crept toward their town with each day. Maybe he too wondered if they would be alive to see spring.

Lisl whispered into the song, her eyes closed, her fingers crossed. "I wish that we all live to see next Christmas–with Papa."

Opa put his hand on her shoulder, nodding as though he could hear her whisper.

Aunt Anni looked like a child, although she was nineteen. She stood with Charlotte and Ellen near the tree. Her sky blue dress matched her eyes and made her hair look golden.

Although Kurt's eyes hung on the presents, he managed to sing a few words now and then. But when his sisters started another carol, he glared at them, his head to one side. When it was over, he quickly asked, "Can we open our presents now?" He was afraid they would start another song.

Mama nodded with a smile. Within seconds, Kurt discovered a rocking horse with a red woolen mane hidden behind the tree. He squealed with delight when Dieter helped him pull it out into the middle of the room. His little hands tenderly stroked the red mane, looking into its big painted brown eyes as though the horse had winked at him.

Opa could not see the excitement his creation brought, but he certainly could hear it; he looked as happy as Kurt. Opa was good with his hands even without his sight. Aunt Anni had helped paint the eyes on the horse.

Aunt Anni locked the window shutters tightly then turned on the light. Now it was Kurt's turn to blow out the candles to save them for the next day. Anni lifted him as high as her arms could reach.

Charlotte and Ellen sorted through the gifts and as the oldest, Charlotte opened hers first. She pressed her face into her cardigan with a smile and tried on her mittens. However, it spoiled the surprise for Ellen because they always received the same kind of gift, only in different colors. They wasted no time in trading to match with other clothing–at least for now.

Each of the children took their turn while the family watched. Dieter, with a big smile on his face, unwrapped his gifts–mostly things to keep him warm. He pulled his new knit cap over his face, making monster noises, chasing a squealing Kurt around the room.

Lisl loved the anticipation of a concealed treasure. She found it more exciting than knowing what was inside. However, when all other gifts were opened and everyone looked at hers, Lisl had no choice but to unwrap it. She discovered hand-knitted woolen stockings and mittens. "Oh look at that," she gasped. "A beautiful sweater." Lisl recognized the color. She had helped her mother unravel Grandmother's shawl, unaware that Mama was going to use the wool to knit her a sweater. She had always loved Grandmother's heather-colored wrap, but brightened at the sight of her new stockings.

"Mama, now the kids won't laugh at me anymore." She held the stockings to her waist. "I love them."

"Aunt Anni made them for you." Mama said.

"*Vielen Dank* Tante Anni."

Her aunt laughed. "I didn't think they would make you so happy."

"Some of my classmates tease me because my old ones have too many darned patches at the knees."

"Oh Lisl, that is mean," Aunt Anni said.

"It's all right. I guess they don't know that my stockings belonged to Charlotte and Ellen before they were mine. Other girls wear hand-me-downs, but maybe with just one previous owner and fewer patches." Lisl laughed.

Anni hugged Lisl. "I'm glad you like them."

Lisl held up her sweater. "*Danke* Mama." She hugged it against her chest. "It's so pretty." She carefully folded it and placed it back in its wrapper. "I have a gift for you, too."

Lisl ran from the room. She had hidden Mama's gift in the sitting room behind the curtain on the window ledge.

Two weeks earlier, before the heavy snow, Lisl and Dieter had explored the quarry and stumbled on the sweet violet plants. They dug up the ones with the most buds and Lisl planted them in a little basket she found in the attic. Now a wonderful fragrance escaped from behind the curtains before she ever saw the small blue flowers. She ran to her mother and handed her the gift. "*Frohe Weihnachten*, Mama."

Her mother held the little violet basket in both hands, closed her eyes and inhaled the delicate scent.

"How wonderful," she said, "a little bit of spring." She put her arm around Lisl's shoulder and held the flowers under her nose as well. Lisl took a deep breath and said, "Dieter helped me dig them up."

"I have something for you too." Dieter went to the basement and returned a minute later, dragging a big sack into the room. He plunked it down in front of his mother.

"This is to start the fire in the mornings. I collected them for you. Pine cones," he explained, after seeing his mother's puzzled expression. "Lisl helped."

He stood in front of Mama, wrapped his arms around her waist and looked up at her the way he always did.

"*Danke schoen, mein Liebling*. That is just what I need," she said, kissing him on his forehead. He smiled proudly.

Charlotte and Ellen had been practical, working for farmers, cleaning, sewing, and mending. Their payment was a thick slice of ham, a half pound of butter and some sugar, which made the Christmas goodies. Lisl admired her sisters' determination and hard work to ensure a wonderful Christmas feast.

Aunt Anni brought in a big bowl of hazelnuts and walnuts, mixed with little red and green apples, and placed it on the table.

Ceremoniously, Charlotte set a plate of cookies onto the table. Kurt's eyes grew big. "Oh look at all the cookies." He hovered over the tempting treats, trying hard not to touch them.

Mama served hot apple cider and her special potato soup, and this time she had added diced ham. After they had finished they were allowed to help themselves to the goodies.

Lisl sat on the floor beside Opa's big chair. The living room was warm and would be so for the next three days. Christmas Eve was filled with magic, carols and stories. Opa knew the best ones. Tenderly he reminisced about Papa, and all the funny things he used to do when he was a small boy.

"When your Papa was about your age, Kurt, he too wished for a rocking horse." Opa settled back in the chair. "Well, come Christmas Eve he found one in front of the tree. I had collected a dustbin full of frozen horse biscuits from the neighbor's barn and put them, on paper of course, under the horse's tail." Opa laughed so hard he could barely finish his story. "Oh, you should have seen little Karl's eyes. He gave that rocking horse such funny look."

Lisl loved to listen to her grandfather's stories about her father when he was a child, although she had heard them many times before. But despite her grandfather's laughter, there was a worry in his voice and tears glistened in the corners of his eyes. His laughter almost sounded like a cry.

Lisl often forgot her grandfather was blind when his cloudy blue eyes smiled right at her. Today he looked handsome. His unruly thick gray hair, usually sticking out in the back, was neatly combed to one side. His cheeks were always flushed when he was excited, but his cheekbones seemed in motion today as he ground his teeth together.

Lisl stroked his long, leathery-looking fingers and Opa wrapped them around her hand. She loved this gentle man. Kurt climbed onto Grandfather's lap.

"Opa, I was in the kindergarten play this morning."

"*Wunderbar.* What did you play? A shepherd?"

"No. Opa, do boys *have* to be angels?"

"Why, didn't you want to be an angel?"

"Opa, don't you know? Only girls can be angels. Mama has to cut my hair so I don't look like a girl." He pulled on his mop of blond curls.

Opa laughed, running his hand through Kurt's hair.

Lisl thought Kurt made a very nice little angel in the kindergarten play. He resembled the painted angels on the church ceiling, except for his cheeks; they were not chubby.

Lisl had watched the Christmas play with her family. She remembered wearing the long gown and ferry-like wings when she was in kindergarten. Dieter had always played a shepherd; except when he was only two years old and he wore a wooly white suit and was a little lamb. He was supposed to crawl across the stage, but when he reached the middle he froze, staring out into the audience. Sister Rosa had to give him a little push to get him started again. And, like a wind-up toy, he crawled to the other side, turned and said his line, "Baaa, baaa."

Then it was a warmer, more loving Christmas. Sister Rosa would hug each child and wish them a *Frohe Weihnachten* as she gave them their presents. Now the hugs were replaced with a *Heil Hitler* salute, expecting a salute in return.

So Dieter and Lisl gave Kurt his hug instead. He smiled at them as he proudly walked home with his family.

Kurt was good at remembering to say Heil Hitler now. He had finally learned to greet the townspeople that way– after much prompting from Sister Rosa. Still, he thought of it as a game.

∽

On Christmas morning, Lisl awoke to a familiar sound. Tante Anni was scraping the ashes from the stove to set the fire. Lisl had to listen hard when her mother did this chore. Mama always took great care not to wake her children.

An hour later, the family gathered around the breakfast table in the warm dining room. Because it was Christmas Day, Mama served a *whole* slice of bread, topped with delicious homemade fruit preserves Aunt Anni had brought with her.

The Christmas tree stood like a cherished visitor in the corner of the room. Mama opened the shutters and the wintry scene outside appeared like a beautiful painting through the window.

After breakfast the family bundled up to go to church, wearing their Christmas mittens, caps, and scarves. Lisl ran down the path, her feet didn't hurt. Her new stockings were warm and thick enough to form a soft cushion between her feet and shoes. Still, she slowed down to a dignified walk. Mama had actually bought the shoes new for her a year ago, but they were stiff and hurt her feet. Her old torn hand-me-downs would have been more comfortable, but Mama would not allow her to wear them to church. The family trudged through the deep snow along Muehlenweg.

Lisl skipped along the clean-swept cobblestone street as they entered the town. Friends and townspeople wished each other a *Frohe Weihnachten* along the way, and thoughts of war seemed far from their minds.

Ellen and Charlotte held Opa's hands as they slowly led him along Adolf Hitler Strasse. Grandfather stood tall without his cane, looking directly at whomever talked to him. Some people did not realize he was blind. Opa liked to fool people.

He seemed to enjoy Charlotte's chatter as she described the small square patch of thick snow in front of old Herr Strohheim's house. "It looks like a thick white rug," she giggled in his ear. The street had been swept clean. But

Herr Strohheim had not cleared his side of the street. The old man was known for being stubborn and too proud to let his neighbors help. Sometimes his friends sneaked out at night and cleared the snow for him. He always acted annoyed even though Lisl noticed he looked relieved when no one was watching.

Opa chuckled when Charlotte and Ellen told him that Frau Hofreich's big hat flew off her head the minute she stepped out of her house.

Lisl heard Opa's happy laughter now and again as he and the girls trailed farther behind. Charlotte and Ellen were on their best behavior today; they did not quarrel.

Kurt's little voice chattered non-stop, now that he had Mama's and Aunt Anni's full attention.

They entered the church and Lisl, her sisters, and Dieter joined their classmates in the front rows to sing in the children's choir.

Lisl wiggled her warm toes. Even the beautifully painted walls and ceiling seemed more vivid today, Lisl thought. Baby Jesus in his manger looked warm and glowing in the unheated church.

Most of Lisl's classmates were there, except her friend Gisela. She did not go to Lisl's church, but to her Synagogue with her parents. Lisl wondered where she had moved to. The last time Lisl saw her in class was when they were in first grade.

Lisl never understood why some of the children had been so mean to Gisela. They called her a stinky Jew and sang hurtful, nasty little rhymes.

She still could see her friend's sad face. Gisela did not know what she had done to make some of the children so angry at her, and neither did Lisl. A few of the mean boys threw rocks at her and at Lisl, too, for being Gisela's friend. They would not attack openly, but launched little sneak attacks from behind trees or garden walls. Lisl knew them, but even after telling on them, no punishment followed.

Some of the older boys who lived within the town wall were joined by other boys from nearby towns. Together they threw rocks through the beautiful stained glass windows of the Synagogue.

Lisl shivered. She felt cold when she remembered the hatred on some of the children's and grown-ups' faces. Sometimes Lisl walked by her friend's house still hoping to see Gisela come running out the door, ready to play. But her friend had not lived here for several years. Refugees from northern cities had taken up residence in Gisela's house, peering blankly through the windows at Lisl. There were no Jewish families left in Mainbernheim.

Ellen's elbow landed a painful jab on Lisl's ribs that tore her from her depressing thoughts. She quickly looked at her book and sang along.

჻

Christmas Day is for church and family, but Second Christmas Day, a German holiday, is for having fun. Excited, Lisl, her sisters and Dieter joined the neighborhood children to go sledding. The absence of air raids made this Christmas special. Lisl hoped Frau Burlein had gone to bed by now because it was late afternoon. The old woman owned most of the land in the area, including the field just right for sledding. She had never chased the children in the late afternoon when it started to get dark.

Frau Burlein always wore long dark dresses and coats down to the tip of her shoes and a head scarf wrapped low on her brow. Lisl often wondered what she looked like–she would have liked to see her expression, discover her mood.

But no one ever came close to her because she always chased them off her property.

"Maybe a monster lurks beneath her shrouded garb," Charlotte once said in a poetic but spooky voice. The woman seemed to sense when the children were playing on her fields, anticipating their every move.

"How does she know?" Lisl asked Ellen.

"Maybe she's a witch."

Lisl ran in her torn shoes, trying to keep up with her sisters and brother. She was eager to show off her new mittens and stockings, but most of the children had mittens and stockings, knit hats and mufflers they wanted to show off as well. Lisl laughed and patted her hands against her friend's mittens, they looked very similar. Maybe Mama had shared some of her wool with Traudel's mother. It seemed everyone had received gifts to keep them warm–mostly made with reused wool. Laughing and shouting, they pulled their sleds to the top of the field.

The snow brightened the landscape, creating instant magic in the twilight. A row of barren apple trees stood at the edge of the field, silently observing the children's activities. Glistening, frost-covered branches reached toward them like outstretched arms wanting to join in the fun.

The neighborhood children with sleds at the ready waited until everyone reached the top of the hill then tied a long sled train together.

"All aboard," Erich called out.

They took their seats on the train. Charlotte, Erich, and Anna, the oldest children, took the lead. Ellen, Hansi, and Helga were right behind. Fritz and Robert were near the back, and Traudel, Dieter, and Lisl rode the caboose. Lisl found it more exciting when the train's tail whipped from side to side or spun out wide around corners. She held on tight to Traudel as the train raced down the steep hill.

Lisl and Dieter laughed and shrieked as snow whipped up and into their faces. Traudel joined in. Ever since her father was killed in the war two years ago, Traudel had been sad and quiet and did not want to play. Lisl smiled. It was nice to hear her friend laugh again.

The train whooshed past trees and hedges, barely missing them on the way down. A small opening in the thorny sloe hedge allowed access to a narrow steep road, making the ride twice as long, but even longer having to walk back up again.

They reached the top and lined up for a second ride down. They screamed with fright and delight as the train flew into curves leaving snow clouds in their wake.

Faster, faster they sped toward the hedge opening. But to Lisl's horror, they could not find it. The older children tried to slow the locomotive, but it had too much speed. In a chorus of screams the train and its passengers slammed into a tangle of prickly hedge parts.

Children, sleds, and cut branches all piled into a mound. Charlotte jumped to her feet first, checking on everyone. "Are you all right?" She dug through the pile until she discovered her brother and sisters laughing. Except for a few minor scratches, no one was hurt. Their winter clothing had protected them from the thorns.

Lisl wiped the snow from her face and laughed, spitting snow. All the children rolled in the soft powder while sorting themselves from sleds, branches, and each other. Now Lisl knew Frau Burlein was not asleep.

The woman had cut parts of the sloe hedge earlier and dragged them across the opening while the children were on their way up again.

The ongoing war between the children and Frau Burlein had become an exciting game. She had never complained to their parents, leaving Lisl to suspect that maybe Frau Burlein enjoyed these games as much as the children.

CHAPTER 3

Winter's Fury

By mid-January, winter's grip became unbearable. The temperature inside the house was not much warmer than outside. Even the milk in the pot had a frozen cover. Lisl and her sisters huddled in blankets on the couch with their mother, anxiously listening to news reports on the radio.

Lisl prayed for the announcement that the war had ended, that food and heating material would be available again. Instead, a plea for more sacrifice crushed her hopes. In desperate efforts to halt the enemy's advance, coal and other heating fuel were in high demand by the German army. Weapons factories and train transports had depleted the nation's fuel supply. Schools and other public places felt the chill as well.

"Mama, will we ever get warm again? When will the war end?" Charlotte asked.

Mama shook her head. "I don't know." She rationed their dwindling food supply, not knowing how long before the pantry would be empty. No longer could she afford to trade eggs for coal with Herr Schweizer. Now, on an almost daily trek after school, Mama took the children to the railroad tracks to search for coal.

These long outings became increasingly difficult for Mama. She often felt faint from bending over for long periods and going to the woods seemed to exhaust her even more.

The forestry service allowed the citizens to cut dead trees. Now many people were searching, which made it even harder to find dry dead trees. The family had to walk much deeper into the forest.

When Mama finally found a dead tree, usually about eight to ten inches thick, she cut it with a hand saw into meter-length pieces to fit into the wagon or onto the sled.

Charlotte and Ellen took turns when Mama's arms got too tired. Depending on the height of the tree, not all of the pieces would fit into the hand wagon and sled.

"I think we should carry whatever doesn't fit into the wagon," Ellen said. "By the time we get back to get the rest it will be gone."

Lisl loaded her sister's arms with the wood pieces. Although Mama looked concerned she smiled proudly at her girls.

Dieter helped Mama pull the wagon and Lisl used the sled. She had to move slowly around corners and over rough patches to keep the high load from tipping over. Lisl followed Mama, watching the narrow little wheels on her wagon, wondering how long before they would collapse under the heavy load. By the time they got the firewood to the house, everyone's energy was drained, especially Mama's.

There were times Lisl could not sleep thinking about her mother. She was always exhausted, more so than usual even without strenuous tasks. Maybe she was ill. She did not laugh as often and Lisl missed her songs that always seemed to calm everyone. Sometimes Lisl caught Mama looking sad and depressed when she thought no one was watching.

Charlotte noticed Lisl's concern. "What's the matter, Lisl?"

"I think Mama is ill. She always looks so sad and tired lately."

"Well, I'd better tell you. Mama is going to have a baby in March."

"Yes, I guessed that when I watched her in the woods, but that's no reason for her to be so depressed; I still think she doesn't feel well," Lisl insisted.

Although Lisl looked forward to having a little baby in the family, she could not stop fretting. When her sisters insisted Mama should stay home on their fuel searches, Lisl felt better.

Of course Kurt was happy to stay with her. "I have to keep Mama company so she won't be lonely," he said.

Kurt smiled, trying to convince his sisters. He hated the long, cold coal-searching afternoons, and often ended up crying before his bucket was half full. In the cold wind and snow, he found no place to warm his little body. At least at home there was no wind, and even in the cold house, he could keep warm by wrapping himself in a blanket.

Lisl's spirits were high. Now she didn't have to worry about Mama and Kurt anymore. With buckets and sacks loaded on the sled, the girls and Dieter headed for the railroad tracks.

Charlotte and Ellen stood on one side of the tracks and Dieter and Lisl on the other, waving to the engineers. Most of them stared somber-faced, straight ahead, trying not to notice them. But sometimes one would throw a few shovels full of coal off the train to help shorten their time in the frigid weather. Lisl smiled and waved at the generous engineers.

Dieter was good at making the time go quicker and the search more fun. He invented a game of dragons when steam-blowing locomotives thundered by spewing fire and steam, dragging their long tails behind. They counted the dragons, always hoping that some might spew a little coal with their fiery breath.

After hours of searching and the sack still not filled, their enthusiasm vanished along with the dragons. Instead, other monsters sprang to life. The monsters called Reality, Freezing Cold, and Gnawing Hunger–and no matter how hard Lisl tried to ignore them she could not wish them away.

⁀

Near the end of January, on one of their searches, a sudden freezing snowstorm raced across the fields and caught them by surprise. Strong gusts hurled stinging icy needles at their faces.

Lisl wrapped her coat tightly around her shivering body. Her hands felt like icicles, ready to drop off and shatter to pieces.

Dieter pulled his knit cap over his forehead and the girls tightened their scarves around their heads. They turned their backs against the wind and continued walking the tracks.

Lisl thought of her warm slippers behind the stove, and maybe a pot of hot soup–it made the cold bearable.

They found some coal between snow-free patches the locomotives' steam had uncovered. But the new snow came down hard and fast. They had to work quickly before the white blanket covered the black treasure.

Charlotte was more concerned about Lisl's and Dieter's wellbeing than finding coal and often checked on them. Ellen, on the other hand, gave all her concentration to the spilled chunks. In her determination she filled her bucket in half the time. Now and then, barely visible in the drifting snow, Ellen slapped her arms around her shoulders, trying to warm herself. Lisl tried it, but it only made her feel sore.

Suddenly the air-raid sirens whined in the distance along with the wind, interrupting their search. Charlotte raced across the tracks, pulling Dieter and Lisl along. They dropped their almost-full buckets and scurried into the nearby woods.

"I hope the air raid won't last too long. Look at the sled and buckets, Lisl. We've got to remember where they are in case they get snowed under," Ellen said.

"Let's put a stick in the snow," Lisl said, but sadly discovered there were no sticks in sight. They, too, had been collected for firewood.

Ellen reluctantly walked toward the woods. They had lost their collection several times in the previous winter when darkness or snow had covered their find.

The pine woods offered some relief from the wind as they huddled together. Lisl gazed between the treetops toward the sound of British bombers, but all she saw was the swirling snowstorm.

Frightened by explosions nearby, Charlotte put her arms around Dieter and Lisl, moving them farther away from the tracks and deeper into the woods. "Ellen, come on," she called.

Every now and then, with the sound of explosions, a glow of fire flashed through the storm, but finally the bombing stopped. Charlotte wanted to wait a little longer to be sure.

"I think it's safe to come out," Ellen called. They walked back to the tracks before the night spread its dark blanket over the landscape.

Lisl listened for the all-clear siren, but heard only the howling wind.

Although the bombers had moved on, a British observer plane appeared suddenly, flying low over their heads along the rails and vanishing into the twilight of drifting snow.

In the distance, fire and smoke remained. In the thick blanket of snow, the rails became a visible target, cutting clear dark lines through the white landscape. The enemy's efforts to interrupt the supply to the warfront had failed. The heavy snowstorm had caught them by surprise as well.

"I think they missed." Dieter looked down the tracks while blowing warmth into his cupped hands.

Lisl gazed down the rails, pulling her oversized, flapping coat tightly around her. "Where would we find coal if the tracks were destroyed?" She whispered into the wind.

The bright whiteout that had whipped around them earlier turned to dark gray, fiercely tearing at them as darkness crept closer.

They searched beside the tracks, but found no sign of sled, buckets or the almost-filled sack of coal. Tears of anger glistened in Ellen's eyes as she pushed one snow mound after another only to uncover shrubs instead of their collected treasure.

Lisl stood ankle-deep in snow; her arms wrapped around her chest. Her teeth chattered. "We have to go home or we won't find our way back."

They walked along the rails while looking for the buckets. In some areas they sank waist-deep into the snow drifts, and soon it became too dark to see the outline of the mounds. The snow had swallowed buckets, sled, and coal. No longer sure if the place they were searching was the right location, Ellen finally gave up.

"We'd better come back in the morning before someone else finds it." She kicked the snow-covered shrub mounds she stumbled on.

They turned from the tracks and slid down the embankment, hanging on tight to each other. They made their way toward the trail beside Eichelsee, a small frozen lake. The storm intensified, screaming along with the all-clear siren. Danger had passed.

The blackouts allowed no lights from the town to guide them in the right direction. But the sound of the all-clear siren, however brief, pointed the way.

Ellen was determined to find her way back and grabbed onto Charlotte who had Dieter and Lisl in tow. Staying together was important in approaching darkness.

They found themselves against hedges that surrounded the fields and soon realized they had lost the trail.

Charlotte looked panicked. Lisl was not concerned; her sister always reacted that way even though she was the oldest.

"Don't worry; we'll make it home," Lisl yelled. But Charlotte couldn't hear through the howling wind. She wiped her tears with the back of her mitten, smearing coal dust across her face.

"We should have left earlier, before it got too dark," she shouted at Ellen.

"It was your idea to stay in the woods so long," Ellen snapped back.

Lisl knew it was normal for her sisters to argue. Sometimes it even calmed Charlotte, and Dieter and Lisl found comfort in their squabbling.

They stumbled over snow-covered shrubs, fighting their way out of snow drifts. When one fell, the others tumbled down as well.

Dieter followed blindly, pressing his face against Charlotte. At least he kept the hurling, stinging snowflakes from his eyes. Lisl wanted to close her eyes as well, but she was convinced that they were walking in circles. Yet she stumbled aimlessly along, holding on tight as they tried to find the narrow trail. They backtracked often when they found themselves in ditches or against hedges.

Soon Lisl could not feel her feet at all. She closed her sore eyes and just followed along, falling and stumbling through the snow.

Finally the ground turned smooth.

"I think we've found the road," Ellen shouted. Their strides became faster, more confident.

When they approached their garden path on Muehlenweg, Lisl was surprised to see a single, small light. "Look," she shouted, "Look up there." Mama stood by the window holding a candle, even though she risked being arrested for exposing light. Mama closed the shutters and ran outside. "Are you all right? I was so worried." She pulled them into the house, dusted the snow off their clothing, and peeled them out of their coats, mittens, and shoes as they were too cold and stiff to do so themselves.

"You should never stay out in a storm. Next time come right back before it gets so bad." Mama did not seem to care that they had lost the sled and the coal.

Lisl no longer could hide her tears. Now as she warmed up, the feeling returned along with the pain. Her feet ached to the bone.

While in the woods the snow had melted in her shoes and then froze again on their way back, freezing her knit stockings to her feet. A long, painful process followed. Her mother put Lisl's feet into cold water, although it felt warm. Gradually as her feet adjusted to the temperature, Mama added warm water a little at a time.

"There, it won't be so painful if we do it nice and slow." Then Mama rubbed everyone's hands and feet until they felt warm again. Lisl stood by the stove, the warmth from the coal they had collected the day before made going out in the freezing wind and darkness all worthwhile. As long as the trains were running there would be a warm stove—at least in the evenings.

Mama had warmed their slippers and served hot goat's milk and bread.

Lisl heard the howling wind and freezing snow tapping against the window as though it too wanted to come inside.

She gazed around the room and felt safe. Dieter looked happy too even though his face was red and sore. Ellen and Charlotte smiled triumphantly at each other with an invisible bond like mountain climbers who had reached the highest peak against all odds.

"Mama, Charlotte and I will go back in the morning, before school. We have to get the sled and coal," Ellen said, unwilling to lose her treasure to the morning searchers again.

Charlotte reached across the table, holding Ellen's hand in agreement.

"I'll come, too." Lisl raised her hand.

They were exhausted, yet willing to play with Kurt who brought a game board to the table with a hopeful look in his eyes.

Lisl leaned toward the candle's flame. The warmth felt good on her sore face and even the fierce storm outside sounded comforting. But the wail of the air-raid siren cut their game short, and Mama extinguished the candle on the table. The family listened in darkness as bombers flew across the sky toward their target.

Mama did not appear to be concerned. "Don't worry Kurt. The planes fly on to bigger cities. Our little town is safe for the time being."

This did not stop Kurt from crawling under the kitchen bench into his safe little corner.

Lisl peered through the window into the storm. "I hope we don't have to go outside again to the shelter."

"No, Lisl. Tonight you can sleep in your bed no matter what," Mama promised.

With the monotone of the all-clear siren, Mama lit the candle again, but Kurt remained under the bench, "just to be safe," he said.

෨

When Lisl awoke next morning, her sisters' beds were empty. She ran downstairs. Even though the dawn shed little light, Charlotte and Ellen had already gone in search of the sled and coal.

Lisl opened the front door and found a frosty calm in the early morning light. It was still, a magical transformation from the night before.

The snow was pasted against the threshold and halfway up the door. But a few steps farther out, the wind had swept the snow clear to the frozen ground. High snowdrifts against the west side of the house almost covered the windows, while the northeast side had very little snow on the ground.

Lisl saw her sisters' footprints mark a trail down to Muehlenweg. She sighed. Charlotte had promised to wake her so she could go with them. Maybe her sister had forgotten her promise, or maybe she thought that they would be faster without her. Now she could only worry about them.

An hour and a half later, Dieter and Lisl were on their way to school. Charlotte and Ellen came toward them, pulling the sled along Muehlenweg. Lisl ran with Dieter to help them. Charlotte and Ellen looked tired with strained red faces and steam in their breath like an over-worked locomotive. They had pulled the heavy load through the deep snowdrifts and welcomed the help. Still, they wore triumphant smiles when Mama came running, beaming at the sight of coal.

With only a short warm-up period while eating their small breakfast, Charlotte and Ellen were ready to leave for school. At least they could rest up in school, Lisl thought.

When they arrived at the schoolhouse, a group of students had gathered in front of the closed door reading an attached sign. Charlotte read aloud: "*Due to frigid cold and frozen water pipes, school will be closed until further notice.*"

Lisl did not mind. Lately her fingers were too stiff to hang on to her pencil, and her feet ached from sitting motionless in the cold classroom in her snow-soaked stockings and shoes. Now they could stay in their warm beds a little longer before going out to search for fuel and return in plenty of time before nightfall.

∾

Spring seemed so far away and, to Lisl's disappointment, the first day of February seemed even colder. Her thoughts drifted to daydreams of shedding her shoes and running barefoot through the warm sunny meadow.

The long periods of freezing weather and lack of food numbed her mind. Her brothers did not notice when she found the simplest words hard to spell during word games.

Ellen thawed a big pot of ice on the kitchen stove for drinking water and to wash up. It was strange seeing Ellen move in slow motion–she disliked slowpokes.

Charlotte sat wrapped in a blanket. Her knitting needles, too, clicked in slow motion. Ordinarily they moved faster than Lisl could watch. Now, Charlotte stared at her work when her hands did not cooperate. Lisl felt sorry for her. Charlotte always felt the need to keep busy.

Charlotte and Ellen were not fighting much lately. Little remarks that usually erupted into insult-screaming battles passed unchallenged.

Mama sat quietly mending stockings and socks for farmers who were willing to give food in payment. A saddened expression swept across Mama's face now and then as she watched her children through hazel eyes.

"Wouldn't it be wonderful to go to sleep when it gets cold, and wake up when it's warm again just like bears?" Lisl asked.

"You wouldn't want to sleep your life away," Mama said.

"I would. Better than being so cold all the time," Ellen said through chattering teeth.

Charlotte nodded, pulling her blanket tightly around her shoulders.

"It will soon pass," Mama promised. But Lisl knew she was trying to cheer them up. Many more cold weeks lay ahead.

Mama put down her mending and stood up. "It's time for bed."

The upstairs bedroom walls and ceilings glistened with frost. Yet, Lisl and Dieter found magic in their frigid surroundings. The glow of a candle set the frosty rooms sparkling, creating walls of diamonds.

Dieter was lucky. He slipped into a bed that Kurt had already warmed, because he went to bed an hour earlier. During the cold weather, the boys slept in one bed with Kurt's comforter piled on top of Dieter's.

The girls undressed under the covers after their beds warmed. Lately, however, they stayed half-dressed because the sirens often chased them out of bed and into the shelter in the middle of the night.

Still, once they warmed up in their big feather beds, they stayed cozy until morning. During the night, however, a frosty patch developed, sticking cold and stiff where their breath touched the covers.

Before Lisl went to bed she gazed through the window in the dark, blowing against the glass to see outside through half-opened shutters. She admired the beautiful art work the frost had painted on the glass. Crystal patterns of flowers and ferns in intricate detail covered the window.

Maybe Mama was right about not sleeping my life away and missing this icy creation. And even as she stood admiring nature's painting, a new masterpiece covered the void her breath had left.

"Lisl, are you frozen to the floor?" Charlotte mumbled from under her covers.

"Did you see the pretty pictures on the window?" Lisl stood shaking, her arms wrapped tightly around her chest.

"You said that last night. They look the same to me—cold!" Ellen's voice quavered.

"Goodnight, Lisl. Go to bed before you freeze," Charlotte said.

"Goodnight." Lisl crawled under the blanket. Her body tightened into a cold shivering ball with clenched teeth until her jaw ached. She thought of a beautiful snow princess skating on a sparkling flower-design ice rink. Finally she felt warm and slowly uncurled.

She liked the stillness of the night when it remained undisturbed by air raids. Her sisters must be warm, she thought, as she listened to their loud, deep breathing as they slept. The boys in the next room were quiet as well.

She wondered if her mother had fallen asleep by the kitchen table again. Sometimes, when Lisl went downstairs to use the bathroom, she found her mother with her head on her folded arms over an open book. Only when the fire died and the cold crept in did she wake up coughing, and Lisl heard her go to bed.

CHAPTER 4

Witches and Willow Branches

Schools remained closed to Lisl's delight. She relished the sunny day, running with her sisters and brother down the garden path to the creek behind the Burlein Mill in search of firewood.

A bright stillness froze the landscape motionless like a Christmas card. Only the laughter of her sisters and Dieter, and the forlorn call of a crow, interrupted the silence of this sunny winter afternoon.

Lisl stood in awe. The weeping willow trees were magically transformed into bridal veils, reflecting their frost-covered branches on the icy surface of the creek. She lifted her face toward the warm sun, gazing through the glistening twigs of the willows.

Her sisters were busy reaching under the snow cover, pulling out branches that Frau Burlein had cut off her trees in late fall. The thin little branches lay scattered, hidden under the white blanket. Lisl and Dieter gathered what their sisters freed from the frosty hold and piled them in a stack.

The snow shook off like downy feathers, and when Dieter tried to make a snowball it fell apart in his mittens.

"I'll bet you can't do this." Dieter swung on a branch and dropped down on the other side of the creek–the witch's side. They always collected whatever was within their reach for cooking fuel, even if it meant searching on Frau Burlein's land.

"How will you get back over here? The branches are much shorter there," Ellen called.

"Oh, let's go over there," Charlotte said. "That's where Frau Burlein cut the bigger branches."

"I don't need a branch." Lisl took a running leap over a narrow part of the creek, barely clearing the frozen surface.

"That looks easy." Charlotte had no trouble making the jump with her long skinny legs.

"Well, what makes you think that's such a great accomplishment?" Ellen fished for an argument. "Even if you didn't make it, the creek is frozen solid, so you can't fall into the water." Ellen took a few deep breaths, ran toward the bank and jumped, but slipped on the ice.

"See what I mean." She lay on the ice, smiling at Charlotte. Lisl was not at all sure that Ellen had fallen by accident. She had to prove her point. But when she struggled to her feet, her legs slid out from under her, and the surface cracked. With a yell, she fell through the ice into the moving water. Charlotte and Lisl tried to grab hold of her, but they could not get her out without falling in themselves. Ellen's water-soaked clothing weighed her down.

Dieter held out a branch.

"Grab it, Ellen," Lisl shouted in panic.

Ellen looked dazed. Waist deep in the frigid water, she tried to climb out but the edge of the ice kept breaking away.

"Grab the branch, grab the branch," Charlotte shouted.

Finally Ellen held on tight and they slowly pulled her out of the water.

Ellen's teeth chattered, her body shook as the frost started to stiffen her clothes. Before they had a chance to get Ellen to the other side again, Frau Burlein appeared.

Lisl shouted, "run," but stood frozen like a statue as did Charlotte and Dieter. They had not seen the old woman coming. Now it was too late.

"How many times do I have to tell you not to play around here?" Frau Burlein waved her cane above her head.

The old woman grabbed Ellen's arm and hastily dragged her away.

Lisl shouted, "Let go of her."

Ellen tried to get away but her coughing made her limp and without a struggle she stumbled along. It all happened so fast. Charlotte looked as though she were about to cry.

Frau Burlein's long coat swept a wide trail in the snow, flanked by Ellen's small footprints on one side and the poke mark of the cane on the other.

Then, as if on cue, the children followed Ellen's footprints across a bridge. The trail disappeared behind a high wooden door where horse-drawn wagons entered for grain processing.

Dieter rushed to the door, grabbed the handle and tried to open it–he could not. They all pulled together. Still it would not budge.

"Ellen, come out right now." Charlotte shouted. "Do you hear me? Ellen! Ellen!" She pressed her ear against the door, as did Lisl, but all they heard was a door slam inside the mill's courtyard. Dieter looked worried. "What's she going to do to Ellen?"

Charlotte cried, "If anything happens to her, I will never forgive myself. Mama will be so upset. We should have run her home as soon as we got her out of the water." Charlotte blew her red nose and sniffled, pulling on the big iron ring handle again.

"You know Ellen! She will get away from Frau Burlein if she wants to." Lisl laughed, acting as if she knew that Ellen would be all right.

It did not work. Charlotte kept crying.

Dieter peeked through a knothole in the door.

"Do you see anything?" Lisl tried to look through a crack.

"Yeah. A big wagon . . . and a plow . . . and two sawhorses and . . . wow, what a big pile of firewood."

"Let's try the front door." Lisl hoped to find Ellen before Mama missed them and came looking.

They ran up a trail around the mill to the other side of the house where the living quarters were located. A small bridge a few meters from Muehlenweg led across the creek to the front door. They stopped on the bridge, watching the water beneath the frozen surface flow into a low opening beside the building. The water rushed over the icicle-laden waterwheel where it joined the lower creek–the place they had been searching for firewood. There, under the ice cover, the water ran on to the next mill two kilometers away.

Frau Burlein had closed operation of her mill about three years ago when her son was killed in an accident at a threshing machine. Except when chasing the children, the woman was seldom seen in public.

They were waiting by the entry, hoping to see Ellen walk out, when Charlotte realized the door was ajar. Dieter knocked but got no reply. Lisl pushed the door open and peeked in. Charlotte and Dieter stood close behind.

Silently they stepped inside and found themselves in a narrow, long hallway with a row of high little windows on one side. Dusty shafts of sunlight filtered through the dirty glass, and spread in even spaces across the floor like railroad tracks. The scent of straw and apples hung in the air, and the gurgling of water behind the opposite wall reminded Lisl of a summer's day, although she shivered from the cold.

They followed the rail pattern and came on a single door at the end of the hallway. Dieter looked wide-eyed at Lisl and Charlotte when they heard a muffled voice behind the door. Charlotte had stopped crying and motioned for Lisl, who stood closest, to knock. Gingerly she raised her hand and Dieter gave her an encouraging nod. Lisl wrapped her knuckles on the door. Her heart pounded in her throat as she listened.

Slowly the door swung open into a big room with a crackling fire in an open fireplace. The heavy wood-planked floor creaked under Frau Burlein's weight with every step.

She looked down at Lisl from under her headscarf. "Don't just stand there letting in the cold, get in here and shut the door."

As soon as they had stepped inside, the woman slammed the door shut. Lisl jumped as if a trap had sprung.

"You look like you could do with a little warming up." Frau Burlein grabbed Dieter and Lisl by their shoulders, pushing them ahead of her, closer to the fireplace. Charlotte followed, a worried look on her face.

The story of Hansel and Gretel came to Lisl's mind and when she looked at Dieter she knew he too thought of it.

But then they saw Ellen wrapped in a blanket, sipping a hot drink. Her clothes were spread over chairs around the fire.

Lisl and Dieter stood motionless where the woman had placed them. When Frau Burlein left the room, Charlotte ran to Ellen, fussing over her, pulling the blanket tightly around her.

"What happened?" Now Charlotte looked more curious than worried.

"We had her all wrong; she is really very nice." Ellen looked cozy in her blanket, but her teeth still chattered behind her blue lips. The bottom part of her long braids hung wet and heavy alongside her pale face.

Frau Burlein returned carrying a small wooden tray with three mugs filled with hot apple cider. The towel draped over her arm she handed to Charlotte, pointing to Ellen's hair.

Dieter looked at Frau Burlein suspiciously when she handed him a mug.

The woman bent down, looking at him closely, her face in front of his. "Are you the boy who threw rocks at the icicles on my water wheel?"

Dieter stumbled backward. His eyes widened and he shook his head vigorously.

Frau Burlein straightened up again. "No, I don't think you'd do that. You're Irma's boy. She does a good job of raising you kids. Besides, you're always too busy digging in the stone break."

Her statement seemed to unnerve Dieter. How did she know, his eyes asked Lisl. When the old woman was not looking, he whispered, "She's a spy."

Charlotte had loosened Ellen's braids and towel dried them until she cried out in pain.

"How long will it take for her clothes to dry?" Charlotte asked. "We should be getting home."

"We still have to get the wood." Lisl regretted her words as soon as they came out of her mouth.

Frau Burlein came close to Lisl. "What wood?"

"The willow branches down by the creek," Lisl said meekly, "that is if you're not using them. If you need them we'll be glad to bring them up for you." Lisl felt small as the woman stood over her.

Frau Burlein backed away. "That stuff is wet, and even when it's dry, it doesn't burn too well." She thought for a moment. "You can take some of the wood down by the lower entrance. Erwin was supposed to get it, but he never showed. I guess they don't need a warm church," she mumbled to herself.

"*Danke shoen*, Frau Burlein." Lisl curtsied, looking up at her, trying to see her expression underneath her scarf. Lisl thought she saw her smile, and shyly smiled back.

"Turn the clothes over to dry the other side. And spread them out good," the woman told Charlotte and Lisl before she went into the kitchen.

"She must have put them through the wringer, they're almost dry," Charlotte whispered to Lisl as they turned the clothing.

Dieter sat obediently on the bench near the fireplace, his hands wrapped around the warm mug. He gazed at all the wonderful things on shelves and open cupboards. Beer steins–some that looked like old men's faces, and others like fancy castles, and others like cats. Wood carvings of bear, deer and other animals were displayed throughout the room.

Sunlight flooded through four tall, narrow side-by-side windows dressed in faded lace curtains that reminded Lisl of fragile spider webs. She looked through the dirty glass and saw the creek below with the wide expanse of the meadow. The built-in window seat, covered with worn cushions, held an open book and reading glasses. She pictured Frau Burlein reading there in the afternoon sun. Lisl smiled when she thought of Mama and her reading chair by the window.

A clock in the middle of the fireplace mantel chimed three times and the play began. A little door opened on one side of the clock and two tiny figures marched out on a turning platform. The little couple danced around each other to a glockenspiel and marched back in.

"Did you see that?" Dieter whispered, his eyes wide, just as Frau Burlein came back into the room.

She handed each a cookie, and when she gave one to Dieter, Lisl was sure this time she did see the woman smile.

Lisl was famished. They all took great care not to miss a crumb of the unexpected treats. The warmth of the fireplace and the cookie reminded Lisl of her grandmother, but her house always smelled of fresh-brewed coffee.

Ellen smiled her sparkling smile again. She had stopped shivering and coughing.

Charlotte braided Ellen's hair. Her clothes were still a little damp, but Ellen did not mind. She was thoroughly warmed up.

One by one they shook Frau Burlein's hand.

"*Vielen Dank*, Frau Burlein."

"*Danke shoen*, Frau Burlein," Dieter said.

The woman held Dieter's hand just a little longer, looking at him as though she wanted to say something. Then abruptly she let go.

"Don't forget the wood," she said in her gruff hoarse voice. "Here, I'll let you out the other door." She walked down the steep stairs ahead of them with surprising agility for someone with such long skirts and a cane. As they came to the lower part of the mill she led them to the woodpile near the big door.

"Hold out your arms," Frau Burlein commanded and stacked meter-length pieces of wood onto Dieter's arms. The girls helped each other load up.

Slowly Frau Burlein pushed the heavy, creaking door open and let them out.

"*Vielen Dank. Aufwiedersehen*," they called to Frau Burlein.

Lisl heard the door close behind her, but she was unable to turn; her arms were loaded too high. She barely could wait to see Mama's reaction when she saw all that wood, and hopefully she would not be too upset when she heard about Ellen.

They all were happy to carry the wood, especially since it was only a short block home. Still, the wood was getting heavy.

Lisl walked beside Dieter, careful not to drop any wood.

"Have you ever seen her at the stone break?" Dieter peered at Lisl over his stack of wood.

Lisl shook her head. "No, never." She wondered why she would want to.

"Do you think there are two of them?"

"I don't think so." Lisl laughed, almost dropping her wood.

"Do you think she will be nice from now on?"

Lisl brightened. "Maybe she only pretends to be mean."

"Yeah."

They walked in the tracks their sisters had left in the snow, but stayed well behind because Charlotte and Ellen were arguing again.

CHAPTER 5

The Wine Cellar

"Wake up. Hurry. We have to go."

Charlotte stood over Lisl, shaking her awake.

"Come on, get up," Ellen joined in.

"Not again." Lisl covered her head to drown out the blaring sirens and her sisters' shouting voices.

Charlotte pulled the covers off. "Get up or you'll be left behind."

Lisl would rather have taken her chances with the bombers than go to the cold, smelly air-raid shelter. But she knew her family would not leave without her. It seemed she had just closed her eyes a moment ago, but it was close to midnight.

Mama poked her head through the door. "Are you ready, girls? Hurry."

Lisl had barely set foot on the floor when she noticed her sisters were dressed in extra clothing, ready to go. She never understood how they managed to wake from a sound sleep and jump into action at a moment's notice.

In the dim light of blackout Lisl struggled into her clothes, often ending up wearing them backward or inside-out. No one cared as long as she got out of bed and dressed to keep warm.

Shivering and frightened, they gathered by the door where suitcases, bundles and one blanket stood ready.

Kurt cried. His little nose was running. "I don't want to go to the '*dungeon*'," as the neighborhood children called the wine cellar.

Dieter was still half asleep. He leaned against the door quiet and pale, but ready to go. "At least we don't have to carry the heavy load any more," he mumbled.

About a week ago Mama had decided to store her heirlooms and photographs in the big empty metal-lined box they used to store flour and other dry goods. Now it was Mama's treasure chest, filled with her precious mementos. She had slid the box under the basement stairs for safekeeping.

Lisl had watched Mama handle her special things before she packed them away. It was a hard decision because she might lose them if their house got bombed. Now she brought only important papers, a few photographs, and clothing the family might need in case they found themselves homeless. Still, the tablecloth grandmother had embroidered for Mama's wedding always found a little space in her suitcase.

Mama opened the door and looked back as if to memorize her home in case she would find a pile of rubble in its place. She took the lead through the garden's narrow path down toward Muehlenweg. The family eased their way along the snowy border of the path in the dark because flashlights were not allowed. Charlotte carried Kurt on her back. She had to hang on to him or he would have run back to the house.

Unlike the townspeople, Lisl and her family had only a short distance to walk to get to the shelter. Lisl heard people down by the road, crunching along on snow-covered Muehlenweg. The sirens still blared as Mama with her family merged with the stream of townspeople.

A procession of dark, ghostly figures moved like sleepwalkers. Lisl could not see their faces, but she heard their muffled voices and whispered words. Were they crying or praying?

Women clutched babies or bundles of possessions. Lisl wanted to comfort the trembling woman beside her. Yet Lisl was shaking as well, but mostly from the cold, not fear. They had made this trip many times before so Lisl and Dieter had adjusted to the routine.

Night air raids were still frightening for Charlotte. But she was always fearful when sirens blared no matter what time of day, and Kurt cried predictably. Lisl just crossed her fingers, hoping the bombers would not notice their insignificant little town.

In the cold, dark night, Lisl felt comforted by the grip of her mother's warm hand. When they arrived at the shelter, Lisl pulled her hand from a woman who had a panicked look on her face. "Walter," the woman shouted.

"He's here with me." Mama stood by the narrow path leading into the shelter, holding a little boy's hand. Mama headed for the underground wine cellar with Charlotte, Ellen and Kurt.

Lisl and Dieter trailed behind. "Here we go again, into the dungeon, the dragon's lair," Dieter said.

The rounded opening of the tunnel that led into the wine cellar did resemble a dragon's long, outstretched neck with its entrance mouth wide open. "Oooh, we got swallowed," Lisl wailed as they walked through the neck of the dragon.

Charlotte shook her head. "Can't you ever be serious?"

They entered the low curved tunnel, about five meters long, into a large dome-like room beneath a shrub-covered hill. Big empty barrels, some broken, stood against the walls. Lisl and Dieter thought of them as dragon eggs. "The broken ones have already hatched. We'd better watch out," Dieter said.

Lisl compared the size of the dragon eggs with the narrow tunnel. "Mama, how did they get these barrels in here?"

Mama looked up at the barrels. "I know. They're tall. They probably were constructed inside the cellar."

Lisl remembered three winters ago, when she and her sisters had followed some of the older neighbor boys into the dragon's lair and sneaked out with some loose staves. With strings fastened on each side, they became wonderful skis. How mysterious and spooky this place had been.

Now the wine cellar seemed different. The excitement was gone, replaced by stifling odors of stale wine, soiled diapers and too many people crammed together. Lisl felt nauseous just thinking about all the foul odors.

The dimly lit dome room was about twenty meters across. A circle of heavy support pillars, about six meters high, stood in a circle halfway between the walls and the center, reassuring people that this dome would not collapse on their heads.

The tunnel was the only entry to the cellar, but in the middle of the rounded dome ceiling was a small square ventilation grid. The shelter was dark except for one bare dim bulb dangling where the tunnel met the dome.

Since Mainbernheim had no air-raid shelter, old Herr Reinhard volunteered his wine cellar. Reinhard's father had built it a long time ago to keep the wine at a perfect temperature. The winery was no longer in use and the cellar had become neglected. Lisl tried to imagine the cellar when it was filled with huge barrels of famous Franken wine.

Mama spread the blanket at the far side of the cellar to keep out of the flow of people. Charlotte and Ellen piled the luggage and bundles against the barrels.

Dieter and Lisl watched flashlight beams crisscross through the darkness of the dome.

"It looks like the big artillery searchlight looking for British and American bombers," Lisl said.

Dieter shook his head. "Yes, but not in here. Here they search for the hatched dragons."

But soon they tired of the light show and concentrated on the sounds outside, anxious to hear the all-clear siren.

Coughing, crying and shouting filled the cellar. Lisl covered her ears with her hands, trying to shut out the noise. It did not help.

A long hour of waiting and listening followed. Dieter sat with Lisl on her little suitcase.

Sometimes in past trips to the dungeon, they'd barely settled down when the all-clear siren sounded and they rushed back to their still-warm beds. But other nights they waited for hours before they were allowed to go home.

Dieter pulled Lisl's hands away from her ears. "Can you hear any bombers yet?"

She listened, then shook her head. "I don't think we could hear them over all that yelling."

But soon a loud roar of British bombers brought sudden silence.

"I hope they don't drop the bombs on our house," Charlotte whispered, moving closer to her mother.

The bombers passed without releasing their bombs. Lisl wanted to get back into her bed while there was still a little warmth left. She fastened her headscarf tightly around her hair, afraid the lice would find her again. She could almost feel them crawling into her hair the way they did a year ago. It took Mama a long time to get rid of the pests.

Mama sat on the blanket, her back against the luggage, her children gathered around her.

Lisl thought of the red hen sheltering her little chicks under her feathers. She felt like one of the chicks as she huddled closer to her mother.

They nodded off a few minutes at a time or until Kurt started to cry again.

Mama rocked him in her arms, trying to calm him. Even after he had fallen asleep she continued to rock. When Mama dozed off, her rocking stopped and Kurt started to cry again. She kissed his forehead tenderly, trying to get him to sleep again.

"Liebling, just try to sleep a little. Time will go so much faster." She stroked his hair and hummed a lullaby.

"Mama, why can't we stay in our own cellar?" Lisl asked again. But her mother only stroked her face without an answer, the way she always responded.

Lisl tried to stretch. Even sitting on her suitcase, her bones ached from the damp, cold ground until she felt numb and stiff. Although a flimsily constructed outhouse stood a few meters outside the entry, some mothers brought their own version of toilets for their little ones. The foul smell made Lisl clench her jaw. "I feel sick," she whispered through her teeth.

"Think of something nice so you don't smell that horrible stink anymore," Dieter said.

She tried to remember the wonderful scent of the lilacs in their garden and the fresh air after a spring rain, but the noise in the cellar interfered with her imagination.

Dieter pulled Lisl's hands off her ears. "Do you want to sneak out for a while to get some fresh air and stretch your legs?"

She nodded and tried to stand, but found that there was little room to move. They might step on someone in the dark.

Charlotte rested on her mother's shoulder. Every once in a while she fell asleep for a few minutes, but awoke with a start at the slightest sound of airplanes–even German planes.

Ellen always found a little rest with her head on one of her sisters' laps. She could sleep in any position, and under any circumstance. All the noise and turmoil did not seem to bother her. Lisl wished she could do that.

Dieter lifted Lisl's hands from her ears again so she could hear the all-clear siren.

Her face brightened, she sprung to her feet and grabbed her suitcase before the rest of her family realized they could go home now.

CHAPTER 6

Bringing Opa Home

A relentless freeze kept the ground solid although it was late February. Patches of snow clung stubbornly to lower areas where the sun lost its reach. The fog had lifted; a clear blue sky greeted the morning.

On her way to school, Lisl admired the frozen wonderland. Sparkling ice crystals covered every twig, every blade of grass with winter brilliance. The big weeping willows sparkled like crystal clouds in the morning sun. *Would they break if I were to touch them?*

Lisl's breath hung like a cloud, slowly floating toward the sky. There she saw a white stripe marking its way across the blue morning like a chalk mark on a blackboard. Her gaze traced the line to find its origin. A small plane, barely visible, flew from the direction of Iphofen toward Kitzingen. The smoke stripe trailed like a long banner in a parade.

Mama had sent Dieter off earlier worried that, together, he and Lisl would play along the way and bc latc for school. Lisl started to run when she realized she was late even without Dieter.

She slid into her seat right after the bell rang. Her teacher frowned at her–a reminder to be on time in the future. Staying after class in the cold room was something Lisl hated more than the air-raid sirens.

At recess, Lisl played with her classmates in the schoolyard. A low rumble in the distance brought their games to a stop, their eyes searching the sky.

Soon it escalated into a roar. Full alarm blared at the same moment the bombers appeared over the rooftops from the direction of Iphofen, following the still-visible smoke line in the sky.

"American bombers," a student shouted, pointing at the huge planes. They flew in close formation and when they were out of sight, another wave appeared.

The students stood stunned, the sight of these huge bombers had a hypnotic effect. Lisl wanted to run, but her feet felt too heavy to move. The rumble of bomber engines vibrated through her body. She had not seen the enemy so close and so clearly before.

Finally a few students ran, ducking beneath the barren branches of the hedge surrounding the playfield. But they provided little protection.

Herr Kiefer came running into the schoolyard.

"Children leave your school bags and get to the shelters." Yet he too stood motionless in the middle of the playfield, watching the bombers fly so close together they almost touched. But when Herr Stolz ran out, blowing his whistle, shouting, "Run, children, into the shelters," the spell was broken. Lisl's head filled with the sound of the wailing sirens, the ominous rumble of propellers, and her teacher's frantic whistle as she ran from the schoolyard.

She caught up with her sisters and Dieter as they raced through the town along Adolf Hitler Strasse. The bombers had moved on, the roar of their engines replaced with the sound of explosions in the distance.

Most of the children headed for the wine cellar shelter. Charlotte grabbed Dieter's and Lisl's hands as they ran after Ellen on the way home.

Out of breath, they made it up the path. Mama stood in the open doorway holding Kurt. She hurried them down to the root cellar.

"I think they bombed Kitzingen," Mama said. She paced in and out between the root cellar and the basement hallway. Finally, she ran upstairs and out into the garden with her children after her. They hurried to the hill behind their garden. Together they watched the bombing from the cover of a shrubby little forest. From there they had a good view of the surrounding towns. The ground defense artillery attacked from every direction.

"Oh no," Mama cried as she watched a thick smoke rise in the distance after thundering explosions. The beautiful clear sky now looked like an upcoming storm as smoke spread in threatening clouds across the horizon.

Kitzingen had a military airport and an artillery installation, the Flack Caserne.

Mama sighed. "I hope Opa and Anni had time to go to the shelter. Maybe the military installations were the targets." The sirens still blared although the bombing had stopped.

"Do you think their house was hit?" Lisl whispered, not breaking her gaze from the rising smoke columns.

"I don't know," Mama said. "I hope Opa and Aunt Anni are all right."

"Can Charlotte and I go to Kitzingen to check on Opa?" Ellen asked even though Charlotte vigorously shook her head.

"No. You'd better stay here. I'll take the bike, it's faster."

Kitzingen was six kilometers northwest of Mainbernheim. Grandfather's house was on the other end of town, making the distance close to ten kilometers. They had walked often to visit Opa and Aunt Anni, but riding bikes took only half the time.

"Charlotte, keep the children near the house. When you hear the alarm, get everyone into the root cellar," Mama said. She maneuvered her bike down the steep garden path onto Muehlenweg and rode away.

Lisl and Dieter returned to the fields to see if the rising smoke had stopped.

Two small planes flew low overhead and sent them scrambling for cover. Lisl stopped when she recognized the sound of German planes.

Dieter gazed at the rising smoke over Kitzingen, his forehead wrinkled. "What if they bomb Kitzingen again and Mama is right in the middle?"

"I don't think so. The bombers can't come back that soon. They have to go home to get more benzine," Lisl reassured him. Still, they sat near the edge of the field by the garden entrance, watching the smoke rise, waiting for their mother's return.

Two hours later Mama pushed her bike up the path, looking pale and exhausted. "Opa's house is all right," she said, gasping for breath. "The old and new Main River bridges are still standing." She stood by the window, gazing across the garden, trying to calm her breathing.

"Mama, you shouldn't have taken the bike in your condition," Charlotte scolded. She set a cup of tea on the little table beside Mama's chair. "Did you see Opa?

"Opa is all right and Aunt Anni had to go back to the hospital. They need all the help they can get."

"Did Opa make it to the shelter?"

"No, there was no time, no warning." Mama sat in her chair by the window and picked up her cup. They gathered around her while she told them that no significant damage was done to the town, only the military installations.

The afternoon stayed quiet and the family stayed close together.

Charlotte still looked pale and frightened, biting her nails. "Mama, could the bombers hit Mainbernheim by mistake?"

"Don't worry, Charlotte. Our little town is not worth bombing. I'm sure they know which town to bomb."

By evening Charlotte had calmed herself after a few arguments with Ellen who had teased her for being afraid *after* the bombing was over.

The air-raid siren remained silent. The family could sleep in their beds, although they stayed fully dressed.

The next morning came with a frosty, sunny brilliance just like the day before. Lisl searched for another marking stripe like the plane had left the day before, but saw only clear blue sky.

Dieter skipped beside her on their way to school.

The frosty designs on the shrubs and trees were not as elaborate without the fog. Lisl stopped. "Look, it's like the frost dipped the edges of each leaf in sugar."

Dieter laughed. "I'll bet the sun licks it off by the time we get out of school."

When Lisl arrived at school her classmates told stories about the bombing.

"Lisl, did you go to Kitzingen?" Inge asked.

"No, but my mother went to check on our Opa."

Leo ran between them. "Just wait. Soon it will be our turn. Bang." He made an awful sound, scaring Inge.

"Did you go?" Lisl asked her friend.

"No, we went to the shelter."

As Lisl listened to her classmates, she learned that most of them had gone to the wine cellar shelter. Others, like her mother, had gone to Kitzingen to check on relatives and friends.

Class began with a warning siren. Lisl jumped to her feet and some of the students ran to the door waiting for full alarm. But after a few minutes the all-clear siren brought them back to their seats.

Still, Lisl kept her book bag close, ready to run. Her classmates were distracted as well, unable to concentrate on their lessons.

Two hours later the warning siren sounded again, followed by full alarm a few minutes later. Lisl ran out of school with her classmates who scattered in all directions.

Sirens screamed from Kitzingen as well as other smaller towns in the area. They reminded Lisl of a discordant concert as she raced toward her home. Many children and their families ran along Muehlenweg with her, but went on to the wine cellar shelter. Mama was waiting by the door and hurried her into the root cellar to join the rest of the family.

The bombers had returned. Kitzingen seemed the selected target and was bombed again.

Mama sat at the bottom of the basement steps, waiting out the alarm. The bombing seemed to go on forever.

After the attack had stopped, the singular tone of the all-clear siren rang out and again Mama made the trip to Kitzingen. This time Lisl and Ellen walked with her, leaving Charlotte in charge of the boys.

The girls ran beside their mother, trying hard to keep up with her fast pace. People on bikes and on foot raced toward Kitzingen. Lisl wondered why some of them pulled empty hand wagons.

As they neared the town Lisl saw flames, and sporadic explosions rocked in areas where fire found fuel. The Main River bridge that led into Kitzingen was undamaged, at least the new one.

Now even Ellen looked scared as screaming aid cars and horse-drawn wagons tried to reach the injured and the dead. Choking smoke and dust brought on coughing fits and made their eyes water. Lisl stared stunned in all directions while panic-stricken citizens pushed their way past.

"Keep up, girls," Mama called out.

Scrambling over smoldering piles of debris after their mother, they searched for familiar street signs.

Lisl thought they had entered hell. She could only guess which buildings the crumpled ruins might have been.

Some areas showed no signs of damage, while right beside them, whole sections were flattened to burning rubble. Empty roofless shells of large brick buildings stood hollow with blackened holes where windows used to be.

Lisl stared at the ruins, hoping to see some sign of life, but Ellen pulled her away to catch up with Mama. Through flames, smoke, and dust they searched for Opa's house.

"Dear God," Mama cried out.

Ellen and Lisl scrambled to her side, looking at a pile of rubble.

"Opa, Anni," Mama called frantically.

They made their way across the pile.

"Look," Lisl shouted when she saw Aunt Anni sitting on the concrete steps, the only part of the house still in one piece. She appeared to be in a daze but unharmed. She clutched something close to her chest, rocking back and forth. Aunt Anni did not look up when Mama approached.

Opa crawled on his hands and knees in the middle of what used to be their living room. Tears ran from his blind eyes. His cane lay beside him. Blood dripped from his fingers as he sorted through broken glass and debris.

Mama called out his name then knelt beside him. She hugged him, cradling him in her arms.

When he realized Mama was with him, he cried, "I was born in this house, and so were Karl and Anni. Everything is gone. Karl will be devastated." Opa wiped his tears.

Lisl thought that her father would not feel too bad when he saw that Opa and Aunt Anni were still alive.

Mama patted his arm. "Thank God you made it to the shelter."

"Where will we go?" Opa said, mostly to himself.

"You're welcome to stay with us. You know that." Mama put her arm around his shoulder. "The children will be happy to have their Opa there. And I will feel safer having a man around the house."

Ellen searched through the scattered belongings, looking for undamaged items. Lisl held her sleeve across her mouth to filter the smoke. Smoldering pieces of fine old furniture lay scattered among the ruins. Only a small part of an inner wall stood like a monument, clinging to a section of crumbled chimney. Their precious crystal, stained with her grandfather's blood, lay like shattered ice among the rubble. Now the frost on the willow trees she had admired the day before had list its magic. She walked slowly through the demolished house and saw a piece of the porcelain head of a beautiful china doll. Aunt Anni had allowed Lisl to play with it when she came to visit, but always reminded her how old and rare it was.

Lisl joined Anni on the steps and put her arm around her aunt's shoulder. Anni lifted her head. Still disoriented, she looked at Lisl for a moment, and with a soft moan Anni hugged her, cradling her in her arms. Without a word, Anni opened her hand and Lisl saw a piece of the doll's head.

"I saw the other half over there. I'll get it. Maybe we can put it back together." Lisl made her way across the debris. Her aunt followed. They searched for every little piece of the doll. Anni took the scarf from her blond curls and wrapped the pieces carefully inside. The thought of not having to leave even the tiniest part of the doll behind seemed to make her feel better.

Mama wrapped Opa's hands with strips she tore from a partially burned sheet. "Lisl, you'd better take Opa home.

And walk slowly. Ellen and I will help Aunt Anni search for their belongings. We will be home soon."

Lisl led Opa by his bandaged hand away from the only home he had ever known. She put her other hand over his to still his shaking. Her heart ached, seeing her grandfather so helpless. He always wanted to get around on his own with the use of his cane. His cane! "Opa, wait here." Lisl ran back into the pile of rubble and just as quickly returned.

"Here, your walking stick." She put it in his hand. He stroked her hair and tried to speak, but only swallowed hard through his tears.

They stumbled over rubble that blocked the streets. People rushed past, their faces empty, stunned. Some with gaping wounds yet still determined to piece their lives together.

Aid cars and oxen-drawn wagons drove over fallen brick walls, trying to get to the injured and dead. Broken mains shot water high into the air like fountains gone wild while firemen stood helpless. Women and children rushed with water buckets trying to drown fires too close to undamaged property.

A woman stood in her house without walls cradling a lifeless child. Lisl could no longer hold back her tears. She wanted to go to the woman, but what could she do or say to comfort her? Other women stood tearlessly stunned, covered in blood, patiently waiting for help.

Lisl gagged and swallowed hard when she smelled the sweet, sickly stench of human blood. She cried quietly. Now Opa put his hand over Lisl's when she held his too tight, squeezing the blood through his bandages. Opa could not see the terrible sights, but he could hear the cries and smell the horror. His expression mirrored the devastation.

Carefully and slowly, trying to avoid obstacles that lay in her grandfather's way, Lisl led him out of Kitzingen.

Many people walked away from the smoldering town with nothing left to look back on. A procession of hopelessness made its way south on Bundesbahn 8 toward Mainbernheim.

Survivors and their relatives dragged hand wagons loaded high with salvaged household goods—all that was left of a lifetime of accumulation.

Periodically, Opa stopped to wipe his tears with his bandaged hands. "Smoke," he said.

Grandfather's stride slowed as they neared Mainbernheim. Lisl patted his arm. He must be exhausted. They had been on the road for almost three hours. Most of that time was spent making their way across the rubble that once was Kitzingen.

They reached Mainbernheim, going through the north tower along Adolf Hitler Strasse. Townspeople were busy getting their homeless relatives and friends settled.

Lisl saw their tears and heard their worries as citizens called out to each other, wondering when it would be their turn.

Opa held Lisl's hand tight. She felt a comfort in his grip. They walked slowly through town and through the gate of Weiderturm, the south tower, toward their housing area on Muehlenweg.

"Opa, would you like to rest a while before we go up the path?"

"Opa," Dieter called out, running down the path with Kurt in tow.

"I'm here, too, Opa." Kurt ran right at his grandfather, almost knocking him down. He still didn't understand that Opa could not catch him when he hurled himself at him.

"Oh, steady there," Opa said, trying to catch his balance. The boys looked shocked when they saw his face where he had brushed his tears with his blood-soaked bandages. They took his arms and pulled him up the hill and into the house the way they always did when he came to visit. It seemed to make Opa feel better.

Charlotte cried out at the sight of him.

"His face is not injured," Lisl said quickly to calm her sister.

Charlotte hugged him, and then wiped the dried blood off his face, relieved to see that he had only minor injuries from sorting through broken glass. She hovered around him, trying to ease his pain and made a cup of tea from the chamomile leaves she had gathered the summer before. Opa always enjoyed that. She loosened his bandages to make it easier for him to lift his cup.

He finished his tea in silence. Then slowly he told them about the bombing.

"When the bombing was finally over and we came out of the shelter, everything was different. We couldn't find our home." Opa wiped his tears. "It was terrible. When Anni found the site she just cried and wouldn't tell me what was going on."

Charlotte stroked his bandaged hands now and then and cried along with him.

Just before dark, Mama, Ellen, and Anni returned exhausted and dirty. Each carried still usable household items. Mama looked tired. She had carried more than she should have in her eighth months of pregnancy.

Ellen quietly put down an armload of pots, bowls filled with blackened silverware, and utensils that had survived the fire. She sat on the kitchen chair and rested her elbows on the table, her chin in her hands, staring at nothing. Her hair fell around her sooty face and her usually sparkling blue eyes were red and filled with tears. She did not react to Charlotte's gentle touch.

Anni, too, sat unresponsive, staring at half-burned photos in her hand. She did not put them down until Opa needed her help.

At first Lisl thought it odd he would need Aunt Anni with little tasks she had seen him do many times himself. But then she saw how her aunt came to life when she thought she was needed. Opa was smart.

Mama dropped metal boxes with important papers and the bundle of slightly singed towels and tablecloths on the floor, almost falling down as well. She swept the hair from her face and sat in her chair by the window, trying hard to hide her tears. But Lisl saw her brown eyes turn hazel. She stood behind her mother's chair and wrapped her arms around her neck, putting her cheek against her mother's.

Mama held Lisl's arms tightly for some time before she said, "You did well today, Lisl. You got Opa home safe."

CHAPTER 7

Trapped

March arrived on a chilly breeze of fear as the war front steadily moved toward Mainbernheim. Still, Lisl found something to be happy about; the biting cold had lost its teeth. However, new worries were on everyone's mind–staying alive through air wars, bombings and artillery attacks. Rumors of neighboring towns being attacked kept people on edge.

Charlotte wrinkled her forehead, "Why do they attack the little towns that have no military installations?"

"I suppose they're searching for German ground troops in outlying areas," Mama said.

Now when the children left the house for school, Mama gave them little time to dawdle. Lisl and Dieter got a big lecture on how quickly they could get killed making side-trip to the stone break. Mama never had to worry about Kurt or Charlotte though; they were too frightened to go very far from home.

Sleepless nights followed anxious days and most of their nights were spent in the shelter. On rare occasions, Mama allowed them to stay in their beds, but they slept fully clothed, except for their shoes, to escape quickly in case of an attack.

One night just after Lisl had fallen asleep, the door flew open. Sirens blared and Mama shouted into the dark room, "Hurry girls, get ready." Lisl and her sisters grabbed their shoes and coats, trying to slip them on while stumbling downstairs.

Lisl heard Mama's soft voice in the boy's bedroom, urging them out of bed.

Kurt cried because he could not tie his shoelaces in the dim light.

"Come on, Dieter. We have to leave." Mama sounded impatient now.

Opa and Aunt Anni had left the house with the first sound of the siren because they needed more time to get to the shelter. Lisl wondered if they were getting any sleep at all. She imagined them waiting by the door, fully dressed and ready to run with the sound of the alarm.

Dieter came downstairs still half asleep. He looked like a limp rag doll when he tried to lift his suitcase. After a few more tries he finally managed to pick it up. They all grabbed their suitcases and bundles that always stood ready by the door. Charlotte lifted a crying, struggling Kurt onto her back.

"The cellar smells bad. Put me down." He cried as the family fled into the cold night.

Ellen tried to distract Kurt by tickling while they walked down the garden path; he pushed her hand away squirming to get down.

They followed Mama to Muehlenweg. Lisl heard Dieter's teeth chatter and put her arm around his shoulders.

The mood of the townspeople seemed to have changed– they seemed more alert, no longer trudging along like sleepwalkers. Some people ran, eager to secure a good place in the wine cellar.

Lisl and her family came to the entrance where the usual crowd of women had gathered outside the tunnel. They chatted animatedly and their heightened conversation resulted in brighter light as they squeezed vigorously on the power handles of their flashlights. The pumping of the flashlight handles created an eerie wheezing sound.

"It's the dragons breathing," Dieter said.

Lisl's face reflected Dieter's fear, her eyes grew large. She too felt the danger–not from the dragon's breath, but the possibility of becoming a target because of the exposed light.

Mama peered into the night sky, listening. Lisl followed her mother's gaze but could not see anything. Then a faint sound of a small airplane engine caught her attention. Mama seemed to sense when English observer planes searched for ground movements.

"You'd better go inside; it's not safe out here," Mama warned the chatting women.

Mama took her family into the tunnel.

Lisl looked back, but the women lingered near the entrance to breathe fresh air a little longer, still lighting up their surroundings. Halfway into the tunnel Lisl heard the small plane coming closer, circling above the shelter and then disappearing.

Just as Mama found a spot and all the suitcases and bundles were stuffed between the barrels, a horrific bang shook the shelter.

"Artillery fire," someone shouted.

Seconds later, another explosion hit the entrance. The tunnel collapsed, trapping everyone inside the cellar. Dust clouds billowed into the dome. The dragon spewed its ugly breath from the shattered tunnel. Lisl held her hands over the top of her head and stood like a statue.

Coughing, choking, and screaming filled the dome. Flashlight beams crisscrossed through the cellar like frantic fireflies getting swallowed by dust.

Shoving and pushing, fighting to get fresh air, people searched for a way out. Women scratched hysterically at fallen rocks and earth that blocked the tunnel, only to create more dust with nowhere to go.

Lisl became separated from her family as people rushed in all directions. She tied her headscarf over her face to keep from choking on the dust. "Mama! Charlotte!" She called over and over.

"Stay on your feet or you'll get trampled," someone shouted. Lisl fought hard to keep from falling, trying to free herself from the crowd that wedged her between their tall bodies, pushing her along with them.

Lisl recognized Kurt's panicked screams over all others. She could not see him, too much dust. "Kurt, where are you?" With her fists held at her chest, she pushed her way through the crowd until Kurt's screams were right in front of her. He was alone, holding his hands over his ears, his elbows pulled close to his sides. Thank God he was on his feet.

When Kurt realized Lisl was beside him he grabbed her clothing and would not let go. She wrapped her arms around his shoulders, but the pull of the crowd kept dragging them apart. "Ride piggy-back," she shouted, trying to help him climb on. His small body trembled, but he made no effort.

"Find Mama," he kept screaming and coughing. Lisl pulled his knit cap from his head and held it over his nose as an air filter, but he pulled off again, screaming louder than ever. She did not tell him to stop. Mama might be able to hear him. After a while Lisl too called for her mother almost as loud as Kurt. Her calls brought Dieter who grabbed onto Lisl's arm.

Ellen and Charlotte called out from the other side of the shelter. Lisl feared that she and her brothers would get trampled if they tried to make their way to them. She did not want to get caught in the human landslide that rolled over fallen bodies.

"I've got Kurt and Dieter. We're all right." Lisl shouted several times, hoping her sisters could hear her.

She pulled her brothers with her toward the wall until she felt the barrels at her back. They squeezed between the barrels, away from the moving crowd, holding onto each other.

Lisl listened for her mother's voice, but could not hear her. She hoped that her sisters and Opa and Aunt Anni were with Mama.

Suddenly a bright light filled the dome. A silent calm fell over the crowed. Some of the women fell to their knees, praying. Lisl soon realized that a powerful searchlight shone through the ventilation opening in the ceiling. The illuminated dust looked like the clouds painted on the church ceiling. Even Kurt calmed down at the sight. People stood frozen, shrouded in gray veils of dust, their faces lifted toward the light.

Kurt's eyes grew big when he saw the gray ghost-like figures standing motionless. He did not cry.

A voice called through the opening in the ceiling. "We will pull you up one by one, but you must not panic."

A German soldier, dangling at the end of a rope like a spider, descended slowly through the dust. The crowd pressed back, creating a landing site for the spider-soldier. He tied the rope around a small boy's waist, and told him to grab hold of the rope. The soldier signaled with a sharp whistle and the boy floated up to where hands grabbed him and pulled him to safety through the ventilation square. The rope was lowered again and the next person was secured to the rope.

One woman hung on tightly to her suitcase while she was fastened to the rope, but the soldier took it from her. "You have to leave your things in here," he shouted to the crowd. "Once the tunnel is cleared you can come back for your belongings."

Most of the children were brave and some even enjoyed the ride. But a few of the women screamed in fear, thrashing their arms and legs in mid-air like puppets on a string. Others screamed on their way up yet kept stiff.

Lisl and her brothers stayed tucked in the corner, quietly observing the action. Kurt was curious, watching light patterns dance past the people as they squeezed through the opening above, temporarily shutting out the light.

The crowd finally thinned and the dust settled. Lisl took the scarf off her face; she could breathe again without coughing too much. Ellen came rushing over, still coughing–maybe because of her fear, although Ellen would never admit that she was scared.

"Are you all right?" She stepped between the boys and put her arms around them. Charlotte ran toward them in tears. She held the boys' faces between her hands, giving them a close look, then lifted Kurt onto her back. This time he willingly let his favorite sister carry him.

Kurt was still excited. "We watched the soldier pull the people up."

Charlotte seemed surprised that he wasn't crying.

Neither Charlotte nor Ellen mentioned Mama, and Lisl was afraid to ask. She held her breath when Dieter said. "Where is Mama?"

Ellen pointed. "Over there."

Lisl face brightened as she rushed to the other side of the dome and flung herself at her mother. Mama held her close.

"Mama, we saw the soldier pull the people up. Are we going up there?" Kurt scrambled from Charlotte into Mama's arms. They gathered around their mother who looked pale and shaken. Lisl tried to find a place for her to sit down. But there was only dust.

Aunt Anni led Opa to the children. He reached out to them and the children surrounded their grandfather.

"Opa, we're going to be next," Kurt said.

Only a few families remained.

Dieter bravely volunteered to be next, waving to Kurt on his way up.

After Charlotte and Ellen were safely lifted from the dome, Mama said, "You're next Kurt."

He backed into his mother's arms, his eyes grew big.

"Kurt we all have to go up. You don't want to be left behind, do you?" He shook his head and quickly agreed to have the rope tied around him. Mama cheered him on when his expression changed to panic.

"Kurt isn't it wonderful, you'll fly like a bird up and up you go to the top of the world." She kept talking until he was safe.

Mama wanted to follow Kurt, but the soldier thought it would be too risky in her advanced pregnancy. But Mama insisted. She wanted to be with her children. The soldier finally gave in and tied a loop on the end of the rope that she could step into to avoid having the rope wrapped around her waist. She was lifted standing up, with both hands grabbing onto the rope. Halfway up her legs flipped sideways, and she ended up in a horizontal position.

"Mama, don't let go," Lisl screamed.

Her mother struggled to hang on, but managed to pull herself upright again. She was pulled through the opening and Lisl wanted to follow Mama, but other women pushed ahead of her. Lisl looked around and realized some people had been injured, trampled by the panic-stricken crowd and could not be hoisted up. The frail and elderly had to remain as well until the tunnel was cleared. Opa was among them as well as Aunt Anni, who did not want to leave her father.

When it was Lisl's turn she tried not to wiggle, afraid the rope would break. She closed her eyes tight as she was lifted off her feet. But then she felt like an angel flying up

toward the cloud angels in the sky. She opened her eyes
and saw Aunt Anni smiling up at her. The higher she flew,
the more of the cellar she saw. All the remaining people
looked up at her, even some of the wounded. She smiled.
Is this how God sees everyone because he is so high in
heaven?

As she reached the top, hands grabbed her arms and
pulled her through the opening. As soon as the soldier
untied the rope, he lowered it again for the next person.

Lisl stood under a small tent placed over the ventilation
square and someone pushed her outside through the tent
opening.

Although it was dark she saw the faint outline of a
swastika between the sparse trees. As she came closer she
realized it was on a small army truck with a rope tied to the
back. A soldier gave a sharp whistle and the truck moved
slowly halfway down the hill. Now she knew how they pulled
the people up so quickly. She stood outside the tent, unsure
of what to do next.

"Go join the others down the hill." Someone nudged her
toward the tunnel entrance at the bottom of the mound.

Fighting her way through darkness, stumbling through
small trees and shrubbery, she ran in the direction of
muffled voices. In her panic she lost her footing, slid
downhill and landed on something soft. She screamed
when she saw dead bodies of women that were placed beside
the road. Lisl scrambled to her feet, her stomach churned.
Here again she recognized the sickly-sweet smell of human
blood.

"Mama, where are you?" She ran. Stumbling and falling,
she made her way toward sounds of digging, holding out
her arms to avoid running into obstacles.

As her eyes adjusted to the darkness she saw the outline
of a farm wagon standing by to transport the wounded.
A horse whinnied, stamping his hoofs while some of the

injured were loaded onto the wagon to be taken to the Iphofen hospital three kilometers south on Muehlenweg.

Lisl heard voices around her. Someone pushed her toward the tunnel entrance.

"Everyone dig, hurry, faster." An anxious voice called.

It was a race to free the buried victims in the collapsed tunnel before they ran out of air. Everyone dug with their hands. One soldier called out, "Hurry, we don't know the extent of the damage. The dome might collapse at any moment."

"Oh no. Opa and Aunt Anni are in there." Lisl frantically dug until her fingers hurt.

The cellar was underground with a ceiling of heavy fitted rocks curved overhead, creating a dome-like ceiling. The added weight of a thick layer of dirt supporting growing shrubs and small spindly trees made it even more dangerous. If the dome were to collapse, it would mean certain death for everyone inside.

Even the smaller children helped form a human conveyor belt, moving the debris away from the tunnel.

Lisl pulled and scratched loose rocks and dirt from the blockage and placed it in someone's waiting hands—the beginning of the conveyor line.

Hard digging tools could not be used, not so much for the lack of them, but to avoid injuries to the people still trapped in the rubble. Most of the people rescued from the dome had fled the scene in panic; some were willing to lend a hand to free the buried victims.

Lisl felt many working hands beside hers, sometimes touching each other. But when she felt unmoving, limp fingers, she jerked back. "Someone is buried here," she cried out.

She was pushed aside and some of the older women and one of the soldiers started to scrape around the trapped body. Now Lisl saw many hands moving quickly as a small spotlight illuminated the area. The lifeless fingers gradually became a whole arm as debris was removed. Lisl stood back, watching in a daze.

Some of the women covered the small area with their coats to keep light from escaping into the night sky.

Lisl felt dizzy. She could not tell the moving hands from the lifeless one as people pulled and scraped to free the body.

After about twenty minutes of excavation the woman was freed. It was too late for Frau Hauser, one of the women who had lingered too long outside the tunnel with her flashlight. Her body was placed in line with the others by the roadside. Lisl moved farther back on the conveyor line, afraid of discovering another dead body.

A small tunnel through the rubble took shape. Now Lisl was part of a long line moving the debris from hand to hand away from the tunnel. She could only feel the hands. Maybe her family was right in front of or behind her. But no one dared use a flashlight outside. It could bring on a repeat attack. A dim flashlight could be used as the digging advanced a few meters through the debris.

Now and then Lisl heard joyful cries. She recognized her sisters' voices among them when they found live victims among the crumpled rocks.

Three women and a small boy were taken to the hospital, but two more women were placed with the dead. Soldiers, old men, women and children scratched and dug through the night until they reached the dome.

Guided by one of the soldiers, Opa and Aunt Anni emerged on their hands and knees. They were among the few still able to crawl through the narrow opening that had been dug inside the collapsed tunnel. Cheers rang out as they took their first breaths of fresh air.

In the dim light Lisl recognized her mother and brothers standing next to the entrance hugging Opa and Aunt Anni.

Lisl ran through the crowd. "Opa, you're all right." Although grandfather looked shaken, he held out his hands toward Lisl. "Good you are all here now. Everyone is all right," he said.

Anni looked back through the small crawl passage.

"There are more frail and injured still in there." She, along with a soldier, had given them first aid as best they could. "Now they have to wait until the opening is wide enough for a stretcher to pass through," she said.

A soldier came crawling through the opening. "Frau Meisner is dead," he said. "I think she died of a heart attack."

Her body was left in the dome until more rubble was cleared.

Mama picked up Kurt. "Let's go home. We'll come back tomorrow for our suitcases." Mama sounded exhausted.

It felt good being home again. Lisl, still wrapped in her coat, peered through the window into darkness.

Aunt Anni came over and took her toward the light where she checked everyone's hands for open wounds. After washing off the dirt she discovered only scrapes and bruises. In a few hours Anni would ride her bike to the Kitzingen hospital where she worked.

∿

After that frightening ordeal, Mama converted the family's root cellar into an air-raid shelter.

Empty shelves, once laden with homemade preserves, lined the cellar walls. Charlotte and Ellen moved them from the root cellar across the cemented hallway into the laundry kitchen. Mama was afraid the shelves might fall on her sleeping children during an attack, but it also made more room.

The dirt floor, which in better days was covered with a mountain of potatoes, was covered with empty potato sacks topped with two side-by-side mattresses. They used up the entire floor space except for a little space at the end of the beds where Mama placed a wooden box to serve as a table.

The root cellar was the safest place in the house, and probably could withstand a hit, Mama explained.

Lisl rubbed her hands together with a smile. Here, she knew she could fall asleep. But what she liked most was that it was so quiet and with a mattress under her a lot warmer than the wine cellar. The bathroom was just upstairs. The familiar smell of earth and the lingering scent of potatoes did not make her nauseous like the stench in the wine cellar.

Kurt hopped around on the mattresses, visibly happier as well. But when the alarm sounded Mama could not keep him in the bed. He squeezed himself in a small space behind the mattresses, like a frightened little animal, and stayed there until the all-clear siren sounded.

⁓

Soon after the wine cellar disaster, the army engineers inspected the cellar and cleared away the collapsed part of the tunnel. After reinforcing the structure, they declared it safe to be used again, but without the tunnel leading in.

Opa and Aunt Anni still walked to the wine cellar shelter every time the air-raid sirens sounded. Whenever Aunt Anni wanted to stay at home, Opa reminded her of their house in rubble. He thought that the shelter would be safer than the already-cramped root cellar.

CHAPTER 8

The Search for Wood

Mama looked helplessly at the dwindling food supply in the pantry. The store shelves were empty. The only way to get groceries was on the black market and Mama had only Reichsmark, a worthless currency.

She did not let her children go to the railroad tracks anymore because of frequent attacks on trains. Besides, the chance of finding coal was slim since most of Mainbernheim's citizens were out looking for these treasures in spite of the danger. The dead trees in the forests had all been cut down. Some of the people–like Mama–had cut live trees. Now Mama had to be thrifty, using whatever little wood she had for cooking only.

In the past few weeks, Charlotte and Ellen went to Willanzheim where on occasion they were allowed to do chores in exchange for food. Although Mama was reluctant to let them go, in the end hunger outweighed the risk of getting caught in an air raid.

Ellen was determined to bring home some food. Charlotte, who was as frightened as Kurt, would have liked to stay home. Still, her pride would not allow her to let her sister go by herself.

In March farmers needed Charlotte and Ellen to help with household chores and to watch small children while the women worked in the fields. Their husbands were in the army.

Mama let Dieter and Lisl search for firewood as long as they stayed close by. They went to an area beside the stone break because Dieter insisted he saw wood there. Mama did not mind because in case of an attack they could run home in a matter of minutes.

"There used to be a railroad here a long time ago." Dieter remembered seeing strange-looking wood on the outer edge of the stone break. "You can't really see it anymore now, but I think that old road leads to the old rails."

"Where did you hear that?"

"Willie's grandfather told me."

"Are you sure he said railroad? Here, in the stone break?"

"Yes. He said a small train with flat cars used to run into the quarry. They moved big rocks that way and loaded them onto trucks. But that was a long, long time ago. Willie's grandfather was only a boy when he helped with the loading."

Lisl wondered why she had never seen it before. A few years ago, when her sisters had collected metal for the war effort with the Hitler Youth, they had mentioned a fallen-apart railroad track. And when they reported their find, soldiers with equipment came and removed whatever iron they could. But her sisters never said it was in the stone break.

After they searched the area for a while Dieter said "Here it is—I think."

The wooden parts of the rail and flat cars had been left behind. Lisl could barely recognize the partially buried wood under shrubs and rocks; she could see how they had overlooked it because it was mostly rotted away.

Dieter wasted no time. He picked up an old rusty rail spike that lay nearby and hammered it with a rock into the wood to split it into smaller sections.

"I think this was once a rail tie." He pointed with the spike at the piece of wood pinned under his foot.

The wood broke easily into smaller pieces they could carry. Age and weather had made the wood light and porous.

They had found similar wood here before, but had never made the connection. Mama had used this rotten wood like briquettes. Although it did not burn very hot, it kept the fire smoldering for long periods of time. Then, when a hot fire was needed for cooking, a few dry sticks revived the flames quickly.

"Here, you try to get some off. I have to warm my hands. This spike is cold." Dieter handed it to Lisl. He took off his mittens and rubbed his hands together, then stuck them under his arms.

Lisl hammered the spike into the wood until it split. They took turns. One worked while the other warmed up.

They stacked the pieces at the edge of the slope near their garden so when they were finished they could just scoop it up and carry it home.

"Dieter, how come we never get this cold when we're looking for petrified seashells?" Lisl stuck her hands inside her coat, watching Dieter take his turn.

"I don't know. Maybe the spike is too cold." He stood up and looked toward the sheltered area inside the stone break. "Maybe it's warmer inside," he reasoned. "Do you want to warm up in there?" He had a twinkle in his eyes. "We can look for shells while we're waiting to get warm." He rubbed his hands together, more in anticipation than because of the cold. "We can say that we went there to get warm, in case Mama catches us."

"I guess so, but I don't think you can fool Mama." Lisl laughed. "You know she worries when we climb too high up the embankment."

Lisl forgot the cold as soon as they walked into the stone break. She imagined a prehistoric ocean with beautiful seashells on its banks as she looked at the layers of calcium deposits between the gray rock walls. Maybe today they would find that perfect petrified seashell.

The sunken stone break was their special amphitheater where fantasies made harsh reality disappear.

"Do you think cavemen lived here?" Dieter stood gazing about with magic in his eyes.

"Yeah. And caves dug into the rocks. They would have been safe here. Maybe they looked for wood too." Lisl smiled. "I can just see their fire in the middle of the rocky floor where they warmed up and cooked their food."

"And maybe roasted meat and huge clams." Dieter licked his lips.

They climbed the steep rock embankment until they reached the ledge of the shell layer.

"Maybe that's why there are so many shell pieces in that layer. They had a feast here." Lisl looked at Dieter. "Maybe we'll find something that proves that they lived here once."

Dieter brightened at the thought then busily excavated some of the rocks. "Even if we don't find a sign that they lived here, I still want to find a perfect petrified shell, not just little parts."

Lisl used the old bent fork she kept hidden nearby. Happily she stabbed at the layer for a while, but found only small particles. She watched Dieter digging between the stones with the old rail spike.

"Dieter, are you cold?"

"No." He looked at her, puzzled.

"Look what you're using."

He laughed. "All right, so it wasn't the spike that made me cold."

When shadows crept across the rock wall, the cold followed.

"It must be getting late." Lisl made her way down to the stony ground. Dieter slid down behind her.

When they stepped outside the stone break, Dieter said, "Now do you believe me?"

"What? About the cold?"

"It's freezing out here," he said, sticking his hands in his pockets.

"I think we should try to get a little more wood before we go home." Lisl headed back toward the old rail.

Dieter followed, wrapping his arms tightly around his chest.

They walked along the area where they thought the tracks might have been. But dried weeds, shrubs, and patches of snow made it impossible to recognize its location.

Lisl examined a pile of rocks that looked out of place with the surrounding area. "Look, Dieter, there's some wood buried under there. I think it used to be an old rail cart."

"Wow, look at this." Dieter climbed onto the pile. "I wonder what happened here."

"It looks like they loaded too much on that cart and it collapsed." Lisl tried to pull out a piece of wood, but it was stuck.

When Dieter jumped off the pile to help, he set a rock in motion that rolled onto Lisl's foot.

She cried out in pain, trying to pull away, but her foot was wedged tight between two rocks.

Dieter stood helpless. "Just yank it out."

"No. It hurts." Lisl cringed.

"I'll get them off. Don't worry, I'll be careful." He removed the smaller ones, even though they were quite heavy. But the big rock wedged between another one prevented Lisl from moving.

"If you lift this one a little to the side, I'll get my foot out," she said.

Dieter tried, but it just would not budge. Lisl bent over, trying to help move it, but the rock stood fast.

"I guess we have to get Mama. Boy, will she be upset. I'm just glad it didn't happen inside the stone break or she would never let us go near it again." Dieter started to walk away.

"Dieter, wait, just wait a minute," she called him back. "I have an idea. Sit down here, beside the rock, and bend your knees." Lisl pointed to a spot. "Now put both feet on the side of the rock and slowly straighten your knees." Dieter sat down. His feet firmly planted onto the rock, he looked at Lisl for further instruction.

"Now, stretch your legs, but do it very slowly."

Dieter pushed until his face turned red and slowly the rock started to move. Lisl quickly pulled her foot out.

"Liiiisl . . . it'll fall on me if I let go," Dieter shouted.

Lisl tried to help push the rock, but she knew that she could not hold it.

"Just lower it by bending your knees as slowly as when you lifted it . . . very, very slowly." The rock settled back on the ground. "There, you did it."

Dieter stood up, looking at the rock, then at Lisl. He walked around the pile of rocks, posing heroically when he realized what he had done. But his glory quickly faded when he saw blood soak though Lisl's stocking around her ankle. "Can you walk?"

"I think so. Oh, look at my stocking. I tore my good stockings." She stood, grimacing. "I think we'd better go home now. I'm glad we don't have too much wood to carry." She hobbled toward the road.

"Here, I'll help you. Hang on." Dieter put his arm around Lisl's waist while she put her arm around his shoulder.

They reached the end of the field. The wood pile was bigger than Lisl remembered.

"Are you sure you can carry some of that?" Dieter said.

"Just pile some on my arms. You can carry the rest." Lisl was determined to get the wood home. Someone else might take their neatly stacked pile. However, they could not carry it all, and had to leave some behind. "Don't worry Lisl, I'll get it later."

As they came to the front door, Dieter knocked with his foot, his arms so filled he could not turn the handle.

Mama appeared in the doorway. "Oh, look at all that wood."

"This isn't all. We still have to get the rest," Dieter said meekly, waiting for his mother to discover Lisl's injuries.

Dieter's tone made Mama suspicious. She watched them come through the door and spotted Lisl's limp right away.

"What's the matter with your leg?"

"It's just my ankle, a rock rolled on it–well not on it just beside it."

Mama took the wood from Lisl's arms and stacked it beside the door, then lifted her onto the table to look at her foot.

When her mother took off her blood-soaked stocking, Lisl said, "I'm sorry Mama. I tore my new stockings."

But her mother did not seem to care about the stocking. "Oh my God, how did you ever manage to walk on that?" She moved Lisl's foot in all directions. "At least it's not broken."

Lisl tried not to show pain, but tears gave her away when her mother cleaned off the blood. Lisl's ankle was swollen with bruising and open gashes. Mama soaked a towel in vinegar water, put it around Lisl's ankle, and carried her to the couch in the living room.

"Poor Lisl. Now you have a sore ankle to go with your sore feet." Mama sat beside her, putting her arms around her. "Now lie down and try to get some sleep." She covered her with a blanket.

Dieter hovered around Lisl and whispered to her, "I'm glad Mama didn't think it happened in the stone break." He patted Lisl's shoulder. "Don't worry, I'll get the rest of the wood now." Dieter walked out the door with an eager-to-help Kurt beside him.

Her ankle throbbed. She was sure she could not fall asleep.

"Lisl, wake up; it's time for dinner," her mother called softly stroking her forehead. "Do you feel better after your nice long nap?"

CHAPTER 9

Escape to the Woods

Lisl gazed through the classroom window, where dark clouds chased across the sky. It was early March and she hoped for rain to thaw the frozen ground.

Marie, Lisl's classmate, sat with her head resting on the desk, fast asleep. Her heavy loud breathing made Lisl sleepy as well. She stared at the blackboard to keep from dozing off, but the numbers ran together in a blur. Even her teacher's voice sounded too far away to understand.

The classroom was dark, which made it even harder to stay awake. But the teacher was not allowed to turn on the lights.

A faint rumbling that slowly grew louder brought Lisl fully awake. The children lifted their heads from their desks, frightened, looking at each other. Several of the boys ran to the windows, but were quickly ordered back into their seats.

Lisl recognized the sound of British bombers. The pencil on her desk vibrated as the planes flew overhead. With the wail of full alarm, Lisl, as well as the other children, jumped from their seats, hurried into the hallways and down the stairs.

Dieter was waiting for Lisl by the entrance. His class was usually the first to leave the building. Together they ran outside, their faces toward the sky.

Dieter looked in all directions. "I can't see them."

"They're hiding above the clouds."

Although Lisl's ankle still hurt, she had learned to step softly to lessen the pain.

The sound of heavy artillery fire seemed closer than usual as they hurried across the fields toward their home. A smoke pillar rose from the other side of town. Lisl could not see the bombers, yet the sound of the engines told her that they were British.

An explosion near the town set their feet racing. Now a second column of black smoke, outside the north wall, reached for the sky.

"Look, Dieter." Lisl pointed to the area without slowing her pace.

Dieter's eyes grew big. "Do you think they dropped a bomb?"

"I don't think so. We would have heard a much louder boom. They would have dropped their bombs by now. Just listen, Dieter, there are far too many bombers flying overhead."

"Yeah, they would only need two or three planes to wipe out all of Mainbernheim." Dieter sounded relieved.

"I wonder where they're going. They've already bombed Kitzingen."

They slowed down near the stone break as three of their playmates came running across the field. Lisl saw neighbors hiding under the sparse wild cherry trees and shrubs at the edge of the fields with suitcases and bundles beside them.

"Look, there's Mama," Dieter called out. Their mother ran toward them carrying a big suitcase. Charlotte carried Kurt on her back and a bundle under her arm, trying hard to keep up with her mother. Ellen, who carried two smaller suitcases, followed close behind.

When Lisl came closer, she saw that most of their neighbors had gathered under the little trees.

Mama motioned Lisl and Dieter to fall in step with her.

"Come on you slowpokes. We got home a long time ago and we didn't take the shortcut," Ellen said.

"Yeah, but they let you out before us," Lisl said. "What happened? Why are all the neighbors out here in the woods?" Lisl looked around. "Where are Opa and Aunt Anni?

Ellen shoved one of the suitcases into Lisl's hands. "They went to the shelter."

They joined their neighbors in the woods. But below the field, past the housing area, townspeople ran along Muehlenweg on their way to the wine cellar shelter.

Mama squeezed under the shrubby trees, gathering her children around her. The neighbors too sat in little family groups.

Lisl thought of bird nests as each of the women was closely surrounded by her chicks. They huddled in the thick dry grass under the bushes and thin spindly trees where the snow could not reach. Their chatter reminded Lisl even more of birds as the ladies called out to each other. They described an air disaster–a burning British bomber that had slid into the north side housing area, flattening all six buildings. So the women decided not to stay in their homes and root cellars, or the wine cellar shelter; they thought it would be safer to hide in the woods. At least out here they could see which direction a bomber would fall when it was hit, and hopefully get out of the way.

Kurt pressed his hands over his ears when the thundering noise of planes sounded overhead. Every time Lisl thought they had passed, a new group came across the sky. She gazed into the clouds, but the overcast was too thick to see.

"How will the bombers find their target if they can't see the ground?" Lisl asked. But no one had an answer.

German artillery marked trails of fire into the dark afternoon sky from several locations across the landscape.

At first Lisl thought it senseless because the bombers were not visible. But when she heard sputtering airplane engines she realized the artillery's aim was not as aimless as she had thought.

"Watch out," one of the neighbors cried as a big bomber silently glided through the dark sky. Smoke poured from the plane and mingled with the clouds. Lisl could not tell where the clouds left off and the smoke began. She held her breath. She thought the smoldering sky was ready to burst into flames. This ghostly bomber, silent without the power of its engines, descended slowly toward the woods.

The neighbors scrambled farther back under the shrubs, leaving their suitcases and bundles where they had dropped them. Their chatter stopped as they watched the disabled plane glide over their hiding place. Lisl wanted to run, but looked at Mama who gave a sigh of relief. The smoking bomber drifted away from the woods, out over the fields, gliding a few meters above ground. Then suddenly, while still airborne, the plane burst into flames and plowed into the field, almost digging itself under. Several explosions followed even before the debris from the first one came to rest on the ground. Fire, smoke, and dirt spewed high into the air as the bombs aboard the plane exploded one by one as though the plane were unwilling to stop fighting and accept its doom.

The families huddled together, watching the explosion. Some of the neighbor children fell to the ground or crawled deeper into shrubs.

Lisl and her brothers and sisters knelt on the ground with their hands folded behind their heads, making themselves the smallest targets possible while falling dirt and burning fragments showered around them.

Shreds with bits of metal were scattered across the field. The biggest piece Lisl could recognize was part of a wing in the midst of flames.

Stunned, the families watched in silence, the fire's glow reflecting on their faces and even in the cold, Lisl felt the heat.

Kurt hung on to his mother, shaking in fear, but Charlotte tried hard not to show her panic in front of her playmates and neighbors.

Another bomber hurled through the clouds like a fireball spiraling to the ground on one wing, leaving a fire-and-smoke corkscrew pattern hanging in the air.

Lisl stared at the falling firebird. "They're trapped. They're going to burn alive." Her eyes followed the burning plane while she bit her lip. The bomber hit the ground a few kilometers farther out in the fields. All she could see was the fiery glow from the explosion and, like a black ribbon of mourning, a dark pillar of smoke rose to the sky.

To Lisl's surprise, parachutes floated out of the clouds, slowly drifting down behind the hill. Lisl smiled. They had not burned. She did not wish that horrible death on anyone, not even the enemy.

Fast-moving trucks mounted with guns and German troops raced across the fields to intercept the parachutes. Lisl heard no shots and hoped they had surrendered peacefully.

Artillery fire pounded relentlessly into the sky like shooting stars as the next wave of bombers rumbled like a thunderstorm above the clouds.

Mama gathered her children and belongings around her. She seemed uncertain now and looked like she was ready to flee to a safer place. Too much was going on all at once. There was no time to react or think about what might happen next. The neighbor women too looked as though they were ready to run. They watched, crouching low to the ground, but seemed too frightened to move.

Sputtering engines with fire and smoke in its wake, a bomber came slowly out of the clouds. At first it seemed to hang in midair, huge, threatening. Then the plane came toward them, slowly, relentlessly lower and lower.

"It's coming straight for us." Lisl started to run, but her mother caught her skirt and pulled her back under the shrubs.

Charlotte and Kurt screamed, pressing their faces into their mother's coat. Lisl and Dieter stood frozen, holding tight onto their mother's grip, as they watched the plane heading toward them.

Lisl cringed, her hands over her ears. "Why is it taking so long to hit us?"

Ellen shouted, "Let's get out of here," but Mama grabbed onto her as well.

The neighbors squatted paralyzed, watching the burning plane fly overhead, almost touching the tops of the little trees under which they were hiding.

Lisl stared at the underside of the bomber above her. It seemed to cover the sky. The sound of its coughing engine and loud whoosh of flames went through her like a wave of fear.

Fire and smoke filtered down between the trees and bushes. Lisl closed her eyes. "The woods are going to catch fire." She clenched her teeth and opened her eyes with a sigh of relief. Smoke drifted between the trembling trees and it looked as though they too were shaking in fear.

The bomber stayed airborne a few more seconds, just long enough to reach the field before it crashed, breaking apart on impact.

The neighbors stayed frozen in their hiding place a few minutes longer before they dared to move.

Lisl gazed into the cold afternoon sky as she followed a few snowflakes swirling without settling on the ground. Then, between the clouds, she caught sight of parachutes – five, six, seven, floating down through the dark clouds. The airmen had escaped their burning inferno and now floated like puppets on strings among the snowflakes.

Silently they drifted into the next field–motionless while in the air. But once they hit the ground, a frantic struggle to free themselves began. The parachutes, caught by the breeze, dragged them across the snow-covered field like feathers blowing in the wind. Finally they came to rest against a sloe hedge where they gathered the parachutes into small bundles.

Old farmers and women armed with pitchforks ran toward them. Lisl saw the enemy's desperate expressions as they confronted the farmers with their weapons–guns against pitchforks–but neither would make the first move.

Trucks with German soldiers finally arrived to take the British soldiers away. Lisl was happy there was no bloodshed on either side.

The air war that seemed like such a very long time to Lisl had actually been less than fifteen or twenty minutes. The bombers had moved out of the area and on to their destination, but not all would arrive to bomb their targets.

Smoke and fire still poured from the crashed bomber like blood draining from a dying body, staining the clean white sheet of snow. On the opposite side, the other bomber lay scattered across the entire field.

Lisl wished the war would end. She wondered if all of the airmen had made it out before their planes crashed. She felt empty, disconnected, as if she were watching a sad, scary movie. Unable to tear herself from the sight of disaster, she stood shivering until the touch of her mother's hand on her shoulder turned her away from the scene of horror. The sight of her family and playmates gave her comfort. It felt good to see that no one was hurt.

The neighborhood children chattered nervously on their way home. They seemed to draw strength from each other. To hide their fear, forced laughter rang without joy.

Lisl and Dieter followed Mama and the rest of the family, carrying their belongings back to their undamaged homes to the sound of the all-clear siren.

"Mama, what will happen to the British airmen they captured?" Lisl asked.

"I don't know. I think they will be put in a prison camp."

"What will they do with them when they get there?" Dieter asked.

"I think they will hold them until the war is over."

Lisl could tell by her mother's face that she too was wondering how long that might be.

The evening remained calm. They slept in their beds for a few hours. But with full alarm they spent the rest of the night in the root cellar–cold and hungry.

CHAPTER 10

Premonition

Daylight filtered through the little window of the root cellar when Lisl awoke. Charlotte and Ellen had already left the bed. They had a way of sneaking out without waking the rest.

Through half-closed eyes Lisl watched Kurt next to her slowly waking. He wiped the sleep from his eyes and gazed around.

"Mama?" he called softly. When he could not find her, he scrambled out of bed.

Lisl listened to the familiar sound of his footsteps running up the stairs. The non-stop chatter of his little voice started the minute he entered the kitchen.

Dieter stood by the window watching sparrows hopping on the ground close to the glass and then quietly left the root cellar.

Lisl closed her eyes and almost fell asleep again. Now that everyone had left the bed she could stretch out. All night long she felt like a sardine in a can, frozen in the same position as not to disturb her brothers and sisters.

Mama was used to Lisl being the last one up and called several times down the cellar stairs. But when her voice turned harsh, Lisl dragged herself out of bed.

When she got upstairs, Charlotte, Ellen and Dieter had already left for school. Lisl ate her half-slice of bread on the run to be on time for school.

At school, after a few hours of uninterrupted lessons, Herr Stolz walked through the rows of desks, stopping now and then to look out the windows. Maybe he too found it hard to believe they had come halfway through the day without an air raid. Still, most of the students were distracted.

Lisl listened for the sound of bombers instead of to her teacher's voice. He slapped his pointing rod hard on the desks of inattentive students.

Hilde and Susanna, who sat in front of Lisl, shivered, glancing toward the windows. Some students had fallen asleep. Finally, between naps, lessons and listening for bombers, the long school day came to an end.

When Lisl came home, Charlotte was about to go get field salads called *Schafsmaulchen*, or sheep's mouths. Lisl decided to go with her.

Armed with a basket and little paring knives they walked through the field behind their garden, cutting off tiny plants that grew wild and were winter hardy. They even grew under the blanket of snow. Now that the snow was almost gone, the small plants were easy to find. Lisl loved the tasty salads–although a little tough–they grew before anything green could be found.

Lisl sat on her heels in the middle of the field, watching as the sun cast a red glow in the late afternoon sky. Even the sparse snow patches looked as though someone had run across the fields spilling red paint here and there. She always loved to watch the sun sink behind the hills, yet today the sight overwhelmed her with sadness. Tears welled in her eyes.

"What's the matter? Did you cut yourself?" Charlotte rushed to Lisl's side to examine her hands.

Lisl shook her head and wiped her tears on her sleeve, but she could not stop crying. "I don't know why, but the sunset makes me feel so sad."

"Oh, but it's beautiful. It lights up the sky all orange and red."

"It doesn't look pretty today." Lisl found no words to explain her emotions. So she kept silent, trying hard to keep from crying again. She watched the sun paint the sky blood red as day gave way to night.

Charlotte picked up the basket. "I think we have enough. We'd better go." She watched Lisl out of the corner of her eye.

"Here, you carry the basket. We found some good ones today." She looked uncomfortable and stroked Lisl's hair.

Lisl tried to smile. "Don't worry, I'm all right."

For the rest of the evening, Charlotte kept an eye on Lisl, trying to cheer her up.

But the field salad that Charlotte had prepared had lost its taste.

Mama put her hand on Lisl's forehead. "No, you don't seem to have a fever. Don't you feel good?"

"I'm all right, I'm just not hungry."

Her mother looked concerned because Lisl usually loved the salad.

The evening was quiet, without air raids. Mama told them they could sleep in their beds, but to keep their clothes on. After a few hours a warning siren hurried them from their beds into their root cellar.

Frightening nightmares of red sunsets haunted Lisl's sleep. She awoke often.

Shortly before midnight, explosions rumbled in the distance like a far-away thunderstorm. A few minutes later, a soft rapping on the front door awoke Lisl. She slipped out of bed from between her brothers and sisters, careful not to wake them, and went upstairs.

The front door was ajar. She heard her mother's voice in the garden. As she stepped through the door she saw Frau Nagel, her neighbor, talking excitedly with her mother. A faint red glow reflected on their faces in an otherwise dark garden.

Lisl stepped beside her mother and followed their gaze to the west. There on the horizon she saw the same sunset she had seen in the field.

"Lisl, Wuerzburg has been hit." Mama put her arm around Lisl who held on tight to her mother. It was a frightening sight–a red glow in the distance lit up the night. The overwhelming sorrow she had felt in the field took hold of her again. She could not feel the frosty chill on her bare feet or the cold breeze on her face, but stared at the unsettling sight of a sunset that had fallen out of its time frame.

Her mother noticed Lisl's bare feet and sent her back to bed. But Lisl found no sleep. Her tears ran onto her pillow. She did not know what made her cry or why she felt so sad.

The next morning, on March sixteenth, a radio report told of the terrible bombing disaster. A large part of Wuerzburg had burned. The Wuerzburg children's hospital was in flames and the little patients had run into the dark streets, screaming and on fire. Most of the hospital's patients had perished. Wuerzburg lay in ruins. Civilian casualties and damage to Wuerzburg were devastating. The kind of bombs that had been dropped exploded above ground, spreading their fiery destruction across the city.

Mama put her arms around Lisl as if to protect her from the report. They sat motionless. Tears rolled down her mother's face, but now Lisl could not cry as she listened to the radio.

"Charred, unrecognizable bodies littered the streets." Lisl felt like covering her ears yet listened to the horrifying details. "I will never get the screams of the children out of my mind," the reporter sobbed.

Lisl felt nauseous and her mother's face turned white. Lisl could smell the burning cloth and flesh. She was not sure whether it was her imagination, or if the wind had carried the stench of human blood over thirty kilometers from Wuerzburg to Mainbernheim.

The reporter's voice kept repeating in her thoughts. Lisl was afraid to fall asleep, afraid she would dream of the red sky. Not even the promise of spring could ease her mind.

She wandered listlessly along the garden path, peering into the sky. Enemy bombers flew across the horizon toward another target while the warning sirens blared. *Where will they drop their bombs this time?*

Dieter looked left out and lonely as though he had lost his playmate. Still, Lisl was grateful that he had not heard the radio report.

Today Mama did not object when Dieter tried to cheer Lisl up with a trip to the stone break. But even there the reporter's sobs haunted her. She poked around the layers of rocks under the residue of snow just to please her brother, but her thoughts were elsewhere.

Dieter looked at Lisl, he seemed unsure of how to cheer her. He showed her small pieces of petrified seashells he had found, and even though she looked, she did not see them. But when she saw Dieter's disappointed face she tried to pay attention.

Two days had passed; still, when Lisl closed her eyes she saw a sunset on fire and heard the screams of children. Charlotte took her aside and told her that a baby brother or sister would soon arrive.

Her sadness finally gave way to joy as excitement filled the house. Everyone was busy getting ready for the baby's arrival and Ellen raced on her bike to inform the midwife of the happy event.

Kurt waited impatiently by the front door for someone to knock and hand him the baby.

Charlotte checked the baby clothes she had mended and laundered weeks before. She spread the little garments out on the table, then lovingly folded them again, running her hands over the soft material. She brought the little cradle down from the attic and Ellen cleaned it meticulously. Together they fluffed and rearranged the bedding, the way they used to when they played with their dolls.

"This is a doll's bed." Kurt gave Charlotte a dubious glance as he rocked the little cradle.

Charlotte scooped him up. "I'll bet I can fit you into the doll's bed." She held her giggling, squirming brother over the cradle.

"I'm not a baby."

"Oh, I think you're a doll."

It was close to noon when Frau Kreidel, the midwife, knocked on the door. Kurt rushed to open it. "You forgot to bring the baby." He stood in her way, his palms up.

Frau Kreidel laughed. "I think we need your Mama's help here." She walked past Kurt toward Mama, took her pulse, then ordered her to go to bed.

As Mama's labor pains became more severe, the children, who had gathered near the doorway, became more upset.

Frau Kreidel looked at their worried faces. "Your Mama will be all right. I'll call you when you can come in." She pushed them out into the living room and closed the door.

Charlotte took care of the younger children and Opa while Aunt Anni was at work.

Ellen kept a fire going with pots of water at a boiling point.

"We'll get a surprise for Mama." Lisl grabbed Dieter's hand and they quickly ran outside, up to the hedge where the violets grew. But when they returned, Frau Kreidel would not let them in to see their mother.

As evening approached, the children and Opa sat around the kitchen table while Charlotte prepared red beets and potatoes.

Dieter went to his mother's bedroom and tried to listen through the door. He looked at Lisl, shook his head, and sat down again, but his eyes stayed on the door.

After dinner Ellen and Lisl collected the plates from the table and washed them, taking great care not to make any noise.

Opa sat in the big chair, but only minutes at a time. He paced between his chair and the bedroom door without tapping his cane to the floor. He stood quietly for a while then went to his room.

Charlotte got Kurt ready for bed. She carried him around the kitchen, then seated herself in Opa's chair, but jumped up again when a tiny cry came from behind the door. They gathered outside the bedroom, whispering to each other until Frau Kreidel came out.

"You have a baby brother," she told them, yet she still would not let them in. She took the hot water and disappeared behind the door again.

After some anxious moments and restless pacing, Frau Kreidel opened the door. "You can come in." She stepped aside, watching the children tiptoe into their mother's room.

Charlotte carried Kurt to Mama's bedside and Dieter set the bowl of violets on her dresser.

Their mother looked pale, and although Frau Kreidel had washed Mama's face, her sweat-soaked hair told of a hard labor. But now Mama smiled as they all gathered around her. "This is your little brother." She uncovered his little head beside her as she watched her children's faces.

Lisl brightened when she looked at her mother and put her hand on hers. Then she gazed at the little miracle lying cradled in her mother's arms.

"What's his name?" Kurt wanted to know.

"I think we will name him Werner. What do you think?"

"I like Werner," Ellen said. The others agreed. Charlotte stroked Werner's little hand and sang softly.

Frau Kreidel sat in the chair by the window observing the children with tears in her eyes, talking to herself about doom.

"Oh Mama, he is so small. Just like a doll," Lisl said.

"Charlotte got the doll bed," Kurt whispered to his mother. "She wants the baby to sleep in it. Does he have to?"

"It's a baby crib. Werner will like it," Mama told him.

Dieter gazed in astonishment at the tiny boy. He held his hand over the blanket to feel the baby's little feet. And when Werner moved his toes under his hand, he looked up and smiled at his mother.

Charlotte lifted Kurt so he too could get a good look at his brother.

"The baby doesn't look very happy. He looks like he's going to cry," Kurt said.

Werner moved his arms across his face and started to fuss.

"See, I told you he won't like the doll bed, so don't put him in," Kurt whispered.

"Babies always cry. But that doesn't mean they're unhappy," his mother assured him.

Charlotte picked Kurt up. "The children are ready for bed, Mama." Their mother gave them a tired but happy smile as she kissed them goodnight. Dieter and Lisl took one last look at baby Werner.

"The violets are beautiful, but I would like them a little closer, I want to smell them all night."

Lisl rushed to bring the flowers to her mother's bedside, happy that she had noticed them.

Mama held the bowl between her hands and with closed eyes she inhaled the violets' sweet fragrance. Then she set them on the little table beside her bed.

The warning siren sounded. Lisl and Dieter quickly hugged their mother again before they went to the root cellar for the night. Although Lisl felt happy that Mama and the baby stayed in the bedroom, she hoped that the bombers would not come near Mainbernheim.

Lisl could not sleep. She wondered why Frau Kreidel had been so upset. Why had she mumbled to herself, "this small life, born into such a cruel world only to have it end too soon"? Was the baby sick? But her mother had told her that Werner was a wonderful healthy baby. She knew her mother would not lie. Frau Kreidel must have meant the war. She probably thought of Wuerzburg. But Lisl did not believe that the enemy would kill a baby so tiny. She kept thinking about the children burned in Wuerzburg and wondered if there were any babies among them.

Explosions rumbled in the distance. She hoped the bombing would not come too close tonight. A baby's first night of life should be spent in his mother's bed, not the root cellar.

She said her prayers and forced herself to think of happy things–the beautiful new baby, the violets she and Dieter had picked underneath the hedges, and her mother's happy face when she smelled them. Violets were her mother's favorite flower because they started to bloom in late winter.

Still the happy thoughts were pushed aside by thoughts of Wuerzburg, the terrible fire, and Frau Kreidel's prediction of doom. Even after saying her prayers again, Lisl lay sleepless on the mattress beside her brothers and sisters, still and stiff, careful not to wake them. Then finally toward morning she fell asleep.

CHAPTER 11

Dancing in the Mud

The air-raid sirens had been silent for the past two nights and Mama allowed her children to sleep in their bedrooms.

Lisl awoke to the sound of running water. She opened the window and flung the shutters back.

"Charlotte, Ellen, come quick. Look, spring has arrived."

"Close the shutters, Lisl," Ellen mumbled from under her covers.

"Can't you smell it?" Lisl insisted.

The scent of pine trees drifted from the west on a warm breeze along with the smell of fresh rain. But Lisl saw no sign of rain, only melting snow gurgling down the drainpipe.

Charlotte slid out of bed and came to the window. "Oh, it's going to be muddy again. The frost is gone."

The south side of the roof, where the sun reached with strength, had been free of snow for over a week. Lisl watched a slushy layer of snow slide down the roof tiles, teetering on the edge of the gutter. She dressed and hurried outside. With her eyes fixed on the gutter, she waited to see the last of the snow drop to the ground. But the slush clung tenaciously in soggy, dripping wads like wet laundry.

Winter's frost had loosened the earth but kept it hard and stiff, like walking on a frozen sponge. But now with the thaw Lisl felt the softened soil beneath her feet–plants could grow now. She twirled along the muddy pathway.

Mama stood in the doorway. "Lisl, what on earth are you doing out in that mess?"

"Mama, look, spring is here."

"I think you have to wait a little longer before you go dance about in the garden. Come in and get ready for school."

Ellen poked her head around her mother and looked at Lisl's shoes.

"Oh no, not the mud again," she moaned. "Now we have to wash our shoes every night."

Charlotte stepped out. She sighed, glancing down at her clean shoes with a pained look on her face.

After breakfast, Dieter and Lisl ran across the fields, on their usual shortcut to school. Lisl looked for signs of green, but the wild rose shrubs dividing the fields showed no new growth yet. A little disappointed, she knew it would take a few warmer weeks before the rosebuds would appear.

"Do you want to go to the meadow after school? Maybe we'll find some wild primroses." Dieter tempted Lisl with his bright smile. "They might be blooming right through the slush. They're always early."

Lisl nodded and skipped along beside him in her torn, muddy shoes.

Spring lingered in her mind when she arrived at school. She could see the sky through the classroom window, that is, if she craned her neck.

Strong gusts chased gray, wispy clouds across the heavens. Usually her mind was on bombers hiding above the overcast on a day like this. Today, however, she contemplated whether these clouds would bring rain or snow; after all, she had smelled rain this morning. Every time the snow had almost melted, a new snowfall called winter's freeze to return. Today felt different, much too warm for snow.

Herr Stolz's voice sounded somewhere in the distance. But Lisl's attention was on a little sparrow hopping on the window ledge shaking his feathers with excitement–a sure sign of spring.

"Lisl!" Herr Stolz shouted. She turned and came face to face with her teacher. "You'll stay after school to catch up on the lessons you ignored." Her classmates giggled.

Suddenly a loud explosion shook the building. The children jumped from their seats and bolted out the door. Herr Stolz tried to stop them, but the students stampeded out of the classroom and down the stairs. But when they came to the exit, Herr Kiefer stood with his arm stretched across the door.

"Get back to class," his voice boomed. "A thunderstorm does not dismiss class." After hearing a few more thunderclaps rumble in the distance, Lisl and her classmates sheepishly returned to their seats. Still, their concentration had been broken.

After a while, the bell rang and the students hurried out, leaving Lisl sitting alone.

Herr Stolz slammed a book onto her desk. "Open to page 38 and write out the answers of the next three pages." With a stern look and loud clap of his hand on the book he left the room.

Lisl heard the storm rumbling as the heavy, low clouds tried to make their way over Schwanberg. She could not take her eyes from the window until she saw fat raindrops hit the window pane. She smiled and watched the rain streak sideways across the glass like a curtain of gray pearls blowing in the wind.

She had promised Dieter they would go to the meadows, but it was too wet. She signaled to him from the window to go on home. She had no idea how long it would take to finish her assignment. Yet she kept watching the rain, winter was finally over.

Reluctantly Lisl slouched over her workbook, but her mind was on Mama and how to tell her why she was kept after school. Even when her mother did not scold her, her silent disappointment made Lisl feel worse. Lisl preferred the scolding.

She finally concentrated on her lessons and found the answers were easy. Herr Stolz came back into the classroom, sat at his desk correcting papers, but paid no attention to Lisl.

Almost an hour passed. Lisl sat up straight and noisily closed the book. She was sure that her answers were correct.

Her teacher came over and looked at her work. "Good, there are no mistakes. You work well if you put your mind to it."

Lisl sat still, expecting a lengthy lecture about paying attention.

"You have done your homework for today that your classmates have to do at home. Now you can take the rest of the afternoon off and go bird watching." His tone was kinder now. But his smile disappeared with the sound of the warning siren. "Go, quickly."

Lisl slung her book bag over her shoulder and hurried out ahead of her teacher.

With the wail of full alarm, Lisl ran home through the pouring rain. There were many people running along muddy Muehlenweg to get to the wine cellar shelter.

When Lisl got to the front door her mother stood in the doorway.

"*Gruess Dich* Mama," Lisl said with a cautious smile, slipping out of her muddy shoes. But Mama did not smile. With a disappointed expression she pushed a towel into Lisl's hands. Lisl knew she was in trouble. Her mother pointed to the basement stairs. Lisl ran down ahead of her mother while drying her hair and joined the family in the root cellar.

"Lisl," Mama sounded harsh. "What happened at school today?"

"I did my homework there."

"Lisl! You know what I mean."

"I only looked out the window and didn't hear Herr Stolz when he asked me a question. It was only about our homework assignments." Lisl tried to make it sound like a minor reprimand. "But you know, all he had me do was my homework, so I don't have to do it now." She hoped her mother would see the advantage as well.

"Oh Lisl, I wish you wouldn't always have your head in the clouds."

Lisl knew by her mother's softer tone she was not all that angry with her.

"Lisl, you'll never get to be an archeologist if you don't pay attention at school." Ellen always knew how to make Lisl feel like a failure when she thought Mama did not punish her enough. Schoolwork came easily to Ellen who often helped Lisl and Dieter with their homework, and sometimes even Charlotte—but not without making them feel stupid.

Explosions rumbled in the distance. Kurt hid behind the mattress in the corner, and Charlotte hovered around the baby, trying to hide her fear. But a little involuntary sound of distress escaped her lips with every explosion.

Dieter sat beside Lisl on the foot of the mattress. "Don't pay any attention to Ellen," he whispered, "she doesn't know anything about petrified seashells."

"Don't you have to do your homework now?" Lisl asked as she watched Ellen do hers near the little window.

"I already did mine. Mama made me do it as soon as I got home." Dieter, wearing his secret little smile, moved close to Lisl. "I've got a surprise." He pulled a little book out from under his sweater. "I got it from the school library, but I have to return it next week."

Although the book contained nothing about *petrified* seashells, it held an abundance of information and pictures on shells from around the world. Eagerly they searched for seashells of Europe. Now, with the help of the book, they could identify the petrified seashells–just in case they found a whole one in the quarry.

"Do you think shells have changed much since they turned to stone thousands of years ago?" Dieter asked.

"Could be, but I hope we'll still be able to recognize them."

The air raid lasted into the late evening but Lisl and Dieter were too wrapped up in the book to pay attention to explosions. They sat side by side with their heads together, reading by the glow of a single candle on the little wooden box. They fantasized about which of the seashells might be in the stone break. Of course they picked the most beautiful shells in the book.

"You know, the little pieces we found could have come from that shell." Dieter pointed to a picture.

"It's hard to tell, they're such tiny sections."

They tried to remember and compare them. Dieter's eyes sparkled. He looked at Lisl. "We should go back to the stone break before we forget what the pictures looked like."

Lisl smiled, whispering, "Yeah and soon."

CHAPTER 12

Working for Food

Ellen and Lisl–armed with a one-liter milk can and a cloth bag–walked to Willanzheim, about four kilometers from Mainbernheim. This small farming community consisted of about ten farmhouses with large barns attached. Lisl could hear the cows mooing in the barns and smell the manure. A dog came running and circled around them while barking a friendly, tail-wagging greeting. He tagged along after Lisl, hoping for affections.

Ellen's forehead wrinkled when she looked at Lisl's torn, mud-soaked shoes. "We had better get our shoes real clean before we come to the door; otherwise they won't let us in–and get rid of that." Ellen pointed to the dog that had attached himself to Lisl.

"Go home." Lisl motioned to the animal. The dog looked sad, but stopped following.

Ellen pointed at the farmhouse. "Let me do the talking. Frau Weigand will remember me; Charlotte and I worked here two weeks ago."

Ellen sat at the steps and pointed at clumps of dry grass under the eaves. Lisl pulled some out, handed some to Ellen, and wiped off all traces of dirt from her shoes and some of the mud that got on her knit stockings. Of course it did not come clean, but she stuck her feet back into her shoes, hoping no one would notice.

Ellen knocked on the door and whispered to Lisl, "Try to look sad." She looked at Lisl. "Not pouting."

An old woman peeked through the curtains on the front door window and then opened the door. "Yes? What do you want?" She looked at them suspiciously.

"I'm Ellen, remember me? This is my sister Lisl."

"Hello girls. Yes, I have seen you before." She pointed at Ellen.

"Yes, Frau Weigand. I have been working for you with my sister Charlotte. Do you have any chores we can do for you today? Maybe you need your dishes washed or your windows cleaned in exchange for some food?" Then with a weak gesture Ellen brought her hand to her stomach. "We haven't eaten for two days now. We're very hungry." Ellen looked as if she were about to faint.

"Oh, poor girls! Come in," the woman said, walking ahead of them into the kitchen. "Here, you sit down, and I will get you something."

Ellen knew that around noon cooked food was on hand for the old woman's family when they came in from the fields for lunch. Frau Weigand was more likely to be generous in sharing.

Ellen's voice sounded weak and her acting ability was outstanding as usual. Ellen's pale complexion and her light blue eyes made her look frail, and she knew how to take advantage with that. At times she fooled Mama, pretending to be sick to avoid having to go to school.

Lisl received little sympathy with her rosy cheeks, but was often treated like a waif; her hand-me-downs were too big and made her look smaller, much like a stray animal.

Ellen and Lisl sat at the kitchen table. A blue-and-white checkered tablecloth gave a clean appearance to a not-sotidy kitchen. Still, Lisl felt cozy. She welcomed the chance to warm her cold, wet feet. The wooden floor showed traces of dried mud. Dirty overalls hung on the back of the kitchen door and muddy boots lay in the corner. A big basket of firewood stood beside a warm oven. Lisl wondered where they had found the dry wood.

The old woman placed a bowl of split pea soup in front of them with a big slice of homemade bread. Lisl looked at the meal. It could feed the whole family at home.

Ellen kicked Lisl's foot under the table when she saw that Lisl was about to say something to that effect and quickly said, "Would you mind if we took some of it home? We have a milk can with us."

"No, you can eat it here. I'll fill your milk can when you're finished with your chores." The woman smiled.

Lisl was famished. The soup smelled delicious and tasted of pork although she found none in the soup.

Ellen savored every spoonful and winked at her sister. Lisl ate the soup, but slipped the big slice of bread into the pocket of her loose-fitting coat. She was not used to eating so much at one time so she saved the bread for later. But the thought of her family not being able to share the meal made it hard for her to swallow.

After they had finished, Ellen scrubbed the wooden floor in the living room and polished the furniture. Lisl washed windows, but not without Ellen helping to clean the spots she had missed. After a while, Frau Weigand's daughter and her two young sons came in to have their lunch.

Lisl scrubbed bed sheets on a wooden table in the basement. Frau Weigand had boiled them in a big laundry kettle earlier. With little soap available, boiling the sheets was one way to get them clean and germ-free. After rinsing the laundry in a big bathtub of cold water, Ellen and Lisl worked together to wring them out and hang the sheets outside on the line to dry.

The lady was delighted, gave them a thick slice of bacon, some bread, and filled their milk can with soup.

"Would you like us to come back to help you with your chores again?" Ellen asked.

"That would be nice, but not too soon. Maybe in a couple of weeks." Frau Weigand walked the girls to the door and watched as they headed through the mud to the main road.

Ellen's faint voice vanished and her humor and energy lightened the walk home. Her pity act always worked when it was needed, and sometimes it even fooled Lisl.

Ellen pulled in her cheeks and looked as if she were about to drop. "You have to learn to look starved," she said.

Lisl could see why it always worked; Ellen was good. "How is this?" Lisl pulled in her cheeks and crossed her eyes.

Ellen broke out in laughter. "Now you look like a cross-eyed rabbit."

"How do you learn to look starved?"

"I can see you'll never pass for starving, even if you are." Ellen gave up on the idea, but still laughed at Lisl's attempt.

On their way home the sound of bombers above the low cloud cover caught their attention.

Lisl stopped for a moment. "I think they are American planes." After listening and worrying for many months, she had learned to tell by the sound whether they were small planes or bombers, British, American or German. "We'd better hurry. Mama will be worried."

"Well, if we can't see them, they can't see us either. Besides, it's not the bombers but the little planes we have to watch out for. They can swoop down and shoot at us. Bombers can't do that."

When they got home, Mama had set the table. She had great confidence in Ellen's ability to bring home food. Mama hummed, winking at the girls while she fried the bacon slice Ellen had proudly set on the table.

The tapping of the cane on the floor announced that Grandfather was on his way to the kitchen. He sniffed the air. "What's cooking?" he asked Anni.

"Soup, I think."

While the soup heated, the family gathered around in anticipation. A few minutes later it was served with the big slice of bread from Lisl's pocket. The bacon grease was saved for next day's dinner along with the bread Frau Weigand had given them to take home.

Ellen and Lisl washed their shoes and stockings while the rest of the family had their dinner. Lisl sat with her elbows resting on her knees, her chin in her hands while she soaked her feet in a pan of warm water. Her washed stockings were draped over the stovepipe. She hoped they would dry overnight. She hated her other pair with too many mending patches on the knees. Although her new ones had mending around one ankle as well, it was not that noticeable.

The monotone of the warning siren interrupted the family meal. Opa and Aunt Anni hurried out to the wine cellar. Mama allowed the children to finish their dinner before they went to the root cellar in the basement at the sound of a full alarm.

They sat on their mattress and listened for planes.

Mama engaged them in a song so they would focus on the words instead the roar of the bombers.

Die Gedanken sind frei, wer can sie erraten.
Sie fliehen vorbei wie nachtliche Schatten.
Kein Mensh can sie wissen, kein Jager ershiessen.
Es bleibed dabei, die Gedanken sind frei.

They sang quietly, listening for bombers in the distance.

Close to midnight, with the all-clear siren, they returned to their beds, but stayed fully dressed.

CHAPTER 13

Seashell Treasure

"Class dismissed." Herr Stolz smiled as he watched his students *walk* from the classroom. He had been in a good mood all day. Lisl was not sure whether he was happy because he'd had a chance to teach the whole day without air raid interruptions, or because his students had actually paid attention.

Lisl walked from the classroom as well, but once outside, she raced down the stairs, ahead of all her classmates. Today was a perfect day to visit the stone break.

Dieter, who had been waiting for her by the entrance, fell in step with her. They smiled at each other, and without a word, raced out of the town and across the fields toward their special place.

The frost was gone and because the air-raid siren did not scream at the moment, they knew it was a good time to dig for petrified seashells.

Dieter smiled when they came to the edge of the quarry.

"We probably would have found a good shell by now if the air raids didn't always interrupt us. We just don't get enough time."

Mama always worried when they dug for shells. A few weeks ago, she made Dieter promise that he would not climb the embankment. He had promised to stay only on the lower part of the cliff.

Breathless, they entered their fantasy place–the large sunken stone break. The school bags slid off their shoulders and dropped to the ground as they ran through the entrance. With a quick dash across the stony surface they reached the rock wall with its calcium layer.

Lisl climbed up the high embankment, feeling only a little guilt. After all, *she* had not promised to keep off.

A surprise interrupted her climb. Tiny white flowers on fragile stems trembled in the breeze, seemingly growing out of bare rocks. She smiled and touched a flower petal.

"Did you find anything?" Dieter called to her.

"Not yet." She continued her climb until she made her way to a ledge, just a meter below the shrubby field above. The layer of calcium deposits, revealing particles of petrified seashells, sloped off in an angle between layers of brown rock.

Lisl gazed at the shell fragments, excavating small areas while Dieter dug industriously on the lower level.

"Lisl, do you think there was an ocean here a long time ago?" He looked up at her, shading his eyes.

"You know there could have been a deep blue sea with lots of shells," Lisl said.

Dieter stopped digging. "Yeah, do you think there were people here? You know people who came in tall ships with big sails?" He rubbed his hands together.

"I don't think so. We haven't seen any sign of humans, like tools or pots. Not even bones. I think it was too long ago."

"Yeah, or maybe it was a place where people couldn't go because of danger." Dieter still seemed hopeful.

"Like what? Like sea monsters?"

"Well, no. Maybe the cliffs were too steep for boats to land." Dieter started to dig again and when Lisl took a break he called. "Did you find anything yet?"

"Nothing yet." She kept one hand on the shrubbery roots she had exposed earlier while scraping at the rock wall with the other hand. Then she saw a round form partially exposed. She pulled on the embedded object and carefully loosened particles of rock and dirt until it was free.

"Look at this." She held it out between her fingers.

"Let me see." He scrambled up the embankment, sliding backward on loose rocks several times. Lisl grabbed his hand and pulled him up to the narrow ledge where he could hold on to the roots. His face was red from the cold March winds, his blue eyes sparkled in anticipation. She put the disc-like object, almost the size of her palm, in his outstretched hand.

Dieter held his breath at the sight. "It's not only whole, it's perfect," he said. "Not even a scratch or nick. But I don't remember seeing this one in the book." He held it up and turned it in all directions. "It looks like a big flattened snail shell."

"Maybe there were different shells here a long time ago. Maybe they're extinct now." She looked at Dieter whose eyes grew big at the thought of finding something that may have lived there millions of years ago.

"Yeah, they don't exist anymore," he whispered.

Lisl caressed the shell, tracing the snail design with her fingertips. "I wonder how old it is? What color do you think it was before it turned to stone?"

"Maybe blue. It almost looks like glass, but stone too." Dieter put it back in Lisl's hand and gazed at it in awe. They handed it back and forth. Each time their imagination grew bigger.

"It's like a piece of marble," Lisl said.

Air-raid sirens blared. Explosions rumbled in the distance like a thunderstorm. Without a word they slid down the embankment, grabbed their school bags, and ran toward the garden–about two hundred meters away.

The sounds of heavy artillery came from neighboring towns. Lisl heard no planes. Maybe the shots came from tanks attacking Michelfeld or Rodelsee. She knew Mama would be out looking for them, although there was no immediate danger without planes overhead.

When they came closer to their garden, Lisl saw Mama standing by the clothesline, calling.

They rushed to her and Dieter put his arms around her waist to assure her that they were all right.

"Where have you been? School let out over an hour ago." Mama looked angry, her strained expression dimmed Lisl's joy at finding the treasure. She tried to help by hanging the rest of the diapers onto the line.

"We just wanted to see . . ." Lisl tried to explain, but her mother cut her off.

"I know what you wanted to see. You were in the stone break again. I told you not to play in there. It's dangerous. You could fall and break your necks."

The sound of gunfire from neighboring towns did not seem to worry Mama. They had heard it many times before.

"Mama, guess what we found." Dieter smiled wistfully, his arms still around her waist, his face turned up.

Mama brushed the hair from his forehead and her expression softened.

He reached into his pocket and presented the shell to her.

"What am I going to do with you two?" she said with a smile.

"Yes, Mama, but look at it," Dieter insisted.

She took the petrified seashell from his hand and wiped it with the corner of her apron. "Oh, that is beautiful." She held it against the sunlight. "It's almost transparent." Her amber eyes sparkled as the sun cast a golden glow across her face.

They stood in awe, admiring the shell.

Mama's eyes had a faraway look. "We are so far from the sea it's hard to imagine an ocean here."

"Maybe the sea was right here where we are standing now." Lisl tapped the ground with her shoe.

Mama's face lit up at the thought. "There are enough rocks in the garden." She gazed toward the stone break with a smile. Lisl thought her mother would have loved to go there with them and escape into their fantasy world. Maybe, for just a moment, she was able to forget the horrors of war and the lack of food. Or maybe it was a magic seashell. But then, Lisl remembered, her mother was a dreamer too.

A small British observer plane flew low over the neighborhood gardens and the spell was broken. They quickly ran into the house.

CHAPTER 14

No Escape

Explosions thundered in the distance like an impending storm. It was late March now and the advancing war front made its presence heard.

"Enemy ground troops have moved close to Michelfeld," Herr Brunner, a neighbor, shouted as he rode past on his bike. He had just visited his daughter and grandchildren who lived in the little town.

Michelfeld was about six kilometers from Mainbernheim. Lisl wondered how long before the enemy would find their little town.

The town crier rang his big bell on every street corner– as usual. Lisl heard no panic in his voice, so it could not be that bad.

"Keep gatherings indoors," he shouted. "Blackouts will be strictly enforced. Stay in the shelter. Keep off the streets." He walked off in long strides, followed by neighborhood children who mockingly stalked behind him.

"Mama, what does he mean by keep off the streets?" Lisl asked.

"I suppose he means not to stand around in groups. You still have to go to school though."

At school, the teacher told his class, "The playground time will be short from now on. And please do not dawdle or walk in groups on your way home."

Well, that would be hard to do, Lisl thought. Did that mean she could not walk home with Dieter? But two was not exactly a group and would probably be all right.

Now she had to take the warnings seriously. She knew the danger was real if Herr Stolz showed such concern. However, when the sirens blared, Lisl and her classmates, along with other classes, ran out of the building in large groups, hurrying through the streets to get to their homes or shelters.

That evening, an impatient knocking brought Mama running to the front door. Frau Nagel, her next-door neighbor, stood outside the door, shaking in fear. She was surrounded by her five children, a grouping the town crier had said "was forbidden".

"Frau Lindner, we are leaving to go farther to the southeast." Frau Nagel motioned toward her hand wagon piled high with big fluffy bedding. She was proud of her goose down comforters, and had often pinned them on the clothesline for all to see, instead of hanging them through the open window the way other neighbors freshened their bedding.

Loaded down by heavy suitcases and bundles, the Nagel children already looked tired just from carrying them from next door.

"I hope this will give us a new start somewhere safer. Will you please come with us?" Frau Nagel begged, "We still have a chance to get away from the enemy. They're getting very close."

But before she could continue, Mama pulled her and the children into the house.

A small British observer plane had been circling overhead since dusk, dropping flares that lit up the landscape to detect ground movements of German troops and tanks.

Frau Nagel did not seem to realize the danger she had put her family, as well as Mama's, in.

"Where would you go? There is no escape to the southeast. The Russian army will be waiting for you. They are known to do terrible things to German women."

Lisl was startled. She seldom heard such harshness in her mother's voice.

The Nagel children, visibly shaken, turned their pale frightened faces to Mama, then to their mother and back to Mama.

Fifteen-year-old Helga Nagel turned to her mother, "Mama, let's go back home. Frau Lindner is right. We will be safer at home."

"Yes, listen to Helga. Go back to your house and take your chances. There is no safe place to run." Mama paused, waiting for an argument from Frau Nagel.

The woman looked crushed and small, sitting hunched over on the hallway bench.

Lisl felt sorry for her neighbor. She looked as if she had been crying and was about to cry again.

Mama sat down beside her and put her arm around her shoulder, patting her gently. "How far do you think you'll get in the dark, with a hand wagon, all that luggage, and five children?" she said softly.

With her head hung low, Frau Nagel twisted her handkerchief, concentrating on her hands, dabbing at her eyes now and then. Finally she lifted her head, looked at Mama, and started to laugh until she cried again.

Mama stood up. "Let's go in the kitchen. It's warm there. I'll make some chamomile tea."

"Look outside, it's all lit up," six-year-old Herman Nagel shouted, pointing through the half-open shutters. Mama rushed to close the shutters tightly and moved him away from the window.

"It would do no good to go at night. It's as bright as day out there," Irmgard told her mother.

Helga went to the crib and picked up baby Werner. Cradling him in her arms, she sat down by the kitchen table where Mama poured the tea.

Frau Nagel had calmed herself. She seemed relieved that Mama had talked her out of going. They chatted with each other the way they used to in more peaceful times. With her husband at war, Frau Nagel found it difficult to make decisions on her own, and often asked Mama for advice.

"Do you want to play, *Mench Aerger Dich Nicht?*" Dieter whispered to the Nagel children. They quickly spread the game board on the floor, crowding around the candle Mama moved from the kitchen table to the floor.

The Nagel children played against the Lindner children. Their mothers cheered them on, looking over their shoulders. Muffled laughter filled the small kitchen and Lisl forgot about the war until she heard that rumbling coming from the southwest.

The warning siren screamed and the game ended. The Nagel family hurried home to get ready to go to the wine cellar. Charlotte and Ellen helped them push their hand wagon next door again.

Full alarm blared by the time Mama got the smaller children ready to go to the root cellar and Charlotte and Ellen returned, running, from next door.

Again, they faced a long sleepless night.

CHAPTER 15

In the Trenches

When Herr Stolz heard the eerie up-and-down wail of full alarm and the sound of heavy artillery fire, he hurried the children out of the schoolhouse. Most of the students ran along Adolf Hitler Strasse. Lisl took the shortcut through one of the smaller tower gates when she saw Dieter dawdling along the path waiting for her to catch up. His class had been dismissed before the alarm sounded. Together they took their usual route that led them across the fields and along the stone break to their home.

Lisl had never heard gunfire quite that loud. Wide-eyed, she turned in circles trying to see where the enemy was shooting from.

"I hope we don't have to spend the night in the root cellar again. Do you think it will last all night?" Dieter asked as they hurried across the barren fields.

Lisl didn't respond. An artillery shell hit the next field, throwing dirt high into the air. She stopped running, covered her ears, then ran again.

"Hurry, Dieter, they're getting close."

They raced until their lungs ached. Lisl hoped Mama would not come to look for them and get herself killed.

Halfway through the field, they found themselves surrounded by heavy gunfire. Artillery shells tore into the ground. Soil and shrubbery from hedges that surrounded the fields spewed like fountains and showered down on them.

Lisl dropped her book bag from her shoulders, held it over her head to keep the flying dirt off, and just kept running and panting.

Clouds of smoke mixed with the smell of gunpowder hung in the air. The sounds of explosions were deafening.

Suddenly Lisl felt herself being pulled into a muddy hole. She let out a terrified scream. Dieter tumbled down beside her.

"Don't you have a better place to play than right in the middle of an artillery attack? You should be in a shelter," a German soldier shouted. Out of breath, Lisl pointed toward her home, gasping, but could not make a sound.

Finally she squeaked as she pointed to the housing area again, "We live right over there."

The houses were not visible from where the soldiers were stationed, since the Siedlung was downhill from the fields. Still, the edge of their garden was only about two hundred meters away.

Lisl was sure the ditches in the fields had not been there this morning. They must have been dug after she and Dieter had passed through on their way to school.

"We live right over there," Lisl shouted again. The soldiers did not listen to her. She scrambled out, trying to help Dieter out as well. But one of the soldiers pulled her back down and stuffed her, along with Dieter, into the corner of the ditch. The narrow hole was already crowded with three soldiers and wooden boxes – some filled with big ammunition shells.

A heavy gun, mounted beside the hole, was halfway covered with netting and shrubs.

"We have to get home or our mother will come to search for us." Lisl tried again.

"You'd better wait a while until things calm down a little," The soldier pushed them both back into their little space.

Heavy gunfire hit all around the fields and the soldiers fired back.

Lisl knew there were more ditches spread around the field by the sounds of soldiers calling out to each other. They shouted commands to each other between gun shots. She poked her head up and saw shallow mounds of camouflaged tents hiding their cannons. She quickly ducked down again and covered her ears as they prepared to fire one of the guns nearby. Lisl realized they had stumbled into a war zone.

Although Lisl was scared of the noisy guns that stood only a few meters away, she was more worried that her mother would come looking for them at any moment.

Dieter's face was ashen. He stuck his fingers in his ears and squinted when the soldiers prepared to load a heavy shell into the gun.

Lisl saw her chance. While the soldiers were distracted, she grabbed Dieter's hand and together they scrambled out, running, stumbling, falling, and running again toward their house.

"Get back, you little fools. You'll get yourselves killed," the soldier shouted.

Lisl looked back to see if the soldiers were coming after them. An artillery shell hit near the ditch they were in and sprayed the dirt high into the air. Lisl screamed and dragged Dieter along with her. The frightful explosions behind them only made them run faster. Lisl was afraid to look back, afraid that the soldiers had taken a hit.

At the end of the field they slowed down. Dieter bent over to catch his breath. Lisl's lungs ached. She turned to see where the last artillery hit had exploded. She saw a gaping smoldering hole only a few meters from their garden. She worried that the next hit would be their garden or even the house. They ran again.

Dieter pointed to the road below, where Charlotte and Ellen ran along Muehlenweg. They always took the longer way through town.

Mama was halfway up the garden path while Kurt stood screaming in the open doorway.

Dieter looked at Lisl. "You don't have to cry any more," he gasped, "we made it home."

"I'm not crying." Lisl wiped her tears with her sleeve. "I've got something in my eyes."

When they reached Mama, she grabbed their hands and ran into the house. Then she stood silently by the open door and took a terrified Kurt in her arms, waiting for Charlotte and Ellen.

Although her mother looked shaken, Lisl noticed anger in her eyes as well. Mama herded them down into the root cellar without a word.

Kurt screamed even louder when Mama put him on the ground in the root cellar. He scrambled behind the mattress, trying to hide from the noisy explosions.

The baby lay in his laundry basket, looking curiously at Lisl when she stroked his soft little face.

A few moments later, Charlotte and Ellen came tearing down the stairs. They too could see that Mama was angry, but did not dare ask why.

"What happened?" Charlotte asked Lisl.

"I don't know," Lisl whispered.

"How did you two get so dirty?" Ellen noticed the mud on Lisl's and Dieter's clothes.

Dieter started to explain the muddy foxholes, but when Mama came down the cellar stairs, he just shrugged his shoulders.

Mama realized the counterattack was fired from the fields above their home. "Why did they have to dig the trenches so close to the houses?" But when she looked at her children she quickly went silent.

"That's why Mama was angry," Lisl whispered to Charlotte. Her sister stroked Lisl's hair.

Opa and Aunt Anni had gone to the wine cellar dungeon with the first sound of the sirens.

Now Mama sat with her children on the mattresses in the root cellar, waiting and listening. Some of the hits came so close and so loud that even Lisl and Dieter covered their ears.

Mama's anger turned to sadness when she lifted Kurt from his little prison behind the mattress and cradled him in her arms.

After about an hour the shooting stopped and everyone rushed upstairs to find something to eat. But a few minutes later the attack started again with full force, so they scrambled down again.

When a pattern of on-again, off-again attacks became apparent, they stayed in the cellar.

Some of the explosions sounded as though they were right outside the door. Lisl was not sure whether the enemy fired from tanks or artillery. But whatever it was, the soldiers in the trenches launched counterattacks.

Every time someone had to go to the bathroom, Mama told them when to run upstairs. She could hear when the enemy fired the shot, then a whistling sound followed by an explosion. After that explosion was the safest time to run upstairs so they would not get caught on the stairway during the hit.

Kurt crawled into the smallest corner of the root cellar between the wall and the mattresses when Mama put him down. With his little hands pressed firmly over his ears, his small body shook in fear.

Lisl wished she could take away his terror. Since there was nothing she could do about the attack it was easier not to be scared. She tried to engage him in play, but he only got more frightened. Wild eyed, he pressed his hands even harder over his ears when she tried to get him to come out of his corner. He screamed whenever Mama went upstairs to get something.

With every explosion Charlotte let out a little squeak. She looked as though she wanted to run to a safer location, but found no place to hide.

Ellen tried to calm everyone by entertaining them with funny faces. She usually stayed calm to the point of being heroic or even unfeeling. But Lisl noticed how her eyes closed tightly when the explosions came too close. Lisl knew by her sister's nervous cough that she was frightened as well, although she tried to hide it. Ordinarily, Ellen lectured everyone on how to stay strong, not to be frightened. Today she did not even try.

Charlotte, who laughed hysterically at the silliest things, also cried just as easily when she became frightened.

Ellen always knew how to make Charlotte laugh by wearing her mother's big hat and long coat. Exaggerating a lady walk she pranced across the mattress then tripped over the long coat. She did manage to get a smile out of Charlotte, or rather a worried grimace vaguely resembling a smile. At least she stopped crying. When one loud explosion shook the house, Ellen let herself fall onto the mattress, but Charlotte failed to see the humor and started to cry again.

Dieter and Lisl sat at the foot of the mattress and started to count whenever they heard a shot being fired.

"Can't you two ever be serious? How can you play at a time like this? We might all be dead by morning," Charlotte shouted at them.

"We want to know how far away the enemy is." Dieter tried to calm her. "We're counting the seconds between the shots being fired and the hits in the fields."

"I think they're about three to five kilometers away, give or take a few," Lisl said, "You know, the way we count the seconds between lightning and a thunderclap to figure the distance of the storm."

This however, did not calm Charlotte. To hear how close the enemy had advanced made her near tears again. So Lisl quickly added, "Of course we could be wrong; I think they're still a long way off."

Charlotte looked at Dieter and Lisl as though they had lost their minds. She shook her head and was about to complain to Mama about their lack of concern.

Mama just smiled. "Charlotte, they're taking a scientific approach to the problem," she joked. Mama was hoping Charlotte would see the humor as well, but Charlotte shook her head.

To Lisl it wasn't a scientific approach, just Dieter's new game, and it made the attacks easier to bear.

With another break in the on-again, off-again attacks, Mama hurried up to the kitchen to prepare dinner. After a while she brought fried potatoes, red beets and hot linden tea to the cellar. She called the potatoes "chased" potatoes because she chased them around a greaseless frying pan to keep them from sticking. Her humor calmed everyone except Charlotte and Kurt.

Finally, at two in the morning, the attack stopped. The stillness screamed in Lisl's ears. They sat on the mattress on the cellar floor, waiting for that next shot, the one that might hit their house. But the calm lingered.

One by one they ran upstairs to wash and get ready for bed back in the root cellar.

They stayed fully clothed, suitcases by the cellar door.

Kurt had worn himself out worrying and screaming. He was the first to fall asleep. Yet even in his slumber he cried and thrashed about.

Lisl could tell by Ellen's steady and loud breathing that she had fallen asleep as well.

Dieter's eyelids looked heavy. Still, he tried to show Lisl shadow creatures against the wall from the light of the candle on a wooden box. When the show stopped, Lisl knew he too had fallen asleep.

Explosions thundered in the distance and Lisl wondered if Michelfeld or Rodelsee had been taken, or maybe one of the other small towns near Mainbernheim.

A low-flying airplane thundered noisily over the house. Charlotte sat up.

"German plane," Lisl whispered sleepily and Charlotte settled down again.

Lisl listened to the familiar sound of the plane's engine. She stared at the flickering candle flame, wondering if she would ever be able to go back to her bed upstairs again.

Mama changed the baby's diaper. When she was finished she warmed milk over the candle's flame and poured it slowly from the metal cup into the baby's bottle, careful not to spill a drop. She fed Werner and put him back in the little oval laundry basket. Mama's face looked happy in the candle's glow as she covered the baby with a warm blanket. She sat on the foot of the bed to keep a watchful eye throughout the night, ready to get her children out of bed at a moment's notice.

Lisl reached out to her mother and stroked her hand, whispering, "*Gute Nacht*, Mama."

"*Gute Nacht, Liebling.*" Slowly Mama pulled the covers over Lisl as not to wake the sleeping children beside her.

Lisl felt safe knowing that her mother slept across the foot of the two mattresses, the only place in the cellar where she had room to lie down.

Silently Lisl prayed they would not be killed. She wanted to see the end of the war. To be here when their lives returned to normal. When Papa came home. She tried to think of what normal used to be like, but sleep interrupted her thoughts.

∾

Next morning, with the click of the front door closing, Lisl awoke. She slipped into her shoes, went upstairs and out into the garden.

Mama stood motionless in the misty, gray dawn, staring at a hole an artillery hit had torn into the ground at the edge of the garden.

The still moist air caressed Lisl's face. Quietly she stepped beside her mother, whispering "Mama?"

Her mother took Lisl's hand. They did not go to the end of the garden where the fields began. The unmistakable smell of gunpowder hung in the air on this last day of March.

Mama took no notice of Lisl who watched the softness on her mother's face disappear as she looked toward the fields where the trenches had been dug. Then, hastily she pulled Lisl back into the house.

"*Guten Morgen,* Mama,*"* Ellen said, rubbing her eyes.

"*Guten Morgen,* Mama." Charlotte came up from the cellar stairs behind Ellen.

Although Mama glanced at her daughters for a moment, she did not seem to see them either. She gazed out across the garden toward the fields again.

"I'm going to have a talk with the soldiers," she finally said. "They need to know the danger they put us in as well as our neighbors by digging trenches so close to our homes."

"Can we come with you?" Ellen asked.

Mama nodded.

They strode through the garden and out to the fields. Deep holes dotted the landscape around the trenches and across the fields. And as they approached the ditches, they saw German medics take away the wounded and dead soldiers, place them in two trucks, and then slowly drive away. The few remaining soldiers lay slumped in the trenches.

The stillness reminded Lisl of a funeral. Only the gray mist cried.

Mama watched the mud-covered soldiers.

Lisl wanted to ask her mother whether they were dead or alive because they did not move, yet she was afraid to break the silence.

Her mother and sisters looked stunned, standing like statues in the field. The soldiers became aware of them and stirred.

"Heil Hitler," Mama said, her hand held high as she approached.

With vacant expressions, the soldiers looked at her without returning the salute. "You shouldn't be here," one of them said in a low, quiet voice.

A tear trickled down Mama's cheek. She swallowed. "Please, could you move a little farther away from our homes? I'm afraid that with the next attack we won't be so lucky, our homes will get hit." There was no hint of anger in her voice now.

"Where are your homes?" The exhausted soldier struggled to his feet.

Mama pointed toward the Siedlung. "Only about two hundred meters below the fields."

"We will be gone by evening. Other troops will replace us but not in this location," a young soldier said, not stirring from his position.

Ellen and Charlotte looked at each other. These soldiers looked almost as young as Charlotte's classmates. Why were these boys here and in uniform? Lisl had not noticed their ages the day before when they had pulled her into the hole. But then she had only seen three of them up close. She wondered if they had been wounded or killed.

Mama looked at the skinny soldiers. "When did you eat last?"

One of the soldiers shrugged his shoulders.

Mama walked away; no longer could she hide her tears.

"Couldn't we bring them something to eat?" Charlotte asked.

"What could we bring them? We have so few potatoes left."

"We could make them a soup," Lisl suggested.

"Yeah, there is a little bacon grease left in the jar. We could put some of that into the soup," Ellen said.

"All right." Their mother agreed. "But remember it will make our rations very skimpy."

"I don't mind skipping a meal," Lisl said hastily although her stomach growled.

"I'll skip mine, too," Charlotte echoed, her eyes welling over.

"I can always try to get more food from the farmers." But a hint of doubt was in Ellen's voice. Now even she found it hard to exchange chores for food. The farmers had discovered the black market. Now they traded the food for clothing and things that their families needed.

Charlotte was eager to get started. She ran ahead of them across the field on her long skinny legs.

By the time Lisl came through the door, Charlotte had already brought some potatoes into the kitchen. Enthusiastically they peeled and cut them into the pot and set them to boil.

Lisl ran into the garden with Dieter on her heels.

Dieter helped dig up the last of the over-wintered brussels sprouts from the vegetable pit in the garden. "What are we making?" he asked.

"Soup for the soldiers up there." Lisl pointed toward the fields, then ran back into the kitchen and slipped a handful of the washed vegetables into the pot. When the bacon grease was added, it even smelled like soup–or at least like something to eat. Dieter saved the rest of the brussels sprouts for the family dinner.

When it was done, Mama put the soup into the milk can. Ellen grabbed the can and ran up to the field, followed by Charlotte and Lisl.

"Heil Hitler," they greeted and stood at attention. Lisl caught a disapproving look from one of the soldiers. She was afraid he would chase them away. She quickly said, "We brought you some soup."

Mama came across the field with some ersatz coffee, which she handed to the soldiers.

"Are you sure you can spare the food?" one of the soldiers asked, looking at Lisl and her sisters.

"It was their idea," Mama said.

Slowly the soldiers came out of the holes and shook the girls' hands, tying to hide their tears. "*Herzlichen Dank . . . Vielen Dank.*" Then they quickly divided the soup. One of the soldiers pointed at his small portion with his mouth full. "This is the best soup I've ever tasted." They finished within minutes and Lisl realized they could have used a lot more.

Farmers came running across the field. At first Lisl thought they were bringing food. But they were empty-handed, shouting at the hungry troops. One old woman said, "Get away from here. The enemy will destroy our fields along with our homes."

Another one walked close to a tired soldier, shouting, "You've got to get out of here."

Lisl cried. How could they be so heartless? These young men had risked their lives to defend their town. Her mother had also asked them to move farther away, but at least she had given them something to eat.

Before nightfall, Dieter and Lisl went back to see if the soldiers were still there, but all traces of guns and equipment had been erased except for the big holes. Artillery hits of various shapes and depths scattered across the fields and around the trenches, obliterating some of them beyond recognition. Now the trenches looked morbid, like freshly dug graves. Lisl wondered how many soldiers had died.

She stood at the edge of the field, overlooking the neighborhood. One shell had hit only about eight meters from their house. None of their neighbors' houses were hit, although some came very close. What would happen when the attacks started again? Where could they go if their house was destroyed?

Dieter walked around the holes. "I bet you have to be brave to fire those big guns. I wonder why they didn't wear earplugs." He searched for spent gun shells. Disappointed he walked away. "I think the other boys beat me to it."

Lisl's mind was on the starving soldiers who had looked so sad and tired. She grieved for the dead soldiers' families. Would they be told of their deaths right away, or would they have to wait and worry? Lisl wiped her tears. She thought of her father. Was he still alive? She would rather not know, and be able to hope a little longer.

CHAPTER 16

Charlotte's Confirmation

All through the cold hard winter Lisl had longed for her favorite month. April had finally arrived.

The big cherry tree stood waiting, ready to burst into bloom, while the sour cherry tree under the window dared to show a few of its white blossoms. Trembling daffodils blew their golden trumpets defiantly into the cold breeze.

A chilly gust swept through the cobblestone streets as Lisl walked with her family to church on the Sunday of Charlotte's confirmation.

Ellen stayed at the house to take care of Kurt and Werner so Mama could attend the confirmation. Opa and Aunt Anni were too frightened to leave the wine cellar shelter.

Mama had prepared for this special day since Christmas when she started to save eggs, putting them in the glycerin barrel to keep them fresh.

Two dozen eggs bought a pair of black shoes and stockings for Charlotte. Although the shoes were not new, Lisl could not tell them from brand new unless she looked at the soles. She hoped she too would have fine shiny shoes when her confirmation came around in four years.

She had watched her mother create magic on her sewing machine, transforming grandmother's old black dress into a confirmation gown.

Charlotte had tried it on almost daily when only pins held it together. "How do I look?" she would ask, twirling around.

"Skinny," Ellen had replied.

"I'm not skinny. Mama, is it too tight?"

This went on while the dress took shape. But now Charlotte proudly wore her special outfit to church.

On their way through town, Lisl noticed soldiers stationed all around town–more troops than usual. Some sat around the outdoor tables of Gasthof Zum Falken, a hotel and restaurant. Maps, instead of food, covered the outdoor tables, and the soldiers struggled against the wind to keep the maps from flying away. A somber-faced commander leaned restlessly over a table, his finger tracing routes across the papers.

The town's mayor looked over the commander's shoulder. Lisl heard him arguing with one of the officers who did not want to listen. However, the mayor seemed unwilling to give in. He shouted, but Lisl was too far away to understand what was being said. The officer brushed him aside.

Everywhere Lisl looked, troops moved into position around the town. She felt the unrest. The uncertainty made her jumpy, yet excited–something was about to happen.

Dieter trailed behind, observing soldiers.

"Dieter, come on, stay with us," Mama called.

"I just want to see if some of the soldiers are from Mainbernheim."

Townspeople scurried through the streets, looking for familiar faces as well, and a few citizens tried to get information from the busy, nervous soldiers only to be motioned out of the way.

Charlotte trembled, walking arm in arm between Mama and Lisl. She did not appear to be frightened and seemed oblivious to all the commotion. Not wanting to cover her pretty dress, she had gone without her coat and was shaking from the breeze.

The photographer rushed about in front of the church steps. He pulled Charlotte out from between Mama and Lisl and arranged her with other participants he had gathered. By the time Dieter called out "smile Charlotte," the photographer had already taken the picture.

In church, Charlotte and her classmates disappeared into a side room while their families seated themselves in their usual places.

Frau Hoffman whispered to Mama, "The SS is in town."

"Are you sure?"

The woman nodded.

"American troops have invaded Michelfeld," another lady said. She waited for the song to end before she continued. "Enemy tanks are moving toward Mainbernheim." Heads turned to listen.

Lisl shook her head. She could not imagine tanks on that narrow road between Michelfeld and Mainbernheim. Besides, Michelfeld was not even half the size of Mainbernheim. Enemy tanks would not bother with such a small town.

Poor Charlotte. No one paid attention. Even during the service, people whispered to each other, glancing toward the entrance where an old man stood watch. Lisl too kept her eyes on the open door where two boys talked to the watchman. But no matter how hard the congregation concentrated on the action outside, they could not hear.

The organ music started again. The girls in their black dresses and flower crowns and boys in their black suits and boutonnieres walked down the aisle and lined up in front of the altar. Songbooks in hand, they were ready for their confirmation celebration.

Lisl and Dieter waved to Charlotte who looked so happy, smiling at her family. She looked painfully thin and frail in her black dress and black stockings. But she sang like an angel in the front row, holding her head straight and stiff to keep her flower crown from falling off, although Mama had fastened it securely to her curls.

Suddenly explosions and screams interrupted the serenity of the ceremony. The sirens wailed in eerie contrast to the church organ, but the organist stubbornly kept playing.

"Mainbernheim is under attack," an old man shouted.

Charlotte hurried to her family as the congregation ran screaming out of church and into the street.

Outside they collided with German troops rolling heavy guns through the streets to position equipment at the edge of the town wall. They were ready to fire back at the enemy.

Lisl looked all around, not sure where the attack was coming from–maybe from right outside the wall.

Civilians and soldiers ran in all directions. Families became separated dodging guns and equipment the soldiers dragged into place.

The church bells rang as always when worshipers left the church. It was a strange mix of calm and chaos. Lisl concentrated on the calming sound of the bells to shut out gunfire and Charlotte's screams. Lisl could almost imagine a peaceful Sunday morning, had it not been for the German soldiers pushing her out of their way and the screaming sirens.

Through artillery fire and soldiers scrambling into defense positions, Lisl and her family hurried along Muehlenweg and finally made it home.

Ellen had bundled Werner in a warm blanket and stood in the doorway ready to run in case the house got hit.

Kurt ran screaming to his mother as soon as she came near the door. She picked him up and hurried everyone ahead of her into the root cellar.

Charlotte threw herself onto the mattress, shaking in fear. "Oh, Mama, why did it have to happen today?" She lay face down on the pillow.

"I know, but war does not wait for anything," Mama said.

"I've lost my flower crown," Charlotte sobbed, still face down.

"Never mind."

"I tore my nice black stockings on the way home." She rolled to her side and sat up. "I know how much food you had to pay." She cried louder now as she looked at her torn stockings again.

"It doesn't matter. At least no one got hurt." Mama consoled her.

Lisl wished she could think of something to make her sister feel better. Tears welled up in Lisl's eyes as she watched Charlotte bury her face in Mama's shoulder.

Dieter seemed unnerved by his sister's sobbing. "Do you think the shooting will be over soon or do we have to stay in the root cellar all day?"

Lisl shrugged. She had looked forward to Charlotte's special day. At least someone had taken a picture of her and her classmates in front of the church.

The church bells still rang along with the screaming sirens as explosions continued to rock the area.

Dieter sat on the foot of the bed with his head hung low.

Lisl sat down beside him and put her hand on his shoulder.

Kurt had fled into his little safety nest behind the mattress, covering his ears, screaming louder with every explosion.

"Come here, *Liebling*," Mama said, holding out her hands to him. Slowly he crawled out from behind the mattresses and into her arms. She rocked him and hummed his favorite lullaby, and soon he calmed down.

Lisl knew it broke her mother's heart to see him so frightened all the time.

Mama held Kurt most of the day and Lisl wished she could comfort her mother. Although she seemed strong, Lisl could not help thinking there must be times when even Mama needs comfort and love. She wished Papa could be here.

Carefully, Lisl picked up the baby and sat down beside Dieter again. She wondered why Werner was never frightened, even when Kurt screamed. Maybe he was used to all the noise, or maybe he was the world's best little baby. He looked at her with big curious eyes whenever she talked to him, as if he understood. And when she sang to him, he often held his breath to listen.

Dieter rubbed the baby's cheek and pressed his face against Werner's head.

"He is so soft, and smells so good." Dieter smiled again.

Ellen and Charlotte tried to do most of the chores between attacks so Mama could stay with Kurt. Ellen boiled a few potatoes to serve with the goat cheese–Frau Weber's gift for Charlotte's confirmation. Mama had hoped to eat in the dining room, but now they would have to eat their special dinner in the root cellar–the attack would not stop.

Lisl laid the baby back in his basket. She realized that she heard no arguing from the kitchen. Curious, she peeked in. She wanted to make sure that her sisters were really in there. She found them silent, Charlotte trying hard to keep from crying.

Lisl had picked some daffodils in the garden before they left for church. She now brought them to Charlotte, hoping to cheer her up. But when she took them from Lisl's hand with a surprised look, she started sobbing again.

Ellen glanced helplessly at Charlotte now and then. She could not think of a thing to make Charlotte feel better either.

If only they would start to quarrel, Lisl thought. Charlotte's crying always stopped when she had to defend herself and think of a snappy answer for Ellen. But Ellen was kind to her today, which made Charlotte feel even worse.

The attack on Mainbernheim stopped in the late afternoon, and so did Charlotte's crying.

"I know it will start again. I don't even care because I know we'll all be killed." She stared ahead, pale, resigned to her doom.

"Don't even think such a thing," Mama said. "We will be all right. You'll see."

They stayed in the root cellar throughout the night. The town remained calm.

In the morning Charlotte's dark cloud of doom lifted when she heard the town crier shouting, "The enemy has retreated. Michelfeld is free again."

The calm lasted all day and through the night.

CHAPTER 17

Bird Watching

The next day, Lisl and Dieter walked to school through town instead of taking the shortcut through the fields.

"See, I told you the town is still standing."

Dieter was right. The northeast side, mostly outside the wall, showed the most damage. Judging by the sounds of explosions the day before, Lisl thought the town would be destroyed. Most of the hits were in the fields and in the little garden plots around the outside of the wall. The highway beside the gardens was damaged too, but one lane remained open to traffic–mostly German military convoys. The town, as well as the schoolhouse, showed only minor damage.

When Lisl arrived at her school desk everyone told of their experiences until the teacher called the class to order. Lisl tried to concentrate on her teacher's lectures, but it was hard to ignore the sound of war raging in the distance.

But there was something else that distracted Lisl. Her mind was on a sparrow, sitting on the window ledge. The little bird chirped and fluttered every time another bird flew by, unaware of the war, only that spring had arrived. There were nests to be built and families to be raised. Oh how Lisl would have liked to be a little bird.

Herr Stolz's voice tore her from her thoughts. "Lisl, are we bird watching again, or are we getting our math into our distracted little head?"

"Sorry." Lisl felt her cheeks turn red.

"I'm waiting." He tapped his pointing stick against the blackboard.

"I'm sorry, I didn't hear the question." She waited for the snickers, but her classmates did not giggle today. They too were preoccupied, twisting in their seats to peer through the window, but not to look at the birds.

Suddenly an explosion shook the schoolhouse. The children sprang from their seats. Some ran to the windows, while others ran out the door.

"Stay in your seats," Herr Stolz shouted, hitting his stick loudly on his desk. "We are not getting out of school until the enemy bursts through the door." But with the wail of the air-raid siren, he had to let them go. "Dismissed. Go to your shelters. Fast." But most of the children had already fled.

Students from all grades rushed out of the schoolhouse, down the courthouse steps and onto the main street where they scattered in different directions.

Artillery shells hit sections of the wall, hurling heavy rocks, bricks and debris high into the air as though they were little pebbles.

Lisl screamed. She had expected more protection from such a thick, strong stone wall. She called out to her sisters when she saw them running along the street ahead of her. Together they hurried along until Charlotte shouted, "There is Dieter." Dieter slowed, then stopped, so his sisters could catch up with him.

"Hurry! We've got to get into the root cellar." Ellen shouted over the noise of screaming people and explosions.

Charlotte held Dieter's hand so she would not lose him in the frantic crowd.

An old man sat on a stone bench in front of his house asleep.

Ellen pulled on his sleeve to wake him. "You have to go inside," she shouted. She shook him, and with her hand on his shoulder he slumped over and fell to the ground. Blood oozed from a head wound.

Lisl felt numb, staring at the old man.

Charlotte screamed, unable to move, her hands over her ears. Ellen pulled her away.

They ran along Adolf Hitler Strasse toward Muehlenweg among many students and townspeople.

Two small, low-flying planes roared overhead, shooting at the group of people.

Lisl was amazed by the quick reactions of the children. They threw themselves on the ground or under farm wagons that stood against buildings. Motionless, they waited until the planes had passed before they dared to move and continue their run toward the shelters.

The two planes reappeared as Lisl and her sisters and brother reached the outside of the wall. A small group of children ran with them. Some headed for the Siedlung while others raced for the dungeon shelter.

Lisl saw the planes circle overhead. She barely could keep up as she kept losing her shoes.

Now *they* were the target of a second attack as the planes swooped down.

Dieter and Lisl threw themselves under the sloe hedge alongside Muehlenweg. Other children followed. A few fell flat on the ground as bullets marked a line of flying dirt beside them.

One of the children cried out in pain but none of them moved as they watched the planes circle overhead for a repeat attack.

Lisl peered out from under the hedge. A sharp pain in her head made her ears ring the way they did when she dove under water at the lake. Yet, calm settled around her as if time had stopped.

A small group of children ran for cover. They reminded Lisl of baby chicks that, even at just a few days old, knew to take cover when a shadow flew above them. How did they know about hawks on the attack? How did they know when to hide under their mother's feathers? Now she knew how they felt. She swore never again to fool them by casting shadows.

A thousand thoughts went through her mind and again, she became only an onlooker, detached. It all happened so fast, but Lisl observed in slow motion, although her heart drummed loud and fast in her ears.

Charlotte and some of the other children who had taken cover on the ground in the middle of the road scrambled on their hands and knees to get under the hedge before the next attack.

The planes swooped down with a horrible whine–this time closer than before.

Charlotte screamed and Lisl closed her eyes. However, the planes did not attack. Without a shot, the planes hurled up through the sky and were gone within seconds.

Lisl lifted her head and looked through the hedge branches. "I wonder why they didn't fire."

"Maybe they didn't see us." Dieter looked up through the hedge.

"Or maybe they came close enough to see we're not ground troops?"

No one dared to get up.

Finally, Lisl wiped her eyes and crawled out from under the hedge. She felt as though a thorny branch had torn at her head. She could barely see the road. Her eyes burned, and her vision blurred. She brushed the dirt off her face with her sleeve.

Dieter crawled out after Lisl, wiping his face.

Charlotte rolled onto her side and peered out from under the shrubs, spitting dirt.

"Ellen," she screamed, when she saw her sister lying face down in the middle of the road.

Lisl wanted to hear that cough. "Please, Ellen, get up," she prayed.

Ellen raised her head and coughed, "Shh, not so loud. They might come back." Charlotte laughed when she heard Ellen's voice.

Lisl wiped her tears and ran to Ellen who stood sweeping the dust from her face and coat.

Slowly the other children got to their feet, straightened their disheveled clothes and, with a watchful eye on the sky, cleaned themselves off.

Traudel, Lisl's friend and neighbor, remained motionless on the ground. She lay on her side with her knees pulled to her chest like a little ball. Her unblinking eyes stared ahead in horror at something that Lisl could not see.

"Traudel? Traudel, you can get up now," Lisl called to her. But Traudel remained motionless, her head was bleeding. Hansi was lying next to her, trying to get up, but looked too weak to stand. He did not take Lisl's hand. His words ran together. Lisl could not understand him. When she asked him what he had said, she realized he did not see or hear her at all.

Blood soaked through the scarf on his shoulder. His jacket was torn at the hip where a small blood stain slowly grew larger. Lisl stood up and looked around, and for the first time she was scared. "Ellen! Charlotte! Help! Mama, where are you?"

Ellen rushed to Lisl's side and bent over Hansi, her classmate. "Hansi, Hansi," she called out to him, but he did not hear or respond to Ellen's outstretched hand either. He just kept talking incoherently.

Charlotte stood frozen, staring into the sky.

Ellen coughed and looked at her sisters and other students who stood staring in a daze at their two schoolmates that lay bleeding on ground. She screamed, "Don't just stand there, we have to go. Come on."

"We have to get help," Charlotte yelled still staring at the injured.

Ellen ran ahead, but kept close to the hedge, ready to scramble under. Now the other children started to hurry after her.

Women from the Siedlung came running to take care of their children.

"Hansi is hurt," Ellen shouted as his mother rushed toward her.

"Where is he?"

"Back there." Ellen motioned to him lying in the dust.

Traudel's mother ran toward Lisl. "Where is Traudel?"

Lisl pointed to the ground a few meters behind her. She did not turn when Traudel's mother cried out in despair. Lisl held her hands over her ears and raced after her sisters and brother. She was afraid to look back. But she could not outrun the woman's grief. "Oh no. Not you, too," Lisl heard her cry. Now she had lost her daughter as well as her husband in the war.

Mama came running along Muehlenweg toward her children. Charlotte cried out at the sight of her. Mama hugged them one by one as they reached her. Holding on to each other, they hurried toward the house.

As Lisl ran up the garden path she looked back and saw many people hurry past on Muehlenweg now. A few were crying, running toward the shelter, no one carried luggage or bundles. Some had no time to put on their shoes or coats.

Mama had left a screaming Kurt in the root cellar. When she came through the door she picked him up and calmed him, cradling him in her arms.

Baby Werner was awake, but did not seem upset at Kurt's screaming. Charlotte picked the baby up and put her tear-soaked face against his little chest.

Then, all was quiet. Artillery attacks had ceased. The small planes that had appeared so suddenly had left the sky.

When they washed up, Mama discovered that Lisl was bleeding from a small wound behind her right ear.

Lisl thought that she had scraped her head on the hedge branches when she dove under it. A tiny piece of scalp was torn away, exposing her skull between blood-soaked hair. Now that her mother cleaned around the wound, her head felt sore.

"Oh, we have to see the doctor."

"Mama, I don't want to go to the doctor. I feel foolish. It's just a little scratch."

"I need to be sure that nothing serious has gone into your skull," Mama said.

"No, there's nothing except some dirt."

Her mother, however, thought otherwise. She put Lisl on the back of the bike and rode her to the doctor's office.

Squirming, Lisl sat among blood-covered, moaning women and crying children.

"Mama, I don't think I should be here. It's only a little scratch."

Mama said nothing. She put her arm around Lisl's shoulder. Lisl was not sure whether her mother was trying to comfort her or keep her from running out of the office.

Aid cars and farm wagons pulled up in front of the doctor's office as more people were brought in. The severely wounded were sent on to the hospitals–one in Kitzingen, six kilometers to the northwest, and one in Iphofen about three kilometers to the south.

Mama waited patiently with Lisl who felt weak and tired and just wanted to leave. Her mother pulled her into her arms to rest her head, where she promptly fell asleep.

Lisl woke when her mother moved. It was her turn to see the doctor. She dragged her feet. "Mama, the doctor will laugh and chase us out of his office when he sees me." But to her surprise the doctor determined that a small piece of shrapnel or metal had made the tear in her scalp.

He shaved a large area around the wound, removing dirt and what he thought was a small piece of metal. "You're a very lucky young lady. You could have been killed."

Lisl did not feel all that lucky. Her head ached and she was afraid she might throw up after he had finished dressing the wound. There were still many people in the waiting room and more arriving when Lisl and her mother walked out the door.

Mama put her on the bike. "Lisl, you've got to hold on to me. Make sure you stay awake." She did not need to worry. Now that they were out of the doctor's office Lisl felt all right, but still not convinced that it was shrapnel and not a thorny branch that had injured her. She was more worried about her appearance and would have given anything for a scarf to cover her half-bald bandaged head.

When they arrived home, Lisl looked into the mirror. "Did he have to take off so much hair?"

"You should be thankful you're alive," her mother said, teary-eyed, holding her close.

"You can always cover your bandages with your scarf." Dieter sounded logical when he realized that her hair was not long enough to cover her bald area.

Ellen and Charlotte examined her bandages. Ellen shook her head, looking as though she saw something horrible.

"Don't worry. It will grow out in a year—hopefully." Charlotte petted Lisl's head with a sad look.

After her sister's consoling words, Lisl felt ugly and self-conscious.

The artillery attacks began again and lasted into the late night. Charlotte could not help herself and started to cry again—a lot more normal. Her silent submission to doom made everyone nervous.

The family stayed awake most of the night. No one seemed to be able to sleep, always waiting for the next attack. But the night was still.

CHAPTER 18

Brunner's Report

Lisl awoke to loud shouting. Curious, she sneaked from the root cellar, hurried upstairs to the window, and joined her mother.

"What's going on?" Lisl asked.

Mama put her arm around Lisl, "It's Herr Brunner." Together they watched him run from house to house shouting, "Tanks are heading toward the town."

When he reached the front door, Mama asked him in.

"Herr Brunner, if you don't slow down you'll have a heart attack."

"I was on my way to Michelfeld to see my daughter and grandchildren." His voice failed and he gasped for breath. "When all of a sudden I heard the loudest screeching noise you can imagine. American and English tanks were everywhere, all over the fields." He motioned, wild-eyed. "Well, you can imagine I got out of there, fast. There was no way I could get through to see my family."

Tears glistened in his eyes. He slumped into a kitchen chair. His hands and voice shook.

Mama listened calmly while she made him a cup of linden tea. As she handed him the cup, he looked up at her. "Do you think they're still alive?"

Mama's eyes turned hazel. "I don't know." She patted his shoulder and turned away.

"I don't know how to tell Hedwig that I didn't get to see her sister. I haven't gone home yet." He looked out the window across the gardens toward his house. He emptied his cup with a few gulps and walked out the door without another word, then pushed his bike down Muehlenweg toward his home.

Lisl peered through the window, but saw no one. Ordinarily the neighborhood children played soccer on Muehlenweg or in the meadow. It seemed everyone was afraid to leave their homes. They had no way of knowing when the attack on Mainbernheim would start again.

School had been closed since the last attack so Mama kept everyone in the root cellar on the mattresses, sometimes all day, but always through the night.

Lisl went back to the root cellar to put her shoes on in case they would have to leave in a hurry. Lisl and Dieter kept their fingers crossed.

"This cellar is strong, it's not going to get crunched," Dieter told Lisl. Yet, he sounded more like he was convincing himself than Lisl.

Charlotte played with Kurt to keep him occupied and out of his little hiding place, although sometimes she looked as though she were ready to join him there.

Ellen tried to sing to hide her fear, but her nervous coughing gave her away.

The day went slowly into night and everyone was nervously waiting for something to happen. Exhausted, with the dawning of a new day, they finally fell asleep.

A few hours later, Lisl woke to the ringing of the town crier's bell, which he rang loud and long on every street corner. Lisl tiptoed out of the root cellar and ran upstairs into the living room where her mother stood by the open window. Mama seemed more curious than worried as they listened.

The town crier shouted in monotone, void of emotion as though announcing a town meeting. "Enemy troops are on their way. Please stay in your shelters. Do not use lights. Keep the shutters closed and stay off the streets. It's only a matter of hours before the enemy will be at your door."

Lisl watched him walk off in long deliberate strides, as if pacing off measurements, but today without the giggling children in his wake. Farther down the street he recited the same speech. Lisl craned her neck–there were no children in sight.

Earlier that morning the air-raid siren had sounded, but no attack followed. Lisl listened for the all-clear siren that never came. The church bells rang and did not stop. How nice it would be to be called to church on a peaceful Sunday, Lisl thought.

Most of Mainbernheim's citizens remained in the big wine cellar around the clock. Grandfather and Aunt Anni stayed there as well, only returning to the house for something to eat. Sometimes Aunt Anni took food back to the wine cellar to spare Opa the trip.

In the evening, Opa and Aunt Anni stumbled through the door. "We've got to get some sleep," Anni said. "I'd rather take my chances with the enemy than go another night without sleep." She put her suitcase by the front door. "I think our troops have left. I saw no sign of them on our way home."

Without a word, Opa walked into his room, banging his cane on the ground and walls. He dropped face down onto his bed. His shoes hung over the side of the bed. Aunt Anni slipped them off his feet, he did not react.

Now that the German troops had moved out of the area, Lisl hoped that the enemy would stop shooting at Mainbernheim. She replayed images of the last few days when troops were stationed all around town and the consequences the townspeople had suffered. Maybe the mayor had been trying to save their lives when he had argued with the officers. Maybe he, too, wanted the soldiers to leave town.

Explosions still tore through the night, although Lisl did not hear the sound of defending counterattack. It turned into another restless night.

Lisl's head ached and her side of the feather pillow turned into a pile of rocks. Her bandages kept coming loose and her mother fastened them again and again, which made Lisl's head hurt even more.

Because they all slept on the same two mattresses, she tried to stay still, but her tossing kept the rest of her family from getting their sleep.

Finally, Mama decided to let the children sleep in their own beds upstairs. But they stayed fully dressed except for their shoes.

Their bedrooms, however, were no better. Lisl and her sisters lay wide awake, listening to frightening sounds. Mama came into their room several times during the night trying to calm Charlotte. Lisl heard her mother talking in the boys' bedroom as well.

Kurt's panic did not lessen as the sound of heavy machinery mixed with sporadic rifle fire tore though the night. He seemed calmer when they all slept in the root cellar, tucked into his little safe space with his mother close by.

Dieter's calming voice had no effect. Kurt wanted to be in his mother's room where the baby lay peacefully sleeping.

Mama finally gave in and took him to her room where he quickly calmed down.

Charlotte cried quietly and Ellen coughed most of the night with her head under her pillow.

Lisl was not sure whether Ellen did this to silence her coughing or shut out her sister's cries, and the terrible screeching of machinery that invaded the night.

Lisl tried to peek through the shutters during the night, but Charlotte quickly pulled her away. "Don't look out; they might shoot when they see someone in the window."

They lay awake in the darkness of their shuttered room until almost three in the morning when they finally fell asleep.

Just before dawn, Lisl awoke with a start. The horrible noises had stopped, yet she feared the sudden silence even more. She held her breath, listening. Her heart pounded in her ears. Before, she had been able to tell by the sound of moving machines where the enemy was. Now they could be right outside the door.

CHAPTER 19

Enemy at the Door

Mama stood in the dark by the open window. Lisl stepped beside her and without a word put her arm around her mother's waist.

Brown fog hung in the early light of dawn. Everything smelled different. A stench of gasoline, oil, and gunpowder replaced the scent of the flowering cherry tree. Tears rolled down Mama's face and onto Lisl's. Lisl did not dare ask why, but as she looked across the fields she realized the reason.

Tanks waited on the higher field ridges around Mainbernheim. The enemy had moved into position during the night, cutting heavy tracks through the greening wheat fields like open scars–an attack on Mother Nature, Lisl thought.

The landscape, pockmarked from earlier artillery attacks, somehow appeared softer in the morning mist. Even the gaping wounds torn into the fields three days before already seemed to be healing.

Lisl felt no panic as she looked at the hazy outlines of the tanks. She thought of a strange, silent movie she had seen on her fifth birthday. The picture show was about Indians. With a shudder she remembered the nightmares it gave her. She had not liked this movie with the many Indians wearing big feather hats and swinging hatchets while circling a compound of wagons. Now the tanks reminded her of the Indians, and the high wall surrounding Mainbernheim, the wagons. In the movie, the Indians managed to kill all the people in the compound. She also pictured the crumbling wall after the first attack only a few days ago. How easily the enemy could force their way into town. She stood as if frozen, watching the motionless tanks in the misty fields.

Usually the robins started to sing at dawn. Today even they were silent. Truly, this must be the end. Mama seemed caught in her own thoughts, yet she held Lisl tight.

They both jumped when one of the tanks suddenly fired into the town. Just one shot, then silence again. Kurt screamed in his mother's bedroom and this time he made the baby cry as well.

Mama wiped her tears as Charlotte, Ellen, and Dieter came running downstairs and crowding around her.

Aunt Anni, with Opa in tow, burst though the door fully dressed. They too rushed to the window instead of the root cellar.

Mama swallowed and held up her hand to reassure everyone. "I want you all to put on extra clothing. We don't know what will happen. Just stay quiet and close together."

Lisl watched her mother. She was calm yet pale, looking at her children in silent reverence as if saying goodbye.

"Go," she ordered when they lingered in her gaze too long. They ran upstairs, and within minutes gathered around the window again, shaking even though they were dressed in coats and scarves. Opa and Aunt Anni had put on warm coats too.

Now the family stood by the window in the advancing light of dawn, waiting for that next shot. No one thought of seeking shelter. Mama probably knew that the time for refuge had passed, and in a way Lisl found it less stressful to see where the enemy was. She crossed her fingers, closed her eyes and whispered, "I wish that we'll be alive tomorrow."

"Me too." Dieter whispered back.

Even Charlotte stood without tears. She seemed stunned rather than panicked as she stared out the window. Ellen could not stop coughing.

The brown-gray haze of exhaust and fog slowly lifted. The tanks looked threatening now, revealing more detail in the gathering light of the morning. Some of the tanks bore a star and some were covered with dirty netting and twigs.

"American," Mama whispered.

The Siedlung housing area stood on a higher elevation than Mainbernheim and was also surrounded by a circle of menacing-looking tanks.

The higher observation point of their home focused more clearly on the enemy, which made Lisl feel more isolated and excluded. She would have felt safer within the town walls with many people. The families in the five-house Siedlung had no means of defense. The only men here were old Herr Brunner and Lisl's blind Grandfather.

Opa finally broke the silence. "What's going on? What are they doing?" But no one answered.

After what seemed like an eternity, the mayor came through the tower door and waved a white flag as he gingerly made his way up the hill toward the tanks.

Mama sighed in relief. "I think the shooting will stop now." She stroked Grandfather's hand.

"Opa, are you afraid of the tanks?" Dieter asked.

"I guess I am afraid of what I can't see."

"I'll tell you what they look like, so you won't have to be afraid anymore." Dieter patted Opa's arm.

Mama glanced at Charlotte's stunned face. She looked as though she were about to scream. Aunt Anni saw it too and said, "Come Charlotte lets make some tea." She took Charlotte's hand and went into the kitchen with her. After a while, they brought linden tea to the dining room table and four slices of bread that Aunt Anni cut in half and passed around.

Mama stayed at the window while the family had their breakfast. Lisl brought her a cup of tea. She could not read her mother's face as she observed the enemy. Lisl held out the cup to her. "Mama, what will happen to us now? Do you think they'll let us live?" She studied her mother's expression.

Mama took the cup from Lisl's hand and smiled. "I think there's a good chance we will see tomorrow."

Lisl heard hope in her mother's voice–hope that had not been there for some time. The color in her face had returned as well.

"Just think, Mama, if we do get to live, we'll be able to sleep in our beds all night long. No more air raids."

"Oh, that would be wonderful, but the baby will still wake me." Mama laughed her happy laugh the way she used to. Still, Lisl felt sorry for her. Even without air raids her mother could not sleep through the night.

She wanted to ask if Papa would come home soon, but she knew it would only make Mama sad again. They had not seen or heard from him for ten months. They did not know whether he was dead or alive.

The screeching noises started again when the American tanks moved closer to town. Lisl watched through half-open shutters, wondering if they would get stuck trying to go through those narrow tower gates. But they stopped outside the wall and set up roadblocks.

A convoy of jeeps and covered trucks rolled through the tower gate and into town where Lisl lost sight of them. A smaller convoy moved slowly along Muehlenweg.

Sporadic rifle shots panicked Charlotte and Kurt into crying fits. Even though Ellen coughed, she tried to calm her older sister with her funny little dancing act. It usually set Charlotte into wild laughter, but today Ellen's performance went unnoticed.

Lisl and Dieter ran upstairs to peek through the cracks of shutters and get a better view of the tanks.

With the sound of rifle shots nearby, Dieter looked alarmed. "Do you think they will shoot us?"

"Look, Dieter." Lisl pointed at a group of soldiers as one fired his rifle. "They only shot through the barn door. Maybe they think our soldiers are hiding in there."

"But who would shoot at the enemy now? All our soldiers have left."

"Yes, but they don't know that."

Frightened, yet curious, Lisl and Dieter watched foot soldiers walk cautiously beside jeeps along Muehlenweg, their rifles pointed at buildings and hedges.

"They're coming up the path." Lisl's voice cracked and she pulled Dieter from the window. As they ran down the stairs, they heard soldiers' footsteps coming around to the front door.

A loud hard knock that sounded like a rifle butt hitting against the door startled Grandfather and Aunt Anni. They fled into their room and locked the door.

Charlotte and Kurt started to cry again and huddled behind their mother. With the baby in her arms, Mama quickly opened the door before the soldiers could break it down.

Four men rushed into the house, nervously pointing their guns in all directions.

Ellen, Dieter, and Lisl stood behind the kitchen door, but Ellen's coughing gave their hiding place away.

One soldier shouted loud commands at Mama that seemed to confuse her.

At first Lisl was not aware that he was shouting in German as his German words were hard to understand.

"*Haben sie Gewere? Sind Soldaten hier?*" one of them shouted.

Mama shook her head. "There are no soldiers or weapons here."

The soldiers pushed past while one stayed to keep an eye on her. The rest of the troops discovered Lisl, Dieter and Ellen in the kitchen and pushed them toward the hallway, grouping them with the rest of the family, then they continued their search.

Mama stood quietly cradling the baby in one arm and holding the other children steady with the other.

In all the chaos and the uncertainty of their survival, Lisl felt safe in her mother's grip. Her sisters and brothers stood close by, and even Kurt and Charlotte were quiet.

"Where are the men and weapons?" the soldiers kept asking. Mama put the baby in the crib and told them again that there were no weapons or German soldiers in the house.

When one of the men could not open Opa's door, he alerted the others. They all grouped around the door, preparing to shoot it down.

Mama quickly put herself in front of the door, shouting, "Anni, unlock the door."

The soldiers rushed into the room before Anni could step out of the way. She screamed at the sight of four guns pointing at her. Grandfather cried quietly.

"Here is your man, but there are no weapons here," Mama said calmly as the soldiers rushed to Grandfather.

Opa held his shaking hands over his face, as if that could save him from getting shot.

One soldier gave a signal and the others relaxed their attack pose when they realized Opa was blind.

"That's okay, Pops," he said, patting Opa's shoulder.

Although Opa did not understand what the soldier meant, it did calm him.

Three men went through every inch of the house while another held the family at gunpoint.

Lisl felt numb, detached, seeing their actions through a blur. Half-open shutters allowed a view of sunny daffodils and forsythias. The sight of flowers took her to a more pleasant place. Dieter followed her gaze and smiled as if to go there with her.

The soldiers systematically dumped the contents from drawers and cabinets onto the floor in their search for weapons.

Dieter, Ellen, and Lisl stood silently with their mother as they watched the soldiers' actions.

With every crash of silverware and kitchen utensils hitting the floor, Charlotte let out a little sound of distress. Her hands flew to her lips as if to stifle it, and sometimes she covered her ears to shut out the noise the soldiers made, or maybe her own squeak.

Kurt buried his face into his mother's dress. He looked bewildered and frightened at the soldiers' destructive behavior.

Finally the soldiers were satisfied and left the house, telling Mama that the family was under house arrest, and if caught outside, would be shot.

The door slammed shut. The enemy soldiers were gone. The family stood silent, listening, still holding onto each other for a little while longer.

Lisl heard banging on their neighbors' doors, followed by sharp commands. But no shots were fired. Farther away however, sounds of gunfire rang out. Lisl crossed her fingers, hoping that only barn doors, or maybe just locked doors, were the targets.

Mama loosened her hold and looked into the worried faces of her children.

"The worst is over. We're alive," she said with a little smile.

Like magic Ellen stopped coughing, Kurt and Charlotte stopped crying and smiled back at their mother.

Lisl thought her mother would be upset at the mess, but she was surprisingly cheerful. She pointed to the light fixture on the ceiling, its lampshade made of six mirror sections to create a brighter light from a dim bulb. Every section reflected the hunting knife on top of the wardrobe.

Mama laughed. "I was afraid that the soldiers might see it. I tried hard not to look at it." She had hidden the staghorn-handled knife on top of the high wardrobe. The knife was the first gift she had given to Papa before they were married and she did not want to give it to the enemy as required. Although Papa never went hunting, they took the knife on hiking trips in the Alps. Mama pushed a chair in front of the wardrobe, climbed up and covered it with a sheet of old newspaper.

"Oh, just look at the mess they left!" Dieter said.

Mama broke into laughter they hadn't heard for a long time. "You didn't really expect them to clean it up."

Lisl noticed her mother's hands were shaking as she steadied herself against the chair. However, her eyes remained brown.

Opa came out of his room, nervously tapping his cane on the floor and walls. He wanted to make his way through the kitchen, but the dumped kitchen utensils got in his way.

Aunt Anni tried to lead him around obstacles, but he pushed her arm away. He reached out, trying to find the boys who quickly came to lead him into the living room. Opa wiped his eyes, sat down in the big chair, and Kurt climbed on his lap.

Lisl knew he needed the children and Mama, to hear their relieved chatter, to be in the midst of the action, to feel their relief.

Mama sat in the rocking chair by the window. She held baby Werner in her arms. Her chest rose and fell in deep breaths as she observed her family, but now her eyes turned hazel.

"Look, Mama, they mixed it all together," Ellen called from the kitchen, staring at the piles on the floor. Confused, she picked a few things from the pile then dropped them again, throwing her hands in the air, coughing again. "Just look at this mess," she shouted.

Lisl found her sister's actions puzzling. In the face of real danger she had performed a little dance, but now the disorder seemed to unnerve her to the point of panic.

Charlotte handed a dishpan to Ellen and sat down on the floor beside her. Now Charlotte was calm as she placed the spilled household items in the container. Ellen always needed everything in its proper place and would get angry when her sisters messed up their bedroom.

Mama put the baby in the crib. "Well, now is a good time to organize. We can't go outside, so let's all help together."

"Mama, do they really expect us to stay out of our own garden?" Lisl asked.

"You heard him, stay in the house or you'll get shot."

But Lisl loved this time of year when every plant and tree awoke from a long cold sleep. She had waited so long for spring when the flowers showed off their spectacular colors one by one. Was she to miss all that? But her mother locked both doors and put the keys in her apron pocket.

"How long will we have to stay locked up?" Lisl asked.

Mama looked at her, shrugging her shoulders.

Dieter frowned. "House arrest! Pfui."

Lisl felt like a prisoner. She was not allowed to enjoy the garden or talk to other neighbors and playmates. Not knowing what was going to happen made her restless.

She saw no sign of Frau Nagel or her children, not even through their window as she looked across the garden toward their house. Their shutters were still shut, even now, when blackout was no longer necessary. She wondered if they were still alive.

౮౨

The food was almost gone except for a small sack of shriveled seed potatoes that were to be planted soon. Mama found a few jars of green beans and peas hidden in the back of the laundry room shelf.

"Today's menu, chased seed potatoes and peas," Mama announced. She had to ration the food carefully. She had no way of knowing how long the house arrest would be in effect.

The day went slowly. Mama tried to keep her daughters occupied with organizing drawers in all the rooms, even the drawers that were not dumped on the floor. They were busy folding clothing, dusting, organizing and sweeping. At times they sang quietly. Charlotte even laughed again. She was unusually cooperative with Ellen.

Lisl looked out the window a good deal of the day, hoping to catch the flight of a bird or see signs of unfolding spring. Her mother joined her at times looking for the same things. But what they saw was a dreary day advancing into a gray evening and the ever-present enemy soldiers watching; a reminder that the war was not over.

But at least the nights were bright again and reading books a pleasure. There was no need to take the candle to the bathroom.

To Lisl it was a celebration of light as she ran from room to room, turning on lights and opening window shutters. At least she was allowed to look out into the garden. Dieter and Kurt followed with laughter and squeals, delighted as the mirror shades magnified the lights like the glass ornaments on the Christmas tree.

Evenings were still cold. What little firewood was left was reserved for cooking. So, the small kitchen remained the family room in the evenings.

Some time ago, the bedroom walls had lost their frosty sparkle. Lisl and her sisters were able to wash up in their room again.

Lisl opened the window and saw soldiers standing watch down on Muehlenweg, keeping an eye on every house. With hands on their rifles, ready to shoot at unexpected threats, they seemed on high alert.

"What if the German army reclaims Mainbernheim again like they did Michelfeld?" Lisl said.

Charlotte looked up from the washbowl, her face dripping wet. "Oh, I hope that won't happen." Her eyes widened. "I hate the thought of having to go through artillery attacks and the occupation again."

Ellen coughed again. "Maybe we wouldn't be so lucky a second time."

Charlotte stepped beside Lisl and peered out the window while drying her face. Then she nudged Lisl away, closed the window, and with a sudden pull she closed the drapes as if to shut out the scene outside as well as her fear.

Lisl lay on her bed with her arms folded behind her head. Her mother's words, "the worst is over," echoed, comforting, in her mind. She hoped Mama was right.

Oh the luxury of going to bed without the worry of having to run to the shelter in the middle of the night. The softness of her nightgown on her body felt good now. It was a luxury to no longer sleep in her street clothes.

After washing up, Ellen pulled her nightgown over her head and sat on the stool in front of the dresser. Slowly, as if in a daydream, she brushed her hair and looked through the mirror to a far-away place.

Charlotte took her time, to the point of fussing, folding her clothes, arranging them neatly on her chair by the foot of her bed. She fluffed her featherbed and pillow ceremoniously and dropped her head on the softness with a smile.

All the little things they used to take for granted had become very special. They were ready for a good night's sleep.

After two hours, a shrill sound pierced the night and sent Ellen and Charlotte scrambling out of their beds and down the stairs. But Lisl, who had always been slow in getting up, only got as far as putting one foot on the floor when she heard her sisters laughing. They came back into the room halfway dressed. They had realized on their way to the root cellar that there was no air raid.

Lisl fell back into her bed and huddled under the covers again.

Halfway through the night the wind slammed a loose shutter against the house. Lisl and her sisters woke with a start. Ellen and Charlotte turned in their beds and went back to sleep, but the shutter kept banging. Lisl opened the window and fastened the latch, attaching each shutter to the outside wall instead of latching them together. The night was quiet and as she looked out she wondered where the enemy soldiers were sleeping. In the glow of the streetlights she saw trucks nearby. Guards with rifles walked silently along Muehlenweg, keeping an eye on every house.

Lisl took a deep breath. A stiff breeze had cleared the air of the stench of gasoline and gunpowder. The wind carried the scent of pine woods and fresh rain, although the ground was still dry.

She left the window slightly open and was soon lulled to sleep by heavy drops hitting the red tile roof.

∞

It was close to nine when Lisl awoke the next morning. She had even slept through her mother's routine of warming the baby bottle several times during the night.

"*Guten Morgen*, Mama."

"*Gut Morgen, Liebling*. Did you sleep well?"

"Yes I did. Can I watch you bathe the baby?"

"I'm afraid I'm already done." Mama slipped Werner's little arms through his shirt. "Are the others still asleep?"

"Yes."

"It's amazing how well you slept through all that noise the tanks and trucks made early this morning. They've been on the move since dawn."

"I didn't hear them."

By ten the family sat around the table. Lisl felt weak from the lack of food. She knew her brothers and sisters felt the same. Even though no one complained, Lisl saw the pain and hidden tears in her mother's face as she looked at her hungry children. Hunger had become a way of life.

Only a small heel of black bread was left in the bread box and the apple sauce that served as bread spread was getting low as well.

Grandfather and Aunt Anni insisted that they were not hungry. Mama divided the food into five parts for the children.

Lisl choked when she tried to swallow her bread, knowing that the adults were just as hungry. But to argue would do no good.

At times Lisl smuggled some of her food to Dieter under the table. He was always so hungry. Mama had caught her once handing bread to Dieter. "Lisl, I try very hard to see that everyone has an equal share. I don't want you to do it again."

"But Mama, he's . . ."

"I don't want to hear anymore about it. Don't do it again, understand?"

Lisl had wanted to cry when she saw the guilty look on Dieter's face.

After breakfast Opa went to his room and Aunt Anni and Charlotte started to clean the windows. They all tried to keep busy to take their minds off food and the fact that they were not allowed to leave the house.

The two pet angora rabbits had not been fed for a day or so. Lisl was worried that the lack of food may give her mother the idea of *Hasenpfeffer*. The two chickens must have been starving by now too. But because her mother needed their eggs, they were safe for the time being.

Mama went down to the basement and out through the side door. She opened the chicken coup to let the hens out to fend for themselves. She gave the two white angora rabbits some of the cattle beets the family had received in exchange for helping the farmers with their harvest last fall.

The children were relieved to see Mama come back in through the side door.

"Mama, you're not supposed to go out. You'll get shot." Kurt shouted.

"It's all right, *Liebling*, I was very careful. Look." She showed him two eggs. "Hoffman's chicken has not laid an egg since he brought it last week. If it doesn't start soon, we'll save that one for when Papa comes home." The two eggs were the family's meal for the day.

The next day Lisl slipped out through the basement door to the cages. She cut pieces off the cattle beets and fed the rabbits. They seemed to enjoy their meal so much that Lisl took a bite. It tasted delicious. A little woody perhaps, but it would fill their stomachs.

Excited, she brought one of the beets upstairs to the family. They found it tasty as well. Now their diets consisted of cattle beets, sometimes with eggs scrambled with some water to stretch them a little, and seed potatoes.

CHAPTER 20

The Lost Secret

A week later, Lisl heard the town crier's voice, sounding much louder than usual, yet with no ringing bell. She ran to the window. He was sitting on a jeep shouting through a bullhorn while gun-bearing British soldiers kept him company. He looked proud; maybe he thought the ride was just to make him more comfortable.

All the neighbor women peered out their windows, listening to him shouting, "Citizens will be allowed to leave the house for two hours, from nine to eleven. Curfew will be strictly enforced. Anyone caught after curfew will be shot."

"Did you hear that? We can go outside again." Lisl ran out the door. Dieter and Kurt followed her into the garden although it was only ten to nine.

The chickens needed watching to make sure they did not leave the yard. They seemed happier being free and searching for worms and insects.

Now that the family was allowed to leave the house, Mama wasted no time. She hurried with Ellen into town to find food.

Charlotte took charge of the younger children. She was good at giving the baby his bath and Kurt loved playing with Charlotte.

Lisl and Dieter told her they would be in the garden, but wandered out to the stone break. Now at least they could go back to their secret playground outside their garden without the fear of artillery attacks.

But as they came closer they heard voices, and when they peeked down from the rim into the stone break, they saw a bonfire in the middle of the level stony area.

"They're English soldiers," Dieter said.

"How can you tell?"

"They have flat helmets. Mama told me."

The soldiers were shouting and laughing, warming themselves by the open fire.

Lisl and Dieter sat on their heels, watching, but stayed well out of sight.

"How did they find our secret place?" Dieter whispered. "What are they doing here?"

"Yeah and where did they find the wood for the fire?" Lisl said.

The soldiers seemed to be having their own private party, drinking wine and breaking the empty wine bottles on the rocks. They roasted chunks of meat on sticks over the fire.

"Why are they hiding down there?" Lisl whispered.

"What do you think they're cooking?"

"I don't know. Maybe army rations or something. Whatever it is, it smells delicious." Lisl's stomach growled.

Dieter licked his lips and took a deep breath with his eyes closed, as if trying to taste the smell of the roasting meat.

Lisl ducked down, pulling Dieter with her. The soldiers lined up empty bottles on the ledge of the embankment near the place where Lisl and Dieter were hiding. Their secret place had been invaded too. Fighting back her tears, Lisl hung her head and looked back at their sanctuary.

"Lisl, they won't stay there forever. The war won't last that long."

Lisl nodded. "Let's go home." She ran ahead of Dieter.

When they came to the house Charlotte was standing by the door, hands on her hips. "Where on earth did you disappear to?" she shouted. "I told you not to leave the garden."

Lisl did not like to upset her sister and quickly said, "Charlotte, we discovered some really good field salads. We came back to get the basket."

Charlotte looked at Lisl suspiciously. "And just how far away are these field salads?"

"They're right outside the garden. We can hear you when you call us," Dieter said.

"All right, but don't stay too long. You only have an hour left before curfew starts."

Lisl grabbed the basket and ran toward the fields with Dieter.

"I sure hope we can find some," he said.

"Yeah. I think I saw some, but a few fields over. From there we won't be able to hear Charlotte. So we'd better hurry."

Charlotte was delighted when Dieter and Lisl came back with a good portion of *Schafsmaulchen* and ten minutes to spare.

Dieter searched hungrily around the kitchen, but there was no food in sight. He watched through the window, waiting for Mama and Ellen to return. Charlotte and Lisl came to the window off and on to look over his shoulder.

Opa walked through the house, tapping his cane on the floor. Now and then he played with Kurt but always ended up by the window, listening.

"Do you see them yet, Dieter?" he asked.

"No, not yet."

Lisl knew that Opa was extra hungry after skipping so many meals for the sake of his grandchildren.

Aunt Anni finally had a chance to go to the hospital. However, curfew did not allow her enough time to work and return home in the same day. She had to stay there. At least she would get some food.

"They're back," Dieter shouted when he saw his mother and Ellen walking along Muehlenweg toward the house. He ran outside and down the path.

Mama walked through the door a few minutes past curfew. Her smile told Lisl that she had managed to get some food.

Ellen put the bag on the table and slowly pulled out a head of over-wintered cabbage, a half loaf of black bread and a pair of bratwurst. She watched all the hungry eager faces and smiled proudly.

Lisl brightened. "Oh, Ellen, that's wonderful. Now all of us get to eat."

Ellen ruffled Lisl's bangs until they stood out like a little umbrella. Usually, Lisl hated that, but today she didn't care.

Mama had gone to several farmers who still owed her payment for the mending she had done the year before.

"Some gave me nothing but excuses. But I got bread from one, bratwurst from another, and cabbage from the one who promised to give me more later," Mama smiled.

Lisl was sure that the farmers with excuses would not get Mama's help again. It was hard for her to have to ask for a little food. In the past they had given her flour, split peas or beans in payment for her work. Sometimes, when they had butchered a pig, the farmers filled a two-liter milk can with soup and sausage.

Mama seemed happy, singing while boiling half of the cabbage. When it was tender, she ran it through a meat grinder and thickened it with a little flour, usually to make a creamier and more filling dish whenever she had no meat. But today she fried the sausages, saving the grease that collected in the pan as bread spread for later. Charlotte prepared the field salad.

Although Lisl's mouth watered, she took her time and set the table in a manor befitting the meal. She even rushed into the garden to get a few irises to dress up the table. Now they were celebrating. Everyone had a small piece of sausage on their plate. Grandfather smiled when Mama told him that the children would have more food from now on. But Lisl could tell by her mother's expression that she only told him that so he would enjoy his meal. Good thing Opa could not see her face or he would have felt guilty eating his little piece of sausage.

After dinner, Grandfather sat in the big chair, telling stories to the boys. Lisl gazed out across the garden, the shutters wide open. Muehlenweg looked different now. The absence of long lines of people making their daily or nightly trek to the dungeon felt reassuring. They too could sleep safely in their own beds again. But now Muehlenweg was occupied by American and English military vehicles. Now and then a farm wagon, on its way to the fields, joined the convoy.

Lisl saw her mother put her face close to the bowl of dried-up violets, trying to capture the last sweet scent.

"We will get you fresh ones tomorrow, Mama, if they are still in bloom," Lisl said. Her mother joined her by the window, stroking her short stubble hair.

Now, as they looked out over the ruined wheat fields, Lisl no longer saw the sadness in her mother's eyes. She felt a sense of new beginning and hope in Mama's attitude. Lisl put her hand in Mama's, they smiled at each other.

Mama seated herself in the rocking chair by the window, overlooking the scene within the room. She looked happy and leaned back in her chair, closing her eyes. Lisl thought maybe she was counting her blessings that everyone had made it safely through the war.

The baby gurgled in his crib when Lisl played with him, his tiny hand wrapped tightly around her finger. Werner was a good baby. He rarely cried except when he was hungry.

Ellen and Charlotte were cleaning the kitchen, their voices raised in argument. But Mama did not interfere. Maybe she too found their arguing reassuring. Life was back to normal.

CHAPTER 21

Bone in the Ash

Next morning Dieter poked his head through the door, whispering, "Lisl are you awake?"

"What?" Lisl lifted her head.

"Do you want to go to town?"

"Yeah, in a little while." Lisl dropped her head on the pillow and dozed off again.

"Lisl, wake up. We haven't been in town since the occupation. Don't you want to know what's going on?"

Reluctantly Lisl got out of bed and, after a skimpy breakfast, she watched the clock impatiently with Dieter until curfew was lifted for two hours. They pretended to go in the garden, but ran up through the fields to get into town.

All over the trails and fields, American soldiers stood watch. At first Lisl was afraid to pass the jeeps and convoys on the move toward the fighting front to the southeast. It seemed the war had ended, but Lisl was reminded by explosions in the distance now and then that the soldiers were still fighting and the war raged on.

People in town usually swept the street clean every Saturday. But when Lisl and Dieter entered they found the narrow cobblestone streets clogged with military vehicles, barely leaving room for a bicycle to pass. Gun-bearing soldiers still were on full alert even though they already had checked every building. By the shape of their helmets, Lisl knew they were American — Ami soldiers as the townspeople called them. Somehow she had imagined the enemy to be more frightening. The difference was they wore soft boots, she thought, when one of the soldiers sneaked up behind her without making a sound. It made her jump. American soldiers walked silently, whereas the German soldiers wore hard boots that could be heard a long way off, especially on the cobblestone streets.

Ami soldiers watched as children scrambled and fought over tidbits the soldiers had thrown from the jeeps. Hordes of little beggars had gathered around the vehicles, eagerly awaiting handouts. Lisl saw a chocolate bar fly through the air and a crowd of children scramble after the treat. She tried to remember the last time she had eaten chocolate, but she could no longer recall the taste.

One of the soldiers threw chewing gum to the children. Although he tried to make it clear that gum should be chewed, not swallowed, the hungry crowd gulped it down just to fill their empty stomachs.

Dieter and Lisl observed the frenzy for a moment.

"I wonder how it tastes." Dieter licked his lips, but made no attempt to fight over the candies.

Lisl felt sad that the children would behave like they did. She would rather starve than end up an amusement. Still, she would have loved to bring home a chocolate bar to share with her family.

They made their way out of the main road onto a narrow side street. Lisl realized how naïve she'd been to think that everything would be back to normal when harsh realities stared in her face everywhere she looked. Old Frau Kleinlein wandered the clogged streets, looking for her home that now lay in rubble. Over and over she called out for her family, too disoriented to remember that they were no longer among the living. Tears welled up in Lisl's eyes at the sight of this helpless woman. Frau Manfred made her way across the street and took Frau Kleinlein's arm, gently leading her to a safer place.

Lisl and Dieter squeezed past military vehicles and soldiers with rifles. And when Dieter examined the enemy jeeps too long a soldier came toward him.

Dieter stumbled backward shouting, "Look, Lisl. He's a Moor."

Now Lisl saw the dark-skinned soldier as well. He looked different from the other soldiers although he wore the same uniform. She wondered where he came from. The Moor acknowledged their curiosity by exposing his big, white teeth with a frightful grimace.

Dieter ran up the side street and through a narrow door in the wall.

Lisl could barely keep up. When they were outside Lisl stopped to catch her breath. "He's just an Ami soldier with dark skin, that's all. He just tried to scare us because he knew that we've never seen a Moor before. That doesn't mean he'll get us."

They took the shortcut through the fields where military convoys moved on the higher ridges toward a still-raging warfront.

As they came close to the stone break, Lisl crossed her fingers, hoping that the English soldiers had gone. Cautiously they approached their no-longer-secret place. It was quiet. Lisl gazed at the embankment where they had found the petrified seashell. She was relieved to find it undisturbed. Empty German wine bottles lay broken, littering the ground around a pile of ashes where the enemy troops had the bonfire the day before.

Dieter poked through the burned-out cinders with a stick. His eyes grew big when he stirred up a charred bone. He held it up to show Lisl just how large it was and then measured it against his leg. It was almost from his ankle to his knee. He stared at Lisl for a moment then whispered, "Do you think the enemy eats people?"

"Don't be silly."

"Do you think the Moor eats people?"

"There were no Moors by the fire. They were English, remember?"

"Well maybe *they* eat people."

"I don't think so."

"Let's show it to Opa; he will know if it's a human bone." He hurried out of the stone break.

Lisl ran after him. "But don't let Mama see it."

Dieter peered over his shoulder to make sure they were not being followed.

When they got to the house, he hid the bone outside in the bushes near the front door.

"Where have you been? Mama was worried. It's past curfew," Charlotte scolded when they came through the door.

"We were in town to see what's going on," Dieter said, trying to hide his sooty hands.

When Lisl saw her mother completely absorbed in the joy of bathing her kicking, gurgling baby she realized that her sister worried more than she liked to admit.

Charlotte pulled Dieter's hands from behind his back. "How did you get so black?"

"Where is Opa?" Dieter tried to avoid the answer.

"I think he's taking a nap."

That did not discourage Dieter. When he thought no one was looking, he went outside to retrieve the bone.

Dieter and Lisl slipped into Grandfather's room. Opa sat in his chair, but opened his eyes when he heard the door. Lisl sat down in the chair beside him and put her hand on his. He always knew whose hand touched his.

"Lisl," her grandfather said, holding her hand between his.

"Opa, guess what I found today," Dieter said.

"Hmm, let me think . . . I give up."

"Here, I'll put it in your hand and you have to guess what it is." He placed the charred bone in Opa's hand.

"Oh . . . I would say it's a bone." He ran his fingers over it, getting his hands sooty as well.

"Yes, but what kind of a bone?"

"Oh, probably a leg bone."

"Yes, but where did it come from?" Dieter went on impatiently, still trying to sound as though he were playing a game. He stared into Opa's face, holding his breath.

"I would say . . ." Opa ran his hands along the bone again, "I would say it came from a sheep. I don't think it's from a deer. There are none left in this area." He handed the bone back to Dieter.

"It couldn't have been from a larger animal? Or even a person?" Dieter asked just to make sure.

Grandfather laughed. "You have a wild imagination, Dieter."

Dieter relaxed and smiled—a little sheepishly Lisl thought. The bone no longer held his interest.

CHAPTER 22

Don't Shoot Mama

The sun lingered in the sky a little longer each day. Lisl too wanted to linger in the garden. But whenever she ventured outside past curfew, American soldiers walking around the garden motioned toward the door with their guns and she had to go inside again.

In the past, the garden had been an extension of their house as the weather became warmer, and the outdoor table under the big cherry tree served as the dining room. It was a place to discuss the day's activities. Lisl found it hard to think of the garden as off limits.

Mama broke the rules on more than one occasion.

One afternoon, after washing the diapers, she took her basket to the clothesline near the end of the garden. After hanging a few diapers, shots rang out.

Charlotte raced to the door with her brothers and sisters, crowding in the open doorway. But Mama had left instructions to stay inside no matter what.

Charlotte pleaded with her mother. "Mama, come back. They will shoot you."

She calmly went about her business as one of the soldiers fired a few more shots from the field above. Mama refused to rush inside until she had hung every last diaper. Only then did she pick up her empty basket and slowly walk into the house.

Charlotte and Kurt were crying.

Mama quickly calmed her upset children. "I know I shouldn't have gone outside, but don't worry, they just want to scare me; they're not monsters, they wouldn't shoot a woman for hanging diapers. But they have to scare us to make their curfew work."

But Lisl had seen defiance in Mama's slow walk back to the house. She was familiar with her mother's stubborn side, and also her uncanny insight into human nature.

༄

Strange noises in the garden had Lisl lying awake and listening in the night. She peeked through the half-opened window and realized that Ami soldiers were all around the house, garden and neighborhood. They walked across the garden, paying no attention to flower beds. She wondered, with all the soldiers in the garden, if the birds would return to their usual nesting sites. Lisl had not seen a single robin in the garden, and no matter how hard she looked, the little songbirds did not show themselves either.

A sound came from below the window. An Ami soldier sat with his back against the house smoking a cigarette, his rifle propped against his knee.

Werner cried for his bottle, and the soldier knocked loudly on a window shutter. "Baby's crying," he called. This frightened Kurt and he started to cry as well.

Lisl found it unnerving to have the soldiers right outside the doors and windows. The peace she had experienced the first night after the occupation was now replaced by new worries; nights of listening to strange sounds in the garden.

She heard footsteps and sometimes loud voices shouting and laughing. The smell of cigarettes and beer drifted through the open window.

Every year a nightingale built its nest in the thicket of the sloe hedge by the edge of the garden. Lisl looked forward to its song that rang with brilliant clarity through the stillness of the night. She would miss the little nightingale.

CHAPTER 23

Swastika

On Sunday morning Lisl got ready to go to church with her family. She dreaded having to force her sore feet into her hard Sunday shoes.

April days were warmer now; however, the old stone church remained unheated.

In church Lisl took off her shoes. Better cold feet than pain, she thought. With every note she sang, her breath rose like a cloud toward the painted sky on the church ceiling.

Lisl loved the beautiful voices of the choir, and the powerful sound of the pipe organ vibrated through her body like a warm wave. The pastor delivered a short sermon–his first since the occupation–in a quiet, somber voice. At times Lisl felt as though he spoke only to her. The sound of his voice took her to a different place–a place where barefoot angels walked on soft warm clouds.

But pain brought her back to reality. It was time to leave the church and slip her icy cold feet into her stiff Sunday shoes.

"Why on earth did you take them off?" Ellen snapped.

"You go on ahead. We'll catch up with you outside," Mama said.

When Lisl and her mother finally walked through the church door, they were greeted by music coming from the main street below.

Lisl wanted to run down to join the rest of her family and to see what was going on, but her feet were too sore. She stared at the seemingly endless steps that lead from the church down to the city hall, and more steps from there down to the main street where the music played. Although tempted to remove her shoes again, she decided that too many people had gathered and would probably laugh if they saw her walking around in her knit stockings.

The military vehicles that blocked the streets earlier had been cleared, leaving room for movement.

Mama took Lisl's hand as they walked down to join the rest of the family and the townspeople who had lined the street.

An American military band, followed by English and American military vehicles, rolled through Adolf Hitler Strasse, now called Herrn Strasse again. The swastika that used to top the church steeple was fastened to an open car—the focus of the parade.

Lisl looked up to the church tower and smiled when she saw the gleaming golden cross again. Adolf Hitler was no longer in charge of their little town or church, although the war was not over.

Mama too lifted her face to gaze at the cross. She sighed with a smile and squeezed Lisl's hand. But her eyes turned hazel when she looked at the car.

At first Lisl did not recognize the group of men, their heads shaven, sitting in the open swastika car. But at closer look she recognized the two teachers from her school, Herr Kiefer and Herr Stolz, and other distinguished townspeople—even the doctor sat among the group.

"Why do they have to be punished?" Charlotte said.

"Because they were Nazi sympathizers," a woman said, seemingly enjoying their humiliation.

Mainbernheim had been divided into two groups, the Socialists and the much larger group, the Nationalists.

Or as they were called, the Sozis and the Nazis. Now the Sozis felt courageous, shouting rude remarks, pointing and laughing at the bald group. Some even threw rocks at the men seated in the open car.

Lisl did not understand why they were acting so hostile toward people who had served their community well. Maybe the Sozis wanted to show the enemy they were on their side all along.

The bald mayor sat with his face buried in his hands. Most of the men sat with their heads bowed except for Herr Kiefer, he stood defiantly in the open car.

Lisl felt cold at the sight of the car slowly rolling through town with the Sozis mockingly goose-stepping alongside. However, most of the people stood silent, sad.

The music sounded inappropriate; too cheerful for such a depressing occasion. Lisl wanted to shout, *Gruess Gott,* to Herr Kiefer, but kept quiet. She thought back to the time when she was in first grade and Herr Kiefer, who taught seventh and eighth grade, also taught *her* a lesson, but of a different kind. She had never forgotten the day that in her mind would always be Heil Hitler day.

A week before Heil Hitler day, a German military parade with a marching band had come goose-stepping through town. After speeches and heel-clicking salutes, Herr Kiefer was called to the Town Hall. He was reprimanded for not enforcing the Nazi ways with his students. As a result, Herr Kiefer, who had often taught his students to think for themselves, had to teach what he hated most–blind obedience.

Lisl had stumbled onto the scene a week later, only to be made an example of "reinforcement" of the proper Nazi greeting.

At that time Lisl thought a leader of war did not take precedence over God. She had always greeted people with *Gruess Gott, Guten Morgen, Guten Tag,* or *Guten Abend,* whatever time of day it happened to be. Friends and family were greeted with a warm, *Gruess Gott,* or *Wie gehts,* followed by a hug or handshake. But that all changed that afternoon.

Lisl remembered when her first grade class, located on the second floor, had rushed down one flight of stairs homeward bound. Herr Kiefer and Herr Stolz stood at the bottom of the stairway when the students hurried past.

Lisl slowed down and said, "*Gruess Gott.*"

Herr Kiefer grabbed Lisl's arm and held her back as the rest of the children ran out the door.

"That is no way to greet your teachers," he said, grasping her arm firmly. "What is your name?"

"Lisl Lindner."

Herr Kiefer had a reputation for being strict and Lisl was afraid of him, so she kept quiet. He probably had not understood her greeting.

"Go to the top and start again," he commanded.

She climbed back to the second floor from where she had come. But as she started down she heard his booming voice, "All the way to the top."

She climbed to the fourth floor and stood still for a moment.

"All right, you can come down now. And don't run." His voice echoed through the open staircase.

Lisl stomped down in steady, deliberate steps so he could hear that she wasn't running. When she reached the bottom she looked him straight in the eyes and said, "*Gruess Gott.*"

"No no." He slapped his hands against the sides of his legs. "Up you go again." He pointed toward the stairs.

As she hurried up again, Gisela, also a first-grader and friend, whispered to her, "Lisl, say 'Heil Hitler.'"

Heil Hitler. Yes, she should have known. Lisl remembered the big magnificent military parade marching through the main street of Mainbernheim only a week before. Soldiers goose-stepped in their hard boots on the cobblestone street in rhythm to a thunderous marching band. A truly impressive sight. People had lined the streets, cheering, shouting "Heil Hitler" to high-ranking officers standing in open cars.

Although most people in Mainbernheim greeted with Heil Hitler, Lisl thought it was a choice, not a law. Now she knew what was expected of her.

From the top of the fourth floor she confidently marched down and passed right by her teachers with a big "Heil Hitler."

But Herr Kiefer grabbed her arm again. "Better, but not good enough," he said, pointing to the stairs again.

Now what did I do wrong, she wondered, as she went back up.

Gisela came slowly down the stairs now. She had tried to wait for Lisl so they could walk home together. As she passed Lisl on the stairs, she brought her hand up beside her face, whispered "Heil Hitler," and kept on walking.

Confused, Lisl rushed to the top, turned and hurried right back down, just short of running. With her elbow bent she raised her hand and said, "Heil Hitler."

Herr Kiefer rolled his eyes and pointed to the stairs. And as she turned she heard the teachers talking, but she wasn't sure what they meant.

"You don't have to take it that far," Herr Stolz objected.

"Now do you see how ridiculous this is?" Herr Kiefer said.

On her way up, Lisl thought maybe she had used the wrong hand. And when she marched past them with an insecure "Heil Hitler," raising her left hand, Herr Kiefer pushed her toward the stairs, shaking his head.

By now Lisl felt picked on as she pulled herself up on the smooth, worn handrail, familiar with every imperfection her hand slid across.

A thin string of sunlight trickled through the stairwell from a window above. She wished she could be walking home with Gisela.

Not sure of what she had done wrong this time, she thought of the parade. She remembered when the officer accepted the key to the town, how his hand shot up as he clicked his heels, shouting, "Heil Hitler."

She hurried the rest of the way up, skipping the last two steps, then ran back down again, arriving breathless at the bottom.

With an awkward attempt at clicking her heels in her torn shoes, her right hand shot up straight and stiff as she shouted, "Heil Hitler."

Herr Kiefer and Herr Stolz looked at each other for a moment then broke out in boisterous laughter.

"Well done," Herr Kiefer said between laughter. "You can go home now." Lisl remembered running out of the building so fast she almost lost her shoes. She was afraid Herr Kiefer would change his mind. She heard them laughing until they were out of earshot.

Lisl arrived home. Out of breath she flung the door open and managed to shout, "Heil Hitler."

Mama looked puzzled for a moment then she took Lisl in her arms and said, "*Gruess Dich, Liebchen.*"

Lisl wiped her tears and smiled. Things were back to normal again, at least at home. But even Mama tried to hide a smile when Lisl demonstrated the incident by clicking her heels. Mama told Lisl that heel clicking was reserved for the military only.

Now four years later, as she observed Herr Kiefer and Herr Stolz being paraded with shaven heads through the town, she felt no satisfaction. She had to admit, she had learned to salute. Her satisfaction came when she realized she was free to greet anyone the way *she* wanted to.

Herr Kiefer stood tall and proud, showing no humiliation as the car slowly rolled through town. He smiled calmly at his friends, students and most of the townspeople who seemed distressed by his dilemma. He held his shaven head high and one could almost believe the parade was in his honor.

Lisl could still hear the music, fragmented now, as they left the town and turned onto Muehlenweg.

Her sisters walked ahead with Dieter, chatting excitedly about the parade.

Sundays were special for Lisl. It usually meant no hard work and sometimes a little more to eat, but the parade had ruined her joy. She walked slowly, hanging on to her mother's arm to avoid limping. She wanted to take off her shoes, but Mama told her that the ground was still too cold.

When they came close to the house she saw Grandfather by the open window. He must have been worried about the curfew. When he heard their chatter he called to Aunt Anni and Kurt, "They're here."

Kurt came running down the path, excited to have his favorite playmate back. He hurled himself at Charlotte who caught him and lifted him up into the air.

When they entered the house, Lisl took off her shoes and slipped into the soft birthday slippers Charlotte had knitted for her.

Aunt Anni was home. It was her day off. She brought a big bowl of hot soup to the table made from beans and peas with some of the sausage fat for flavor. She had managed to save a little bread from work.

An hour later someone knocked on the door, shouting, "Frau Lindner."

Mama opened the door and her neighbor stepped inside, pulling three of her five children in with her. Mama looked surprised that her neighbor dared come out after curfew. Without a word, Frau Nagel took a cake from a bag and handed it to Mama.

"I've baked this for you and your family. A thank you present," she said.

Mama looked puzzled. "What did *I* do to deserve a cake?"

"You kept us from leaving our home."

"Well, I don't know what to say. Thank you. You didn't have to do that. I had my own selfish reason for stopping you. I didn't want to lose my good neighbor." Mama put the cake on the table. And before she had time to get a knife, everyone had gathered around the cake, including Frau Nagel and her children.

"What did she say?" Opa asked Aunt Anni.

"She brought a cake."

Mama made a pot of ersatz coffee, took out the plates and sliced the cake. Everyone in the room enjoyed the tasty surprise. Mama gave the last pieces to Frau Nagel for the two children she had left at home. Although the cake lacked sugar and butter and tasted more like white bread, it was a rare treat.

Aunt Anni had made a fire while the family was in church; she had managed to get a half sack of coal on the black market. It turned out to be a warm and wonderful Sunday after all, Lisl thought, munching on her slice of cake.

Frau Nagel pulled out a letter from her dress pocket and held it up like a trophy. "I got a letter from Hans yesterday," she beamed. "It's from a prison camp." She took the letter from its envelope and spread it on the table. "He doesn't know when he will be coming home, probably as soon as the war is over." Frau Nagel knew the letter by heart and her hand lovingly stroked the page while reciting parts of its contents.

"That is wonderful. Does he know any of the prisoners there?" Mama asked.

"He didn't say." Frau Nagel looked at the letter again. "No, he didn't say. I'm sure he would have mentioned it."

"Yes I'm sure." Mama looked disappointed.

"Hans is all right. He has not been injured, but he's very hungry, he wrote." She folded the letter and slid it back into the envelope and put it in her pocket. She started to cry. "I hate to think what would have happened if you hadn't stopped me from leaving our house. Hans would have no place to come home to. He would have found refugees instead." She smiled through her tears.

Mama smiled back, but Lisl saw the sadness on her mother's face. She appeared cheerful, trying to hide her sorrow as more and more families had received letters, yet they still had no word from Papa. But when Mama's brown eyes turned hazel she could not hide her grief from Lisl.

CHAPTER 24

A Bucket Full of Coffee

Next morning, Mama lit the kitchen stove to make a pot of linden tea for breakfast. They had picked linden blossoms and chamomile the past summer and dried them in the attic. Black tea and coffee had not been available for years. A half-slice of bread each with a little applesauce had to keep them going until evening.

Anni was at work and Opa just had a cup of tea and went back to his room. He said he was not hungry, but Lisl new he did not want to take food from his grandchildren. She worried about him.

Before Lisl had a chance to clear the table, a loud knock on the front door startled her. Mama and Lisl opened it and found four American soldiers shivering, but smiling, rubbing their hands together. One of the soldiers held a big kettle-like bucket. He pointed at it and told Mama something.

She looked confused and shrugged her shoulders to let them know she did not understand. After a few more attempts, the soldier pulled a little booklet from his pocket and slowly read a few strangely pronounced words in German.

"We make coffee in your kitchen?"

Mama seemed uncertain for a moment. She looked at the soldiers, then at her children. "Come in," she said finally, directing them to the kitchen.

They crowded around the stove. One soldier pointed to the faucet and Mama nodded. He filled the bucket with water and set it on the stove.

Lisl knew it would take a long time for that big kettle to boil since the fire was not very hot.

The soldiers waited, warming themselves, trying to talk to Mama and the children.

At first, no one knew what they were trying say. But eventually between gestures and the little booklet they made themselves understood.

One soldier told Mama that they too were looking forward to warmer weather. "It's damned cold out there in the camps," one of them said before he slowly translated what that meant.

Dieter stood in front of the soldiers, examining their gear. The big rifles and equipment they carried aroused his curiosity. He pointed out the difference between their war equipment and Papa's, although the soldiers did not fully understand him.

One of the soldiers took his rifle from his shoulder and set the rifle butt to the floor with a thud. With his legs slightly apart he stood like a guard so the boys could get a better look at him.

Dieter's face lit up while examining his rifle up close. He smiled at the Ami standing motionless like a statue.

With a sudden motion the soldier brought his big rifle to his chest and crossed his arm over it. He slung the weapon over his shoulder then set the rifle butt to the floor again with a loud thump. Dieter stood in amazement while Kurt backed up against his mother. The soldier picked up the rifle and again slung it over his shoulder. Then in a fast motion he dropped it to his side, then holding it in the middle, he spun it around, and back to the floor, repeating the maneuver with precision.

Lisl clapped her hands, trying to make the stone-faced man smile.

Dieter looked impressed. Even Kurt came closer and asked him to do it again.

Mama and the girls watched amused. One of the soldiers shouted out mock commands to which the entertainer moved like a wind-up toy. The other soldiers joined in, shouting a rhyme in song to match his movement. The rifle butt hit the floor with the definite rhythm of a drum, and the voices of the soldiers sang in rhyme. Their music filled the room.

But it all came to an abrupt end when their company commander came through the door, barking a sharp command. All four soldiers snapped to attention and stood still, not even blinking.

Lisl wondered what the commander had said to make them look like wooden soldiers.

The commander took the entertainer and another soldier with him. The two remaining Amis behaved like soldiers on a mission. The show had ended.

Lisl sat on the bench behind the kitchen table, wondering where they had come from. Was it a place were Indians lived? Did the soldiers' families worry they might get killed in the war? Or did the soldiers worry about the families they had left behind with the Indians? What did their country look like? She had seen pictures in library books where Indians lived in caves of tall cliffs. She would have liked to ask if they had petrified seashells in those caves, but the language barrier made it impossible.

Finally the water came to a boil and one of the soldiers emptied a big packet of coffee into the bucket. He stirred it up with the spoon that Mama had used to scrape out the last of the applesauce. He then picked up a used cup from the table, emptying the few drops of linden tea into the sink.

Mama watched amused as he dipped the cup into the bucket to sample the brew. After he took a sip, he handed the cup over for Mama to taste. She took a few sips, then a few more, before she handed it back to him. "Very good," she said.

Lisl could tell her mother was tempted to finish the whole cup; she had not tasted real coffee for a long time. The soldier poured the coffee back into the bucket. He set the cup back on the table, thanked Mama, and left with the bucket of coffee.

The whole house smelled of fresh brewed coffee for the rest of the day.

CHAPTER 25

The Good and the Bad

Mama worried when none of the stores had sugar for the baby's formula. She had no soap, coffee or cigarettes to buy groceries with on the black market. She was out of luck.

"Mama, did you know the Ami soldiers have little envelopes of sugar in their pockets to put in their coffee?" Dieter said. "If you think we can spare an egg, maybe I can exchange one for some sugar? I think they would like a fresh egg. My friend told me they only have powdered eggs."

"Well, you can try." Mama thought for a moment then handed Lisl one egg. "You go with him," she said.

Lisl and Dieter went on the search for American military campsites. Although Lisl could hide her shaven head under her scarf, she could do nothing to hide her oversized hand-me-downs. Her shoes looked as though they might fall into shreds at any moment. So she waited in the background, but kept an eye on Dieter as he approached the camp with the egg.

Dieter's first try ended in disaster. The soldiers did not want to listen and chased him away.

"They probably thought you were just begging," Lisl consoled him.

He had tried so hard to make them understand that to get a fresh egg would be a relief from powdered eggs. Yet he did not give up easily and confidently walked to the second camp. But the jeeps were surrounded by too many begging children; Lisl knew they had no chance there either.

"Maybe there's a camp in the stone break again," Dieter said.

"I don't think we should go in there." Lisl remembered the broken wine bottles and the target shooting.

"Oh, you don't have to worry; they don't eat people. Opa said so," he teased.

Even before they came to the stone break they heard voices. But the soldiers were not as rowdy as the last ones maybe because they had no wine. Lisl noticed that they had not seen English troops lately, only Americans. And here in the stone break there were no children. Lisl thought they might have a chance. She handed the egg to Dieter again and waited a few meters away. He marched right up to the soldiers.

"Would you like to exchange a nice fresh egg for some sugar? The egg is real fresh. It was laid this morning." He spoke loudly and slowly in German, hoping they would understand him. One of the soldiers rose to his feet, held two little envelopes of sugar between his fingers and said, "You want sugar?"

Dieter nodded with a happy smile on his face.

The soldier took the egg and crushed it in his hand, squeezing the raw egg through his fingers. He threw back his head and laughed, but did not give Dieter the sugar.

Lisl's hand flew to her lips. "Oh no."

Dieter stared at the wasted egg and back to the soldier's face. Surprisingly, Dieter did not look upset or angry and Lisl saw that he was trying to make sense of this soldier. The other Amis did not laugh. They must have said something the egg crusher did not like, because he abruptly stopped laughing and got angry at them and at Dieter. The longer

Dieter calmly and curiously stared at him the angrier he became until the soldier pushed Dieter away.

Lisl burst into tears. She grabbed Dieter's hand and pulled him along, putting her arm around him. Now they had to tell Mama they had lost the egg.

Another soldier came running after them, telling them something. Lisl slowly shook her head. She did not understand him. He held out his hand and offered three little envelopes of sugar to Dieter.

Dieter, with a sad look, turned up his empty hands. "I have nothing left to trade," he said. The soldier held Dieter's hands and put the sugar in them. Dieter showed it to Lisl with a smile. He thought for a moment and asked Lisl, "Is it all right if we give him the petrified seashell?"

Lisl was reluctant. It was after all a treasure, but she finally nodded.

Dieter carried it in his pocket for good luck. Now he presented the seashell to the soldier with visible pride.

The Ami looked surprised. He held it carefully, his eyes grew big and then he smiled at Lisl. The soldier wanted to know where she had found it.

When Lisl finally understood, she pointed to the embankment. She could tell he knew how rare it was by the way he examined it again. He must have been an archeologist, too, so she felt better about giving him the shell.

The soldier sat on his boot heels in front of Dieter and Lisl while he admired the shell. He took off his helmet and ran his hand through his dark, short hair, and then he pointed at himself and said, "My name is Ira. Ira," he repeated slowly. Then he pointed to Lisl and Dieter.

"This is Lisl, my sister. I'm Dieter," he said. The soldier shook their hands. Then he dug into his pocket and gave Lisl two little envelopes of instant coffee.

Lisl did not know what it was until she read the letters spelling coffee. She smiled at him. *"Danke shoen."*

Ira admired the shell again, and then felt his jacket pockets, pulled out a full pack of cigarettes and gave it to Dieter.

Dieter beamed, "Do you know what we can buy with a whole pack of cigarettes?" Of course, Ira did not understand, but he smiled back at Dieter's happy face.

"Vielen Dank, Ira," they said and shook his hand again before they ran off.

Lisl could not wait to see Mama's reaction. When Lisl looked back, the soldier still sat there watching them run across the field toward the house.

Dieter burst into the room, waking the baby.

"Mama, guess what we got," he said, trying hard to conceal his excitement.

"Hmm, let me guess . . . is it sugar?" she said, knowing how to play his little game. He reached into his pocket and came up with the sugar.

"You are correct." He handed her the little envelopes. "Guess what else we got."

Mama was curious now. "I think . . . maybe more sugar?" she said.

"Wrong, coffee! We got coffee." He giggled.

Mama took the little envelopes from Lisl's hands and read, "Nescafe. Oh, that is real coffee." She tried to smell through its tight seal.

But Dieter was not finished. "Guess what else we have." He held his hand over his pocket containing the cigarettes.

Mama forgot about the game as she blurted out, "What?"

"We got cigarettes," he said in an exaggerated tone.

Mama took the pack of cigarettes, already figuring what she could buy with it. "Probably a bag of flour . . . a small bag, or maybe some sugar." She thought out loud.

"Mama, I hope you won't get upset," Dieter said.

"Why, what happened?" Now Mama looked worried.

"We gave your shell away."

"Oh, I'm sorry." She knew how much the shell meant to them. "Maybe you can find another one–maybe even more beautiful."

Lisl and Dieter exchanged a secret smile. Mama unknowingly had signaled a go-ahead to dig in the stone break without getting in trouble. That alone was worth giving the shell away. Of course they would not mention it again. Mama might change her mind once she had a chance to think about it.

CHAPTER 26

Eviction

Lisl's grandmother had died a few weeks after Kurt was born. Frau Weber, Oma's best friend, kept in touch with the family.

Lisl and Dieter loved to visit Frau Weber and had often helped out by doing her shopping when food was still available. Frau Weber kept two goats in her backyard. Every other day she shared goats' milk with Lisl's family, and Dieter and Lisl ran to watch her milk the goats. She always seemed so glad to see the children and greeted them with warmth and a happy smile. Today, however, Frau Weber had already finished milking by the time they arrived. She filled their one-liter milk can.

Lisl loved to listen to her stories about Grandmother. But lately, with the curfew, they had to return home all too early.

"*Danke shoen*, Frau Weber." Lisl shook her hand as did Dieter before they ran across the fields homeward bound.

As they arrived at the house, two American soldiers were coming to the front door. They handed Mama a piece of paper then left without a word. Mama read the letter over and over. She looked pale.

"What's the matter?" Charlotte took the letter from Mama's hand.

"Is it from Papa?" Lisl dared ask.

Mama shook her head, her face darkened. "No. We have to leave our house."

Lisl could not understand why they would have to leave now that the war in their area was over. Yet she sighed in relief because she had feared bad news about her father. She peered over Charlotte's shoulder as she read the letter out loud. The official document ordered the family to evacuate their house within one hour because it would be occupied by American troops for two weeks. They were not allowed to take anything other than the clothing they would need.

"Where can we go?" Mama whispered. She looked helplessly around the house. Most of their friends had either already taken in people who were left homeless after the bombings or their homes had been taken over by troops as well.

Charlotte did not cry. She threw the paper to the ground, shouting "Why do we have to go? And just look at that." She picked it up again and pointed at the part most distressing to her. "We're not allowed to take much with us."

Ellen coughed excessively but expressed her anger by cleaning everything in sight.

Grandfather looked confused. He cried when he realized that now the whole family would be homeless.

"Opa it's only for a little while. We still have a home." Lisl patted his hand, but it did not make him feel any better.

"Opa and I can stay in Ursula's apartment in Kitzingen," Aunt Anni said. "Ursula works with me at the hospital and has asked me to move in with her and her little daughter." Anni watched her father wipe his tears.

Lisl knew Opa would rather stay with his grandchildren. He seemed apprehensive about the apartment.

"Ursula's mother died a week ago," Anni explained.

"Oh, how sad, was she sick?" Mama asked.

"No, she knew her mother would not recover from the injuries she got in the Kitzingen bombing." Anni went to her father and put her hand on his shoulder. "Now she feels depressed and lonely. They were very close. She asked me because she needs company right now."

"Is the apartment big enough for four people?" Mama asked.

"I think so. We can stay in her mother's room if we're willing to pack up her things. Ursula can't cope with that."

"Are you sure she wants both of us?" Opa asked.

"Yes, Papa. You'll be doing Ursula a favor by staying with her. She needs someone to watch over her six-year-old in case we both have to work at the same time. It will be good for both of you. You already know the little girl. She likes you."

"Has everyone forgotten I'm blind?"

"Papa, she is very self sufficient. You'll do just fine. You'll help each other."

"Opa stays with *us*," Kurt objected.

"Opa and I can visit you, Kurt." Aunt Anni turned to Mama. "But where will you go?"

"Don't worry. I think we can stay at Frau Weber's house. She had offered her attic in case we were evicted like a lot of families in town."

So Anni and Opa said their goodbyes. Lisl helped with their bags when Opa became too tearful to carry them. Dieter and Lisl put their belongings in a hand wagon and walked to the train station with them. The station had since been repaired. Anni took the written order with them in case they were stopped after curfew.

Lisl and Dieter watched as Anni guided Opa onto the train, then they handed the luggage to Anni. Lisl hoped that there would be a seat for Opa on the crowed railcar. Slowly the train moved. Aunt Anni stood by the window and waved. She said something to Opa and he put his hand against the window.

"*Aufwiedersehen*," Dieter and Lisl called, waving until the train was out of sight.

Lisl felt empty and sad on their way home.

"It won't be the same without them. I'll miss Opa," Dieter said.

When they got back to the house, Mama sorted through children's clothing, packing enough thick sweaters and things to last them through the two weeks.

The attic in Frau Weber's house was much smaller than Lisl remembered. Two old mattresses and a few comforters stored in the corner were welcomed since they could bring no beds.

Frau Weber brought some blankets and pillows up. "Here, these might help for the little ones to sleep on." She put them on the floor where Kurt promptly jumped on them to see how comfortable they were.

Mama took Ellen and Lisl back to the house to get a few more things, including the little laundry basket for Werner.

At the house, Mama tried to find a safer hiding place for the hunting knife still hidden on top of the wardrobe. She was afraid to take it with her; she might get searched.

The wood basket by the stove seemed a likely place. Mama thought it would be safe hidden under wood scraps and a few pinecones–not enough to build a fire. She figured that no one would suspect such an obvious place.

As they walked down the garden path, Mama looked back at the house through hazel eyes.

Although Mama seemed grateful for the warm lodging, the attic felt cramped and the only place she could stand up straight was the two-meter-wide space in middle of the slanted roof. Frau Weber had used the attic to dry herbs and teas for many years, and the still-lingering smell became stifling at times.

The church bells sounded as though they came from the next room instead of two houses down. And in the first few days, Lisl and her sisters scrambled from their beds with the sound of the bells, ready to run to the air-raid shelter.

Kurt surprised his mother by telling her that the bells were nice; they did not keep him awake. Soon Lisl and Dieter stopped counting the hours chime through the night, and Charlotte and Ellen stopped covering their heads with pillows. Everyone adjusted and slept soundly.

But Lisl and Dieter heard strange noises coming from between the walls.

"Mice." Mama told them.

But they would not accept such a simple explanation. Their imaginations ran wild with thoughts of prehistoric monsters that they had accidentally released from the stone break. Now they were hiding between the walls and in secret rooms. Still, after a few nights, even the sound of the monsters faded.

Every day Lisl and Ellen walked with Mama across the fields where they gathered dandelion greens on the way to their house to feed the rabbits and chickens.

Mama laughed when she saw that someone had tried to feed the rabbits seed onions that were to be planted soon. Obviously, the soldiers thought the little onions were rabbit food because they were stored in one of the empty cages.

The soldiers also had given them little bowls of water in Mama's good Rosenthal china. The rabbits had never had water in their cages because the cattle beets and dandelion greens provided enough moisture.

"Good little bunnies," Lisl petted their white fluffy fur, "you didn't break the bowls."

Ellen took out the bowls and Lisl collected the seed onions and hid them under an empty clay pot in the garden. She hoped she could plant them when they were allowed to come back.

Lisl was sure that she had locked the chicken coop securely when they left. Now it was open and the chickens were gone. Usually they came running when she called out their names, but no matter how hard she searched they were nowhere to be found.

Mama walked around the house and saw the front door wide open. She hesitated in the open doorway before she stepped inside with Ellen and Lisl close behind. At first Lisl thought the house was unoccupied.

"Psst." Ellen pointed to the couch where a soldier lay sleeping.

Mama put her finger to her lips and gingerly took a few more steps.

Although the drapes were drawn, Mama still could see the empty space where the radio used to stand. They silently walked through the house and found other things missing, mostly household items.

Mama cried when she discovered that her beautiful tablecloth was gone–the wedding gift her mother had made for her. Lisl thought it so unfair to have lost it now after Mama had taken it to the air-raid shelter so many times to keep it safe. As they left Mama wiped her tears. This time she did not look back as they walked down the garden path.

Next morning Ellen and Lisl ran ahead of their mother to feed the rabbits and found the cages open and the rabbits gone. They searched the garden.

"I found one," Ellen called, grabbing the little angora fluff ball.

"I've got the other one." Lisl shouted. The rabbits seemed happy to be back in their safe cages with dandelion greens.

Lisl was glad the hawks had not discovered them. They had lost quite a few chicks to the hawks a few years ago.

Mama glanced up at the windows. The curtains were still drawn, but she did not go inside the house again even though the door was wide open. The sadness in Mama's eyes made Lisl unhappy.

The two weeks in the attic dragged on forever. Everyone developed cabin fever. Lisl felt trapped in this small living space and often went with Dieter to visit Frau Weber downstairs. Sometimes they watched when the woman milked the goats. She was always happy when they helped her feed the animals. Lisl and Dieter were only too glad to help the old woman just to get away from their quarreling sisters.

Charlotte and Ellen argued constantly, and more viciously than ever. Charlotte yanked a sweater from Ellen's hand as she was about to pull it over her head. "You know that isn't yours, I only loaned it to you," Charlotte screamed.

"I remember clearly that you gave it to me." Ellen snatched the sweater back. "We exchanged them, stupid, or don't you remember?"

"I did no such thing. You wanted yours back, or are *you* too stupid to remember that?"

With the limited supply of clothes, ownership seemed important. Usually they swapped their sweaters and other things they wore since they were close to the same size. But now battles brewed over every item.

"Will you please stop that!" Mama shouted at them. But soon they were calling each other terrible names again.

Lisl had never heard her mother raise her voice like that before. But with the low ceiling and slanted roof, Mama's temper flared as well. She felt cramped and was tired of constantly playing referee. Still, Mama's greatest worry remained–the shortage of food.

Lisl and Dieter had lost interest in the noises between the walls; they no longer sparked their imagination. But they always knew when to disappear–usually as soon as their sisters started slinging nasty insults at each other.

Lisl liked to sit with Dieter outside on a garden bench in front of Frau Weber's house, even when curfew was in effect. Sometimes Frau Weber joined them. She liked their company, amused by their vivid wild stories. She too could spin some fantastic tales to keep them interested.

In the mornings Lisl and Dieter watched American trucks and jeeps roll by on the street below with a swarm of hungry children in their wake. Frau Weber's house was two houses from the church in the middle of town. It was like having a front row seat to all the action. Lisl was not used to seeing so much commotion because the little Siedlung was surrounded by gardens and wheat fields. She preferred the peace and quiet of their garden.

On Sunday morning she and Dieter, along with other children, were allowed to ring the church bells. Herr Koechner took them into the bell tower where he pulled down the ropes to the three big bells so the children could grab onto them. They hung in clusters like grapes, having great fun getting rides high up into the air then back down to the floor. This kept the bells swinging back and forth. Still, Lisl looked forward to being home again, close to the garden and the stone break.

The day before they were allowed to return to their home, Mama and Lisl went to feed the rabbits and again found the cages empty. They searched the garden and the surrounding area but they could not find them.

Mama looked angry. "Now I wish I had roasted them. Someone else had our dinner."

"Maybe the hawks got them," Lisl said. But she still hoped to find them hiding somewhere in the garden. She was glad her mother did not have to kill them for food. Dieter and Kurt would have been upset, and Mama would have been sad when no one in the family swallowed a bite. The white long-haired Angora rabbits with their red eyes and pink ears were much too cute to eat.

Finally, the next day the family moved back home and were greeted by a nauseating smell.

Mama walked through the rooms in disbelief. Nothing had been cleaned in those two weeks. Every dish, including their good Rosenthal china, was piled high in the sink. Rotting food stuck to plates and bowls. Mama found glasses with residue of stale beer and other foul-smelling liquids throughout the house. Some of the dishes and glasses were broken. The floor was littered with garbage.

Ellen felt a little foolish for having cleaned so meticulously before they left.

Mama checked the wood basket to retrieve the knife and discovered the wood chips and pinecones were gone, replaced by candy wrappers and other paper scraps. She was afraid the soldiers had found the knife and she might be arrested for concealing a weapon. When she emptied the paper garbage, she discovered that the knife was still on the bottom underneath the wrappers. The soldiers hadn't seen it. With a sigh of relief she smiled and hid it in a safer place in her bedroom.

Now cleanup work began–washing dishes, scrubbing floors, polishing furniture, cleaning windows and doing laundry until the awful smell disappeared. Gradually the house became livable again. But they also discovered that many more of their belongings were missing than they first thought–even old toys and the children's leather school bags.

Lisl's Sunday shoes were gone as well, which upset her mother more than it did Lisl.

"Now see what you've done. Your nice shoes are gone all because you were too lazy to look for them," her mother scolded.

But Lisl had actually pushed her shoes further under her bed before they evacuated, telling her mother that she couldn't find them. Lisl wanted to save herself some pain on Sundays when she would have to wear them to church.

Lisl looked under the bed again. Maybe they were still there. She scrambled to her feet and frowned, trying to look sad. "I'm sorry Mama."

Most of their books were still in their usual place, although some were quite valuable.

"Good thing all the dishes were dirty, or they would have disappeared as well."

A few days later Mama became suspicious when she recognized some of her belongings in the possession of certain townspeople who had been troublesome in the past.

It made sense to Lisl, who could not imagine that the soldiers would take such items while still on the move toward the war front. After all, the door had been left open so it was easy for thieves to sneak in just as she and her mother had done.

Mama could not reclaim her possessions; no one was willing to help her.

CHAPTER 27

Green Bread

Lisl watched her mother stretch her arms and smile into the sunshine as she came out into the garden. Lisl had sneaked out before curfew lifted. Mama smiled at Lisl. She didn't seem to mind. "Oh it's so nice to be home again," Mama said. "Now we can start the planting."

The rocky ground and poor soil did not discourage Mama who had always vigorously worked the ground in the past, fighting for every square meter of planting area. The garden had provided fruits and vegetables at the times they needed them most.

Mama took a deep breath then sat down beside Lisl on the garden bench. "Ah, can you smell it?"

Lisl sniffed the air. "It smells like spring."

"Yes, it does. The weather is warmer. We can sow spinach and plant the lettuce."

"Shall I get the basket?" Lisl jumped up.

"Yes *Liebling*."

"Where did you get the plants Mama?"

"From Frau Ziegler. She also gave me seeds. She knew I had no food to trade so she only asked for Papa's help with her taxes when he gets home." Mama laughed. "She gave me a lot more than I had hoped for."

"Listen, Mama. The birds are back." Lisl stood smiling, gazing at the trees, listening to the robins' spring concert. "Do you think the nightingales will return?"

"Well maybe not this year. They are very shy birds."

Dieter and Kurt raced through the garden, happy to be home as well. Now the children took care of overwintered plants, shrubs, and flowers. The tulips displayed a brilliant show of color as daffodils bid their farewell. Lisl looked forward to the sweet scent of the lilacs. Their buds were ready to burst into bloom.

"Frau Lindner," a man called from the road below.

Lisl and her mother went to the edge of the garden path.

"*Guten Tag*, Herr Holzbrecht," Mama called down from the garden.

The old man held two squawking chickens upside down by their legs. "I heard you've lost some chickens," he said.

"Yes. I don't know if someone took them or if they just ran away."

"Well, I have a couple I can spare." He lifted the flapping birds up so Mama could get a better look at them.

"Oh, that is very kind of you. I'm very grateful." Mama hurried from the garden down to Muehlenweg with Lisl.

"I owe it to you. I know I haven't been able to pay you for the mending you've done for us. I hope this will help. I don't know why, but some people are so unkind, stealing from folks like you." He handed Lisl and Mama each a chicken. "They are good laying hens." He gasped for breath and pointed to the garden path. "Sorry I can't get up there; it's too steep for me." He turned, concentrating on the road ahead and without turning he waved his arm in the air and called, "*Aufwiedersehen*."

"*Aufwiedersehen und vielen Dank*," Mama called after him.

Lisl held the chicken close to her chest, petting its red feathers. "Poor thing, you had to hang by your feet all the way out here." She watched her mother stroke the other chicken, but Lisl suspected that it was not because it had to endure hanging upside down, but rather as an encouragement to lay eggs. They put them in the chicken coop and closed the gate securely.

"At least we'll have eggs again," Mama said, stepping lightly through the garden toward the house.

∽

The farmers started plowing and planting their fields. Now they needed help and Charlotte and Ellen were more than willing.

Lisl and her brothers were usually waiting by the door when their sisters returned. Mama too was curious to see what goodies the farmers had given them in exchange for their work. Sometimes they brought home flour or a half a loaf of bread. When they returned empty handed, they usually were rewarded the next day with a thick slice of ham or bacon worth two days of work.

Lisl and Dieter worked in the family garden, pulling weeds and cultivating the stony ground, preparing the beds for seeds. They raked the rocks downhill from the beds, creating a little loose wall to keep the dirt from washing away.

After Mama planted the spinach seeds, Dieter and Lisl brought buckets of water from the rain barrel to fill Mama's watering can. She poured it carefully onto the seeded beds. Lisl could hardly wait for the spinach to grow. It was her favorite dish.

"Tomorrow we'll put the string beans in the ground." Mama stood straight, then gazed into the scattered clouds and smiled.

Werner was asleep in his carriage under the cherry tree, which was now in full bloom. Kurt, kneeling on a wooden garden chair, created pictures on a slate tablet on the outdoor table.

Too soon curfew started and it was time to go inside. But lately the family worked a few extra hours when the soldiers were not around and so did the farmers.

Next morning after curfew, Frau Nagel called to Mama over the fence.

"Frau Lindner, I heard we're allowed to get bread at the town hall, that is, if you're not too picky about freshness."

"Thank you, Frau Nagel. I will send the children right away," Mama said.

Dieter and Lisl quickly put their garden tools away. With the promise of bread, they ran along Muehlenweg and into town, hoping to return before curfew.

Disappointed, they found long lines of people in front of the building.

An old man came through the door with two small square loaves. "*Kommis Brot*," he said, slapping the mold-covered loaves together, releasing a cloud of green dust.

Lisl was curious, she had never heard of Kommis Brot. The bread did not come from the local bakery but from the German government–army rations that had not made it to the front lines.

"It's still edible if you cut the green stuff away." The old man hit the loaves together like cymbals.

"Maybe, after the army rations have gone, we'll get some good bread again. So take as much as you can get," a woman said.

"Yes, but then you can only buy it on the black market," another one said.

One woman shook her head. "You're only allowed one loaf per person." She smiled, holding up a big bag. "I have a large family."

Dieter and Lisl waited patiently and by the time they finally got to the head of the line they only had a few minutes before curfew.

"Lindner?" the lady asked reading the name off a list.

Lisl nodded eagerly.

"Well, you'll get seven loaves."

The woman handed the little square green loaves to Lisl and Dieter. Although Werner was still too small to eat the bread, Lisl was glad he was included in the count.

On their way home, Dieter pointed out alternative routes through town to Lisl so they would not get shot by the enemy after curfew. They pretended to be spies on a mission, sneaking in and out of dark corners and narrow side streets.

Dieter ran across the street holding one loaf under each arm and a third one between his hands under his chin. Lisl hugged four little loaves across her chest.

"Pssst." Dieter motioned to Lisl with his big eyes to follow him. He slipped through a narrow stone doorway in the high wall. They signaled each other when one of them had made it across an open area unseen. Planning detours to the next rendezvous, all the while carrying seven loaves of moldy bread, they reached safety checkpoints and felt heroic.

Dieter had run halfway across the cobblestone street when a troop of American soldiers came out from a side street. He quickly backed up and pressed himself tightly against the wall. The soldiers walked right by him, talking to each other, paying no attention to Dieter who stood in plain sight. He looked panic-stricken, trying to hide behind the moldy bread while his eyes followed the men.

Lisl hid behind the fountain, and although the soldiers looked at her, they seemed preoccupied. They passed by and disappeared around the corner.

Lisl ran to Dieter who stood frozen, pasted against the wall, holding his breath. She thought he looked a little blue.

"They're gone," she whispered.

He opened his eyes and exhaled a sigh of relief. The game took on a new dimension–a great rush–because they believed they would be shot if caught. It made the spy game very real and their safe return home a victory.

When Mama saw the moldy bread she looked disappointed. So too were Dieter and Lisl when she did not share in their triumph. Mama did not think that they were in any danger by being out a few minutes past curfew. She showed more interest in the bread.

Mama cut the mold from the loaves until only a small part in the center remained that could actually be eaten. Two of the loaves were moldy clear through. Still, there was enough to go with the soup to make a more filling meal.

CHAPTER 28

Ghost in the Barn

In the last week of April the weather had finally warmed, and Lisl and Dieter searched in the stone break for that perfect shell. Too soon their time was up with the approach of curfew. They skipped through the fields and as they came into the garden, Lisl's heart sank. Mama sat on the front door steps, her shoulders slumped. She held a piece of paper and Lisl knew that something terrible had happened. "Please, don't let it be about Papa," she whispered.

Charlotte and Ellen tried to read over her shoulder, looking as depressed as their mother.

Lisl turned to her. "Mama?" Her mother looked at her through hazel eyes without a word.

"What's the matter, Mama?" Dieter asked. But she did not answer. Instead, she handed Charlotte the paper. All eyes hung on Charlotte's lips, waiting for her to read. After reading a few lines in silence, she shouted, "Oh no, not again!"

Lisl sighed with relief. Charlotte's reaction eliminated her fear for Papa. Whatever was in that note could not be all that bad.

Charlotte stomped her foot. "Why do we have to move out of our house again?"

Since keeping warm was no longer a concern, the loft of the barn across the street suited Mama just fine–at least it had lots of room. The farmer gave her permission to use the loft as long as she needed. This time Mama could keep an eye on her house.

No orders were given on how much they could take with them. Mama loaded the blankets, pillows and kitchen things she needed into the hand wagon and moved them to the barn.

The family waited to see who would move in.

Dieter and Kurt stood guard, peeking through the bullet holes the soldiers had left in the barn door the day they had occupied Mainbernheim.

Mama and the children worked in the garden every morning tending the vegetables, which by now showed a good start. Lisl fed the two chickens and made sure they stayed nearby. Still the family waited for American or British soldiers to occupy their home.

Mama would have liked to use her stove, but she did not dare go into the house. It was hard not being able to cook. Again she heated the baby formula over a candle flame. But this time she had to be careful, the barn was littered with straw.

Frau Nagel offered her kitchen and stove so Mama could cook potatoes. But Mama declined. She knew it would be a hardship on her neighbor since she had very little fuel for cooking. Mama became very skilled with that candle. She even managed to fry eggs. It just took a little longer.

The boys had fun in the barn. They spread the blanket over the straw and jumped around. Kurt amazed his mother. He had a good time in the barn. Since the shooting had stopped, he no longer was that frightened little boy.

Lisl and Dieter heard strange noises at night again, different from those in Frau Weber's house.

"There is a ghost in here, I can hear it moan at night," Dieter said.

Lisl had heard the strange rustling and moaning sounds too. She imagined a ghost floating above their heads when she felt a draft. Although the mournful sound seemed familiar, it kept her awake a good part of the night.

On the second night in the barn, Lisl awoke to frightening screams. She tried to wake Dieter, but he was already wide awake with the blanket pulled over his head.

Lisl wanted to know who had screamed; maybe an animal was hurt. Her curiosity overruled her fear.

"Let's find out what kind of ghost is in here," she whispered. A year ago Lisl had heard similar shrieks in the night, but never that loud.

"Can't it wait until morning?" Dieter asked from under his blanket.

"No, silly, they only come out at night."

"Let's tell Mama. She can come with us," Dieter suggested after hearing a moan.

"Let her sleep. You know she wouldn't believe our ghost story."

"I'll go with you, but only if we can bring the flashlight."

"The flashlight makes too much noise when you squeeze it." Dieter picked "squeaky" up anyway. "All right," Lisl said, "but be careful. Don't wake Kurt; we don't want him to get frightened again."

Gingerly they tiptoed over the carpet of straw. Dieter's hand shook as he pointed the way with the flashlight. Abruptly they froze near the end of the loft when they heard that haunting call close by.

Lisl's heart pounded. Her mouth felt dry. Dieter's eyes were big. He hesitated until they heard the next moan followed by a hideous scream. He dropped the flashlight and started to run, but Lisl grabbed his arm and picked up the flashlight. Then they followed the sound.

Lisl pointed to the ceiling and whispered, "Wait, I see the ghost." Right above their heads were two big shiny eyes staring down over the rafters right into the beam of the light. Hastily, but silently, the ghost took flight and whooshed over their heads, escaping through an opening in the barn where a pulley was mounted outside the barn wall.

"An owl." Lisl let out a long breath.

Dieter looked a little foolish for having been so scared. "Wait, I think there are more in here." Noises came from the heavy wooden beams above their heads. Three young owlets peered down at them. Round little bundles of fluff gazed curiously over the edge of their nest built in the corner of the rafters.

Dieter carefully stepped backward so as not to upset the baby owls. He and Lisl watched from a short distance, and then quietly retreated to their beds.

Lisl was thrilled to be sharing their sleeping quarters with an owl family.

"I hope the mother comes back to feed her young," she whispered to Dieter. They lay quietly, listening to the shrieks of the little owls as their mother approached the nest with food. The screams Lisl had found so frightening a moment ago now sounded beautiful. She felt reassured that life goes on even with bullet holes in the door.

After almost a week in the barn, the house was still unoccupied.

Mama decided to tell the new mayor that she was going to move her family back into her house. He admitted a mistake had been made. The troops had moved on, but he failed to inform Mama.

Mama loaded the hand wagon and moved her family back into their home. It was as they had left it–clean.

Mama sighed. "I hope that's the last time we'll have to move."

CHAPTER 29

Danger in the Stone Break

On the last day of April, Dieter and Lisl brought a basket of vegetable seedlings to Frau Weber. She treated them to a glass of cider and asked if they could stay a while.

"Today we can't stay long because we have to go somewhere before curfew starts," Lisl said. They had planned a side trip to the stone break. Mama did not expect them back very soon. Frau Weber stood in the doorway as they ran down the street and back through town.

Military vehicles still blocked the streets. Begging children swarmed around American soldiers even though they did not hand out candy. Loud music blared from the jeeps. The strange whiny songs the soldiers called country music sounded mournful and sad to Lisl. She had never heard that kind of music before.

Military roadblocks meant little to Dieter as he led the way through one of the smaller towers. Once outside the wall they followed the trail through the fields until they came to the ditches the German army had dug. Now they were gaping holes in which some of the soldiers had died. Lisl stopped beside the morbid monuments for a moment and then started to run to catch up with Dieter.

They came to their favorite place. American jeeps and soldiers rested in the fields above the stone break, but not inside the quarry.

From the field above, Lisl and Dieter slid down into the sunken area instead of walking farther to take the road leading inside their amphitheater.

Lisl felt safe here. Dieter's eyes searched the rock wall and pointed. "This is where you found the good shell." He picked a handful of sticks near the ash pile the English soldiers had left behind. "We have to find another good shell for Mama."

Lisl climbed up the steep embankment and Dieter followed. He used a rock to pound the sticks between a rocky layer and the root mat of the shrubby field above to keep the top from collapsing on their excavation site.

"Wow that is great." Lisl was impressed by how cleverly he had placed the scaffolding.

Dieter looked proud, giving her a big grin.

They dug deeper creating a cavern, all the while removing rocks and pebbles that were in the way of more promising objects. Every time Lisl thought she had found a whole shell, when she pulled it free it turned out to be only part of one. Still, Dieter put them in his pocket if he thought they were large enough to be identified. He had written some of the names and descriptions down before returning the book.

Lisl heard voices from above. She popped her head over the rim and saw an American soldier walk slowly toward them.

"Someone is coming. I think he heard your hammering," she whispered.

"Let's hide." Dieter squeezed himself into the excavated cavern under the layer of rocks and roots.

Lisl squeezed in as well when she heard the soldier's footsteps come closer. He stopped at the edge only a meter above their heads. His gear jangled. She could hear him breathe.

The soldier stood still for a while, maybe listening.

Lisl tapped Dieter's arm and pointed to the scaffolding above their heads. It started to sag. She hoped that the soldier would move away from the undermined area. Instead, he stepped even closer to the edge.

The scaffolding collapsed—almost in slow motion. The soldier let out a scream as he tumbled from the high embankment. He passed Dieter and Lisl while spilling rocks and dirt onto them. Desperately they clung to exposed shrubbery roots to keep from falling after him.

Lisl held her breath. She expected to hear him get up or make some kind of noise, but all she heard was the sound of rocks and debris rolling after him.

Covered in dirt and dry shrubbery, Lisl pressed her face against the stony embankment to keep from falling. The moisture of the rocks cooled her hot face. Carefully she looked down over her shoulder. An unmoving figure sprawled about five meters below.

"Oh my God. Dieter, look what happened. We killed him."

Dieter, unable to look down for fear of falling, seemed frozen against the rocks. They both stuck to the rocky face as though they were glued there.

Why was it so quiet? Lisl expected an alarm to go off, some sort of commotion. But all she heard was the sound of pebbles and dirt still trickling down the embankment. A bird in the hedge thicket sang. Everything seemed normal as long as she did not look down. And when she did, the Ami still lay as he fell. Lisl, convinced the other soldiers had heard his scream, waited in fear. But nothing happened. They waited a few more minutes; still, no one came.

Dieter finally managed to move and quickly slid down the embankment. Almost falling, Lisl scraped her hands and knees on her way to the ground.

"Do you think he's really dead?" Dieter whispered.

"I think so. His forehead is bleeding a little."

"That doesn't mean he is dead."

"He's not moving." Lisl came closer, wanting to feel his pulse, but afraid to touch him. The soldier's chest rose slightly. "He is still alive. We have to get help."

"How, Lisl? They will arrest us for digging. It's our fault he fell."

Lisl thought for a moment then started toward the steep, rocky embankment.

"You stay here and get ready to run when I get back down."

"What are you going to do?" he called after her.

"Just wait there." She climbed up the embankment until she reached the field above.

"Hallo. Hallo," she shouted at the soldiers who stood near a jeep about 30 meters away. She waved her arms, shouting again, trying to get their attention, but they did not hear over the country music on their jeep's radio.

"Hallooo," she shouted through her cupped hands.

Finally, one of the soldiers saw her and came toward her.

She ran back to the edge of the stone break and slid down. Never before had she been able to go down that fast without actually falling. She grabbed Dieter's arm and together they ran toward the entrance of the stone break. She stopped, pulling Dieter behind a pile of stacked rocks a safe distance from the injured soldier.

Lisl watched until the soldier appeared on the rim of the embankment. When he saw his buddy lying on the bottom, he gave a sharp whistle through his fingers to alert the others, and then slid down. Two more soldiers appeared on the top and quickly came after him.

Lisl sighed when the injured soldier regained consciousness. "Thank God he's all right."

The injured man pointed to the top from which he fell and tried to stand up, but collapsed, grabbing his leg.

The soldiers used some of Dieter's fallen scaffolding sticks to make a brace for his injured leg. Two of the soldiers supported him under his arms as they walked him out of the stone break along the road.

One of the soldiers came looking for Lisl. She was afraid to get up and run because he was too close. They had to stay hidden so he would not shoot them. Her heart pounding, Lisl pressed herself tightly against the rock pile, hoping he would give up.

Suddenly he appeared behind them, on his soft, silent boots, telling her something she could not understand, but she knew by the sound of his voice that he was not about to shoot her.

He pointed to the rock wall, "Thank you," he said, and then, "*Danke shoen.*" He shook Lisl's hand and ran off to catch up with the other soldiers.

Puzzled, Lisl and Dieter looked at each other. Apparently the injured soldier had not seen them. Lisl smiled and took a deep breath. They ran home, still shaken, with a few minutes to spare before curfew.

"Let's not talk about it. All right?" Lisl said.

Dieter agreed by zipping his lip.

CHAPTER 30

Wading in Wine

May rushed in on a fragrant breeze. Lisl watched the clock, and then tore out into the garden minutes before curfew lifted. After admiring the flowers, she started pulling weeds with Dieter. She heard Frau Nagel call from across the garden.

"Frau Lindner, are you there?" She peered over the fence. "The Koehler winery in Kitzingen is open," she shouted when she spotted Mama.

Mama put down her garden tool and walked toward her.

"The debris is cleared enough so we can go down into the cellar. My friend said they found undamaged bottles of wine in there." Frau Nagel sounded excited.

"When did that happen?"

"Yesterday, or early this morning, I think." Frau Nagel took off her apron, ready to go. "We'd better hurry before it's all gone."

"What about the owner? I'm sure they won't just give it away."

Frau Nagel leaned over the fence, whispering, squinting through half closed eyes, "Haven't you heard? The Koehlers are missing. No one knows where they are. They could be buried under all that rubble, for all we know, or maybe they left the country." She stood back, looking disappointed when Mama seemed hesitant. So Frau Nagel tried a different approach. "Just think what you can buy with such fine wine."

Mama looked like she was about to give in so Lisl asked. "Can I go with you?"

"Well, I don't know. It doesn't seem right to take the wine."

"If we don't, someone else will." Her neighbor made an appealing argument. Mama was in great need of food and clothing for her children. A few good bottles of wine could buy some food on the black market.

"Can I come with you?" Ellen pushed between Mama and Lisl.

"I asked first. Mama, you said I could come."

Mama nodded. "I can only take one on the back of the bike." She looked at Lisl and at Ellen. "Yes Lisl, you can come."

So Ellen and Charlotte stayed to take care of the boys and work in the garden. Lisl grabbed two cloth bags to carry the wine bottles and folded them on the back of the bike to sit on.

Mama, with Lisl on the back, rode with her neighbor to Kitzingen. Lisl wrapped her arms around her mother's waist. On the road, military convoys seemed to be the ever-present distraction.

When they reached Kitzingen, the rubble of the bombing more than two months earlier still blocked most of the streets. Memories of the attack replayed in Lisl's mind. She felt uneasy, her stomach ached.

The few cleared streets were blocked off. American soldiers supervised removing the rubble. With heavy equipment, Ami soldiers alongside German prisoners of war pushed the remains of demolished buildings to the side, making the roads of Kitzingen passable again.

Frau Nagel and Mama had to push their bikes over piles of rubble and around land-clearing equipment while Lisl stayed on the back of the bike.

"This is as close as we're going to get," Frau Nagel said. Lisl jumped off and took the two bags. She already imagined them filled with bottles of wine.

They leaned the bikes against a ruin and headed toward the wine cellar about two blocks away. Lisl ran beside her mother and neighbor. The rubble was more of an obstacle for Lisl because her torn shoes kept falling off.

"Here we are," Frau Nagel said. They stopped for a moment and then climbed over a huge mound of debris. Large cut rock, bricks and half-burned wooden beams lay jammed together in a pile.

"Be careful Lisl." Mama pointed at broken window glass and pieces of roof tile mixed in the debris.

Lisl recognized the crumbled three-story building by the elaborately-carved wooden posts that once graced the facade. She had always loved the carved decoration and felt sad to see it scattered, splintered and partially buried in ash. The intricate carvings–still visible–had been a landmark and the pride of the winery.

A *Halt, do not enter* sign was half hidden in the rubble. The upper three floors lay in a jumbled mass on top of the once-famous cellar below.

Two women with bottles wrapped in their skirts emerged from a hole in the pile and hurried away. Lisl thought they were running away from something. Maybe they were not supposed to take the wine.

A third woman came out of the same hole and sat down on a tightly-wedged wooden rail. She removed her shoes, turned them upside down, and poured out foul smelling liquid. Then she slipped them back on her feet, picked up her cloth bag, and hurried after her companions. Lisl wondered why her bag was dripping.

Mama, Frau Nagel and Lisl peeked down, and then climbed backward into the hole. The light became weaker. A pungent odor of stale wine took Lisl's breath away as they entered. At first she felt blinded after the bright sunshine outside. After a few moments Lisl's eyes adjusted to the dim daylight sieving through cracks of the debris above. Now she saw they were standing on the top step of a wide stairway–open on both sides. The banisters were gone with nothing to hang onto. The wobbly steps were littered with debris. Slowly and carefully they worked their way down two stories toward the bottom.

Some of the tall, exquisitely hand-carved shelves were standing undamaged against a high wall and were still holding drained barrels. The shelves on the other side, however, hung haphazardly in mid-air, held only by huge broken barrels wedged precariously against them.

A woman waded ankle deep through the stagnant wine, her dress gathered to keep it dry while avoiding broken bottles on the floor. She tried to head for the undamaged bottles on the far shelves.

"Wait for me," a woman called to her, leaving a hollow echo hanging in the dim cellar.

A drunken, one-armed man scooped up some wine from the floor which he drank from the bottom half of a broken bottle. He sang to himself while crying;

Ich hat einen Kameraten,
einen besseren find'st Du nicht.

Lisl was frightened to see him drunk and in such turmoil. His mournful song echoed in eerie repetition through the huge cellar as he waded through the wine.

Lisl and her mother made their way to the lower stone steps. Mama's face reflected uncertainty; she seemed hesitant to step down.

Frau Nagel walked ahead and into the stale wine without a second thought.

"You'd better stay here on the steps," Mama said. But the stairs started to move again, and Lisl could not let go of her mother's hand. As Frau Nagel stood in the liquid, waiting for Mama, a woman's scream echoed through the cellar.

The panic-stricken woman rushed up the stairs, looking back at a bloated body halfway submerged in the wine soup, floating face down.

People stampeded up the stairs, some fell screaming off the sides and into the smelly liquid.

Lisl and her mother sat down on the steps, holding onto the edge of the moving stairway to keep from getting pushed off. Lisl had only seen four people inside and was surprised when about a dozen stampeded up the stairs.

Mama and Frau Nagel led Lisl up the stairs and crawled through the opening.

American military as well as the German police arrived to remove the body.

Lisl overheard the German policeman say, "I don't know how he got in there. By the looks of it, he's been floating in there for a while."

A second policeman said, "But they only opened it last night."

They stood outside on top of the rubble pile. The thought of the intoxicated man drinking from the wine someone had drowned in made Lisl's stomach churn.

Mama held Lisl by her shoulders. "Breathe deeply."

Lisl took a deep breath, but inhaled the stench that escaped through a hole in the rubble pile. She was embarrassed when she was unable to stop gagging and so she vomited.

"Lisl, think of something nice, the beautiful flowers in the garden, the birds singing," her mother said.

Frau Nagel looked puzzled. "Why would that make her feel better?"

"She has to get her mind off the dead body."

Lisl removed her head scarf and wiped her face. She thought of the garden and the fresh air and her stomach settled. As she leaned against her mother, a shadow loomed over her. A Moor soldier stood in front of her. He wore a helmet, with the letters M.P. on it, which made him appear even taller. Frightened, she moved behind her mother, but he came around as well. The soldier had a kind face as he calmly looked at her. "OK?" He put his hand on her head. She looked up at him and her fear disappeared. He offered her the biggest candy bar she had ever seen. She looked at her mother who nodded. Timidly, Lisl took it from his hand and said, "*Danke shoen*," with a curtsy. He smiled, ruffled her short stubble hair and went on his way.

Lisl felt better. She tried not to think of the body floating in the wine, but she had to make a conscious effort. And, she did not look when the police loaded the body into the truck. She kept her head down to read the candy wrapper. She heard the truck drive away, but did not look up.

A policeman pulled the sign from the rubble and propped it up. But Lisl saw a few women sneak past the sign and back into the hole once he had left.

"Frau Nagel, we're going home." Mama said.

"Oh, but you didn't get any wine yet."

"It's better for Lisl if we go." Mama seemed eager to leave. Maybe she was having second thoughts about taking the wine.

"I think I will try one more time to see if I can find some unbroken bottles," Frau Nagel said.

"Do you want a bag to carry them in?" Lisl handed her one of the bags and put her chocolate in the other.

"Yes, thank you. I know I will be late for curfew." She laughed and waved goodbye.

Lisl stumbled beside her mother over the rubble mountain to get to the bike.

Mama lifted Lisl on the back, telling her, "Now you hang on tight." They started to ride along the road but had to get off several times to get around obstacles.

Lisl felt weak from her ordeal but also excited to have something to share with her family. She wrapped her arms around her mother's waist, leaning against her. "Mama, I'm sorry I got sick. Now you didn't get any wine."

"Lisl, after what I saw I wouldn't want any. Don't you worry. Besides, we're already late for curfew."

When Lisl pushed the bike up the garden path, Kurt and Dieter came running toward them. Kurt hurled himself at his mother. She caught him in her arms.

"Wait till you see what Lisl got for you."

Kurt scrambled down again and ran behind Lisl, trying to look into the bag hanging from the handlebar of the bike.

"Let's get in the house," Lisl told Kurt. She winked at Dieter who by now looked as curious as Kurt. Ellen and Charlotte, with Werner in her arms, came in as well.

"You didn't get any wine?" Ellen looked disappointed.

"No, it was a mess there." Mama shuddered.

Lisl felt guilty. Had Ellen gone with Mama, they would have come home with both bags filled to the rim.

"I got something we all can eat." Lisl tried to sound cheerful as she put the candy bar on the kitchen table.

"Oh, what a big chocolate!" Kurt squealed, his eyes fixed on the candy bar. Lisl took the wrapper off and handed it to Mama. She broke it into six even pieces so each had a double square.

Kurt gulped his first piece down in seconds.

"Don't eat it all at once; save one piece for later," Mama told him.

"How did you get it?" Dieter finally asked Lisl who couldn't wait to tell him.

"A Moor soldier gave it to me," she said, "and I wasn't scared of him. He just handed it to me when no other kids were around. He didn't throw it at me. He stood right beside me and just gave it to me." They all seemed impressed and munched on the chocolate slowly to savor the taste.

Mama laughed. "Oh Kurt, just look at you." He had tried too hard to save his second piece of chocolate, smelling and handling it until it was all over his fingers and nose.

"You may as well eat it before it disappears all over you," Lisl giggled.

Frau Nagel knocked on the door way past curfew. Lately the soldiers had not been shooting over people's heads to scare them inside.

Mama went to the front door, but did not invite her neighbor in, and when Lisl went out into the hall, she knew why. Frau Nagel's dress was soaked in wine up to her thighs. She reeked of stale wine but had managed to find two bottles.

CHAPTER 31

The End of the War

Lisl ran to the window when she heard music. Mama joined her. "I wonder what's going on in town."

"Can we go?" Lisl was curious, but she hoped it was not another parade of humiliation for her teachers.

Ellen and Charlotte also heard the music and quickly slipped into their coats. So Mama took her family into Mainbernheim.

The town square was crowded with people, Ami soldiers, and excitement. No one paid attention to curfew. An American band, followed by their military parade, marched through the south tower. American and British soldiers cheered and shouted, throwing their caps in the air.

A platform had been erected in the town square and the new Burgermeister strutted up to make a speech. He fumbled with papers in his hand, clearing his throat several times then called out, "Quiet please. Quiet." When he finally got everyone's attention he shouted, "The war is over. As of today, May eighth, the German army has surrendered." He proudly nodded in all directions, as if he, personally, had a hand in ending the war.

His speech went on at great length, but Mama walked slowly away from the podium, surrounded by her children.

Lisl saw mixed reactions reflected on people's faces. Most of the citizens went quietly about their business while others cheered. But a few looked devastated, crushed.

Lisl did not know how to feel. She looked at her mother whose silence did not tell her much either.

"We have lost the war," an old man said, shaking his head.

Mama pushed the baby carriage through the main street flanked by Dieter and Kurt. Lisl and her sisters trailed behind. After a few more speeches the music started again.

"Can we stay a while?" Ellen asked.

"Yes. But be home in a couple of hours."

Ellen and Charlotte ran back to the town square.

"Don't you want to go too?" Mama asked Lisl.

"No. I know we lost the war." Lisl shrugged her shoulders. "What else can they tell us?"

"Well, let's see now. They can tell us that the killing has stopped. People all over Germany won't have to spend their nights in air-raid shelters anymore."

Lisl looked at her mother in silence.

"And no more curfews." Mama smiled.

"Really?" Lisl brightened. "That is worth celebrating."

"Do you think all the fathers will come home now?" Dieter asked.

"We have to wait and see."

Dieter and Lisl exchanged glances when they saw Mama's sad expression and did not mention Papa again.

They strolled through the big north tower outside of town. Kurt's little voice rattled nonstop even though no one paid attention.

Lisl had expected disappointment from her mother. She remembered her tears the morning the tanks stood in the surrounding field. Now she wondered whether Mama had cried because they had occupied Mainbernheim, or because they had made such a mess of the fields. Maybe

Mama thought the enemy would shoot everyone. Lisl did not see that sadness now.

Mama looked back toward the town as if seeing it for the first time. She seemed relieved. The damage the attack had left on Mainbernheim was most apparent on the outside of the wall where big sections were demolished. Two of the smaller towers had their upper halves blown off. But the east and south parts were still intact as were most of the historical buildings. Some smaller buildings and farm compounds built back-to-back inside the north wall were completely destroyed. Yet, in some areas rebuilding had already begun. The heavy cut rocks that had been strewn over some gardens outside the wall were stacked and ready to be reused.

Lisl heard music coming from a radio in a window. She remembered when her mother had listened to the underground broadcast during the war. She would press her ear tightly against the radio, with the volume so low no one else could hear. The Third Reich had ordered its citizens not to listen to "propaganda, lies and scare tactics," as they had called it.

Weeks before the end of the war, Lisl had turned to that station quite by accident. The regular broadcast was interrupted by an eerie repetition of the first bar of Beethoven's Fifth Symphony, a sound she would not soon forget. And then came that voice.

A somber voice, informing the German people how far the enemy had advanced. "The futility of fighting will only prolong the killing."

But her mother had rushed into the room and turned it off. She did not want her children to listen to these reports in case they were questioned. Now Lisl realized her mother did expect the loss of the war; it came as no surprise.

They walked a trail beside Bundesbahn 8 along the outside of the wall. In olden times the little garden plots were a moat that surrounded the wall. Now some of the gardens were cleared of debris and replaced with vegetable plants. Other plots took a little longer. Still, glorious blooms–ignoring their situation–found their way through the debris.

Mama showed more interest in the gardens than the loss of the war. She seemed to enjoy the walk in the warm sunshine with the music coming from the town square.

"What will happen now?" Lisl asked.

"Nothing, I suppose. People will rebuild their homes and families can hope again. Life will go on." Her mother looked off into the distance through hazel eyes.

Deep in thought, Lisl walked behind her mother and brothers. Mama led them back into town through a narrow side door in the wall.

The parade was still in progress with more music and boring speeches. But Lisl did enjoy one small part of the Burgermeister's speech when he said, "Curfew is lifted as of today."

She grinned at Dieter when he threw his arms up, shouting "*Hurrah.*"

The pastor's wife sprang into action to do her part in the celebration by gathering some of the children. A few of Lisl's classmates came running, asking her if she wanted to sing on the platform. Lisl shook her head; she did not feel like celebrating, not until her father was home safe. She needed a little time to think, to sort it all out.

The loss of the war had come much earlier for Lisl. It came when the tanks surrounded Mainbernheim. When they feared for their lives. When curfew kept her from going into the garden, and when their secret place had been invaded.

Before the occupation, she did not think her family would live through the war. She had often wondered what it would be like to get shot. Now the fear for her family was lifted from her mind, but she still worried about her father.

As Lisl watched American soldiers dance in the streets, she thought the word *enemy* did not fit anymore. She would have to think of a different name. *Ami* would have to do for now, as most of the townspeople called the American soldiers. But she would have to think of a more fitting word.

Slowly, she realized the full meaning of the war's end. The shooting had finally stopped for good. The German army could not reclaim Mainbernheim as they had Michelfeld where families perished in the second attack. It felt good to be alive. She took a deep breath and smiled into the sunshine.

CHAPTER 32

Flowers for Mama

Mother's Day was an exciting time for Lisl. The day before, Lisl, with her sisters and brothers, visited neighbors and friends, asking if they could spare some flowers.

Frau Neumeier gave Kurt three of the biggest red peonies from her garden. Each blossom was as big as his head. He took them slowly, almost breathlessly, from her hand, looked at her with his big blue eyes and made her smile.

"*Danke shoen, Frau Neumeier.*" He held the peonies with both hands, carefully as not to crush them, and proudly walked home. Lisl hid them in the girls' bedroom next to Dieter's jar of white lilacs from Frau Herman's garden, and Charlotte's bearded irises from Frau Nagel's garden. Ellen had collected a mix from many different gardens and hers was by far the biggest and most colorful jar. Some of the neighbors saved the best flowers for the Lindner children, knowing they would do little chores for them in return.

Lisl looked forward to the beautiful peach-colored roses that Dr. Hetzner always saved for her. The doctor and his wife lived on Bahnweg in a big house outside the wall. He had a hothouse in his garden where he grew the most beautiful roses.

In anticipation Lisl raced with Dieter to the doctor's house. She was so excited she couldn't feel the sharp pebbles under her bare feet. She ran up the steps, two at a time, and rang the bell. The door opened and Frau Hetzner looked startled at Lisl.

"Oh, Lisl, I forgot about you. Our greenhouse was hit in the attack. The roses were damaged as well. Maybe my neighbors will give you some of their flowers."

"But they don't have roses," Lisl said.

Frau Hetzner shook her head. "No. But they do have lovely lilacs."

"That's all right. I'm sorry you lost the roses. I'll see if I can find something."

With a sad smile, the woman closed the door.

Dieter walked ahead of Lisl down the wide stone steps. "Sorry Lisl. What a shame," he said.

They strolled along Bahnweg, looking at all the flowers that grew in gardens of big stately homes. The narrow road was lined with lilacs in bloom, but Mama had lilacs in her own garden except for the white ones Dieter had found for her.

"Maybe the lilies of the valley are blooming in the forest. Mama loves them." Dieter tried to cheer her up.

"Yeah, let's get some." They ran along Bahnweg and onto the road that wound its way through the woods toward Michelfeld. It used to be a beautiful walk, but now the fields between Mainbernheim and Michelfeld were criss-crossed with tank tracks and pockmarked with artillery hits. The destruction of the wheat fields and nearby farmhouses told of a desperate battle. Lisl realized how naive she had been to think enemy tanks would keep to the narrow road.

They left the road and fields and walked into the woods. The deeper they ventured into the forest, the more beautiful it became with fewer reminders of war. Lisl stopped and sniffed the air; she could smell the flowers even though she did not see them.

The forest was still. Lisl was aware of the stark contrast between the war-beaten fields and the serenity of the woods. Never had the forest been so clean. Twigs, sticks and pinecones that usually had littered the ground were picked clean by people in their search for firewood. Dead, lower branches of the pines were stripped as well, giving the trees a taller, greener appearance.

"Maybe we'll see a deer," Dieter whispered as they walked softly along the narrow path.

Fragrant evergreens reached for the sky. Steaming shafts of sunlight illuminated patches of mossy ground where lilies of the valley grew through the green carpet.

They stood in awe watching the afternoon sun play in the treetops. A cuckoo called close by, and farther away another one seemed to answer. The moist air and the scent of evergreens and moss, mixed with the delicious scent of the lilies, made an unforgettable perfume. Dieter and Lisl stood in silence, breathing in the air, forgetting the time.

"We'd better pick the flowers and go home before Mama starts to worry," Lisl said.

There was no end to the lilies. They picked flowers until their hands could hold no more.

"At least they don't grow in our own garden." Lisl consoled herself.

༺ა

On Mother's Day morning the girls got up early and set a pretty breakfast table. Lisl circled her mother's place setting with a necklace of wild flowers the way they always did on birthdays and Mother's Day. The table was laden with large bouquets that made Lisl's short jar of lilies almost invisible.

When Mama came into the room she stopped in the doorway.

"*Alles Gute zum Muttertag.*" Overwhelmed by hugs, she stood in awe at the sight of all the flowers, and as she came closer Lisl noticed her mother's eyes searching for the roses that had graced the table in the past. After leaning over the bouquets and smelling their sweet scent, Mama picked up the short jar of lilies of the valley and lingered over them just a little longer. She never mentioned roses.

The week before Mother's Day, Ellen and Charlotte had exchanged work for flour at the Scheck's mill. And Lisl and Dieter had gone from camp to camp, trying to get some sugar from the American soldiers. Dieter, after many tries, had found a soldier who spoke a little German. He understood Dieter wanted the sugar for his mother's cake. The American soldier gave him six little envelopes, but did not take the two eggs Dieter had offered in exchange. The soldier told him to use them in his mother's cake. So they had enough ingredients for Charlotte to make a wonderful bundt cake for Mother's Day.

Now the cake stood like a centerpiece among the flowers. Everyone's eyes were focused on the cake, but no one asked to cut it. Lisl watched her mother trying to hide her tears. She looked like she wanted to say something, but swallowed hard and handed Charlotte the knife.

Charlotte placed the first slice ceremoniously on Mama's plate. Kurt's eyes followed it all the way there. When a piece slid on his plate he smiled at his mother, then at Charlotte, but he did not eat it right away, he admired it first. Mama looked at her children, and Lisl saw happiness in spite of her hazel eyes.

Later that night when everyone was asleep, Lisl awoke with a start. Mama stood over her and gently stroked her face. Lisl sat up, but Mama put her finger to her lips.

"Lisl. Can you hear it?" she whispered.

Lisl held her breath, listening. Then the unmistakable song of the nightingale rang through the night. She scrambled out of bed to join her mother who opened the window. They stood side by side, taking in the beautiful recital. There was movement on the road below the garden. Two American soldiers walked slowly, and then stood still. They too listened and seemed to enjoy the serenade.

"Better go back to sleep now." Mama tucked Lisl in. But she could not sleep. "The nightingale did come back," she whispered. Wanting to hear every note, she waited for the next verse to ring clear through the silence of the fragrant night. But finally she no longer could stay awake and, carried by the lullaby of a little bird, she fell asleep.

CHAPTER 33

Back to School

Mama called her neighbors to her house to organize a repair party. The next day all the residents of Muehlenweg came armed with shovels, picks, buckets and wheelbarrows to repair neighborhood gardens. Lisl was excited to see so many happy faces. The women felt grateful that their homes were still standing, although some neighbors told of cracked windows and foundations.

Lisl thought of all the people in town who were not so lucky. Some of their homes lay in rubble and some people had died. Whenever she thought of Traudel, her heart ached and sometimes she dreamed her friend was still alive. But then Lisl would wake with the pain and vision of Traudel lying motionless in the dust.

The children of their neighborhood were busy digging and scraping the scattered soil from the explosions to fill in artillery holes. Lisl found it puzzling that there was never enough scattered soil to do the job so the neighbors gathered some from different locations to level the ground again. Charlotte and Ellen sang while working and most of the children joined in, all hoping for a better future.

Farmers who had come home from the war and women with no time to mourn took back their fields. Horses and oxen pulled the metal debris of the crashed airplane into a pile and filled artillery holes.

Lisl saw the hope in the farmers' faces. They talked of better crops in the coming years. Others leveled soil the best they could and artfully planted crops around the deepest holes like intended designs, or grim monuments.

Lisl and Dieter watched nature's celebration, a spectacular show of colors–the magic of flowers appeared almost overnight. Down in the meadow by the mill creek grew the most beautiful wild flowers. Mama soon ran out of fruit jars to put them in, but always looked surprised and happy when Lisl and Dieter came through the door with more flowers.

In the midst of joy, Lisl heard the town crier announce that school will be open again the next day. She was excited, but also disappointed. Her time of picking flowers and working in the garden was cut short.

On the first day of school, local doctors came to each classroom. The children were examined and sorted like apples. One group was sent to the right while the other group to the left side of the room. After the doctor had finished with the examinations he announced that the group on the left would be given a school lunch.

Lisl was delighted. She stood among the smiling students. Now she could bring home her lunch to share with her family. But when she looked at the disappointed faces across the room, she wondered what made the doctor pick some children over others.

At noon she was told to go to the main floor. There, the first-grade teacher told children of all grades that they were malnourished and therefore eligible for school lunch. The students looked each other over, trying to see if they could detect this ailment.

"Malnourished," one of the eight-graders repeated. Lisl never thought of herself as malnourished; hungry yes, but so were all the other children. Those children looked no different than the malnourished.

When she realized they had to eat lunch at school she was disappointed. Ellen, who sat in the lucky group with some of her classmates, winked at Lisl.

The children–seated at a long table–were served little bowls of boiled oats with lots of cream and sugar, something Lisl was not used to. A local woman served the food, pouring one scoop into each bowl. When Mama made hot cereal it was made with water and sometimes a little applesauce for sweetener, but even that was not available lately.

Most of the children brought the bowl to their mouths, eagerly slurping the cereal as though someone might take it from them. A few from the unlucky group snuck in, looking hungrily over the shoulders of the lucky children.

Lisl tasted this delicious rich food, but had trouble swallowing. Too many eyes followed each spoonful to her mouth. After she ate a few bites, her stomach started to hurt and she put down her spoon. A small hand from behind her chair took the bowl and within seconds put it back in front of her, empty. But thanks to the boy's speed she had no time to worry if this would get her in trouble. The boy smiled at Lisl, wiped his lips with the back of his hand, and slipped out of the room.

Some of the unlucky children were quite skinny, and Lisl could not understand why the lunch was given to her. She never looked pale like Ellen, or as skinny as Charlotte. Some people even called Lisl "Apple Cheeks." Mama had told her that her face had been exposed to the frosty air too long. That was why her cheeks were red and, in cold weather, purple.

Lisl wondered why Dieter and Charlotte were not included in the malnourished group since they ate the same food at home.

After a few days the teachers did not check on the children to see who actually ate the lunches. Lisl managed to share with Dieter and sometimes other hungry classmates. Charlotte was glad that Ellen was willing to share as well.

When teachers and officials realized they would have to feed all of the children to make the program work, they solved the problem by eliminating school lunches.

CHAPTER 34

Wrong Time for Heil Hitler

Lisl had her eyes on the vegetables long before they were ready to harvest. In early June, spinach, radishes, and some cutting lettuce were finally ready, although Mama thought they could have grown little bigger had she not needed the food now.

Spinach Florentine was Lisl's favorite. Mama cooked the spinach leaves lightly, put them through the meat grinder, and mixed in a white sauce made with flour and water. Home-grown vegetables became the main meal along with some potatoes the farmers paid Mama for her mending. Sometimes Mama made scrambled eggs to go with the dinner. But most of the time the eggs were traded. Almost all of the food the family consumed came from their garden now.

Lisl and Dieter kept the young vegetable plants watered and growing. As soon as one bed was cleared, they planted other vegetable seedlings in their place.

Still, the meals remained meager. Charlotte and Ellen worked for farmers, hoping to get some food in payment for their work. But when the farmers tried to pay with Reichsmark, Charlotte became upset. No one would accept this currency–as Mama had found out some time ago.

Although Charlotte was very thin, she worried more about the family than herself. "I wish I could find a real job. One that pays with more food," she said. "I feel worthless."

A lady from town told Mama about a farm where children could eat good food on a regular basis in exchange for light housework.

"This is perfect for you, Charlotte; at least you could eat well. You are getting too thin."

Charlotte frowned, shaking her head. "I don't want to be away overnight Mama."

"Maybe you would worry less if you had chores away from home." Mama sat beside Charlotte, stroking her hair.

"What about you? You still would be hungry."

"We will have more of our own vegetables soon."

The next day Mama made arrangements and the farmer invited the whole family for lunch. They went by train, about thirty-five kilometers from Mainbernheim. The farmhouse was spotless. The lady served pork roast, mashed potatoes, and a big cauliflower smothered with a thick cream sauce. Lisl had not eaten so well in a long time.

Lisl looked around the kitchen. "Where are all the children who work here?"

"At the moment we only have three. They had their meal earlier."

Still Lisl wondered why she did not see them around the house. Mama looked pleased that Charlotte would be getting that kind of food and so she signed Charlotte on to do light household chores.

Although Charlotte was still a little apprehensive, she packed a few things into her little suitcase and took the train the next morning, farmhouse bound.

Kurt moped. He missed his favorite sister. Ellen looked depressed as well. She gave up on Lisl when she could not get even the smallest argument going. Charlotte's absence was most apparent in the bedroom. Lisl found the silence and the lack of her sisters' squabbling eerie. Ellen was so unhappy she even tried to talk about boys to Lisl.

She whispered from her bed. "Do you remember Heinrich from my class?"

"Is he the one with the silly laugh?"

"He does not have a silly laugh. I think he has such a cute smile." Ellen's eyes strayed to the ceiling as though Heinrich were smiling down on her.

Lisl thought she looked rather weird. "Well, what about him?" She tried to bring her sister back to earth.

"I think he likes me." Ellen tucked the covers around her chin with a dreamy look on her face.

"How can you tell?" Lisl thought Ellen had some insight on boys and she had better pay attention just in case she needed it someday.

Ellen gazed at Lisl with an expression Lisl had never seen. "He pulled my hair at school today."

"What? I thought you said he liked you. Why didn't you smack him? I would have."

"Oh Lisl, you just don't understand. You're too young. Charlotte understood." And that was the end of boy talk. Lisl had always thought her sisters shared some special secret. Now she knew what Charlotte and Ellen always whispered about—boys! Yuck.

Two weeks passed. Charlotte came home for a visit. But to Mama's disappointment Charlotte looked just as thin, only now she looked haggard as well. Her hands and face were rough and sun-dried.

"Are they putting you to work in the fields? I thought you'd only have to do light housework," Mama said.

"Well, they are short of field workers in the daytime. I do housework in the evenings." Sitting slumped at the table, Charlotte rested her head on her sunburned arms.

Mama stroked her hair. "The farmer is working you too hard in the fields, Charlotte. All that good food will do you no good if you're too tired to eat."

But Charlotte's only response was. "Can I take a little nap?" Within minutes she was asleep on the couch.

Lisl watched her sister, gently brushing the hair from her sunburned face. She wondered what had changed Charlotte in such a short time. She had lost her spirit to fight with Ellen or play with Kurt and the baby.

Mama watched her exhausted daughter. "I'm not going to let her go back."

Kurt cheered. "Oh, good! She can stay home and play with me."

"It was way too quiet around here anyway," Dieter said.

Lisl smiled. "We will have lots of vegetables soon for Charlotte. Besides the local farmers will need more help."

Ellen was quiet. She had not voiced her opinion. But Lisl knew by that twinkle in her eyes that she had already thought of a welcome-home argument.

From then on, life seemed more normal. Charlotte was home. The local farmers welcomed her help. But best of all, they paid her with food, which made Charlotte happy.

The whisperings about boys at night, and the arguments and name-calling only reassured Lisl that everything was fine–Ellen and Charlotte were happy again.

The weather was warm and dry and keeping the vegetable bed watered was important. Lisl also watered the flowers on Grandmother's grave every day. She was about to walk to the other side of town to the cemetery where Mama had planted beautiful flowers on the grave.

"Can I come too Lisl?" Kurt wiped his hands on his shirt to show Lisl that he was clean and ready to go.

Mama wrapped the baby in a blanket and placed him in the carriage. "Yes, you can go with Lisl and the baby."

Kurt ran down the garden path ahead of her, oblivious to the pebbles under his little bare feet.

Lisl pushed the baby carriage through town, stopping now and then when people admired Werner. She eagerly told them all about the cute things her baby brother could do.

When Lisl approached the cemetery the scent of the big exotic-looking evergreens was irresistible. It seemed like she was entering a different, quieter world. The evergreen shrubs and trees looked strange and majestic and did not grow anywhere else in Mainbernheim. Mournful-sounding little doves added an appropriate mood.

Two tall stone angels with a headstone between stood watch over one gravesite. Kurt liked the smaller angels better. "They look friendlier," he said. "The big ones have scary faces."

Lisl left Kurt and Werner by Grandmother's grave while she ran to the basin to fill a watering can. On her way back, she saw old Herr Koenig pass her brothers. Kurt raised his hand and said, "Heil Hitler." The old man stopped, turned, and slapped Kurt's face so hard it knocked him to the ground. Koenig kept on walking and quickened his step when Lisl screamed, "Why did you do that? He's only a little boy." But he did not turn and hurried through the gate. Lisl dipped her hand in the cool water and held it on Kurt's red face, trying to console him.

"But Sister Rosa told me to say Heil Hitler." Kurt sobbed. Lisl patted his back. No wonder he was confused. He was still crying when they got home. His cheek was red and swollen.

Mama was furious. "How can anyone be so heartless?" She made sure Kurt understood that he could say *Gruess Gott* again. Kurt cheered up when Mama surprised him with six little chirping baby chicks. She had exchanged some fresh vegetables for them. Kurt was delighted and so were Dieter and Lisl.

"Mama, can this one be mine? Look, it's starting to grow little feathers on its downy wings." Dieter cupped his hands protectively around one baby chick.

"Can I have this one?" Kurt tried to pick one up, but it hopped out of his hands every time he almost had it captured. "I think I'll name mine *Lang-Bein* because it has the longest legs. It always escapes out of my hands." He laughed.

Lisl felt sorry for the babies for not having a mother to take care of them. They named their chicks and gladly took on the responsibility of caring for them.

The chicks chirped noisily. "They must be hungry," Lisl said. She tried to feed them a handful of the grain they had stored in the empty rabbit cage, but the chicks were too small to eat it. Lisl ground the grain in the coffee grinder, letting Kurt turn the handle. When she tried to feed the chicks again, they eagerly pecked at the grain.

೧೨

Summer came with a gentle warm breeze. Schools closed, giving the children more time to help in the fields and work in their own gardens.

Lisl had loved the weekend rituals as far back as she could remember. Mama would scrub the stone-tile kitchen floor on Saturday and Lisl would dust the furniture and put a big bouquet of flowers in the living room. Dieter swept the garden path and everyone looked forward to Sunday.

On Sunday after church, the family sat in the garden, enjoying a day of rest, except for a little vegetable watering. The only thing missing was her father and the cake Mama used to make on Saturday for the Sunday Coffee Klatch.

In summer, with the weather's cooperation, the family ate all their meals outside on a square wooden table under the big cherry tree. Most of their activities and discussions took place there.

Now that the war had ended, the American soldiers gave up their lookout posts on Muehlenweg and confined themselves mostly to larger cities. Tanks and other military vehicles had moved away as well. So the garden became the peaceful country setting it used to be.

Even with so many chores to do, Dieter and Lisl always found a chance to return to the stone break and their fantasies of finding prehistoric shells and treasures.

CHAPTER 35

Rum and Coca-Cola

July arrived on a heat wave and Lisl had her eyes on the big cherry tree in their garden. She loved to help her sisters climb the highest branches to select only the ripened fruit. When they had filled a basket, Lisl and her brothers took it to the American camps in the fields farther away.

After walking what seemed forever, Kurt slowed down and wiped his face. "I'm so hot and hungry." He looked at the cherries and then at Lisl.

Dieter's eyes strayed longingly to the basket as well, but he kept silent.

"All right just a few." Lisl handed the boys some cherries. "But we'll have to save the rest for trading. We can pick more when we get home."

When they neared a camp, Dieter took the basket from Lisl and, in his business-like manner, walked to the jeeps where some of the American soldiers sat listening to their country music.

"Hallo," he said as he approached them, showing them the cherries. "Would you like to trade these cherries for some soap, sugar or cigarettes?"

The soldiers jumped off their jeeps and started to eat the cherries before a deal was made.

"They like them." He smiled at Lisl.

One of the soldiers gave Dieter a bar of soap and a candy bar. He showed it to Lisl with a big grin. Soon the basket was empty. But he smiled when another soldier put five little envelopes of sugar and a candy bar in the basket.

While Dieter was negotiating, Kurt had wandered off to the next jeep where he watched soldiers drink Coca-Cola from a bottle. He stood in front of them for a while and then asked, "Can I have a taste of your drink please?" The Amis laughed at first, not understanding what he had said. Kurt licked his lips while watching the soldiers drink. One of the soldiers offered him a drink. He and his buddies laughed when Kurt, who had never tasted Coca-Cola, drank the rest of the bottle.

The soldier kept giving him more until Lisl noticed Kurt seemed to be having trouble standing. She took him by the hand, trying to lead him home, but he staggered and fell to his knees. Lisl picked him up and put him on his feet. But again he slumped down. She helped him up again, supporting him under his arms, but he collapsed.

"I think he has heat stroke," she shouted to Dieter who came running to help stand him up. But Kurt's legs were like putty. Lisl, close to crying, picked him up and carried him away from the jeep. She could not understand why some of the soldiers were laughing. Could they not see he was sick?

Ordinarily she would have carried him piggy-back, which was easier because he would hang on to her. But now he was limp and lifeless and she had to hold him tight to keep him from slipping out of her arms.

"Kurt, hang on to me." He did not respond. Tears rolled down Lisl's cheeks while she struggled along. After a while, he got too heavy. Dieter took his turn while she carried the basket. They switched every hundred meters or so. The road back to the house seemed endless. When they finally got to their garden, Dieter ran up to the house ahead of

Lisl, shouting, "Mama, come quick. Something is wrong with Kurt."

Mama hurried down the garden path, took Kurt from Lisl, carried him into the house and laid him on her bed. She smelled his breath and shouted at Lisl, "Who gave him the drink?"

"Some soldiers gave him Coca-Cola," Lisl said.

"Oh, Lisl, they gave him alcohol with the Coca-Cola. Did you and Dieter have any?"

Confused, Lisl shook her head. "No."

"Good." Mama felt Kurt's pulse.

Lisl did not think this was necessary. She only had to look at his chest to see how fast and irregular his heart was beating.

Mama scooped Kurt into her arms ran for the door. "Take care of the baby. I have to take Kurt to the doctor."

"Will he be all right?" Lisl asked. But her mother had already left. Lisl watched from the window as Mama ran down the path with Kurt in her arms and soon disappeared along Muehlenweg.

Dieter came to the window beside Lisl. "Do you think the doctor can make him better?"

"I don't know. Mama couldn't even take him on the bike," Lisl thought out loud. "It would have been so much faster." They both stood frozen by the window for more than an hour while baby Werner slept peacefully.

Finally they saw Mama carrying Kurt in her arms. Lisl ran down to her, took Kurt from her arms and took him up the path and into the house. He was sound asleep.

"What did the doctor do to him?" Lisl asked.

"He got some of the Coca-Cola out of his stomach and gave him a shot." Mama's voice sounded tired. "He said it will take a day or so to get the alcohol out of his system. If he doesn't improve in a day, I must bring him back."

Lisl put Kurt on her mother's bed. He still had a racing heartbeat, only now he had red splotches over his face and body as well.

Mama lay down beside Kurt. Poor Mama. She had run to the doctor's office with Kurt in her arms and then back again. She looked exhausted, breathing almost as hard as Kurt.

"Mama, go to sleep. We will keep working in the garden and look after the baby," Lisl said. She motioned Dieter out and shut the door.

In the late afternoon Charlotte and Ellen came home from working in the farmers' fields. "Where's Mama?" Charlotte asked.

Dieter told them what had happened, but Lisl did not let them in to see Kurt so as not to disturb Mama's sleep.

She came out of the bedroom an hour later. "Kurt is still asleep, but his heart races and he thrashes around."

Charlotte fixed dinner–potatoes and spinach. After the meal Mama went back to watch over Kurt.

Charlotte and Ellen went in to see him. They stood somberly at the foot of the bed.

"It's your fault. Why didn't you watch him?" Ellen whispered to Lisl.

"I didn't know they gave him alcohol, I thought it was Coca-Cola," Lisl said. Yet she did blame herself. She should have known that something was wrong when the soldiers acted amused when he drank it.

The girls cleaned the kitchen while Dieter sat on the little kitchen bench, his shoulders slumped. The basket with the soap, sugar and candy bars stood ignored on the kitchen windowsill. They all waited for something to happen.

Lisl hoped to see Kurt come out of the bedroom, chatting away. But no sound came from behind the door.

After washing up they all went to bed. But Lisl could not sleep. After an hour of silence Charlotte sat up in her bed.

"Lisl? Are you awake?" Charlotte whispered.

"Yes."

"I can't get to sleep either," Ellen said.

"I'm sorry. I should have watched him better."

"It wasn't your fault," Charlotte whispered again. "How could you have known?"

After a while Ellen whispered, "Lisl, I'm sorry. I didn't mean what I said. I was just worried."

"I know. It's all right."

Off and on throughout the night Lisl heard Kurt trying to vomit even after nothing was left in his stomach. He slept most of next day, and when he awoke, he complained of a bad headache. By evening he felt better.

"Kurt, promise me you will never take a drink from anyone." Mama tried to impress on him.

"Why?"

"Because it was the drinks the soldiers gave you that made you sick."

"It was Coca-Cola," he said. "It was good."

"No Kurt, the Coca-Cola had alcohol in it. I don't want you to take any more drinks. Now promise."

Reluctantly, he said, "I promise, Mama."

CHAPTER 36

Keeping a Secret

In late August the landscape looked tired, but the dry heat was the perfect weather for harvesting sugar beets. The cool mornings made the work in the fields easier. Charlotte and Ellen, who were used to getting up early, woke Lisl. She was not an early riser, especially when the sun was not up yet. Still Lisl preferred to work in cooler conditions.

The farmer had dug the beets the day before. Now they lay in lines on top of the field between dry chunks of soil. Frau Zimmerman drove the oxen-drawn wagon carefully between the rows of exposed beets.

Lisl and her sisters scrambled after the wagon in their bare feet, trying to keep up with the fast-moving oxen. The sugar beets were about the size of a head and the girls needed both hands to pick them up. After a few hours of lifting them over a high-sided wagon, the beets seemed to be getting bigger and heavier. At least Ellen and Charlotte had no energy to argue with each other. Lisl's feet felt sore from walking over the hard chunks of dried earth and she could see her sisters suffered as well.

"I wonder what they'll pay us," Charlotte whispered without looking up from her work.

"I hope she doesn't pay us with these beets," Lisl said. "Maybe we should tell Frau Zimmerman we don't have rabbits anymore."

Ellen looked up with a smile. "I think they have red beets and carrots too. Maybe we'll get some of those."

The wagon was filled to the top, and they had a chance to rest while waiting for the next wagon.

Ellen had brought a bottle of water and bread to share with her sisters.

"If we get done early, maybe Mama will let us go swimming." Ellen motioned a dive.

Lisl brightened. "Maybe she will come with us."

The thought of a cool dip made the work go faster. By three in the afternoon the field was cleared.

"Girls, you have done a great job, and fast too," Frau Zimmerman said. "If you want, you can bring a hand wagon this evening, and I will fill it up for you."

"Will you be harvesting red beets and carrots soon?" Ellen asked. "We would like some of those instead. We don't have rabbits anymore."

"If you come back tomorrow, we will be moving to the north field to harvest the red beets. And if you help, I'll give you some of those. You can have some carrots too, but we've already got them out."

"Oh, we'll be there," Charlotte said.

The sun spread its hot rays over the dry fields and Lisl was happy the work was over for the day. She stretched her arms above her head and stood up straight. It felt good after bending over so long.

Dust clouds flew up behind their bare, running feet on their way home.

Ellen laughed, pointing at Lisl and Charlotte.

"You should see yourselves. You look like you've been dragged through the dirt."

"Look who's talking. You look just as dusty," Charlotte said.

Lisl took off the head scarf she still wore to hide her uneven haircut and dusted herself off.

"Do you want me to clean you off?" Lisl offered, but Ellen took the scarf from her hand.

"No, leave it. I think it will make a perfect reason to go swimming. Let Mama see us like this," Ellen said. Her blue eyes sparkled from her dirty face as she threw a handful of dust on Lisl. As usual Ellen was right.

As they entered the garden Mama cried out, "Oh, look at you; you've been working too hard." She pointed to the table under the cherry tree. "Sit down while I get you something to eat and drink."

Lisl could tell Mama did not want them inside the house.

She brought cold linden tea and some bread, but also a towel. "You'd better wash up before you eat." She pointed to the rain barrel.

"Wouldn't it be nice to go swimming now?" Lisl asked.

Mama looked at her daughters whose eyes stayed fixed on hers, eagerly awaiting her answer.

"Yes. You can go. I'm sure you would like to cool off," she said. "You can take the boys along."

Excited, Kurt hopped around, and Dieter dropped his garden tool. He too was hot and his face brightened when Lisl mentioned swimming in Eichelsee–a small lake near the railroad tracks.

"Don't you want to come?" Lisl asked her mother.

"No. I'll stay here with the baby; maybe take a little nap." She brought out some large towels and the girls' swimsuits. Lisl and her sisters wasted no time and ate their bread on the way after gulping down some tea.

Charlotte's and Ellen's arms became a swing for Kurt on their way to the lake. When he tired, they took turns carrying him piggyback.

The three-kilometer hike through fields to Eichelsee had no shade along the way.

"By the time we get there, we'll really need that swim," Dieter said, his face red.

When they came to the lake, hordes of children were splashing and squealing in the water.

After the girls had changed in the booth they ran down the wooden steps and jumped into the lake to join Dieter who always was the first one in the water. The boys had worn their shorts all day; they now became swimming trunks.

Kurt stood on the edge of the dock, hopping around, but would not jump in.

Charlotte swam around the lake and back to the dock where Kurt still hovered, trying to get up enough nerve to get into the water.

"Kurt, come on in, I'll catch you," Charlotte called to him.

"It's too deep."

"No, it's not. Come on." She splashed water on him to cool him off, but he just ran farther back to avoid getting wet.

Tall water irises and other aquatic vegetation grew in the far end of the lake. Ellen, Lisl and Dieter swam to the back near the reeds, where the water was deep. Not many children dared to swim there.

Dieter showed off his diving skills, disappearing in one place and popping up in another–sometimes behind his sisters.

"Dieter, where are you?" Lisl shouted when he stayed under too long. But soon his head popped up between the root mass of the water irises, laughing at Lisl for worrying.

Lisl dog paddled in circles–she was tired and wanted to swim where she would feel the ground beneath her feet. She gazed across the water, looking for Dieter, who had disappeared again.

Now Ellen too seemed alarmed when he did not come up. They swam near the weeds where they last saw him.

"Dieter, it's not funny anymore," Lisl called out. She saw a disturbance between the reeds, a hand reached up.

"He is in trouble!" Ellen shouted. They splashed through the water to get to him, but again he had disappeared.

"He must be there." Lisl searched the place where she had seen his hand.

Frantically they dog paddled the area until Ellen saw his hand again. "There he is," she shouted. She grabbed onto his hand and pulled, but he was entangled in roots.

Lisl fished for his other hand. Together they yanked his limp body lose and swam with him toward the dock.

Lisl sobbed. He had surely drowned. "Why didn't I watch him more closely?"

But then he coughed, took in a big gulp of air and spewed water from his mouth. He suddenly panicked, thrashing about. Ellen and Lisl could barely hang on to him. Eventually they pulled him to the dock. Charlotte came running and started to cry along with Ellen and Lisl.

"Put him on his stomach," Charlotte commanded. Then she pushed down on his back until he threw up more water and started to cough again.

Dieter tried to turn over, but Charlotte kept pushing down on his back. He sat up, trying to say something, but could only cough. Annoyed, he motioned his sisters away.

"I'm all right. I got caught in the weeds." His words sounded weak between violent coughing fits.

Kurt walked around Dieter, silently observing his brother, and when he saw Dieter smile, he looked at him and said, "You swim like a frog."

Dieter's laughter brought on another coughing spell, but eventually he calmed down.

After Dieter had fully recovered he wanted to get back into the water.

Charlotte blocked his way. "No more diving. Promise?"

He tried to smile when he looked into her frightened face. "All right. I promise."

Charlotte finally talked Kurt into climbing on her back and she swam around the lake with him. When she held him around the waist he kicked his legs. "Look Lisl, I'm swimming," he shouted to her. After a while he wanted to go back to the warm dock. Lisl too stood on the boardwalk shivering although the sun was still hot.

"We'd better go home now," Charlotte decided.

They stayed in their bathing suits to stay cool for their walk back on the hot and dusty road.

Ellen whispered to Charlotte, who then whispered to Dieter and Lisl, "Let's not tell Mama about Dieter, or she will never let us get near the water again."

Kurt pouted when no one told him. "I want to know the secret too."

Charlotte whispered, "Dieter swims like a frog. Shh, don't tell anyone." She put her finger on her lips.

When they got home Mama asked, "How was the water?"

"Fine." Dieter said without looking at her. "But we're just as hot now as when we left." He finally lifted his head and smiled at her.

They hosed themselves off before they went inside to change. No one mentioned Dieter's near drowning.

"Mama, do you want to know a secret?" Kurt whispered to his mother.

"What's the secret?"

"Dieter swims like a frog."

CHAPTER 37

Snake in the Grass

Rhythmic motions of swinging scythes in graceful dance of summer, the farmers walked the fields. The wheat harvest had begun. After the wheat was cut, oxen dragged big rakes across the field to gather the treasure into rows where it was loaded onto wagons and taken to the barns.

Dieter and Kurt looked forward to the big threshing machines operating in the barn with the bullet holes in the door. Lisl hoped that the owl family had left their nest because the noise would surely be frightening.

Now Lisl and Dieter's work began. With the farmers' permission they collected the wheat the rakes had missed.

Today they got up early to be first in the fields. Charlotte and Ellen had already left to help farmers harvest red beets. Lisl envied her sisters for being able to spring out of bed with the first sign of daylight.

Kurt got up, rubbing his eyes. When he saw Lisl and Dieter getting ready to leave he ran to his mother. "I want to go too."

Mama pulled his pajama top over his head. "Well, I don't know. They may stay a long time. Are you sure you want to stay all day?"

"Yes. I want to help too." Kurt was getting himself ready, struggling into his clothes.

"Kurt, if you want to come with us you'll have to put on your shoes," Lisl said.

"You don't have your shoes on."

"It's because they're all torn up. If I wear them now they will fall apart and I won't have any shoes for school."

"But Dieter's shoes are not torn."

"They will be soon," Lisl said.

Mama wrapped a half slice of bread for each and gave them a bottle of cold linden tea to take along.

Lisl loved the fresh, clean air of the morning when the dust and heat had settled during the night. Although she was not an early riser, she did not mind getting up early in summer when the birds woke her with a song and the rising sun made it hard to sleep in.

Kurt watched Lisl and Dieter slide their bare feet across the stubbles of the cut wheat, bending the stubble over to avoid getting pricked.

"I want to slide too." Kurt tried to take off his shoes.

"Oh no, Kurt, you have to leave your shoes on. We need you to run across the field with our bundles," Lisl urged. "You know we can't run with bare feet, so you have to do it for us."

Kurt thought for a moment. Then with a proud smile he said, "Yeah. You need me."

"We sure do. You help a lot," Lisl assured him.

He clumsily retied his laces and stood ready to run.

"Kurt, you can be our scout," Dieter said. "You can tell us where the wheat is so we don't have to walk too much."

Dieter and Lisl walked from side to side in the field, collecting wheat, holding it by the stems, plump grain up, like flowers.

"If we were giants, we wouldn't feel the stubble even if we stepped right on top of it," Dieter said. Lisl thought maybe his feet were sore.

"I don't want to be a giant." Lisl motioned an imaginary stick. "I would like to have a magic wand and have all the grain come to the side of the field already bundled."

"If you had a magic wand you could just turn the grain into bread or even cake," Dieter theorized.

"I'd grow a cake tree." Kurt hopped up and down in the dusty field, trying to join their game.

"Cake doesn't grow, Kurt. It has to be baked," Dieter said.

"I would bake a giant cake." Kurt motioned the size of the cake.

"I guess we'd better just get the grain for now. We still can have bread when Mama bakes some, if we find enough wheat," Lisl said.

Kurt wandered off scouting for the grain.

Lisl silently dreamed of flying to far away places where stores had shelves stocked with food. Dieter, of course, would fly with her.

Dieter was the first to tie up his bundle. His hand no longer fit around the stems.

"Kurt, come and get the first one," he called out.

"Here I come, fast as the wind." Kurt came stumbling across the stubbles, arms stretched.

"If you wait a moment you can take mine, too." Lisl tied her bundle, and, along with Dieter's, put it in Kurt's arms.

Kurt had to lean backward when he walked to avoid dragging the stems on the ground. He took the bundles to the edge of the field where he lined them up neatly until they faced just the right way. His light blond curls bobbed up and down in his eagerness and his face flushed from the heat. He ran back to wait for the next bundle.

They worked all morning and collected more than two dozen bundles each.

But now the sun made its presence felt. Lisl felt dizzy from the heat and from bending over too long. She stood up stretching, and looked around. They had zigzagged from the top by the sloe hedge down to the bottom of the field were the meadow began.

"Lisl, come quick. I found something," Kurt shouted. Dieter and Lisl made their way across the stubble field.

Kurt pointed at a clump of grass. "Look. Something's in there. I saw it wiggle."

Lisl parted the clump. "It's only a little garden snake, a pretty green and yellow one." She picked it up, and it twisted around her wrist like a bracelet. With its head raised and curled in a striking position, Lisl thought it acted amusingly fearsome for such a tiny, harmless snake. "We'd better get it out of the field before the farmer plows it under."

Her brothers followed her out of the field, while admiring the pretty bracelet that still graced her wrist.

Lisl set the snake free on the meadow grass, where it disappeared within seconds.

"I'm going to cool off by the water." Lisl walked toward the creek. After walking on hard stubble all morning, the soft green grass of the meadow felt soothing under her feet. She kneeled beside the creek and put her hands in, bringing them cupped and filled with water to her hot face. She could not resist and took a sip of the cold liquid.

Kurt lay on his stomach, splashing his hands around in the water. He too drank some of the water.

"Kurt, don't drink too much or you'll get sick," Lisl said, but she knew they all would sneak a little sip. The water rushed so clear in gurgling temptation over the rocks. The linden tea had turned hot in the bottle after lying in the sun for hours. They sat by the creek and ate their bread, splashing their hands and feet around in the water.

Refreshed, they went back to collect their bundles on the side of the field. Kurt carried the tea bottle.

With both arms wrapped around the wheat bundles, Dieter and Lisl proudly carried their treasure to the Scheck mill, a kilometer farther south of the field.

Tall poplar trees surrounded the big white mill compound with its heavy red tile roof. High painted wooden doors and woodwork throughout the mill gave it a cared-for, cheerful look. The water splashed noisily over the big waterwheel, keeping it in full motion. The Scheck's mill was a busy, friendly place, unlike the Burlein mill, which was in great need of paint and repair.

Dieter set his load on the ground and knocked on the front door. After several more loud knocks, Herr Scheck's mother opened the door. Dieter started to say something, but she shook her head. "I can't hear too well." When she saw the bundles of wheat, she said, "You have to go see my son about the flour." She smiled and pointed them toward the stairs leading to the lower part of the mill.

Dieter hastily gathered his grain bundles and followed.

Kurt moved closer to Lisl when he heard the noisy commotion of wheels turning. But his curiosity won out and slowly he peeked around her to watch the proceedings.

They set the bundles on the ground and looked for Herr Scheck.

"*Gruess Gott*, Lisl." Startled, Lisl turned and saw Herr Scheck standing beside her. He held out his hand, and Lisl and her brothers shook it vigorously. He stood tall, with red-blond hair and blue eyes smiling from under bushy red eyebrows with a dusting of flour.

"Well, what have we here?" He looked at their bundles. "Did you do all that?" he asked Kurt.

"Yes. But they helped."

"Not bad for a morning's work. I wouldn't mind having workers like you in my mill."

"We would like to help," Lisl said.

"Me too," Kurt agreed.

Herr Scheck looked at Dieter. "What about you?"

"I want to help. What do you pay?" Herr Scheck laughed a hearty belly laugh, but quickly tried to look businesslike. He scratched his head. "What do you think you're worth?"

"How about some flour? Whatever you think we deserve." Dieter was at his best when he was negotiating a deal.

"Tell you what. I'll pay you two pounds of flour for the grain you brought today. But you have to ask your mother if you can come back tomorrow morning to help for a few hours." He pointed to sacks on a shelf. "I'll pay in flour," he said.

"You've got a deal." Dieter shook Herr Scheck's hand and smiled at Lisl. Two pounds of flour was not bad for a day's work.

"Put the bundles over on that shelf." Herr Scheck pointed to a wide shelf. Then he bent down to Dieter's level, and with his head beside Dieter's, he pointed out a woman on the far side of the mill.

"You go see my wife over there, and ask her to give you two pounds of flour."

"*Aufwiedersehen,* Herr Scheck." They made their way between shelves stacked with sacks.

Dust and chaff littered the floor, and the scent of fresh straw hung in the air.

"*Guten Tag, Kinder.* Were you busy again?" Frau Scheck greeted them.

"*Guten Tag,* Frau Scheck."

"How much flour do you want?" she asked Lisl.

"Two pounds please."

Frau Scheck scooped the flour from a big barrel into a bowl on a scale, moving the weights carefully, adding a little flour until she was satisfied. Then she poured it into a triangular brown paper bag.

Dieter and Kurt wandered off. Lisl found them at the grinding stones where they watched wheels–powered only by the big waterwheel–reduce the grain to flour.

Although Dieter had seen the process many times before, Lisl still had to drag him away when it was time to go.

Lisl carried the flour carefully, proud they were able to help add to the food supply at home. Mama might even bake a loaf of bread if they got more flour for helping in the mill tomorrow.

Dieter skipped in and out of the willow's shade along the creek on their way home. "Just wait till Mama hears we have a job."

Lisl realized they had been lucky today. They were the first ones in the field after the rakes had finished. Many hungry people would be out later, scouting for cleared fields to collect wheat. But Lisl and Dieter had a small advantage. When Charlotte and Ellen had helped with the vegetable harvest, they had asked when the farmers cut the wheat so Lisl and Dieter could be there first.

Next morning Dieter and Lisl got up early with their sisters.

Mama decided to let Kurt sleep. "I'm so proud of you." She smiled at her children. "You can go swimming this afternoon."

Charlotte and Ellen went off in one direction and Dieter and Lisl ran to the mill to report for work.

"What do you think Herr Scheck will have us do?" Dieter asked.

"I don't know. I hope it is something we can do well."

"Do you think he'll let us grind the flour?"

"I don't think so. We don't know how to do that. Maybe we can after we've been there for a while."

Lisl knocked on the door. Grandmother Scheck opened it and smiled, pointing to the stairs.

"*Guten Morgen,*" Lisl said cheerfully when she saw Herr and Frau Scheck.

"*Guten Morgen, Kinder.*" Frau Scheck handed her a broom. "Saturday mornings we clean the mill to prepare for next week's load."

Lisl swept the floor around the wheels and shelving, scooping up straw particles and grain chaff and clearing off dust from shelves.

Dieter helped Herr Scheck weigh and fill smaller sacks of flour and do other tedious chores. Lisl saw Dieter's disappointed face. He had hoped for a more challenging assignment. But when their payment was a pound of flour each, he did not seem to mind.

"You've done a great job today," Herr Scheck said. "Would you like to come every Saturday morning until the wheat harvest is over?"

"Oh, can we?" Lisl smiled.

Dieter threw his arms in the air. "Yes."

CHAPTER 38

Storm Cloud on the Horizon

Lisl straightened up and wiped her hot face. Pulling weeds was a never-ending job. Summer held its hot, dry grip into late September. Stagnant heat hung in the air like a chest-crushing weight, and breathing was a chore.

Even the yellow finch on the edge of the roof presented its repetitious call with irritating monotony. Crickets seemed to chirp annoyance. Nothing pleased Lisl except the clouds that gradually piled up like cotton balls on the western horizon. She hoped for rain.

Charlotte and Ellen trudged up the path, tired and dirty from harvesting beets and cabbage in the fields.

Lisl watched as they headed, without a word, for the shade of the cherry tree. Dieter followed Lisl to join their sisters for a rest.

"I'm so hot and thirsty," Charlotte said. She crossed her arms on the table and dropped her head. Her thick auburn hair covered her bare dusty arms. Charlotte and Ellen had worked since dawn. But by two in the afternoon, when the heat became unbearable, the farmer's wife sent them home.

Charlotte did not stir when her mother brought a jug of cold linden tea and glasses to the table. Mama swept the hair from Charlotte's face. "Here, *Liebling,* take a nice long drink."

Ellen came to the table, her face and hair wet from washing up at the rain barrel. She towel dried her hair and wiped her sunburned face, looking through half-closed eyes to a far away place only she could see. Lisl knew that her sisters too wished for better times.

Charlotte finally raised her head. Her soft brown eyes searched for the tea. She barely had the strength to lift the pitcher.

She looked at Ellen. "You washed up already?"

"You know me; once I sit down, I won't be able to get up again."

"Charlotte, you'd better wash too. You'll feel better." Mama handed her a towel.

A slow-running hose kept the rain barrel filled. Charlotte took a long drink and headed toward the water.

"I'm going to wash too." Kurt ran ahead of her. But she caught him and scooped him up in her arms.

"Oh, I will wash you; I will dunk you into the water." Charlotte had found her energy again.

Kurt squealed with delight. His sister was ready to play with him.

"You two are very quiet," Mama said to Lisl and Dieter.

"We're tired too. It's too hot today." Dieter wiped the sweat from his brow with the back of his hand.

Lisl wiped the dust from her face and wrinkled her nose. "I just need a drink. I still have two beds to go." She wanted to jump in the water, but she had to finish her weeding first.

Dieter and Lisl went back to pulling weeds.

"By the time we've done the last bed, the pesky little morning glories have grown back again in the first one," Lisl mumbled.

"Yeah. And there are too many rocks in here."

Lisl glanced toward the stone break. "Maybe it's because the garden is so close to the stone break."

"Every time we rake the rocks out, new ones pop up. I think they grow here along with the weeds." Dieter hit the rake at the pile of rocks.

The garden hugged a gentle slope, and with every hard rain the soil washed down the grade, exposing more rocks.

"Lisl, Dieter, you'd better stop for now. It's too sweltering to be out in the sun," Mama called.

Dieter dropped the garden tool with a sigh of relief, but picked it up again and took it to the storage shed.

Lisl propped her hoe against a small pear tree. She might use it again later in the evening after it had cooled down a little. She went down to the basement wash kitchen, took off her clothes, stepped into the tub and hosed herself off. The cold water felt wonderful as it ran over her hair and body. But when she slipped into her hot dress again she knew it would not last.

The basement door, leading to the lower garden, had been left open for ventilation. When Lisl stepped out of the wash kitchen to go upstairs, she saw Charlotte standing motionless on the stairs.

"Charlotte? What's the matter?"

Charlotte did not answer. She stared out through the open door.

Lisl followed her gaze and saw a man coming up the garden path. Neither Charlotte nor Lisl said a word as they watched him come closer. Long unkempt hair and a thick beard covered his hollow face. He stopped off and on, yet relentlessly came closer. Now *Lisl* felt like a statue as she watched Charlotte slowly walk down the stairs toward the man. He stood in the doorway in front of Charlotte.

"Charlotte, don't you know me?" he said. And when he saw Lisl standing on the stairs he called in a low voice, "Lisl."

"It's Papa." Lisl almost tumbled down the stairs to get to her father. "Papa."

The girls threw their arms around him.

"Papa. Papa. Mama, come quick! Papa is home." Charlotte ran upstairs, excitedly shouting, "Papa is home, Papa is home."

Lisl was afraid to let go, afraid he may turn out to be a dream again. "Papa you're really here? You did come home." She stood back to take a good look at him. "You're all right." She wrapped her arms around his waist.

He sat down on the basement steps. Lisl ran into the wash kitchen and came back with a moist towel, gently wiping his forehead.

Mama came rushing down the stairs. They looked at each other for a long time, and then Mama broke into tears. She sat beside Papa and looked at him with all her love. Gently she wiped the hair from his forehead and kissed him. "Karl, you're here. Thank God, you made it back."

He wrapped his arms around her. They sat in embrace on the cool basement steps.

Finally, Mama stood up, pulling him up with her. They walked upstairs, holding each other tight.

Ellen and Dieter, who had watched him from the top of the stairs, flew at him, hugging him, unable to take their eyes off him. "Is this really Papa?" Dieter said. "It doesn't look like him."

Kurt was afraid of his father and stared at him from a safe distance.

The family gathered around him as he drank a glass of cold linden tea. His red-rimmed blue eyes gazed at his children without that familiar sparkle. They looked back at a sad, frail man.

Mama brought Werner in her arms. "I want you to meet your son." She held the baby out to him.

Papa looked at Werner and a faint smile softened his expression. He held the baby's tiny hand, and Werner grasped his father's finger and looked at him with big curious eyes.

Papa smiled. "He has your eyes."

Mama put the baby back in his crib and took the empty glass from Papa's hand. "Would you like something to eat?"

"Yes. Some nice fresh boiled potatoes," he said with a tired smile. "But I need to lie down for a little while first." He disappeared into the bedroom and lay on top of the covers where he instantly fell asleep. He was too tired to remove his scuffed boots so Mama took them off.

Lisl watched him from the door. All this time Lisl had kept Papa's smiling face in her thoughts. She did not want to forget what he looked like. But this was not how she remembered him.

"Lisl, come help me to get the potatoes," Ellen called from the front door.

Lisl closed the bedroom door and ran outside. "Do you think the potatoes are done?"

"What do you mean done?" Ellen shook her head. "We haven't even put them on the stove yet."

"I mean are they done growing?"

"We'll see. I'm just grateful the farmer gave Mama some seed potatoes to plant or we wouldn't have any to cook for Papa now."

Some of the potatoes were tiny, but they only put the biggest ones–about the size of eggs–on to boil and saved the smaller ones for later.

Charlotte raced on the bike to the house of the farmer they had worked for earlier in the day. She told Frau Herzog the good news. Charlotte beamed when she showed Mama a big slice of ham for Papa's dinner.

Papa is home. Lisl kept peeking through the bedroom door. Her father was home and whole. She had seen other fathers return bitter, some with missing limbs. Others never made it back.

The war had been over since early May. It was mid-September 1945. Lisl had watched her mother become more depressed with every passing month as the townsmen returned home. The uncertainty of whether Papa was alive had been torture for everyone. Now her mother's pain was over and so was Lisl's. Now her mother could be happy: no more hiding her tears.

Lisl looked forward to hearing her father's stories again. She remembered the fun they used to have playing *Fussball*. He had enjoyed playing with his children, endlessly kicking the ball back and forth in front of the house–driving Mama crazy. They had broken the sitting room window that way.

Through spring and summer the family had been eating in the kitchen or outside under the cherry tree. Now Lisl set the dining room table. She picked a colorful bouquet of dahlias from the garden to brighten the table.

"Lisl, please get me some red cabbage; if they're small, get two," Mama called from the kitchen. Lisl brought two.

Charlotte and Ellen raced about, cleaning everything in sight. Dieter picked up Kurt's toys in the garden, while Lisl helped Mama prepare the meal. It smelled like Sunday dinners used to smell a long time ago.

Mama tiptoed into the bedroom. "Karl, dinner is ready," she whispered.

Papa came out on wobbly legs and washed up. Silent and unsmiling, he sat at the table and looked at everyone as though seeing them for the first time.

They looked back at him with somber expressions, reflecting his emotions.

He picked up his fork and slowly started to eat.

Lisl could only gaze at her father. She hoped that he would feel better soon. He had never looked so thin before; she could see his ribs through his shirt. Papa will look more like himself once he shaves off that ugly beard, and puts on a little weight, she thought.

Her father looked at her for a moment, then pointed with his fork to her plate.

Lisl quickly stabbed at the piece of potato on her plate.

The children ate potatoes and vegetables, leaving the slice of ham for their father. They rarely had meat, but Lisl did not miss it now that they had fresh homegrown vegetables and sometimes even an egg.

After dinner Lisl watched her parents walk out into the garden where it was cooler. They sat hand in hand but talked little. Lisl and her sisters cleaned the kitchen, and Dieter kept Kurt occupied.

Kurt's voice sounded agitated and Lisl ran to him as she heard him shouting.

"I will not!" Kurt stomped his foot defiantly, setting his blond curls in motion.

"Shh, not so loud." Dieter tried to calm him.

"What happened?" Lisl asked.

Dieter shrugged his shoulders. "I only said that he has to sleep in our bedroom again now that Papa is home."

"Why can't Papa sleep in the boys' bedroom," Kurt stomped his foot again.

"Because Papa and Mama always sleep in the grown-up room. That's why there is a boys' and a girls' bedroom," Lisl explained.

"The baby is a boy," Kurt argued, "He doesn't have to sleep upstairs."

"You can talk with Mama about it later." Lisl tried to calm him.

"I'll do it now." And before Lisl could stop him he ran to his mother, putting himself squarely in front of her.

"Papa can sleep in the boys' room tonight." It sounded like an order.

Mama laughed. "Kurt, you are the boy. Papa will sleep in his room, our room." She pointed between Papa and herself. But it only made Kurt angry.

"I don't want Papa here." Kurt's face was red and angry.

"Kurt, go to your room, the boys' room," Papa shouted. Kurt ran off crying. Mama looked startled at Papa's harsh reaction, but kept quiet.

Thunder in the distance announced an upcoming storm. Lisl smiled. The rumbling was only thunder now, not an air raid attack. She took a deep breath. The wind carried the scent of rain mixed with the pine forest a few kilometers away. Soon it would be cooler.

Papa went inside. Mama followed. He still was unusually quiet. Mama sat on the kitchen chair watching Papa stand in front of the mirror by the kitchen sink. He cut his beard with a pair of scissors until only stubble was left. Then he picked up the straight razor.

Gently, Mama took it from his shaking hand and lovingly shaved his face.

Lisl and Dieter went out into the garden again. A sudden gust carried the tablecloth from the outdoor table up into the garden where it came to rest on a vegetable bed. Before it could take off again, Dieter caught it. Together they folded it and put it inside then sat side by side on the front step in the open doorway. Black clouds hurried across the sky, the thunderclaps came closer and their counting shorter. Big raindrops–propelled on the wild breeze–hit the powdery ground, raising puffs of dust around each drop.

Lisl ran into the garden to retrieve the hoe she had left leaning against the tree and put it away. Instead of dust, now mud squished between her toes. She poured water from the rain barrel over her feet before she sat beside Dieter again to watch the downpour.

"That feels good," Dieter said, breathing deep. "This is a good day. Papa is home and the rain came."

"Yeah. I'm so glad Papa is home," Lisl said. "Now we can stop worrying."

 ∽

The house cooled slowly inside, especially upstairs under the roof where heat got trapped.

Lisl tossed in her bed. She would have liked to sneak into the wash kitchen to hose off, but did not want to disturb her parents.

Charlotte had opened the windows and doors of both bedrooms as well as the little skylight in the hallway between the rooms. It helped a little.

Kurt was crying. Dieter's tired, soothing voice tried to console him. Finally they both were quiet.

Mama talked softly, but Papa seemed silent. Lisl fell asleep happy, knowing that everyone she loved was here in the house, safe.

Halfway through the night, Lisl awoke. She heard Papa in the bathroom vomiting. Mama spoke to him in whispers. After a while they went back to bed. But not long after, Lisl heard him vomit again. *Poor Papa.*

CHAPTER 39

Mama's Tears

Lisl awoke to the sound of Kurt's little feet running downstairs. She smiled, stretching her arms above her head. Papa was home. She hopped out of bed, washed up and ran downstairs, excited to share breakfast with him.

When Lisl came into the kitchen, Papa was not there and neither was Kurt. Charlotte and Ellen sat quietly at the table, not even casting nasty glances at each other. Their focus, as well as Dieter's, seemed to be on the bedroom door. Papa was still asleep.

Dieter stuck his head under the table "I see you," he said. Lisl lifted the tablecloth and saw Kurt huddled under the kitchen bench the way he used to when air raids frightened him. At first Lisl thought he was just playing hide and seek, but when he did not come out she knew something bothered him. Mama tried to lure him out, but he remained under the bench without a word.

An uncomfortable silence lingered while everyone waited for the bedroom door to open.

"Is Papa getting up to have breakfast with us?" Dieter asked.

"No. Papa is very sick. He'll have to stay in bed."

"What's the matter with him?" Charlotte looked worried.

"He wasn't used to the rich food. I should have known better and given him only the potatoes he had asked for. He went without food for days at times when he was making his way home. At the prison camp there was very little food. Now he can't keep anything down." Mama's eyes darkened with pain.

Charlotte and Ellen looked into the bedroom at their sleeping father, and then left for school.

Lisl peeked at Kurt who still sat scrunched under the bench. He looked like he had been crying. "Kurt, come on out," she held out her hand to him, but he ignored it. "What's the matter with Kurt?" she asked Mama.

"He thinks Papa is sick because he shouted at him yesterday."

"Oh Kurt, it's not your fault. Come out and walk us down to the road." He crawled out from under the bench wiping his eyes.

Dieter and Lisl held his hands as they walked with him down the garden path onto Muehlenweg.

Lisl pointed up to the house. "You'll see, Kurt, Papa won't be angry at you. He's sick because he ate something that wasn't good for him, just like when you drank the Coca-Cola that had something bad in it. Remember, it made you sick?"

Dieter tried to console him. "Yes, Kurt. Fathers don't get sick from little kids' bad tempers, or all fathers would be sick."

Kurt looked somberly at Lisl. "I'll be good today; I'll help him get better." He stood at the end of the path and waved as Lisl and Dieter ran along Muehlenweg.

Lisl could not wait to tell her teacher her father had come home. She waited in the hallway and ran to him when he came up the stairs.

"Herr Stolz, my father came home yesterday."

"Lisl, that is wonderful news. See, I told you not to give up," he smiled. "How is your father?"

"He is sick. He threw up all night long." Lisl studied her teacher's face. She hoped that he may have read about a fast cure for people with this ailment.

But Herr Stolz shook his head. "Oh, I'm sorry Lisl. Don't you worry; lots of soldiers get sick when they come home. They eat too much right away, but I'm sure he'll soon feel better." He smiled at her. "You tell your father that I said hello and wish him a speedy recovery."

After school Lisl found Dieter waiting by the entrance.

They did not discuss the stone break, but ran across the fields, bypassing their favorite digging place without a glance, and headed home.

"Do you think Papa is feeling better?" Lisl asked.

Dieter's face brightened. "Maybe he'll play *Fussball* with us."

But when Lisl saw her mother sitting under the tree by herself she knew he was still sick.

Lisl sat down beside her and put her hand on her mother's. "*Gruess Dich*, Mama." Lisl saw that Mama's brown eyes were hazel yet she was still smiling.

Dieter came up behind his mother's chair and wrapped his arms around her neck.

Mama held on to his hands. "How was school today?"

"All right," Lisl and Dieter said as if on cue.

"Papa is still very sick. I had the doctor take a look at him." Mama tried hard not to cry. "He said it will take time. There was nothing he could do for him. I'm to give Papa tea and *Zwieback* that the doctor gave me. That's all Papa is able to handle for now."

Charlotte and Ellen came up the garden path. They gave their mother a questioning glance but did not ask about their father. They too saw her worry. Now Mama feared for Papa's life all over again.

Papa seemed to get worse and for the next week he did not want to talk or see anyone–not even Opa and Aunt

Anni when they came to visit. Opa was near tears, and Tante Anni, Papa's sister, tried to get information from her brother. Lisl could tell that Anni's feelings were hurt when Papa turned to the wall without a word. Opa and Anni left after trying to encourage Mama.

When Ellen or Charlotte tried to cheer him up he would not respond. The family moved about the house quietly, waiting for him to react to Mama's plea; no one seemed to be able to help him.

Lisl slipped into his room. "Papa? Are you feeling better?" She tried to talk with him, but he seemed to look right through her. She could see that he was in a different place. His eyes stared at the ceiling–at frightening things that only he could see. "Papa where are you? Please come back to us. You're safe now Papa, you're home in your own bed."

∽

The following week, Lisl found her mother crying every day when she got home from school, but she still tried to hide her tears. Soon it became too much for Mama. She told the children, "He has no will to live. I don't know what to do anymore. Now he won't eat at all." She could no longer hold back her tears. "He makes no effort to get better."

Lisl was more worried about her mother now. She too looked ill and thin. Mama had never cried like that, not even when Mainbernheim was under attack.

"Why doesn't he want to live, now that he is home and safe?" Lisl asked.

Her mother looked at Lisl for a moment and stopped crying. "You are absolutely right, Lisl. He has no reason to give up now!" Mama calmed herself, wiped her tears, walked into the bedroom and closed the door behind her.

Lisl thought there was no need because she could hear Mama's shouts clearly.

"How dare you come home and think you can die on us! We know you had to go through hell, but we had our share too."

After an uncomfortable silence Lisl heard Mama again. "Now you eat the toast I brought you and drink the tea! Then you will try to get up, walk a little every day and smell the fresh air in the garden. Look at your children who are half-starved but uncomplaining. Do you understand me?" Mama sounded scolding.

Silence was his only response.

Charlotte and Ellen exchanged a worried glance. Lisl cried and kept her fingers crossed. Kurt was lucky. He bounced his ball on the floor, seemingly oblivious to his mother's pain.

Mama came out of the bedroom a little more confident than when she went in. Dieter rushed to her and wrapped his arms around her waist. She stroked the side of his face, gave him a little smile, and walked out into the garden with him. The girls followed with Kurt chasing his ball through the door. They sat under the cherry tree quietly; the children did know how to comfort their mother.

After a long silence Mama gazed into the sky and wiped her hazel eyes. "It looks like rain again," she said. "Lisl, pick a couple of apples for us."

"I'll help you, Lisl." Kurt ran alongside. She picked two yellow-green apples off the tree and let Kurt carry one. Mama cut them up, and then shared the fresh fruit.

Charlotte lifted the baby from his playpen and cradled him in her arms. In her soft clear voice she sang a lullaby and Ellen harmonized. Soon the whole family joined in the song.

Shlaf Kindchen schlaf.
Dein Vater hueted Schaf.

"Papa," Dieter whispered, staring big-eyed toward the entry. Papa stood in the doorway then slowly walked out into the garden.

The girls stopped singing and nervously looked at their father. He had washed and dressed. He sat down beside Mama without a word. Although he was clean shaven, Lisl thought he looked much skinnier than he had on the day he came home.

When Papa saw the knife and apple core he said, "Dieter, how about getting an apple for your father?"

Dieter jumped up so fast he almost knocked the table over. He climbed after the best-looking apple and came back with a big yellow one. He first polished it on his sleeve before handing it to his father.

"Don't eat too much at once," Mama warned as she handed him the knife.

He put his hand over hers. "You're a tough lady."

Lisl smiled. *Now Papa will be all right.* Although he still looked very ill, at least his smile made him look happy again.

CHAPTER 40

Papa Goes to Work

For the next two weeks, Papa steadily improved. He even kicked the ball back and forth in front of the house a few times with the boys. Mama did not object. He still did not talk much, and the little conversation they had was about everything except the war. Lisl knew he was not ready yet.

When the doctor came to the house, he told Papa he was well enough to go to work. Papa seemed relieved. But when he was told by the American military to work at the Flack Caserne, he became angry.

Papa, along with other former prisoners of war, was picked up in a jeep the next morning and taken to their work place in Kitzingen. The military buildings that had been destroyed in the air raids were rebuilt. It was business as usual, only now the Flack Caserne was occupied by American troops instead of German soldiers.

Papa had worked as a tax inspector before being called into the military.

"Why can't I go back to my old job?" He shouted at Mama, throwing things around, yelling at her for something she had no control over.

"Is that all we're allowed to do?" He hit his fist on the table.

The children stayed out of his way and Lisl felt like a
traitor for not sticking up for her mother. But she knew it
would only make things worse.

"I get punished for things I didn't do. How was I to
know the war was over? We didn't dare talk to anyone when
we made our way across the east sector." He shouted as if
to justify his predicament to Mama. "If the Russians had
caught us, we would have been shot on the spot."

Papa was among survivors who had made their way back
to the west side, to American-occupied Germany, to get
home. They were captured in the Bavarian Alps two weeks
after the German army had surrendered. So Papa and his
fellow company buddies were treated as troops who had
failed to surrender on the eighth of May. They were caught
still bearing arms, long after other German soldiers were set
free. Only when the Americans discovered the reason for
their delayed surrender and their empty guns were they set
free, but much later than the rest. To make their way back
on foot through Russian-occupied territory, undetected,
had taken a long time.

༄

Lisl heard the door slam early in the morning. Papa had
left for work. They did not want to get in their father's way
when he got ready for work. And so they waited in their
rooms, dressed and ready to eat breakfast in a hurry and
leave for school.

After a few days of working in the American PX, Papa
realized that this job was the best thing that could have
happened to him and his family–better than removing
rubble from city streets, which seemed to be the only other
work available. At last he got to eat well and sometimes

was allowed to bring home food that otherwise would have been thrown out. He was allowed to save the bread crusts that were cut off the toast and bread the American soldiers consumed.

Once in a while Mama soaked the white bread crusts in goat's milk mixed with eggs to make a delicious bread pudding. But most of the time the dry bread crusts made a bigger breakfast. Lisl thought the white bread crust tasted almost as good as cake–even all dried out. Mama even made real coffee from used coffee grounds Papa retrieved. It tasted better than linden tea or ersatz coffee.

On occasion, when Papa went to town he took Lisl along. But now they didn't talk or hold hands the way they used to. Sometimes he did look at her. One Sunday Papa ran into friends and former soldiers who now worked with him at the Flack Caserne. Lisl stood quietly beside her father while the men talked about the good food they were allowed to eat at work. Her father even laughed when they exchanged stories about awkward conversation; they tried to learn English and American soldiers tried to learn German.

Lisl remembered the starving German soldiers in the foxholes and hoped they had made it home safely and would not have to starve anymore. Lisl was happy to see Papa and his friends enjoying each other. Her father and his army friends had to endure long periods of starvation as well, and some, like her father, were exposed to the freezing cold for long periods. Tears welled up in Lisl's eyes when she looked at these skinny men. Her father seemed to come to life while he was talking to his friends. She wanted to give him time to talk freely. She touched Papa's hand, waved and walked away. Her father nodded with a smile in agreement.

◦◦

Lisl awoke to Mama's voice. "Children, come down, we have something good for you."

Ellen awoke as fast as she had fallen asleep. She sprang out of bed, turned on the light and looked at the clock. "It's only five minutes to midnight. What's going on?" She ran downstairs in her pajamas.

Lisl closed her eyes again. She must have been dreaming. But then she heard Dieter say, "Is it morning already?" He was in the hallway outside her bedroom. Now she knew she was not dreaming.

Kurt hung onto Charlotte on his way down. It took a little longer for Lisl to open her eyes and leave her bed.

Dieter sniffed the air and wiped the sleep from his eyes. "What smells so good?"

"Pancakes *Liebling,* delicious pancakes." Mama stood by the stove looking at her sleepy brood as they appeared one by one in their pajamas, curiously looking at her.

Papa was getting ready for bed, but stayed to watch his children's faces.

Lisl recalled her mother's sad expression when she, in the past, had sent them to bed hungry. But now she smiled, bringing a plate stacked high with pancakes to the table and dividing them among her children.

"There is a lot more, so eat all you want."

That certainly was something Lisl had not heard her say in a long time, and to think *pancakes.*

"Papa brought a big can of leftover pancake batter from work," she smiled at Papa.

"Remember you have to fry all of the batter or it will spoil," he warned before he went to bed.

"Good. They are very good," Kurt said with his mouth full.

For once they were allowed to eat until they were full. Mama did not have a refrigerator, so when the children went to bed she was still making pancakes for the days ahead.

CHAPTER 41

Eating Like a Prince

Dieter and Kurt ran down the garden path as a jeep stopped on the road below. Lisl watched from the open window.

The driver jumped from the jeep and stood at attention while holding the door open. An American major stepped out, stretching.

"Mama, come quick. Papa has a dog," Lisl shouted.

Mama stood watching with Lisl as Papa was pulled from the backseat by a beautiful dog he held on a leash.

The boys ran to their father. "Is this going to be our dog?" Dieter asked.

"Papa, did you get a ride in the jeep?" Kurt peered from behind Dieter.

"These are my sons, Kurt and Dieter," Papa said to the major, who could speak a little German.

"Hi boys, *Guten Tag.*" He ran his hand over Kurt's blond curls. But when the dog came a little too close, Kurt retreated up the path as fast as his little legs could carry him.

Dieter walked behind his father to the house, trying to pet the dog.

Papa introduced Mama and Lisl. The officer awkwardly shook Lisl's hand. She could tell that shaking hands with everyone was not customary in his country.

"Irma, we'll take care of the dog for a few days until Major Dodge returns from his trip." Papa handed her a big package of ground beef before Mama could object. "This is the meat for the dog," he said.

Mama looked at this big package in disbelief and then smiled at the beautiful, well-behaved animal. After a few attempts at small talk, Major Dodge shook everyone's hand again.

"*Danke. Vielen Dank*," he said. He patted the dog's rump and ordered him to sit. The dog sat at attention like a soldier, his eyes fixed on his master.

"Stay," Dodge commanded and then walked out.

Lisl ran after him. "What's the dog's name?"

"Prince. His name is Prince," the Major said. "He is an Irish Setter."

Lisl ran back to the house where Prince waited for his master's return. The dog paid little attention to Lisl or anyone else in the room, but kept his eyes intently on the door. She felt sorry for him. He sounded so lonely when he whined in a high-pitched whistle. Prince looked at the children, then back to the door again. The jeep drove away.

Mama patted his head. "Now, what are we going to do with you?"

Kurt peeked at Prince from behind the kitchen door, and every time the dog looked at him, Kurt hid again until it became a game.

"Can we take him for a walk?" Dieter asked.

"Yes. But whatever you do, don't let him off the leash. He might run away. After all he is in a strange place." Mama looked at the dog. "Lisl, you'd better go along."

Prince remained exactly where he had been told to sit by his master, making no attempt to get up. He looked at whoever spoke as if he could understand them, and then his eyes fixed on the door again. Mama handed the leash to Lisl.

"Now don't let go of that, wrap it around your wrist." Lisl pulled on the leash, still the dog did not move. "Come," she said, and he jumped up ready to go with her. It was love at first sight.

"Why can't we have a nice dog like that?" Dieter said.

"I know he's a beautiful animal, but you know what the Major feeds him? Ground beef! Now where would we get ground meat for the dog when we can't get any for ourselves? It wouldn't be fair to the dog."

Although Dieter looked disappointed, Lisl knew he would rather not have a dog than to see him starving.

Prince ran ahead, pulling Lisl down to the meadow and along the mill creek toward the Burlein mill. Lisl could not run at the dog's speed. She was afraid of choking him. Dieter could barely keep up. He stopped to catch his breath.

"Wait up," he called.

But Lisl kept running. And no matter how fast she ran the dog wanted to run faster. Prince pulled ahead with a sudden burst of energy and yanked the leash from her hand.

"Catch him Lisl, catch him." Dieter looked horrified.

Lisl stood in awe as Prince ran in long leaps across the meadow. He raced past Dieter, close enough to be caught, but tore away again. He ran back to Lisl who could not hold onto him either. His beautiful long red fur played in the wind like a flame, rushing on waves across the tall yellow grasses. Lisl laughed. "He's playing a game of tag with us."

Dieter threw his hands in the air. "Now what are we going to do?"

"He has to get tired sometime; I think he's just playing," Lisl smiled. "Look, he's having so much fun."

Dieter brightened. "Let's stand farther apart. He'll have to run longer stretches between us and get tired faster." Still, Prince showed no signs of slowing down as he ran back and forth between them, always dodging their reach.

After a while Dieter relaxed. He realized Prince was not about to run away.

Finally Prince grew tired of the game and came to rest beside Lisl who sat in the high grass near the creek.

Dieter came running. "Hold on to his leash, quick." Prince panted as he lay beside Lisl. His long tongue hung out of his open mouth. Lisl snatched the leash and led him to the creek where he had a long drink of water. He settled down between Lisl and Dieter in a regal manner, his front legs extended, his head held high. He looked like a statue.

"His master has given him a good name," Lisl said. "Just look at him. He looks royal."

Reluctantly they took the dog back home where he settled down in the middle of the kitchen floor.

Charlotte and Ellen came through the door arguing, but stopped abruptly when they caught sight of Prince. "What's *that* doing in here?" Ellen pointed at the dog. "You'd better get it outside."

Lisl kneeled on the floor beside Prince, petting him. She put her arms around the dog's neck. "Don't you think he's beautiful?" She tried to make Ellen see how special he was so he would not have to be tied up outside. But now and then Prince did an un-royal thing by getting a few licks onto Lisl's face.

"Yuck! How can you let a dog lick your face?" Ellen asked.

Charlotte pulled a yuck-face and unconsciously wiped her own cheek.

Lisl didn't mind. Still, she wiped her cheek with her sleeve to satisfy her sisters.

"Ellen, we have to keep him inside or he will run away," Dieter kneeled down beside the dog as well.

"So what if he does? What's he doing in here anyway?" She looked at Mama.

"Guess what we're having for dinner. We're having meat loaf."

Ellen and Charlotte's attention shifted to their mother.

"Meat loaf, as in MEAT meat loaf?" Ellen asked. Mama nodded.

"Where did you get the meat?" Charlotte asked. She walked a wide circle around Prince.

"From Major Dodge. It's the dog's food."

Charlotte and Ellen stared at the dog in disbelief, then back to Mama. Ellen tried to say something, but only managed to open her mouth, then closed it, staring at Prince.

"How long is he staying here?" Charlotte kept a respectable distance between herself and the dog.

"Only three days. I think we can put up with Prince for such a short time, don't you?"

"Yes, but does he have to stay in the house?" Ellen wiped her hands although she never had touched the dog. Lisl hid a smile.

"He's so clean and pretty he can stay in my room." Dieter offered. But when Kurt looked alarmed, Mama suggested that he could sleep on the hallway mat.

Mama prepared two big meat loaves, using all of the meat so it would not spoil. She added finely chopped parsley fresh from the garden, two eggs, and bread crusts–water-soaked and drained. It smelled delicious. Prince did not mind eating his meat this way. He even liked the carrots Mama served with the meat. For the family, it was a treat to be eating meat for a change.

"That was so good." Mama petted the dog.

After dinner, Charlotte and Ellen were a little more tolerant of Prince.

CHAPTER 42

GI Laundry

"*Guten Morgen*, Mama." Lisl skipped down the stairs and went to a tall green bag standing in the corner of the living room.

"What's this?" was Ellen's greeting as she came down behind Lisl.

Charlotte came out of the kitchen. She had been up before her sisters. "Laundry," Charlotte said.

"Mama, what is in that sack?" Ellen was not satisfied with her sister's answer.

"Charlotte is right, it's laundry." Mama watched her curious girls.

Lisl inspected the duffel bag. "Laundry? Are you going to wash American soldiers' uniforms?"

"Papa brought it home from work last night. Some of the Amis asked him if he knew where they could have their uniforms washed." Mama wiped her hands on her apron and came into the living room where the girls were gathered around the laundry bag.

"Just look, look what they pay for doing their laundry." Mama opened the bag, took out a big square block and put it on the table. "Soap, to wash their clothes with, and cigarettes in payment for washing them. Of course I'm not going to use the bar soap to wash the clothes. I'll use the same laundry paste that we use."

"Oh, can we use the bar soap to wash with?" Ellen asked.

"I'll cut it in half. We'll use half and the other half we'll trade for food." Mama watched her daughters' curious faces.

The girls were happy to have good soap again, although they were not allowed to wash their hair with it. They still had to use rain water from the barrel outside for softer water, and paste soap from the bucket as shampoo.

"We'll help you with the wash." Charlotte seemed pleased and Ellen nodded, eager to help as well.

Slowly life became easier. The girls showed pride in their appearances, especially Ellen who watched for the searching eyes of boys. She curled her hair with curlers Aunt Anni had given her. Lisl could not understand why Ellen would sleep with those uncomfortable hard rollers tightly stuck to her head. But Ellen treated the curlers like treasures.

Charlotte, on the other hand, had cut strips of cloth to roll up her hair. She slept much better on them.

Lisl's hair was cut into a short pageboy. At last the shaven part had grown out a little. She did not care whether she had curls as long as she had all of her hair again.

After school Charlotte and Ellen helped their mother hang the soldiers' clothing on the line in the garden.

It was late October now. Dieter and Lisl were still working in the garden digging up potatoes and storing them in the root cellar.

Lisl stood in the cellar, broom in hand, sweeping curtains of spider webs off the small window. She opened the window, swept the ledge, and shook off the broom. In the past, she had been scared when her mother sent her down to the root cellar to get potatoes for dinner. Sometimes she saw spiders retreating into corners when she came down.

She wondered why she had never worried about the spiders when they had slept here during the air raids. She rested her chin on the broom handle, recalling those nights. Everything does pass, just like Mama had promised.

"What's the matter, Lisl?" Dieter brought a bucket of potatoes into the cellar to add to the pile.

"I was just thinking about the air raids and when we had to sleep down here."

Dieter's face brightened. "Aren't you glad we don't have to do that anymore?"

"Yeah, but I was wondering where all the spiders were when we slept here."

Dieter shivered. "Don't remind me." He wiggled his fingers in front of Lisl's face. "They crawled all over us when we were asleep."

Lisl pushed his hands from her face. "They could have danced all over us even while we were awake. We just couldn't see them in the dark." Now they both shivered at the thought and quickly ran upstairs and out into the fall sunshine.

They raked the dry wilted potato foliage into a big pile. The garden looked nearly empty now. Most of the vegetables were canned and stored on the shelves in the root cellar. Late cabbages and brussels sprouts were still growing among the fallen leaves.

Orange and golden foliage settled on the ground while a few leaves stayed on the branches as though waiting for summer to return. Lisl shook the tree, hoping the two tiny apples would give up their grip. The mild afternoon air had a gentle feel. Leaves fell softly without the slightest breeze.

Mama came into the garden and lit a fire under the potato foliage. Dieter and Lisl raked leaves onto the slow-burning mound.

Charlotte and Ellen ran up the garden path with Kurt in tow. They gathered around the glowing pile, throwing tiny potatoes, too small for storing, into the fire. After the fire died down, Charlotte retrieved the crispy roasted potatoes. They shared them by the dying flame of the bonfire. This ceremony signaled summer's end for Lisl. She wished that Papa could have joined them, but he was at work. It seemed to Lisl that Papa had lost his joy for the simple things they used to do together.

Lisl stood beside Mama, watching the glowing embers slowly dimming. "Tomorrow we'll prepare the vegetable pit."

The next day Mama dug a hole about a half meter deep and two meters long. It reminded Lisl of foxholes and the sad tired soldiers. She shook her head to bring herself back to the task of lining the hole with straw to keep the frost out and the inside clean. Mama pulled the red and green cabbage as well as the brussels sprouts out of the beds with roots intact. She set them upright in the pit and covered them with a thick layer of straw. This would keep the vegetables fresh and available through fall and maybe into winter.

Lisl hoped for a milder winter this year. Maybe she would get a good pair of shoes that would keep the mud from her toes. Maybe they would have better luck getting wood for the stove now that Mama was able to get cigarettes for doing laundry. And maybe the house would be warmer.

CHAPTER 43

Mouse in the Tub

Dieter and Lisl had just returned from school when a jeep stopped on the road below their garden. Papa jumped out and, with the help of an American soldier, unloaded six boxes onto the garden path.

"Dieter! Lisl! Come take these cans up and wash them out. Mama knows what to do with them. I have to leave again." Papa hopped back into the jeep and drove off before Lisl could ask questions.

Lisl picked up a large box. It was lighter than she had expected.

Dieter lifted one onto his head, acting like it weighed a ton as he carried it through the door.

Mama laughed and took it off his head. "Oh, is Papa here?" She ran to the window.

Lisl shook her head. "No, he had to leave again. Mama, what are these for?"

"What are we going to do with these empty cans?" Dieter brought another box in.

"We have to clean them and take them to the farmers in exchange for food."

"But they forgot to bring the lids."

"No Dieter, there are no lids for them. The farmers know how to seal them."

Mama brought two buckets of water, one containing soap suds, and the children went to work washing the cans. Papa was very creative in finding new ways to provide for his family. He had made friends with some of the American soldiers and found them to be open minded and helpful.

"Mmmm, that smells sooo good. Here, smell." Dieter held one of the empty cans under Lisl's nose.

While she inhaled the fruity aroma, she had an idea. "Let's get a glass." They poured the remaining drops from each can into the glass.

"Mama, look what we've got," Dieter called.

She smelled it. "*Annanas.*"

"It says 'Pineapple.' Does that mean *Annanas?*"

"I guess so, Lisl. I think it's all right to drink." She left them to do their chore. By the time they had emptied six dozen cans, their glass was half filled. Dieter and Lisl shared the treat.

Lisl licked her lips after they had finished it, as if to hang onto the flavor a little longer.

"Wouldn't it be great to have a whole can of this? Not just the juice but the fruit too," Dieter said.

"I don't really know how they grow it. Have you ever seen an *Annanas* tree?"

"No. I think they only grow in America. They must grow a lot of things there. They sure have plenty of food." Dieter looked off into the distance. "Maybe someday we will go there. Wouldn't it be great to see where the Indians live?"

"I wonder what America looks like. We could take a little peek, like in the movies, not really go there, just in case we don't like it."

Dieter brightened. "Yeah, like a bird flying across America and taking a good look."

That evening Frau Wagner came on her bicycle to see what they had for her.

"Frau Lindner, I have a pound of bacon I can give you for these cans, if you think you might get me a few dozen more."

Mama agreed. She was sure Papa could find more.

Dieter and Lisl loaded the boxes into their hand wagon, took them to the Wagner's farmhouse, and unloaded them in a corner of their big kitchen.

"Would you like a pear?" Frau Wagner handed them each a big green pear without waiting for their answer.

"Vielen Dank," Lisl said. Now they had dessert for the family. She pulled Dieter home in the hand wagon.

When Ellen saw the bacon she asked, "Where did you get that?"

After Mama explained, Ellen was not at all happy.

"All that bacon for some empty cans?" She rolled her eyes. "And all you had to do was wash a few cans. I had to work hard just to get a little butter."

Lisl shook her head. "Ellen it wasn't the cleaning they paid for, but the cans."

"What about me, I worked hard too, only I don't feel sorry for myself," Charlotte said.

"Now, we know you both work very hard, but please, no fighting." Mama cut their squabbling short. "What's important is the farmers need cans because they can't get any in the stores."

Ellen and Charlotte still whispered nasty little remarks at each other, but out of their mother's earshot.

Lisl wondered what made her sisters always stay together, even when they didn't have to. Maybe their arguments were more of a game of wits than dislike. Lisl felt left out, never really close to her sisters. They always whispered about boys and other silly girlish things–mixed with lots of squabbling. They seemed to have their own private club in which Lisl did not fit. Ellen rolled her eyes whenever Lisl tried to join.

"You're too young, you wouldn't understand," she would say.

"I don't want to join your silly club anyway. All you talk about is boys." Lisl stomped off. "I would rather think about the stone break and all the secrets that may lie buried. I have more fun with Dieter anyway," she called over her shoulder. She consoled herself that her sisters would not understand *her* fantasy world either.

ɕ∾ɔ

Papa was put on regular shift and no longer worked until midnight. But Lisl thought he would have preferred to work late. When he was home he looked uncomfortable and irritated. Now Papa sat at the dinner table with the family, where his mood swings were becoming more visible. No one was allowed to talk during the meal, and when they dared to speak, he just glared at them.

An American soldier had given Papa a small radio to replace the one that had been stolen. Lisl wished Papa did not have that radio because it gave him another reason not to talk to anyone. Now he listened to the news reports or sports, and everyone was afraid to make any noise.

Lisl missed the dinnertime discussions where the day's events at school became vivid and often humorous conversations, full of laughter and fun.

Mama tried to cheer her children by playing games in Papa's absence. While ironing the American soldiers' uniforms, they harmonized and the boys clowned around by singing along with extra deep or high squeaky voices.

Still the children suffered through their father's periods of deep depression or sudden unprovoked fits of anger.

Lisl longed for the old times when Papa laughed and sang with them. He did not seem to like his family anymore. Maybe he was still haunted by the war. If he could only talk about it he might feel better. But every time she brought up the subject he got angry at her, as if he were protecting a big secret.

One evening Lisl went to the wash kitchen in the basement to wash up for bed, but a few moments later she ran upstairs.

"Mama, there's a mouse caught in the bathtub. It's still alive," she shouted, hoping her mother would rescue the little creature.

Papa's coffee cup slipped from his hand and shattered on the floor. He yelled at Lisl, "Now look what you made me do. Get out." He pointed to the door, shaking, his face pale.

Frightened and crying, Lisl ran to her bedroom. Mama ran after her.

"Oh Lisl, I'm sorry. I'm sure he didn't mean it." Mama held her in her arms and wiped her tears.

"What did I do? I didn't mean to upset him, really."

"I don't know why he snaps at everyone. Maybe he hates to see you so hungry all the time." Mama stroked Lisl's hair. "He tries so hard and in so many ways to get enough food on the table. Maybe he thinks he is a failure and lets it out on his family."

"No, Mama. I think there is something else, because sometimes he is pretty happy, and we do have more food than we did before he came back." Lisl thought for a moment. "Do you think he hates mice?"

"Mice?" Mama laughed.

"Do you remember when I rescued the mouse from the neighbor's cat in the yard?"

"Yes. He had almost the same reaction, only he ran into the house. He felt sick for the rest of the evening." Mama sat on the bed beside Lisl. "At the time I didn't think it was because of the mouse, but you could be right, Lisl, so we'd better not mention mice again."

Lisl had stopped crying. Now she wanted to find out why he still felt so bad sometimes and other times he was quite happy. What could have happened to make him hate mice? He never did before.

Her mother left the bedroom, but Lisl sat on the bed, afraid to go downstairs.

After a while Dieter opened the door and peeked in. "Papa had to go out, you can come down now. I put the mouse outside."

Lisl went back into the laundry kitchen to wash up. Her sisters were ready for bed, and soon the household was quiet. But Mama was still ironing, waiting for Papa to come home.

CHAPTER 44

Fog of Sadness

Lisl stood in the garden. Summer had gone; the golden glow of fall gave way to a dreary gray. November days had lost their early morning light. Fog drifted across the barren fields in quiet resignation. The sun appeared dim and frail through the opaque sky and the smell of decaying leaves hung in the air. Mud clogged Muehlenweg as farm wagons cut deep tracks into the dirt road on their way to spread manure over the empty fields.

Lisl looked at the barren trees. Even the leaves on the ground had lost their color. She had watched them in the harvest sunshine when the wind whipped them into colorful dancing gatherings. Now they lay moisture laden in still piles. Her shoulders slumped; she shivered in the damp air at the thought of another freezing winter.

The boys played *Fussball* in front of the house.

When Papa came into the garden, Lisl felt his eyes on her. She worried he would still be angry with her.

He called, "Lisl catch." She ran after the ball and twirled, catching it. She laughed. *Papa has finally gotten over the war.* But soon she realized that he just felt guilty for shouting at her. She stopped dancing around as she watched his face turn sad. She wanted to tell him, it's all right, you don't have to play with me, but bringing it up would only make him feel bad again.

So she pretended that she had forgotten all about the mouse incident. She laughed and ran after the ball with the boys. Maybe this would get her father back to the way he used to be.

But after a few days, Lisl found him depressed and silent again. The ball in Dieter's hand did not entice him to join in a game.

❦

Papa and Herr Nagel, who had come home much earlier than Papa, volunteered to help with the improvement of the sports field outside of town. American soldiers, who occasionally used the field, helped fill in the artillery-hit holes. Papa worked on these improvements whenever he had a little free time. Lisl thought of it as an escape from his family. Maybe he needed the friendship of fellow prisoners. But even there she never heard him talk about the war.

Lisl and her sisters did not mind that he spent most of his free time away from home. Everything ran more smoothly without him, as he often created arguments between himself and Mama or the children. Mama also seemed happier in his absence as she was often forced to act as peacekeeper between the children and Papa in his unpredictable moods.

Still, Lisl noticed that lately Mama's energy and sense of humor had slowly drained away. And when she looked into her mother's hazel eyes, Lisl knew that she had been secretly crying.

Dieter and Lisl escaped into the stone break without their father's knowledge. The garden no longer needed tending, so Lisl felt less guilty.

She relished the special play times she shared with Dieter, sensing that her days of fantasies and make-believe were about to come to an end.

In the cool mist of late afternoon, Dieter pulled his knit cap a little deeper onto his forehead. "Isn't it great here?" He smiled, running ahead of Lisl and climbing up the embankment.

Lisl searched for the place where they had found that perfect shell. Yes it was her favorite place with Dieter.

"Look, Lisl, I found something," Dieter shouted from a ridge on the rock wall.

Lisl climbed up to him, but she knew by his disappointed expression that it was not the perfect petrified seashell he hoped for. He placed it in her hand.

"Well, at least it's a whole shell." Although it was cracked and chipped around the edges, Lisl acted pleased.

"Not that great," he said, "but better than the little pieces we've found lately."

"Oh, I think it's pretty good." She wiped it with her sleeve, but could not improve its looks. She handed it back and he put it in his pocket.

Lisl no longer cared whether the shell was perfect. She felt good just hiding away in their private little world, daydreaming, free of conflict and hurt feelings. She could tell that Dieter was trying to recapture their dreams as well.

He industriously poked at rocks, smiling at Lisl now and then. "I'm sure this came from a big beautiful shell that was torn apart by cavemen or maybe even prehistoric monsters." He held out a piece to her with a smile, but dropped it again. It seemed his fantasy had worn thin as well with Papa's return.

Lisl had grown up more than she wanted to. It had been a year of many changes for all of them. She missed the simple life, when they were allowed to pretend to be somewhere other than in the midst of war. Lisl knew her mother understood. Mama too looked as though she wanted to escape at times, but she had to hide her feelings because Papa no longer tolerated dreamers.

Dieter had grown as well. Yet they still hung onto that special bond–communicating with each other without words. He had been Lisl's escape companion throughout the war. Their fantasies had made life more bearable.

છ૭

This year the rains came too soon. Mama no longer could hang uniforms out on the clothesline. The area under the roof overhang held only a few uniforms and they took forever to dry.

Mama hammered in nails, zigzagging clotheslines through the living room. The lack of heat in the house prolonged the drying time. Now the room was not only cold but damp as well, and very uncomfortable. Traces of moisture appeared on walls and furniture. Mama often ironed the still-damp uniforms dry to get them out on time. Sometimes some of the heavy seams were still damp when she returned them. But none of the American soldiers ever complained.

One day Papa came home from work with a duffel bag of laundry slung over his shoulder. He plunked it down in the middle of the kitchen. The children gathered around to see what the GI had put in the bag. Some of the soldiers knew by now that Papa had six children, so they put candy bars, along with soap, cigarettes or coffee, in the bag to pay for the laundry. It was a special event, like opening Christmas presents.

Kurt always was the first one to inspect the bags and the most disappointed when the candy bar was missing.

When Mama opened the bag she stared in disbelief without reaching in.

"What is it?" Papa came over and took out an envelope. "Reichsmark! German money. We can't buy anything with that." Papa threw the money onto the kitchen table. He searched the bag, but came up empty-handed. "Not even soap. That's the first and last time I'll bring his laundry home." He kicked the sack. "I'll be at Ehrlich's house, helping them with their taxes. At least Ehrlich pays in food instead of worthless money." He stormed out the door.

By late evening Ellen and Charlotte had finished folding the laundry Mama had ironed, and stacked the uniforms into the duffel bags. Lisl and Dieter had cleaned the kitchen and finished their homework.

Mama glanced at the clock often. Lisl could tell her mother was worried because Papa had left the house so angry.

As the children prepared for bed, Mama started to hang the wet uniforms that she had fed through the wringer onto the line in the living room to dry during the night.

Sometimes when Lisl went downstairs at night, she stopped, her heart pounding when she encountered damp uniforms standing at attention in midair like headless soldiers. She slipped between the troops on her way to the bathroom, but quickly ran upstairs if she imagined one was moving.

The boys had been put to bed a half hour earlier and were silent when the girls went upstairs. Charlotte and Ellen had worked the hardest, and they fell asleep as soon as they laid their heads on their pillows.

Lisl thought about her mother who looked so worried. Whenever she heard a sound outside, Lisl went to the window, hoping to see her father walk up the road. Disappointed, she went back to bed, listening in the night for his footsteps coming up the garden path.

She was about to doze off when she heard the front door unlock. She listened for voices, but it remained quiet. Her mother must have fallen asleep at the kitchen table again. But soon she heard Papa's tender voice as he woke Mama. She sounded happy now. Lisl thought maybe Papa had come home with something good, like a mutton roast, for doing taxes for Herr Ehrlich who kept large herds of sheep.

Lisl pulled the covers under her chin. Now she could fall asleep without worry.

༄

The little sitting room that Opa and Aunt Anni had occupied after the Kitzingen bombing was converted into an office for Papa. Wet uniforms were kept out and it became the only room where Papa could welcome people when they came seeking tax advice. But it also became Papa's escape.

He sat behind the closed door, working all evening long. The farmers paid in food–whatever they could afford. Some could not pay him right away and would let him know when they butchered a pig. Then one of the children was sent with a milk can to get soup with sausages.

Papa's sparse additional tax work was as valuable as Mama's uniform laundry. But when it came to feeding a family of eight, hunger remained a problem.

CHAPTER 45

No Shoes for Lisl

December arrived with a chill of frost. Lisl did not mind, and her sisters were happy as well for not having to wash the mud off their shoes every time they entered the house. Lisl missed her hard shiny Sunday shoes, but when she thought of the pain she had endured on her way to church, she was almost glad they had been stolen.

Her hand-me-downs, although unsightly, at least did not hurt her feet. Still, she wondered how much longer they would last before they fell apart on her feet.

Walking along the railroad tracks would have been hard on her shoes. But Papa did not allow his children to go there any more. It would hurt his pride. They occasionally bought the coal from Herr Schweitzer with cigarettes, coffee, or soap. Herr Schweitzer and many of the townspeople still collected the heating material alongside the rail tracks.

Now, on rare occasion, Mama made a roast and the children got to eat meat. The gnawing hunger they had experienced in the past years had eased. Their root cellar was stocked with potatoes harvested from their garden. Maybe not as much as they usually had stored because they had started eating them before they were fully grown. Still, Mama thought it might be enough to get them through the winter.

The canned vegetables and fruits they harvested in summer stood in neat rows on shelves in the root cellar. Small amounts of flour and sugar could be bought on the black market with cigarettes and coffee. On special occasions, Mama would bake a loaf of bread.

Even with all the advantages, Lisl thought life had been much happier before Papa's return. Even during the bombings, the family was united, comforting each other. Now they had to be careful and think before they spoke so as not to offend Papa accidentally. Then Mama had to try to calm him again, often without success.

Sometimes little things would set him into a rage or throw him into deep depression. So there was little conversation between him and the children. He seemed to prefer it that way.

Lisl felt a different kind of war had invaded their home. She noticed the change in her mother most. Mama gave all of her attention to Papa when he was present.

It seemed to Lisl that her father had stolen their mother's spirit along with her wonderful sense of humor. She too had to be careful around him. The uncertainty of what he might do next was a heavy burden on everyone.

☙

"Lisl, look, it's snowing." Kurt hopped around and pulled Lisl outside to witness the first snowflakes of the season.

"Oh, look at those big flakes." Lisl caught one on her hand for Kurt to admire.

"Look Papa, it's snowing," Kurt ran toward his father as he came up the path.

"Get in the house before you get soaked." He pushed Kurt toward the door. "Where are your coats? Lisl, don't you have any sense at all?" Papa pushed Lisl ahead of him and into the house. Kurt was close to tears.

Mama ran her hand over Kurt's curly hair. "You can play in the snow if you put on your coats and mittens." She waved at Lisl. "You can go with him." Lisl quickly put on her coat.

Dieter dressed warmly and ran after Lisl. "I'll go with you." He frowned, looking back to the door. "Do you think he'll ever play with us? You know? The snowball fights we used to have when Papa was still happy?"

Lisl shrugged her shoulders, her eyes darkened. "Maybe he needs a little more time to get over the war. I wish he could just forget about it and become himself again."

"Look Lisl, I made a snowball." Kurt cupped his little hands around the slushy snow. "I'll show it to Mama." He ran toward the door.

"Oh Kurt, I wouldn't do that." Lisl blocked his way, but when she saw his disappointed face she quickly added, "It might melt inside the house. We'll get Mama to come out to look at your snowball." She opened the door and called, "Mama, come and see what Kurt has made."

Mama came out slipping into her coat.

She smiled at the drippy, soggy thing in his hands. "Kurt, you have made the first snowball." She gathered snow from the outdoor table and threw it at Dieter. Mama frolicked with her children as the new snow whirled around them. Kurt and Dieter were running with Mama, jumping to catch the big flakes. Lisl laughed. She felt happy to see Mama play again even though Papa was standing by the window of his office, watching solemnly.

Lisl stared into the sky, watching the big flakes drift to the ground. It gave her the illusion of floating upward. All the tree branches were covered with wet snow. The rows of barren raspberries and currant bushes looked magical.

Ellen and Charlotte came up the path, shyly glancing at Papa who still stood by the window. But when they saw Mama having a snowball fight with the others, the game had just begun.

Mama laughed and played with her children until they were exhausted. "Maybe Papa will come out and join in the fun. He used to love snowball fights." But after a while it became apparent that he was not coming. They went into the hallway, taking off their wet outer clothes.

Papa stood in the open doorway of the office, and Mama said, "You should have come out for a snowball fight. It's wonderful out there."

"I had enough snow to last me for the rest of my life when I was in Russia." He went back into the office and slammed the door, hiding in his private retreat.

Mama looked crushed and Lisl rushed to her and smiled. "Wasn't that fun?"

෧෨

Lisl had one pair of stockings without a lot of mended patches. Her other pair was in such poor shape that she was ashamed to leave the house wearing them. She had hoped for a better pair of shoes that would not soak her feet in mud and snow. But shoes were nowhere to be found. Her father was well aware of the problem–he frowned every time he looked at her shoes.

One day he came home from work with a package wrapped in newspaper under his arm. "Lisl, come here. I have something for you."

Lisl came running. It was not often her father talked to her or the other children, much less brought a gift. He tore the paper from the package and set a pair of lace-up boots in front of her.

Lisl jumped up and down, took off her slippers and quickly stepped into the boots. But as she looked at her father she could not hide her disappointment. He too saw that they were too big. She quickly folded some of the newspaper and stuffed it into the toes of the boots. Even with the newspaper she still slid around in them, which made it awkward to walk.

He motioned to Charlotte and Ellen. Ellen wasted no time slipping into the boots, never giving Charlotte a chance. Lisl could tell they fit Ellen better and tried hard not to cry. Even though they still looked a little big, Ellen would never admit it.

She marched around the room. "They fit perfectly. Charlotte, I think they are mine." She looked at her father and said, "*Danke shoen* Papa."

Papa looked at Lisl. "Sorry, I know you needed them most. I hope to get another chance at a smaller pair." With that Papa opened the newspaper and the shoe discussion had ended.

Ellen walked to Lisl in shoes that were supposed to be hers. Although she did not need the shoes as desperately, Ellen did admire them. "Don't worry, Lisl, sooner or later I will outgrow them and then they will be yours."

But that was not much consolation for Lisl. By then they would probably look like the ones she was wearing.

Dieter tried to console her. "Don't worry, Lisl, this year will be warmer, at least inside the house." He sat beside her on the floor where she had tried on the shoes and put his arm around her shoulder. "At least Charlotte knitted you nice warm slippers."

"Maybe I should have worn them inside the boots, they might have fit then." But Lisl knew it was too late for that. Ellen was reluctant to take the shoes off–maybe she feared that Charlotte might try them on and find them a perfect fit. Usually the biggest child got first choice, leaving room for hand-me-downs. Lisl resigned herself to another winter with torn shoes.

∽

Lisl looked forward to Christmas Eve, only two weeks away, yet she felt this year would be different. She thought back to the year before, when the house was filled with good spirits and love that not even hunger and cold could drive away.

She hoped her grandfather and Aunt Anni would come again. They had not visited since Papa had refused to see them. The children, however, walked to Kitzingen whenever they had time. Grandfather, with the help of his neighbors and friends, had cleared the house site of rubble. Lisl and her sisters and brother stacked bricks and rocks to the side of the property whenever they visited. Lisl felt the volunteers would have gotten a lot more done without the children's visits because Aunt Anni would try to make a special day for them by cooking something delicious. Grandfather was always pleased to talk with his grandchildren. But as the days grew shorter they no longer had enough daylight to make the trip after school. Opa thought it safer to postpone their visits until spring. Lisl hoped that her father would change his mind and invite Opa and Aunt Anni for Christmas.

The garden lay dormant under a blanket of snow. Dieter used a shovel to clear the path, and Lisl swept behind him with a broom.

"Hallo children," Herr Strohheim called as he came up the path. He carried a white goose under his arm.

"Is your father home?"

"No. Papa is still at work." Dieter dropped the snow shovel.

"Well, I'll go see your mother then." The children went with him and opened the door.

"Mama, Herr Strohheim is here to see you." Lisl called out from the hallway, so Mama could take him into the office and not have to explain the uniforms hanging all over the living room.

"*Gruess Gott* Herr Strohheim, how are you? And how is Frieda?"

"Getting better now, Frau Lindner. She'll be coming home for Christmas."

Mama pointed to a chair and he sat down, holding the goose tightly.

Lisl was curious. Maybe he had forgotten about the goose under his arm. He made no mention of it.

"It has been a long stay in the hospital for your wife."

"Yes. But at least she will be able to get around in a wheelchair when she gets home. She is looking forward to seeing the farm again. I've fixed the damage to the house and put in some ramps so she can get around the place. Now everything looks new. Will she be surprised." His face lit up.

"Yes, you will have a wonderful Christmas with Frieda."

The goose under his arm squawked and struggled. He got up.

"Will you tell Karl I'm sorry it took me so long to pay him? I thought he might like a Christmas goose." He handed the wing-flapping bird to Mama who quickly calmed it.

"That is very kind of you, I'm sure Karl will appreciate such a fine feast for the holidays."

He brushed a few feathers from his sleeve, awkwardly walked to the door, and opened it. Then he came back to the middle of the room as though he had forgotten something. He smiled at the children. "Now don't let it fly away." He shook everyone's hand and headed for the door again.

"*Aufwiedersehen. Frohe Weihnachten,*" he called out.

"*Aufwiedersehen,* Herr Strohheim." Mama was still stroking the goose.

As soon as Strohheim had left, Lisl and Dieter ran to their mother. "You're not going to kill that pretty goose." Lisl petted its neck, taking a good look at it.

"No, at least not right away, it's for Christmas." Mama handed the goose to Lisl and said, "Here, put it in with the chickens. Make sure you lock the gate."

Lisl and Dieter walked slowly around the house to the chicken coop. When they put it in the enclosure, the bird ran a few steps and shook its feathers into place.

"It's so pretty, it looks like a swan," Lisl observed.

"Do people eat swans?"

"I never heard of that."

"Well maybe if we say it's really a swan they won't kill it." With a pout, Dieter stroked the goose as though he knew it wouldn't work.

Papa came up the path and saw the children petting the goose.

"Where did that come from?"

"Herr Strohheim brought it. He said he was sorry it took him so long to pay you," Lisl said.

"Oh yes. Now listen you two, don't get attached to that bird. It's our Christmas dinner." But when the children made no attempt to come out of the chicken pen, he shouted, "Come out of there and finish your chores." He pointed at the half-swept walkway.

"Yes Papa." Lisl went back to clearing the snow off the walk. Dieter gave Lisl a sad look now and then but did not mention the goose again.

CHAPTER 46

A Visitor for Papa

Lisl gazed through the window, watching the swirling snowflakes. The beauty almost made her forget the upcoming long cold winter.

She turned to face hanging uniforms, now dry and stiff. Mama removed the clothespins and Lisl caught the headless soldiers as they fell. Mama folded them, placed them in the basket, and handed it to Lisl. "Take it upstairs please."

Lisl stacked the laundry on the bench in the girls' room, ready for ironing. She smiled when she came back into the living room. Now she could walk through the room without wet uniforms swatting at her face. The moisture on the walls had slowly disappeared from the heat of the stove over the last few weeks.

Mama swept her hair from her face, looking satisfied.

"This is the last load of laundry before the holidays." She unfastened the clotheslines and put them away. Everyone caught the holiday spirit, cleaning and polishing the rooms for the Christmas season.

Papa entered the living room; he shivered, rubbing his hands together and stood by the stove for a moment. Although his office was unheated, he often stayed there too long. He grabbed the newspaper, turned the radio to a soccer game, and sat down.

Lisl wondered how he could read and listen at the same time. She came to the conclusion that the newspaper was his shield between him and his family.

It was Saturday. The room was warm, and the scent of fresh-baked bread filled the air. Lisl wished that every day could be like today–without her father's shield of course.

Dieter sniffed the air. "Can we have a little slice of bread while it's still warm?"

"Yes, *Liebling*."

Kurt came running. "Can I have a slice?" Mama picked him up and sat him on her lap.

"We all can have a little bite now, but we'll save the rest for Sunday."

Ellen and Charlotte argued in the kitchen while rolling out cookie dough. Now and then Mama played referee, but not without more shouting from the girls first. Finally they came to an agreement; Mama suggested shaping half the dough with Charlotte's cutter and the other half with Ellen's.

Lisl worried about finishing Papa's gift. She never liked knitting and had been too slow to finish the scarf in school. Now she needed to hurry to get it done in time for Christmas. Frau Weber had given her some wool unraveled from an old blue sweater that was peppered with moth holes. Lisl had to knot the short pieces together.

Her mother had told her that knitting a scarf would be easy, but Lisl knew better. It was the tedious repetition she hated most. It took her longer just to retrieve a dropped stitch–and she dropped quite a few–than it took Charlotte to make a whole scarf.

"Why couldn't scarves be made from material? It would be so much faster," she complained. Lisl had dragged her knitting around for several days, trying to hide it from her father. Now the short piece of knitting resembled a dish rag.

"Mama, do you want me to do some ironing?" she asked.

"You know you can't do these big uniforms." Mama lifted Lisl's chin and looked at her. "What's the matter?"

"I hate the scarf. Just look at this mess." She held up her knitting.

Ellen walked by at just the wrong time.

"What do you call this?" she snickered.

"Ellen, stop that, I think it will be a very nice scarf–once it's finished," Mama said.

"No, Ellen is right. It's a messy thing."

Charlotte came to look at the scarf. "I'll help you with it later."

"Oh, thank you." Lisl knew that with her sister's help, she would have a chance to finish the scarf and still have time to wash it. Charlotte could knit fast and didn't even have to look at the needles. It was a mystery to Lisl.

There was a knock at the door and Papa put down his paper.

"I'll get it," he said. "It's probably Herr Ehrlich." He opened the door and shouted, "Helmut! What are you doing here?" Before the man could answer Papa grabbed his arm and pulled him through the door. "Come in, please come in."

A thin tall man stood in the hallway. He shook the snow off his coat before he took it off. When he entered the room, he looked at everyone as though he knew them well. But Lisl was sure she had never met him.

Papa seemed overjoyed to see him. Lisl even saw tears in his eyes. He held Helmut's hands with both of his, shaking them vigorously. Then impulsively, Papa hugged him.

"Irma, this is Helmut. We served on the Russian front together. He has saved my life several times."

"*Gruess Gott,* Helmut." Mama shook his hand.

Papa stepped beside Charlotte. "These are my girls, Charlotte and . . ."

"No let me," Helmut interrupted. "This is Ellen and this is Lisl." He finished Papa's count, pointing to them as he said their names. He shook their hands and gave each a long look. Lisl noticed, even through his leather gloves, that some of his fingers were missing.

"And these are my boys, Dieter, Kurt and Werner." Helmut clicked his heels and tipped his hat in mock salute. Dieter and Kurt were impressed. Helmut walked over to look at the baby. Werner was sitting up in his crib, looking wide-eyed at the stranger with the loud voice.

"Karl showed me pictures of the children, so I feel I know them very well." Helmut smiled at Mama. "But I haven't seen the baby before."

"Neither had Karl," Mama said. "You're just in time for coffee and fresh-baked bread. I hope you like goat cheese."

"*Wunderbar.*" He sat down on the couch and stretched his long legs, rubbing his thighs with a painful expression.

He took his hat from his dark brown hair and set it on his knee. Although his steely-gray eyes smiled, Lisl saw them glisten with pain. The fresh scar on his face ran from one cheek across his nose to the other side. His gloved hand unconsciously went to his face to cover the injuries.

Lisl felt sorry for him because he had not learned to accept the scars. She thought all his entertaining jokes and boisterous conversation were to cover how he really felt.

The family sat with their guest around the table now, enjoying the fresh bread and cheese. Mama made coffee from the used grounds Papa had brought home from work.

"How is your family?" Papa asked.

Helmut looked up with a start. His eyes darkened.

"I guess you haven't heard. They died in an air raid in March. After our house was bombed, my wife and daughter stayed with my parents. I was told by a neighbor that my family decided not to go to the shelter that one time because

Renate, my ten-year-old, had become very ill with a fever. That was the night that my parents' house was destroyed."

"Oh, I'm so sorry. I had no idea," Papa said. He looked devastated and put his hand on Helmut's shoulder.

Helmut sank his head. "In just a few moments everything I had was gone. When I got back to Marktbreit, the whole neighborhood lay in rubble." A long and painful silence followed.

Mama broke the silence. "Where do you live now?"

"I'm staying with Horst. He has an apartment in Sommershausen. He lost his house as well."

"How is Horst?" Papa asked.

"He is still taking it hard. He hates the wheelchair. You know him; he always had to be the daredevil." Helmut's eyes darkened. Silently they ate the bread.

After a while Helmut looked up. "Good bread Irma. Coffee's good too."

"Can you stay a while?" Papa asked.

"I have a room at Gasthof zum Falken. I have to leave on Sunday. Horst is expecting me back by then. I have to take him to the doctor Monday morning."

"We can put you up in the sitting room. You don't have to stay at the hotel," Papa said.

"No, no, I have a nice room at the hotel. I can come back here for a while on Sunday, if that is all right with Irma."

Mama put her hand on his. "Helmut, you are always welcome here."

Helmut took a big bottle of cognac from his bag.

"Irma, could we have some glasses? I have saved this bottle for a special occasion. I guess now is as good a time as any." He poured three glasses and handed one to Mama and one to Papa. He raised his glass and seemed at a loss for words or what to drink to.

"Here is to life," he finally said, smiling at the baby.

"Here is to life," Papa repeated.

Helmut refilled two glasses. Mama took hers away and Papa could not keep up with Helmut.

The children sat silently around the table, afraid to speak in their father's presence.

The horrors of war poured from Helmut's lips like the cognac from the bottle.

"Karl, do you remember when you and Horst walked barefoot through the muddy fields because you were tired of pulling your boots out behind you?" Helmut seemed close to tears, but he still pretended to joke.

"Even my socks got sucked. I gave up on finding the damned things," Papa remembered with a forced laugh.

"Oh, I can tell you one thing, fighting the mud was as bad as fighting the Russians." Helmut's eyes looked blurry as he went on. "The infantry didn't get very far. Everything got swallowed up by mud. All our equipment came to a standstill."

"We worked like the devil to dig it out, only to have to dig again twenty meters later." Papa stared into his glass as though he were seeing mud in the cognac.

"Yeah." Helmut poured himself another drink. He then lifted his glass and shouted, "Here is to that damned cold mud." His toast sounded like a curse as he hit his glass against Papa's.

Lisl cringed, expecting the glasses to shatter.

Papa looked up as though he had just remembered something, his face somber. "Can you believe it? Our own platoon left us behind enemy lines. To them we were already dead."

With a far-away look in their glossy eyes, it seemed to Lisl that they no longer were in the living room, but in their own private hell.

Mama sat motionless, but when Charlotte sniffled, she put her arm around her. Ellen glared at her sister, hissing words without sound. But Papa and Helmut paid no attention to the family. They seemed to feed off each other's memories in loud, slurred voices.

"I was glad when the frost came. I thought, 'now we can leave our boots on.' But then came that damned cold and snow," Helmut said.

Papa swayed in his chair, turning in jerks to stare out into the snow. "The frozen bodies," he said. "Oh God, all those frozen soldiers, Bolsheviks and Germans, all lying together."

Lisl and her family sat listening to horrifying stories in silence. Most of the conversation made little sense to Lisl, yet she felt drawn into a terrifying place that brought her to tears. Papa and Helmut were tortured by their memories of lost friends and soldiers. Lisl wanted to change the subject and end their nightmares. But she was unable to utter a word. Now her father was forced to talk about the war he had tried so hard to forget.

Helmut looked off into the distance. "Remember the look on the enemy's faces when we crept into their camp to steal their supplies? They just stared at us. They didn't make a move."

"No, Helmut. They were frozen. They were dead, all of them. They all were frozen." Papa swallowed hard.

"Yeah, they were dead," Helmut echoed in a low, almost inaudible voice. Then he shouted, "But those rats. How come they didn't freeze? I never saw anything like those rats. They could chew a man's face right off of him."

Lisl almost jumped out of her chair. Her stomach turned into a knot. Now she understood the mouse incident and why her father had been so angry at her. Mama put her hand on Lisl's shoulder to keep her calm. Lisl wanted to scream stop when she saw Papa turn white. Yet mercilessly Helmut relived the experience.

"I didn't even recognize Albert and Heinrich. I hope they froze before the rats got to them," he recalled.

Now Papa openly cried, holding up his hand toward Helmut as if to stop him from talking. But Helmut could not stop. He did not see her father's objection or the shocked expressions on the children's faces. He no longer was in the room. He sounded angry. "A lot of good our sacrifice did them. While we were gone stealing the rations for them, they froze to death." He took a drink. "Except for Horst," he said, calmer now. "At least Horst survived. The rats didn't get him."

"We were lucky to get out of there." Tears rolled down Papa's face as he held his glass near his lips but did not drink. He looked ashen.

Lisl looked around the room to keep herself from being pulled into their terror. Kurt's pencil drawings and indifference to the stories felt comforting, and, although Dieter paid close attention, he seemed more curious than upset. Charlotte, on the other hand, was crying with Ellen glaring at her now and then.

But there was no escaping Helmut's loud slurred voice. "And what about Balkan? We lost most of our men there." Helmut gulped down another cognac. "Ironic. We had to play dead to keep from getting shot. Falling on top of dying and dead bodies so the Russians thought they shot us all." Helmut stared into the cognac, his expression filled with horror. "What could we do with no ammo left? We had to keep dead still even when the bodies of our comrades came falling on top of us. We had to stay still. It was the hardest thing I ever did."

Helmut tried to justify his actions–he seemed to feel guilty for staying alive.

Lisl sat paralyzed, unable to wipe her tears.

Papa shuddered. "The thing I remember most was the silence after the shooting," he said. "I was sure I was dead. I couldn't hear my heartbeat anymore. But I think I heard the heart of the soldier lying on top of me, and then it stopped. I felt so sick trying to get out from under the dead bodies." He took a sip and kept staring into the glass. "Trying to get back through the enemy lines without ammunition took some luck." Papa's words were so slurred that Lisl could barely understand him.

"There aren't many of us left," Helmut said.

"Here's to the survivors. We're the lucky ones who have to remember hell for the rest of our lives," Papa said bitterly, lifting his glass.

"Yeah, and if an angel sits on your shoulder you're home free. But if the devil gets on your back, your whole family is gone along with your house. It makes you wonder what it was all about." Glossy-eyed, Helmut pounded his hand on the table like boots hitting the ground and broke out into a mock marching song. Papa joined in.

Lisl felt cold as though she had gone back with them to those horrifying places and times. She wiped her tears.

Charlotte's crying had not stopped since the war stories started.

Mama got up and gathered the children. "Helmut, it's past their bedtime," she interrupted.

Lisl was eager to go upstairs, away from the sadness. Timidly she waved. *Gute Nacht,* Helmut." And the others followed.

He tried to stand up on wobbly legs but gave up when he tipped back in his seat. He held up his hand in a clumsy kind of a wave. "I'll see you in the morning."

Papa made an awkward attempt to hug his children, which surprised Lisl.

Mama went upstairs and tucked in the boys. After a few minutes she came into the girls' room and stayed a while to calm a still-crying Charlotte.

Lisl heard her father's voice calling, "Irma. Where did you go?" Mama quickly went downstairs again.

The girls lay in their beds but could not sleep. They heard Helmut's thunderous voice from downstairs singing:

Auf der Heide blueht ein kleines Bluemelein,
und das heisst, Erika.

Sometimes the conversation sounded soft and sad, sometimes angry and loud. Luckily Lisl could not tell what they were saying. She heard the boys talking in the next room, and by their tones she knew that Kurt had not understood Helmut's and Papa's sad stories. Soon they were silent and she knew that they had fallen asleep–at least Kurt.

Charlotte sobbed. "Why did Helmut have to tell us these stories?"

"Well, that is what happened to them. We should know what happened to Papa," Ellen said.

"I still think they shouldn't tell children," Charlotte insisted.

"You might be the oldest, but you are such a baby," Ellen argued. "Lisl, don't you think she's a baby?"

Lisl did not answer.

"See, Lisl is asleep, so you know she didn't mind listening to the stories."

But Lisl was wide awake, haunted by her father's pain. She wanted to cry silently under her covers. To think about what she had heard and try to make sense of it all.

She did not mind having heard the stories of the hell they had to endure. She felt very sad for her father and Helmut, especially for Helmut who had lost his parents, his wife, his daughter and his house. She wondered if the rats had bitten Helmut's face, those wounds he tried so hard to hide. Lisl hoped they were frostbites or shot wounds. But what about his missing fingers? Had the rats gnawed them off while he was sleeping?

Her mind raced when she thought of all the terrible things that had happened to them. She whispered a promise to God. "I won't pout when Papa gets angry at me. And in the future I'll take great care not to mention mice or rats."

She heard the front door open and Helmut's loud, slurred voice, bidding Mama a good night. Lisl ran to the window and watched him and Papa stumble down the garden path. Her father must have decided to walk Helmut to the hotel. Lisl went back to bed, wondering if her father could find his way back to the house again. She had never seen him drunk before.

The bedroom door opened quietly and Mama stood in the doorway. Lisl sat up. Mama put her finger to her lips and sat down on Lisl's bed. Charlotte and Ellen had fallen asleep.

"Can't you sleep?" Mama whispered.

"I'm all right Mama. I won't have nightmares."

"Good, I won't either. At least now we know what happened to Papa." She swept the back of her fingers lightly over Lisl's cheek.

"*Gute Nacht, Liebling.*"

"*Gute Nacht*, Mama."

After a while, Lisl heard soft cursing from outside. She peeked through the window and saw her father coming through the garden, fighting the snow-covered bushes that blocked his way. Mama came to his rescue. With a soothing voice she led him onto the path and guided him into the house.

The snow had left a soft white cushion on the window ledge. Lisl closed the window and slipped back into her warm bed. She watched the snowflakes dance near the glass until she fell asleep.

CHAPTER 47

Helmut's Promise

Lisl heard her mother's soft voice singing to the baby downstairs. After a while Mama scraped the ashes from the stove to make a fire, a comforting routine Lisl loved to listen to as she slowly awoke.

She lay still, thinking about the stories Helmut and her father had told the night before. How would her father feel? Now the story was told–the horrors he had tried so hard to hide from his family.

Lisl hoped he would not get worse. She was afraid to come downstairs. At least now she knew why Papa behaved like a stranger sometimes. Would he ever be himself again?

Bach's organ music from the radio downstairs reminded Lisl that it was Sunday.

Charlotte and Ellen were still asleep. Ellen's Sunday clothes hung neatly on the back of the chair beside her bed. She liked to plan ahead.

On top of the water in the jug floated a thin layer of ice. Lisl poured the water into the washbowl, holding her finger on the icy lid to keep it from sliding out. After washing up, she slipped into the beautiful blue Sunday dress that Ellen had outgrown. It had belonged to Charlotte once, but Ellen had outgrown it shortly after as they were almost the same size. It was a little big, but Lisl liked it that way; it covered the mended knee patches on her stockings.

Lisl went downstairs. "*Guten Morgen*, Mama."

"*Guten Morgen, Liebling.* Did you sleep well?"

"Yes, Mama, I didn't have bad dreams." Lisl followed her mother into the kitchen. "Mmm the coffee smells good. Can I help you with something?"

"You can set the table."

Lisl set out the good cups and bread plates, arranging them neatly in Sunday tradition.

"Shall I set a place for Helmut?"

"I wouldn't count on him coming for breakfast. I'm sure he'll be sleeping in."

Papa came into the kitchen still in his pajamas. He yawned then moaned in pain, quickly holding his head with both hands.

"*Guten Morgen*." He spoke in a low, quiet voice.

"*Guten Morgen*, Papa." Lisl watched her father get a glass of water and swallow two aspirin. He looked in pain. She prepared herself for the worst.

"How do you feel, Karl?" Mama asked.

"Awful. You should have stopped me after two drinks, you know I'm not much of a drinker."

Lisl found the courage and asked, "Is Helmut coming back?"

Papa looked at her and smiled. "I hope so. He may feel a little foolish today, maybe with a big hangover."

Lisl smiled back. He had actually looked at her and talked to her.

He glanced at Mama. "But then again he could out-drink me any day."

"Maybe you should go by the hotel and invite him for lunch."

"What's for lunch?" he asked.

"I have enough eggs and a little ham. So ham omelets with potato salad and some of the bread I baked."

"Oh I think he'll love that. I'll stop by Falken on our way to church," he said.

"*Guten Morgen*," Charlotte and Ellen said as they came to the table. Dieter and Kurt too gathered around the table, watching their father with fearful expressions.

"Come on now, I won't bite. I just have a terrible headache, so don't anyone start screaming." The children had not expected him to joke and gazed at him wide eyed. Lisl laughed in relief.

After breakfast they dressed to go to church. Papa frowned when he saw Lisl's shoes.

"Can't you do something with those things?" he said.

"I'll clean them up a little." Lisl took off her shoes, but no matter how much she tried to clean them, they remained the same torn monstrosities. She was afraid he would tell her to stay home from church. She slipped into her shoes again and put on her oversized coat, hoping her shoes would not be too noticeable.

Papa walked with his children through the deep snow along Muehlenweg and through the tower gate. The cobblestone streets in town were clean-swept.

Papa turned and motioned toward the church. "You go on; I'll catch up with you in a minute." He headed toward Gasthof zum Falken. The children went slowly on their way and after a few minutes their father caught up.

Quietly the family entered the church. The children sat in the front rows while Papa sat in the back.

The church was still unheated, but Lisl did not mind. At least her feet did not hurt in her old shoes. She watched her breath rise to the ceiling. The painting looked different today. All the angels were smiling. She wondered why she had never noticed that before.

She said her own special prayer, thanking God for sending Helmut. Papa seemed different–better. Now he no longer had to carry that horrible secret.

Ellen poked Lisl without interrupting her singing or turning her eyes from the page. Lisl quickly took her gaze from the paintings to the song book.

On their way out, Lisl saw her father cheerfully talking and smiling with some of his soccer buddies by the entrance. But his smile vanished when he caught sight of Lisl's shoes.

The family walked home together, and this time Charlotte and Ellen did not dare argue. But Lisl could tell it was hard for them. She noticed Ellen poking Charlotte's arm, mouthing some nasty words. Charlotte stuck out her tongue in reply–behind Papa's back of course.

When they got home, Mama had set the table with an extra place setting for Helmut.

"What time will Helmut be here?" she asked Papa.

"I couldn't tell you that. I left a message for him at the desk. He was still asleep."

"Well, the potato salad will keep and I will make the omelets when he gets here."

At one o'clock, Papa was ready to give up. "I don't think he'll come. It's late." Papa looked out the window.

"Let's just wait a few more minutes." Mama arranged the bread neatly on a plate.

A knock on the door announced Helmut's arrival.

"*Guten Tag.* Sorry I'm a little late." He slowly walked through the door as though he wasn't sure if he was welcome. Lisl thought he looked better than he had the night before. With a bright smile he greeted everyone and rubbed his hands together. "I'm hungry now."

Mama brought the salad and omelets to the table and called everyone to sit down. The children looked curiously at Helmut. Lisl hoped he would not tell more of the war stories.

"What? Do I have a fly on my nose?" He said swatting at his nose. The children laughed, and Lisl was happy to see him in a good mood after the frightening and tearful evening.

She noticed that his hand did not cover the facial scars as often. He seemed to enjoy the meal, smiling at the children now and then.

Lisl heard her mother's sigh of relief when Papa engaged the children in conversation, the way he used to.

After the meal, the girls cleared the table. Lisl overheard a conversation between Helmut and her mother after her father had left the room for a moment.

"How is Karl doing?" Helmut asked.

"I think he will be fine now. He needed to face the demons of war. I often felt he was ready to explode." She smiled at Helmut. "I think your visit helped him cope. Whenever I asked him about the war, he would walk away or get angry."

"That was to be expected, Irma. Some of the soldiers never get over the trauma. Horst is going through a very difficult time right now and I have to watch him. He has been talking about suicide off and on. He thinks life without legs isn't worth living. He has a long way to go."

"How are *you* doing, Helmut?" Mama asked cautiously.

"I'm taking it one day at a time. Taking care of Horst helps me as much as it helps him. The fact that someone needs me gives me purpose to go on."

Papa came back into the room and sat across from Helmut.

"I have to apologize for the way I acted last night," Helmut said. "I don't know what got into me. I hope I didn't frighten the children."

Papa shook his head. "I think we both got carried away once we started."

"No need to apologize," Mama said. "The conversation explained a lot. I think everyone feels better for it." Mama glanced at Charlotte. "Well, almost everyone."

Helmut brightened. "You're very kind. But you're right. It felt good and bad all at once to talk about the war. I needed to let it all out. I can't do that with Horst."

"Someday I would like to meet Horst. Maybe you could bring him here when he feels better," Mama said.

"Yes, I think it would do him good to see the children." Helmut watched the boys play. "Especially if they would throw a few balls at him and maybe roughhouse a little. That way he'd know he can still think of having a family." He looked at Lisl. "How old is Lisl?"

"She is ten." Mama motioned Lisl over to the table.

"Lisl, I'll send a Christmas gift just for you. It's something I found for Renate. She was your age."

Lisl saw how he fought back his tears. She didn't want to ask him what his daughter's present was.

"*Danke shoen*, Helmut." She curtsied a little.

Abruptly he stood up. "Well, I have to be off to catch the train," he said. "Oh I almost forgot. I have something for the children." He dug into his bag and took out a small packet. "Charlotte, Ellen, come in here so I can say good-bye."

The girls rushed into the living room. "Do you have to leave already?" Ellen asked.

"Yes, my train leaves in 45 minutes. But I have an early Christmas present for all of you." He handed each of the children a chocolate bar as he shook their hands and said, "*Aufwiedersehen*." The children were delighted and thanked him, wishing him a Merry Christmas. Papa walked him to the station.

CHAPTER 48

Schwanchen's Doom

Christmas excitement filled the house and everyone was busy preparing. Lisl, with Charlotte's help, had finished the scarf for her father. She washed and dried it carefully and now it looked brand new. Lisl found a rumpled up sheet of gold paper with little white angels in the attic. After she ironed out the wrinkles, it was perfect for wrapping Papa's gift.

Dieter stood beside Lisl with a sad look on his face. "Do you think Papa would let us keep Schwanchen as a pet?"

Lisl wrinkled her forehead. "You could try, but they are all looking forward to this Christmas dinner, especially Papa."

Now that Papa was more approachable, Dieter sat down beside his father. Papa didn't notice and kept reading the paper.

"Do you think the goose is really a swan?" Dieter asked.

"Dieter, it's not a swan. It's our Christmas dinner."

"You know, Papa, people don't really get that hungry on Christmas."

"Maybe we can have omelets instead." Lisl joined in.

"Don't you think we all need a good meal where everyone can eat all they want?"

Dieter was not about to give up that easily. "I would be happy with an omelet; even just a small one. And with all the cookies Charlotte has made no one will be that hungry."

Papa smiled and stuck his nose behind the newspaper–the goose subject was closed.

Lisl and Dieter spent a lot of time with Schwanchen, giving the goose extra food and stroking its graceful neck.

Ellen stood by the enclosure. "I see you're trying to fatten it up a little."

Dieter looked shocked. "Oh Ellen, don't you like Schwanchen?"

"Sure I do, especially the nice crisp drumsticks."

Dieter put his arms around Schwanchen as if to protect it from Ellen's words. By now the goose had attached itself to the children and followed them around the yard, or stood by the gate trumpeting loudly when they came into view.

"Maybe we should stop feeding it. Whoever heard of eating a skinny goose," Dieter said.

Lisl shook her head; her eyes darkened. "It's a little late for that. Tomorrow is Christmas Eve and Papa wants to have it for Christmas Day."

❧

Mama arranged a pretty basket with jars of homemade fruits and vegetables. Lisl took the basket and on her way out of the garden she added a few twigs of red berries for decoration.

The snow still fell, getting deeper by the hour. Yet the twirling snowflakes looked like plucked feathers. The dancing flakes had lost their charm for Lisl.

Dieter ran after her. "Let's take the shortcut." They walked past the stone break but could not resist taking a look. The stone wall looked magical; the snow covered the narrow ledges between the gray rocks.

"Look Lisl, it looks like a layer cake with white frosting. Remember when Mama took us to a café once on your birthday a long time ago? They had a cake just like that."

"Mmm, I remember." Lisl's mouth watered. "I think we'd better go before the food freezes."

Dieter looked at Lisl's torn shoes. "I guess we should have taken the street through town, there is less snow."

Frau Weber opened the door promptly at their knocking. "Come in children, I was expecting you."

They stomped the snow off their shoes and shook their coats and knit caps before entering.

Lisl put the basket on the table. "Mama sends you her love and a *Frohe Weihnachten.*"

"*Danke shoen.* That is kind. I have something for your family, too." She picked up a little ceramic pot, wrapped in cellophane tied with a red ribbon, and handed it to Lisl.

Lisl smelled the goat cheese right through the beautiful gift wrap and smiled. "*Danke shoen* Frau Weber."

"You're welcome Lisl. Can you stay a while?" She asked.

"Just for a little while. We'll go to church with Papa later." Lisl sank down into the soft sofa. She felt as though the cushions were swallowing her. Dieter sat down beside her, but fought his way back out to look at the Christmas tree by the window.

"This is a pretty tree. I like the little locomotive." He admired each ornament. "Oh, Lisl look at this angel."

"These ornaments were my son's favorites too when he was a little boy. Now they're my grandson's favorites. They will come for a visit later this evening." A happy smile rushed over her face. "How are your mother and the baby?"

"Mama is fine, the baby too. He sits up in his crib now and watches everything and everyone."

"Well, I know your sisters are as feisty as ever. I saw them in town the other day. They do like to get at each other, don't they?" She laughed a little. "Is your Papa well?"

Lisl beamed. "Yes. Papa is fine. I think he's getting better all the time."

After a short silence Lisl suggested, "Don't you think we ought to go home now, Dieter?"

Dieter went to the door, ready to leave.

"*Frohe Weihnachten,* Frau Weber." They each shook her hand and went on their way.

"She didn't have a single glass ornament on her tree, you know, the ones you like so much," Dieter whispered as they walked toward Herrn Strasse.

The streetlights gleamed in the twilight, illuminating their surroundings with a warm glow.

"Dieter, aren't you glad we have street lights again?"

"We've had them for some time now." He sounded surprised.

"I know that, but remember last Christmas? We couldn't see a single light because of blackout."

They walked home through the town. Windows had open shutters and sparkling candlelight behind curtains. Families decorated their trees, and some decorated around door frames with Tannen twigs. But the stores were closed. They had nothing to sell although some of them had Christmas decorations around their doors.

"Do you think they killed Schwanchen by now?" Dieter abruptly reminded Lisl.

Lisl sighed. "I suppose so."

They walked up the garden path, but could not hear Schwanchen's familiar trumpeting. But it was already dark and the goose would have been asleep by now. Lisl couldn't bear to look.

When they came through the door the scent of cinnamon hung in the air.

Dieter sniffed. "That smells good. What are you making?"

"I'm making Gluehwine with apple cider since we don't have any wine. When you come back from church you can have some to warm you up," Mama said.

"What are we having for dinner?" Lisl asked.

"Potato salad with Bratwurst. Papa got some Bratwurst from Herr Hofman."

"What are we having tomorrow?" Dieter put himself squarely in front of his mother.

"Dieter, you know what we'll have." She tried to brush the hair from his face. But this time Dieter turned away, pouting.

Lisl looked around the room. "Did we get a package today?"

"No Lisl, nothing came."

"I guess Helmut forgot his promise."

Mama did not look at Lisl. "What was that?"

Lisl shrugged her shoulders. "Helmut said he would send me a gift."

"Yes he did. Didn't he?"

There would be no mail tomorrow or the next two days. Lisl wondered what it would have been. Maybe he had made it up or changed his mind.

Kurt helped his mother in the kitchen, keeping very quiet, sneaking little tidbits from the table.

"Where is Papa?" Lisl asked.

"He had to go out for a while. He put the tree up before he left," Mama smiled.

Lisl wondered what awful person would have him do taxes on Christmas Eve.

Ellen carried the box of ornaments to the tree.

The rollaway bed stood near the hallway door. Lisl rolled it to the side. "What are you going to do with this?"

"Papa brought it down from the attic. It was in his way when he got the tree stand and ornaments down," Ellen said. She nudged Lisl out of her way to let her know she didn't want to answer any more questions.

Charlotte came into the room. "Just roll it into Papa's office for now."

Charlotte and Ellen clipped the candleholders onto the tree branches and put in white candle stubs—leftover candles from last Christmas. They would last through a few carols.

Lisl hummed a song and her sisters joined in. For once they cooperated with each other. Ellen handed the ornaments to Charlotte who stood on a chair to reach the top of the tree. They must have come to an agreement not to fight on Christmas. Dieter gazed at the tree in silence. Kurt came out of the kitchen with his mouth full, trying to sing too.

Mama wiped her hands on her apron. "You'd better leave for church. Papa might not be back in time."

"Maybe we should wait a little for Papa."

"No, Lisl, it will be too late. You'd better bundle up. It's going to be cold in church," Mama said.

Charlotte and Ellen walked ahead through town arguing as usual. Lisl and Dieter walked far behind them. Lisl was embarrassed by their shouting. Their truce had not lasted very long. In church, however, Charlotte and Ellen stood side by side, singing with beautiful voices like angels, faces uplifted.

On the way home, Lisl found her sisters in a better mood, and they all walked home together.

As they came through the door, Kurt came running, hopping up and down. "It's almost time for the *Christkind*."

"Yes it is." Mama pointed to the kitchen. "Now you have to stay in there and no peeking." The children were not allowed to leave the kitchen until they heard the bell ring.

Kurt's eyes widened. He heard the front door open followed by footsteps and a commotion from the hallway to the living room. "Is it the *Christkind?*"

Lisl smiled at him. "Maybe it is."

A few minutes later the crystal bell rang and Kurt pushed through the door into the living room.

The curtain billowed in the breeze and the candles flickered. Kurt ran to the window. "We missed the *Christkind* Angel again." Mama closed the window and the dim light bathed the room in a festive glow.

Suddenly Kurt screamed. "Opa!"

Papa had fetched Opa and Aunt Anni from the train station while the children were in church. They all surrounded their grandfather and Anni who had silently sat on the couch until the children noticed. Opa's laughter was no longer laced with sadness.

Papa cleared his throat noisily, bringing his children to attention. "How about some Christmas carols?" He sat on the couch between Opa and Anni and joined the children in song. Opa let his tears trickle down his cheeks; they looked like jewels in the candlelight. Lisl sat beside him and put her hand in his. He held on tight.

Stille Nacht heilige Nacht,
alles shlaeft einsam wacht.

Opa's deep voice rang like the church bells.

When the last note died away, Kurt dashed for the tree. "Look how many packages."

Lisl loved the beautiful cardigan Aunt Anni had knitted for her. She thought it more precious now, knowing how long it took her to knit her father's skimpy little scarf. She also received a new pair of knit stockings.

Charlotte and Ellen giggled over their sweaters and immediately swapped them with each other–at least for now.

With an apologetic look, Lisl handed her father the gift-wrapped scarf.

"What a pretty package." He smiled at Lisl before he opened it. "Ahh, a scarf to keep me warm."

Lisl smiled to herself. He liked it.

Papa put it around his neck, but it did not hang down very far.

Lisl wrinkled her nose. "Sorry. Kind of short, isn't it?"

"Well, not when I tuck it under my coat. At least it won't get in my way when I walk."

Lisl laughed and wrapped her arms around her father. He hugged her back. She would not have dared to do that a few weeks ago. No one could get close to him then. For Lisl, this was the best gift of all.

After a few more Christmas carols the family sat down to dinner.

Papa's office was to become a guest room again for the next three days. Lisl enjoyed hearing Papa tell some of his lighter, more humorous stories to Opa and Aunt Anni. Now he could talk about the war. But he did not mention rats or the horror he had endured. Lisl did not think that he was ready yet.

CHAPTER 49

Sunday Shoes

On Christmas Day, Lisl awoke to the sound of, "Oh Tannen Baum" from the radio downstairs. Mama sang along now and then. Her parents' voices sounded happy. It was a familiar sound from times before the war had robbed Papa of his sense of humor.

Lisl slipped out of bed and stood by the window, blowing her breath on the glass to see through the frosty design. The chimneys in the neighborhood released clouds of smoke into the wintry landscape. The neighbors had found heating fuel to keep their Christmas cozy. Even though the bedroom was frigid, a warm feeling came over Lisl when she heard Papa's and Opa's laughter.

Her view to the outside was cut short. Ice crystal patterns of ferns and feathers crept like magic across the glass, mending the hole her breath had torn into the frosty fabric.

Charlotte sat up yawning. "For heaven's sake. How can you stand there in the cold staring at the window?"

"But Charlotte, the living room is warm. We can warm up again."

Ellen poked at the ice in the water pitcher. "We'd better wash downstairs."

After breakfast the family, except for Mama, Kurt and the baby, walked to church. Ellen and Charlotte took Opa's arms, chatting and laughing all the way through town.

In church, the men's choir sang in the upper section beside the organ. Their powerful voices sounded loud and strong then soft again like an angel's breath.

At the end of the sermon, the organist played almost as loudly as when he had tried to drown out the attack on Mainbernheim on the day of Charlotte's confirmation.

On their way home, Opa said, "Oh, I'm hungry now." Dieter and Lisl exchanged horrified glances. Schwanchen probably had been in the oven for several hours now. By the time they arrived home Lisl would be expected to eat the poor bird. Her stomach churned.

In a funeral march, Lisl and Dieter trailed behind the rest of the family.

Aunt Anni waited up. "Why are you looking so sad?"

Dieter shook his head. "We don't feel like eating Christmas lunch."

"Oh, Schwanchen." She walked with them in silence for a while. But her heart was not in it. She too was looking forward to the Christmas dinner. Anni must have tired of Lisl and Dieter's somber mood. She ran back to Papa's side, leaving the children to their grief.

Ellen slowed down and walked beside them for a few paces. "Don't look so gloomy. It's Christmas. There will be other geese. I know how much you liked Schwanchen."

She finally showed a little compassion, but Lisl thought she sounded far too cheerful for such a serious occasion.

As they walked through the front door Lisl smelled the delicious roast. Despite her misgivings, her stomach rumbled. After preparing vegetables and potato dumplings, Mama called them to the table. She brought out a big golden-brown bird with its legs sticking up and everyone said "Ahh that looks delicious."

Lisl ran from the table. Dieter came after her. He too seemed to have lost his appetite.

"Well, if that's how you feel, you might as well do some chores." Papa motioned to the door. "The chickens are still locked in the coop and haven't been fed yet."

Lisl cried and slammed the door on her way out. How insensitive. Now they had to feed the chickens without being greeted by friendly Schwanchen. It was just too sad. They went downstairs and out through the side door where Dieter fetched the feed. As they opened the door to the coop, they heard an unexpected yet familiar sound.

"Schwanchen!" Dieter dropped to his knees beside the goose, spilling the chickenfeed. He petted its long soft neck as it gobbled up food.

Lisl stepped beside Dieter, laughing. "It's still here." She ran back upstairs with Dieter.

Breathlessly bursting through the door, Dieter pointed at the half-eaten bird. "Who's that?"

"None of ours," Papa said. The family laughed. They must have known all along, Lisl thought. Papa explained that one of the farmers had given him a big duck, already killed, he assured Dieter. Now their appetites had returned. It was the best meal Lisl ever had.

"Papa, you won't save Schwanchen for Easter dinner will you?" Dieter asked with his mouth full.

"You'd better get it to lay eggs in a hurry or I can't guarantee its future."

"But Papa, I don't even know whether it's a he or a she." Dieter looked puzzled. "How will I know?"

"Oh I think I know what it is," Opa said with a little smile. "It's definitely a she."

"How can you tell, you can't even see?" Lisl said.

"It talks too much," he declared. "Females always talk too much."

"Opa, just so you know, the rooster starts screaming before anyone is up, and he is a male." Lisl defended her gender.

"Well, that's different. He's on duty. He has to wake everyone or people would sleep all day."

Lisl laughed and let her grandfather have his joke.

"Oh good. So there is a chance that Schwanchen will lay eggs," Dieter said.

"We'd better get her a mate, that way she will lay," Papa
suggested.

Lisl wrapped her arms around her father's neck from
behind his chair and he stroked her hands.

"Oh, can we really get another goose?" she said.

"Gander," he corrected her.

"But remember, the geese will be your responsibility,"
Ellen reminded them quickly.

Lisl helped clear the table. All of the food had
disappeared. Schwanchen was still alive. Lisl peeked into
the dining room and watched Papa's smile. This had turned
out to be the best Christmas.

Charlotte hummed, nibbling on little bits of duck
still on the carcass as she cleaned the kitchen. Ellen
washed the dishes and handed them to Lisl to dry.
Charlotte put everything back in its place while they sang
carols.

Lisl watched her sisters. Each seemed to know what the
other one was about to do. Dressed in their Sunday best,
ribbons in their curled hair, they looked very grown up.
Charlotte had changed from a frightened girl to a calm and
pretty young lady. She still quarreled with Ellen, but Lisl had
seen grown-ups do the same. Soon Charlotte would find
a job and go to work. She no longer went to school. Lisl
realized how strong her sisters had been all through the war.

Charlotte had often served as a mother substitute when
Mama was too busy. She had worked hard and long hours
in extreme heat and cold.

Ellen had a special talent for bargaining with the
farmers for food after the rest of the family had given up.
Lisl admired her sisters.

Life appeared normal now, but Lisl was not deceived.
She knew it was only temporary. After the holidays, her
mother would take in laundry again. Clotheslines would
crisscross the room with wet uniforms hanging ghostly in

midair. Her mother would work hard just to get a few packs of cigarettes or soap to trade for things the family needed.

Lisl hoped that someday they would save enough cigarettes to buy a pair of shoes for her on the black market. In a few months, the children would work the garden again and help out on farms. Lisl vowed to help more with the cooking and the younger children once Charlotte went to work.

Still she felt sad for her mother. It was very hard on her with six children and Papa—who had not yet fully recovered. But at least he was starting to be happy again, which made Mama happy as well. After hearing Helmut's story of having lost his whole family, maybe Papa felt lucky he still had his.

Lisl sat down on the armrest of the couch beside her father who was reading the paper. Now the paper was in his lap. She could see his face.

"There's still a gift left under the tree," Mama said.

Lisl was sure it was not there a moment ago. By Mama's tone, Lisl knew that it was to be her gift. She retrieved the package wrapped in brown packing paper with a big red bow on it. The brightly colored tag read:

To Lisl.
Frohe Weihnachten,
From Helmut.

"Helmut sent me a gift, he didn't forget." Lisl wanted the magic and guessing to last. She read the tag again and again.

Ellen pulled the string on the gift. "Well, aren't you going to open it?"

Lisl tore the paper from the box and slowly opened it. "Shoes," she whispered. "Shiny black shoes. Aren't they beautiful?"

"They're not exactly for walking in deep snow," Charlotte said.

Lisl caressed their shiny surface. She was afraid to try them on in case they would be too big again and she would have to give them to one of her sisters.

"Look, if you're not going to try them on I will," Ellen said with a teasing smile.

Lisl quickly slipped them on before Ellen could.

"They fit perfectly even in my thick stockings. They don't hurt at all." Lisl walked through the room jumping up and down to make sure.

Mama smiled. "Now you have a new pair of Sunday shoes."

Lisl sat in front of the Christmas tree, admiring her shoes, moving her feet in circles to view them from all angles.

She still could not believe they were hers. But her eyes darkened when she thought of Helmut's daughter. Lisl's joy turned to guilt for wearing them. She wondered what Renate looked like and where these shoes would have taken her had she lived. Poor Helmut. He had to spend the holidays without his family.

Aunt Anni sat on the floor beside Lisl and put her arm around her. "Isn't it a beautiful tree?" Aunt Anni got up and lit the candles that had survived the carols. The children gathered around the tree.

"I'll turn off the lights," Dieter said.

The sound of Christmas songs from the radio filled the room and the children sang along while admiring their favorite ornaments, the special ones they had collected over the years. But Lisl's favorites were still the crystal ornaments. One of them caught her attention, enchanting her with the multiple reflections in its facets. She gazed at distorted images, fragments of her face as she leaned toward it. And when she stood to the side, she saw her family behind her, captured in the glass. She spun it slowly from its bow. Light to shadow to light, hypnotically spinning until she saw the face of a stranger.

CHAPTER 50

June, 1992: A Cloud Angel for Dieter

The twirling ornament sparkled in the bright sunlight. With each turn a glimpse of a strange yet familiar face appeared and disappeared. Bewildered, I stopped the spinning–a grown-up face gazed at me. The reflection was my face, no longer a child. It was June 12, 1992, the day of Papa's funeral. A noise by the front door had brought me back to the present.

A key turned in the lock and the door swung open.

"Lisl," Kurt's deep voice rang out as he came through the door with Charlotte and Ellen trying to hide behind him. "I brought you a surprise."

My sisters rushed to me, taking my breath away as we stood in embrace. Confused I closed my eyes, wanting to return to the childhood I had tried so hard to forget. The Christmas of 1945 lingered in my thoughts. But a bouquet of yellow roses, and Papa's smiling face in the picture beside it, reminded me of the reason I had come back to Mainbernheim.

Kurt stroked my face. "Lisl, are you all right?"

"Well, we did it. She is speechless." Ellen held my hands, looking amused at my disorientation.

"Oh Ellen, Charlotte, I'm sorry. I'm so glad to see you." I hugged both of my sisters again, trying to hide my confusion. We huddled, unsuccessfully hiding our tears. The death of Papa perhaps? The return to our childhood home? Maybe they mourned the loss of time as well.

"What about me? I'm here, too."

I laughed. "Kurt, you sound just like the little boy I remember." The melancholy spell was broken. We enclosed him in our embrace.

To my surprise, my Bavarian dialect had returned with no hesitation. I was home again.

"Being here in this house again reminded me of times when we were all very young. It was wonderful, like going back in time. I was nine or ten years old again." I gazed at the glass ornament still in my hand. "Seeing these ornaments made me feel like I never left." I still felt disoriented but held it tight, afraid to let go of the childhood dream.

Charlotte sat down in Mama's chair by the window.

"Lisl, you haven't changed a bit, you're still daydreaming."

Ellen took the ornament from my hand. "Good heavens look at this old thing. I'd forgotten about them."

"Do you remember Christmas of 1944 and '45?" I asked.

Charlotte shuddered. "Please, don't remind me of those horrible times."

"Oh, but I think they were wonderful times."

Ellen laughed. "You would think so. You and Dieter were always in your own private fantasy world."

"No, it's not that," I shook my head. "It's because the smallest things meant so much to us, everything was special. Whatever happened to all the years in between?"

"We got old." Kurt laughed, running his hand through his graying hair.

"It's wonderful to be together in our house again. Now when I look back, our childhood wasn't all that bad," Ellen admitted.

Charlotte threw her hands in the air. "What is it with you two? Why on earth would you think that? I for one would hate to have to go back there."

Ellen grinned. "Yes, you always were the worrywart."

I walked around the room. "Everywhere I look, memories spring to life, and no matter how sad and terrifying times may have been, part of it was quite wonderful. Especially the close family bond we had."

"Well, yes. I sometimes think about those days, especially on Christmas. I guess it's easier to look back, now that it's all over," Charlotte said. "But I most certainly would not call them wonderful times."

"I have to admit, once I had settled in Seattle I wanted to forget as well. But the memories I had tried to run from were always with me, hiding in that secret place somewhere in my heart."

"I know what you mean." Ellen's eyes moistened.

Kurt got up. "I'd better make you breakfast before you get *me* crying."

"Sorry. I sound morbid don't I?" I laughed. "Well, how was your flight?" I asked my sisters.

"Not bad," Charlotte said. "At least not as long as yours. Kurt picked us up at the airport."

"You wouldn't believe the traffic," Kurt called from the kitchen.

"Yes, it's awful at rush hour." Charlotte agreed. "The entire flight from Birmingham to Frankfurt took less time than the car ride from Frankfurt to Mainbernheim."

Ellen shook her head. "Oh you must have been asleep; it's a bit longer than that."

"You're the one who fell asleep." Charlotte defended herself.

I laughed.

"What's so funny?" Ellen looked puzzled.

"You two. You haven't changed either. You were always quarreling."

"Whatever made you think we were quarreling? I don't remember doing that. Tell her, Charlotte." Ellen pulled her innocent face.

"No, we only had lively discussions, sometimes a little loud, but never a quarrel." Charlotte smiled sweetly at Ellen.

"Never mind Lisl," Charlotte said. "You're not the only one who thinks we're quarreling. Our husbands often misconstrue our discussions as outright fights. Can you believe that?" They both laughed.

"How have you been and how is jolly old England?"

"Not much has changed since your last visit. The kids have gotten older and the grandkids cuter." Charlotte dug in her purse for her latest snapshots.

"Well, I don't have quite as many grandchildren, but they're just as cute." Ellen handed some of her photos to me.

Kurt called from the kitchen. "Let's have breakfast first. I talk better on a full stomach." He juggled plates, fresh hot rolls, and his famous omelets to the table. "You can always fight later over whose grandchildren are cuter."

Kurt had stocked the refrigerator with food, knowing that we sisters would prefer to stay in our parents' house during our three-week stay in Mainbernheim. We had a lot of catching up to do.

Kurt had closed his restaurant in Kitzingen for a week in honor of Papa's passing.

"I will brief you on the funeral arrangements after breakfast," he said. "Werner and his wife will be here a little later. Dieter will be with us in spirit."

We sat around the old dining room table, unconsciously seeking out the same chairs we had used as children. Dieter's chair stood empty, but I still could see his smiling face as I smuggled some food to him under the table.

The house had changed little. Most of the furniture stood in the same place, although some pieces now had a little more character. Even the little wooden bench in the kitchen corner had survived Mama's grandchildren and great-grandchildren.

We ate in silence, each caught up in our own thoughts, remembering when the whole Lindner family sat together.

After breakfast I wandered through the rooms, and the passing of time was apparent. Displayed on walls, tables and desks were photographs of my two children from cradle to graduation. Ellen's and Charlotte's children and grandchildren were smiling from their picture frames.

I wondered if my parents felt deprived of the nine grandchildren–offspring from three daughters too far away–who could not speak German. At least my brothers had not strayed far from home. They had filled the void and had given them seven grandchildren.

Mama's china cabinet was filled with precious figurines. But in the midst of all these treasures stood that perfect petrified seashell that Dieter had found in the spring of '46. I felt a sudden joy but also heartache at seeing it again, thinking back on how persistently Dieter had searched, and how proud he had been to see Mama's smile. It warmed my heart to see that it had been Mama's most prized possession all these years.

Homemade treasures from her grandchildren and great-grandchildren rested right along with the Hummel and Dresden figurines.

A carved wooden box, hidden on the bottom shelf, was filled with the simple gifts that we as children had made for her when times were the most terrifying. Mama had wrapped each gift in silk paper to keep her memories safe.

A photograph in a little silver frame of a man in a wheelchair caught my attention. Two curly-haired girls sat on his lap, and a pretty woman leaned over his shoulder.

Instantly I knew it was Horst, even before I read the names on the back.

Old pictures of my brothers and sisters brought precious memories to life, but were also a reminder of time's passing.

Charlotte and Ellen came into the sitting room and sat down beside me, going through old faded photographs as well. Laughing and crying, they showed pictures to each other of long ago.

I wished we had stayed closer. But the constant reminder of one tragic event, after the war, was more than I could face and certainly more than I could ever talk about without falling apart.

Charlotte and Ellen had moved to England in 1953. There they found their loves and settled down. Four years later, I went to America where I met my husband.

When I watched my daughter and son at play I often thought of the closeness Dieter and I had shared. I'll always cherish the journeys with Dieter into fantasy worlds only children could imagine. My children's dreams and fantasies were much like ours.

Mama loved to explore the beaches and rain forests on her visits to Washington. The last time my parents were in Seattle I watched her play on the beach with my children.

"If you were a bird would you fly away?" I had asked as a child.

"Oh yes," she had replied. "I would fly to a far away place, a place without war and hunger."

"Can I fly with you?" I had asked.

"Yes. We'll all fly away together." But Papa's roots had been anchored too firmly in German soil, keeping Mama's wings clipped.

Over the years we had visited each other often. But this was the first time all of us children gathered in the house where we had grown up.

We walked together through the garden and talked of happy and sad times. The vegetable beds and the hard work of tending them were replaced with shrubs, flowers, and shade trees. Although the now park-like setting had seen better days, the beauty of the quiet landscape was irresistible.

The steep areas were retained by sturdy stone walls to level garden beds. Walks and steps curved through the setting with benches and special plantings, begging us to linger a while. We felt close, as if we had never been separated.

Just before noon Werner came, with his wife Margarete and Kurt's wife Annett, to join the sentimental journey through the garden.

We sat under the old cherry tree, lingering over a refreshing cold drink as we had done as children. I found it appropriate. It was Mama's favorite place to think, cry, and daydream. Now we discussed Papa's funeral under that big tree. I felt Mama's presence.

თ∾ე

The family stood by the gravesite. A steady stream of mourners, people I knew, but also many I had never met, offered their heart-felt condolences. The sorrow I felt as Papa's casket was lowered into the ground was not for him. He had a full and rich life. I wept for Mama. I was haunted by the guilt of being unable to attend her funeral. Health issues had prevented my travel.

I read Mama's name on the gravestone for the first time. Although she'd had a good life after the impact of the war had finally diminished, I felt I had deserted her when I decided to live in America. Mama knew that. Over the years she had sent many photographs while vacationing in her favorite places in the Bavarian Alps. Maybe she wanted to wipe the guilt from my conscience–to let me know she was happy.

Slowly the mourners left the graveyard. I stood before the open grave, concentrating on the mound of single yellow roses friends had placed on Papa's casket. I tried hard *not* to read the first name on the black marble, but my eyes strayed from roses to golden letters.

Dieter Lindner: born 1937, died 1951. Tears ran uncontrollably down my face–still unable to cope with his senseless death from an exploding land mine six years after the war had ended.

I had hoped for rain to hide my tears among the drops. But I knew Dieter would have loved a day like this. I looked into a clear blue sky, trying to compose myself, when I saw a single wispy cloud drift slowly across the heavens.

A cloud angel for Dieter.

Made in the USA
Charleston, SC
14 June 2011